GUARDIAN OF TORMENT

A NYX FORTUNA NOVEL

MICHELLE MANUS

Guardian of Torment Copyright © August 2023 by Michelle Manus
ebook ISBN: 978-1-954400-25-2
Paperback ISBN: 978-1-954400-26-9
Publisher: Seclusion Publishing
Cover Design: Damonza.com

PROLOGUE

Nyx drifted.

She had the sense she'd been drifting for some time, and the equal sense that the knowledge should bother her. But as soon as she grasped the feeling, it slipped away. The whole of her attention was captivated by the knots and lines of power that surrounded her. They formed a brilliant glowing matrix in the darkness, shimmering white strands that stretched between even brighter nodes.

They were woven together prettily enough, but it was a cruel kind of beauty. They didn't belong here. She was certain of it, even if she couldn't focus long enough to remember where *here* was. She trailed fingers that weren't truly physical down one of the glowing strands.

It was a piece of a net. She remembered that now and, having remembered, it was all too easy to see the half-destroyed structure of it around her. A net she had been dismantling because it was keeping her from something. Something she wanted desperately.

There wasn't much of it left—only twelve lines, seven nodes between them. She was close. So close to finishing. It would only take a few more cuts, a few more unraveled knots, and she would have what she wanted.

What...what was it she wanted?

She had a sense of laughter, chime-like and aristocratically brittle, and though she didn't actually *hear* it, the remaining lines of power rippled in sync with it. The sound made her angry. The power that *didn't belong here* made her angry. She reached for one of the nodes. She flinched as she did, an instinctual reaction, but she kept going.

Her fist closed over the node. It was more of a knot, and though the fingers that worked at it were not physical ones, they still burned as she coaxed the bound threads to loosen, little shocks of pain flickering through her.

Stubbornly, she persisted, her nerves on fire as the knot unraveled. Its brilliance dulled and winked out, the threads that connected it to the nearest other knots burning out as well. She ignored the pain, reaching for the next knot, and the next, until she was numb and her entire world had narrowed to the need to be rid of this foreign power.

Shakily, she tore the final piece apart. As the last bit of magic dimmed, she could swear she heard a voice say, "Poor choice, daughter mine."

Then the light winked out and she was alone in the vast darkness. Alone, and confused, and with no idea how to leave wherever *here* was.

1

Nyx Fortuna was lost. Not lost like she sometimes was when Viktor dropped her in the woods, but lost in a different way.

When she was alone in the woods, she could use her surroundings to anchor herself and find her way home. It was supposed to prepare her for a time like this—a time when she didn't know where she was, and had to do her best to orient herself with what was around her.

Except it wasn't working, because what was around her didn't make any sense. Her environment didn't feel truly physical. It was an endless sea of black, the only landmarks in sight the hundreds of disconnected nodes floating in the black depths. She stood on one of those nodes now, and the placement of the others around it felt familiar. Nothing connected them, but if she imagined lines between them, the resulting structure would form a net.

A net, like the kind her mother liked to weave from magic. She stretched mental fingers, her own power washing over the nodes and—*there*. Faint echoes of Elena Fortuna's magic. This had been a Hiding, then. Something larger and more complex than Nyx had ever imagined a Hidden could build.

But then, she had only just started working on Hiding multiple things at the same time. Upping the difficulty and complexity of Nyx's workings had been her mother's twelfth birthday present to her that morning.

So what was this? Some kind of test to see if Nyx could find her way out of the working's core?

She'd stood within the matrix of a Hidden web before, but it had always been one of her own making, so the way out had been well-marked. She couldn't see the way out of this one. Even though this wasn't her own Hiding, finding an exit route should have been simple, because this Hiding wasn't functional anymore. Her mother's power was gone, so why was Nyx still stuck here?

What was it Viktor always told her? *If you find yourself in entirely unfamiliar surroundings, and no one is looking for you, choose a direction and start walking. Do not deviate unless safety dictates that you do so. If you think you are trapped, find the nearest perimeter and make your way to it. Map the confines of your cage.*

She spun in a circle, trying to see an end to the nodes, to determine if they formed a perimeter. To her left, she counted five nodes but couldn't see any past the fifth. Hoping that meant that the fifth node represented the outer edge of the matrix, she crouched, readying to leap to the next node.

"Don't jump." The voice startled her so badly she nearly fell off her perch. She searched, looking for the speaker, but saw no one.

"Who's there?"

"It's Tobi." The voice sounded like it belonged to someone a few years younger than her, while simultaneously sounding as if it belong to someone decades older. If she was forced to pick one, she'd say both, and that didn't make any sense.

Neither did the fact that Tobi clearly seemed to think she should know who he was. Which was hilarious, even if he probably didn't know it. Nyx's world consisted of her mother, Viktor, and Seth. Them, and the random strangers she met every time she and Seth ran away. Even if Viktor never let them stay gone long.

"I don't know a Tobi."

"No, I guess you don't right now." She still couldn't pin down the age, and it almost sounded like more than one person talking in the same voice. It echoed around her. "But you will. You're nice and you found me my moms, so I'm going to help you."

She'd…what? She was pretty sure she would remember if she'd run across a lost boy and helped him find his mothers.

This was either a really vivid dream or… "*Seth.*" His illusions kept getting better by the day. She didn't know how he'd faked her mother's magical signature, or how he'd gotten her into this illusion without her remembering it, but she was seriously going to annihilate him in their next sparring match for this.

"Seth's here," the voice calling itself Tobi said. "But if you want to talk to him, you're going to have to wake up."

"Uh-huh," Nyx said. "And I suppose to wake up you're going to tell me I need to hop on one foot in a circle six times while chanting some nonsense words?"

"No," Tobi said patiently, almost like he'd expected that reaction. "That would never work."

Nyx frowned. Seth never kept trying to fool her once she'd figured out what he was doing. He would just come back with something more ridiculous than hopping on her foot, and tell her that was the price of dropping the illusion. She rarely ever did what he told her to. She had a stubborn streak and a lot of time. With the combination of the two, she could usually make an illusion so difficult for him to hold that he was forced to drop it.

But he always made the ridiculous requests anyway. Except now, he wasn't. So if Seth wasn't doing this, *was* it one of her mother's tests?

"You need to wake up," Tobi repeated. "So I need you to

jump off the point you're on. Not *to* any of the other points, just step off."

She looked down and swallowed. Nothing below, just empty abyss. She looked up and saw the other nodes. They weren't too far away. If she jumped, maybe she could—

"*Please* don't climb." Tobi sounded weary. "You climbed last time and it took us forever to get back here."

"I don't remember that."

He sighed. "I know. Trust me? Your friends are worried about you and I'm getting tired."

Nyx didn't have friends. At least, not any other than Seth. And a disembodied voice telling her she *did* have friends, and that they were worried about her, made her think that maybe this wasn't a test from her mother after all. Maybe it was just a dream.

If it was a dream, stepping into nothing wouldn't kill her. If it *was* one of her mother's tests and she failed it, well, it would hardly be the first time she'd disappointed Elena Fortuna.

She took a breath and stepped off the node.

"**N**yxi?"

Seth. Nyx's heart skipped and she opened her eyes. Seth's face hovered above hers, but something was wrong. Those were his almost-black eyes, staring worriedly into hers, but his face wasn't right. It was…older.

A lot older. This wasn't Seth. This was a man.

She scrambled back and hit a wall, her legs tangling in sheets. They were softer sheets than she'd ever had, on a bed twice the size of hers.

"It's okay," said the guy who sort of looked and sounded like Seth but couldn't *be* Seth. "You're okay."

He wasn't the only person in the room. A boy, maybe eight or nine, stood in front of a woman with auburn hair. Feathers threaded through the locks, almost as if they grew alongside them. Her hands rested protectively on the boy's shoulders.

Next to them was another woman, pale skin and blonde hair, her body packed with muscle. Then a tall, fit Black man with a wealth of slender braids that just brushed his shoulders, and next to him…a *griffin*.

Viktor's voice whispered in her mind. *Your mother and I, we won't always be here to protect you.*

Protect her from what, she'd never been clear on. But this—being in a room full of strangers, one of whom was a mythological creature and one of whom was a creepy older version of Seth —seemed like something she might want to protect herself from.

Another whisper of Viktor's voice. *If you're backed into a corner, make an exit and run.*

She flew off the side of the bed and bolted for the door. Or tried to. Her body felt all off. She tripped over herself twice and then Seth—no, *not* Seth—was there. His hands gently but firmly gripped her shoulders and he was talking in that quiet, easy way that always made everything feel right in the world. Except it was wrong because his voice was deeper than it should be.

She turned, twisted and threw her weight to get out of his grip. Then she stumbled all over herself again because her body felt so wrong. She righted herself and looked up, straight into a large oval mirror, and froze.

That reflection couldn't be her. It belonged to a woman and Nyx wasn't a woman, she was twelve. But those were her eyes, silver-grey and wide as a startled deer's. And when she raised her hand to touch the strange black thorns that pierced her cheek in a spiral pattern, her reflection did the same.

Seth's reflection came up behind hers in the mirror, his hand reaching for her shoulder. She flinched and he backed off.

"It's okay, little Guardian," said the Black man, his voice soft and melodic. It was unnaturally persuasive, that voice, lulling and almost hypnotic.

She struggled against the honey-coated words that assured her everything was fine when *nothing* was fine.

"What's wrong with her?" the blonde woman demanded.

"She's lost," the boy said, and Nyx recognized his voice. Tobi.

"She's standing right there," the woman argued.

"She's not lost *here*," Tobi said, walking to stand in front of Nyx. "She's lost here." He tapped his temple, then held out his hand to her. "Now that you're awake, I can show you the way back."

Nyx swallowed. He looked so small, but serious, his countenance a little eerie, as if something more than just a boy looked out at her from behind his eyes. The hand not held out to her was clutched around a misshapen lump of fabric that looked like it was trying to be a stuffed animal.

She didn't know what made her reach out and take his hand.

A cool wash of magic flooded through her and she was back in that place with the nodes, except it was different this time. She still stood on one, but it was removed from the labyrinth of others, and she was far enough away that she could see them all, floating above a shape below.

The shape wasn't anything she could describe or draw, but she knew, on some instinctual level, that it was her. And most of it was missing. A third or so of it was filled in and glowing softly, but only a few scattered pieces shone in the rest. It looked like one of those children's puzzles that came on a board. Not only was her board mostly unfinished, but the puzzle pieces had been broken into smaller and smaller bits and their edges filed smooth.

"I'm broken," she whispered.

"Your memories are," Tobi said.

She looked at the pieces, floating around her like the debris of an obliterated asteroid. She felt the echoes of her mother's magic, how it had once connected all the broken bits, the broken pieces of *her.* Her mother had *Hidden* Nyx. Hidden her memories…from herself.

She thought of the node she stood on, of Seth looking so much older, *herself* looking so much older... "I'm not twelve anymore, am I?"

"No."

She was just standing on a broken chunk of memory from a time when she'd *been* twelve. A chunk that needed to be fitted back into the board below, like all the rest. She looked at the glowing section of unblemished memory. Her life after the Hiding.

She rubbed her arms. "You're...some kind of healer, right?" She'd never met one. Or, she supposed she had, but twelve-year-old her—and it was all kinds of weird to know she wasn't twelve right now even though she very much felt like it—never had.

"Some kind," Tobi agreed.

"Can you fix me? Put me back together?"

"I'm sorry," he said, which was answer enough. His next words held that double-echo, the sound of others who were older than the boy talking through him. "The mind isn't the body. Bodies within each species are more or less the same. Each physical person is built upon a template that has existed for millennia.

"An individual may have some variations—small-scale mutations or anomalies—but the core concept remains the same. Each mind, on the other hand, is unique. From the moment a child begins learning, their experiences shape them differently from others. There is no template to follow with memories.

"We could force the pieces into the mold and make them stay, but they won't be in the right places. The paths between them will be all jumbled. It would become a maze and you would be lost, skipping from time to time. You might never find your way out."

Nyx swallowed, suddenly very aware of the patch of time she stood on. She looked at the board again, at the pieces glowing in the incomplete section. Slivers, mostly. "Some of the pieces went back where they should."

"Fragments. Ones small enough you could reabsorb them and instinctively put them back where they belonged. Come on." He tugged on her hand, pointing at the section of her memories that were whole. "It will make more sense to *that* you."

Nyx resisted. It was one thing to know in theory that she was older, but the her that she was right now felt like stepping into Future Her's shoes would make Current Her cease to exist. What was this other her like? What if she wasn't a good person? What if—

"Your friends are worried about you," Tobi said, gently squeezing her hand.

Her friends. The people in that room were her friends. And Seth was still with her. Time hadn't changed that. He was her constant, and she was his. So everything would be fine.

She returned the squeeze of Tobi's hand and let him guide her down. It was his magic she felt moving them now, unlike the free fall she'd done earlier to wake up, and she wondered why he hadn't guided her this way before. Had he needed her permission to enter this part of her mind? Had she had to bring him into it with her?

The node they stood on descended with them, like a hover platform that grew smaller and smaller as they approached the unbroken part of her mind. Then her feet were on solid glowing ground, the node a small sphere in her hand, and she was herself again.

Twenty-six years old, staring up at the floating space-debris sea of her ruined memories. She looked away from them, back to the boy beside her.

If Seth had gone to Ankira for Tobi... "How long have I been out of it?"

"Five days."

Relief hit her. Only five days. It wasn't so much to have lost.

"Seth came to get me on the second, but I couldn't find you then. Or the next day, or the next. Not until today."

Because she'd been inside the Hiding as she disassembled it.

He hadn't found her until she'd cut the last thread and her mother's magic was finally gone. On the one hand, it had allowed Tobi to find her. On the other hand, she'd never intended to destroy all of the Hiding at once.

She'd lost ten hours on Lehine, battling her mother as Elena fought Nyx's efforts to reclaim her memories. But this time her mother hadn't fought her. Not really. Nyx had simply gotten hooked on tearing down the net, cutting the strands, telling herself, "Just one more." And it had been one more after that, and one more after that, and she hadn't been able to stop.

Especially since she would swear her mother had been laughing at her the entire time. It had infuriated Nyx, until her focus had dwindled to nothing beyond the Hiding and her determination to have it out at all costs.

So she wasn't surprised she hadn't noticed anyone trying to wake her.

"Thank you for coming to find me," Nyx said.

Tobi nodded, only fidgeting a little. The last six months with Ankira and Diana had made him more accustomed to being thanked for what he did, but he still wasn't used to being appreciated.

"You said you can't fix this." Nyx looked at the glowing sphere of memory in her palm, then at the mostly-empty puzzle board before her. "Do you know how I fix it?"

He hesitated, clearly not wanting to answer.

"It's okay," she told him. "Just tell me."

His voice shifted again, taking on that chorus-like sound it did when the Congregation was really sitting up and paying attention. "We don't know if you can. Not without getting lost in yourself, and there's no guarantee we can pull you out again if that happens. We've been here for hours, waiting to find a version of you we could reason with. Your earlier selves are extremely stubborn and distrustful."

Hardly shocking, considering what she knew about her life.

"So I need to get lost for a while to fix it. How long are we talking? A couple days? A couple weeks?"

Tobi's silence was not encouraging.

"A couple months?" she ventured. The last thing she wanted, after having lost the memories of the first eighteen years of her life, was to turn around and lose an actual few months of it to what essentially amounted to a medically-induced coma. Especially not now, when she had a mass-murderer stashed in the Station's Heart and impossible promises to keep regarding a certain Harvester.

"Years," Tobi said finally. "Almost as many as there are memories."

That…couldn't be right. "But the pieces that are back in place —they didn't take that long." Nor had she gotten lost in her own mind when she'd remembered them.

"They are extremely small pieces of a whole," Tobi/the Congregation said. "Pieces you were likely already reaching for, instinctively needing to recall and managing to free from this"— he gestured at the broken sea above her—"web."

Frustration bit at Nyx. She'd spent years wanting to know who she was. She'd spent six months knowing about the Hiding and desperately trying to regain what had been taken. She'd finally found a way to undo it all, a way that was supposed to fix everything, and now this. "I don't understand. When Seth put the pendant on that let him circumvent the Hiding, all of his memories just came back. This"—she gestured to the sea above, then to the empty board—"why is it separate?"

"We have a theory." Tobi/the Congregation didn't sound like they wanted to share it. "Some number of us worked with Hidden, before the near-elimination of your line. Based on that knowledge of how your magic works, we might be able to explain what you are currently experiencing."

"I'm listening."

"The mind isn't the body, but it is *like* the body. It can be broken the same way a body can. The net that was cast around your memories was meant only to contain them—to Hide *you* from you—in the same way a physical net cast around a person contains their body.

"But if the person caught in the net fights it, and their captor draws the net tighter in an attempt to contain them, eventually it grows tight enough to cut. And if the captive keeps fighting and the net keeps clamping down, and the strands of the net are too strong to break?"

"Then the person inside the net breaks," Nyx finished for him.

"The cohesive whole of your memories was fractured. It appears that, once broken, the pieces became woven into the threads of the net as opposed to resting within it. You have cut the cords of the net, but your memories are still attached to it."

"Then the Hiding is still active?" That couldn't be possible. She'd felt her mother's power dissolving as she cut the strands.

"No. It is more that the skeleton of it remains, and your memories are still stuck to it. Which is fortunate, because that is what is holding them from dropping back into your conscious-ness all at once. Without it, you would have no choice but to attempt to reincorporate them en masse. Given the chaotic tangle they are in, we are not certain the attempt wouldn't fundamen-tally break your psyche."

Her stomach dropped. "That's comforting."

"It was not meant to be." Apparently the Congregation part of Tobi didn't have a sense of humor. "As it is, now that you've broken the bonds, even the skeleton will begin to degrade. As it does, as pieces break free, you may find yourself confused again until you can place the piece where it belongs."

"What do you mean by place it? And how am I supposed to do that when I might not even remember any of this?"

"For the first, instinct." He nodded at the puzzle board. She walked onto it, the piece of memory cradled in her hands, and tried to think instinctively. But that wasn't how instinct worked, so she cleared her mind as much as she could, walking blindly around the space until she felt a tug and followed it. Like playing hot-or-cold with pieces of her brain. She let that tugging sensation guide her until the memory island leaped out of her cupped hands. It settled onto the board, sinking and melding and filling up one of the thousands of hollow places inside her.

She looked up at the sea above her—hundreds of blinking islands and specks of dust and jagged pieces—and knew what Tobi would tell her.

"I can't fix this, can I?" she said softly. Not without losing more years of her life to the process. How much time would she have to spend with each fraction of memory in order to find out where it belonged?

"Everything broken can be put back together. But it is not always worth the time to fix something old, when something new can be made."

Despite everything, a smile tugged at the corner of Nyx's lips. "Are you telling me I should focus on the future instead of the past?"

"If you want to be certain of having a future? Yes."

"But you said this is all going to fall down bit by bit anyway. What does that look like?"

"As pieces break free, your conscious mind will naturally latch onto them, in an attempt to categorize them and fit them back where they belong. If the pieces are small enough, you may simply find yourself arrested by a poignant memory—I believe this is what Seth described you experiencing before, each time you've recalled specific events.

"But if the piece that falls free contains a longer time period, say a span of days or weeks as opposed to a moment, you may once again think yourself twelve, or eleven, or nine, or so on."

Nyx didn't like any of the possible outcomes attached to that scenario. How was she supposed to function if at any moment she could be yanked out of the present? If she was receiving an Arrival and suddenly became a version of herself who didn't know what the Station was or how she'd gotten there, it could be catastrophically bad.

"How fast is this going to happen?"

"We can't say at this point. We have a baseline of the skeleton's composition at present. If we check it daily over the next week, we should be able to establish a rate of decay and give you a better idea."

Rate of decay. Because there was a corpse rotting in her brain. On some level, she understood that all of this—the debris field above, the "skeleton", the puzzle board—were just constructs her mind had created so that she could comprehend what was happening. She wasn't actually in a physical place surrounded by physical things, so she didn't actually have a skeleton inside her that wasn't her own. But knowing that what lingered was only the inactive remnants of her mother's magic didn't make it feel any less…gross.

"I know you said you couldn't put me back together, but can you at least stop the decay? Or, I don't know, put something in place to hold it back?" So she could choose to reabsorb memories at times when she could afford to be lost to the world and potentially confused about when she was in time.

"I'm sorry, but we work with the body, not the mind. Finding you without damaging anything was difficult enough. Any attempt to alter what is here may irrevocably damage your mind."

"So that's it? There's nothing I can do?"

"This was done by a Hidden. *You* are a Hidden. Our best advice to you is to try and recreate what was done."

Recreate what was done. Hide herself all over again. Or, better yet, *not* have spent the last five days cutting her mother's Hiding to pieces.

The poetic injustice of it was so thick that Nyx started laughing. She was still laughing when Tobi pulled her out of herself, until she was no longer looking inward, but out on her room.

The concerned faces of everyone she cared about in the world looked back.

Even then, she couldn't stop laughing. When she doubled over, tears leaking out the corners of her eyes, it was Seth's voice that broke everyone else's stunned silence. "Could you guys give us a minute?"

2

"Nyxi?" Seth crouched in front of her, his dark eyes concerned.

"Don't worry," she managed in between gasps of the laughter she couldn't quite quell. "I'm not having a psychotic break. Yet."

"*Yet?*" he repeated.

The reminder that she would, in all likelihood, have one if she couldn't recreate her mother's Hiding finally sobered her. She pressed her fingertips against eyes gone dry and grainy, and gave Seth the short version of what Toby had told her.

By the time she finished, Seth's jaw was clenched and he had a look she knew all too well. "Don't," she told him. "Don't do that."

"Don't do what?"

"Get that look."

"I don't have a look."

"You do. It's the this-is-all-my-fault look. The if-I-hadn't-wanted-Nyx-to-remember-this-wouldn't-have-happened look. It would have happened. There is no scenario in which I found out how to undo my mother's Hiding and I didn't go for it. So stop looking at me like that."

He blew out a breath. "You know you're a real pain in the ass sometimes, right?"

"I know. That's why you—"

"Little Guardian," Morgen called from outside the room. "I don't mean to interrupt, but there is an upset unicorn-dragon out here about to set someone on fire."

Nyx launched to her feet, tapping back into the Station's senses as she flung the door open. A rush of information and sensation slammed into her, as if the Station was trying to make up for the last few days that she'd been unaware of its happenings.

She shut it all back out before the flurry of information made her trip over her own feet. As it was, she still ran into Morgen. Or rather, she ran into the arm he flung out to prevent her from running down the spiral staircase that was no longer there.

Nyx peered over the edge. Temerex pawed angrily at the floor, sparks flying each time her hoof struck the ground. She saw Nyx and straightened, letting out an excited neigh that was followed by an image of Temerex on the second floor with Nyx.

Nyx sent back an image of Nyx on the ground floor with Temerex instead, and looked behind the unicorn-dragon to where Griff and the others waited. "Do I want to ask what happened to the stairs?"

Griff, currently in what she thought of as his medium-sized form—roughly the size of a full-grown St. Bernard—removed his spectacles, polishing them on his feathers as he answered. "Temerex, in what I believe was a state of extreme concern over your well-being, attempted to climb the staircase. She became stuck and was resistant to attempts to help extricate her. I was worried she would injure herself. Removing the staircase was the most logical solution to the predicament."

Nyx looked at Tem. "You tried to climb a staircase? A *spiral* staircase?" She sent an image of Tem with her legs stuck between the ladder-like stair steps.

Temerex blew out an indignant breath that came with an

image that was the absence of Nyx, with a general sense of panic, fear, and loneliness behind it.

Well, shit. Nyx conjured the stairs back into existence and went down to stroke Temerex's neck.

It had been less than two weeks since Temerex had been rescued from her isolation on Amentia Furor and abandoned by the man she thought of as her father. Then Nyx had disappeared on her for the last five days. Of course she was panicking.

"I'm not going anywhere, okay? I promise. This is your home now." She sent an image of the two of them turning gray together and hoped it translated. It seemed to, because Tem blew out a breath, lipped at Nyx's shirt, then sent Nyx an image of the two of them running outside.

"Give me a couple hours?" She sent an image of the sun in the middle of the sky over an empty field, then one of the sun later in the sky with Nyx and Tem in the field. Tem bobbed her head, then bumped Nyx's shoulder. It was going to take Nyx some time to stop flinching every time the mare did that, since she kept having visions of being accidentally gored by the unicorn-dragon's affections. She patted the finely-scaled neck and watched as Tem turned and trotted to the door that led to her outside enclosure.

"Why does it seem like she actually understands you when you talk?" Morgen asked.

Nyx shrugged. "The whole image communication thing was weird at first, but I think I'm getting a handle on it."

"Image communication?" Morgen echoed.

"I don't know what else to call it. Is there an official term for beings that communicate via mental pictures? Some kind of visual telepathy or something?"

Blank stares greeted her question.

"I told you she said something about talking with pictures," Evra told Morgen, sounding vindicated. She turned to Nyx. "You are saying that the beast sends you telepathic images?"

Nyx would have quibbled with Evra's description of Tem as

"the beast" if the word hadn't been layered in a sort of marveling affection. She had a feeling it was a translation issue.

"Yes?" she answered. "Doesn't she send them to you?"

"No."

"Anybody else?" Nyx asked hopefully.

They all shook their heads.

"I'm not crazy. Jevryn can talk to her, too. Better than I can, actually. She can take complex instructions from him whereas I just sort of send her still images."

Morgen made a hmm-that's-interesting noise and said, "I'll look into it. I'm...still not entirely sure what she is." Considering it was Morgen admitting as much, that was saying something.

Silence descended after that, which Griff broke with a tentative, "Are you feeling better, then?"

Right. They'd seen the Nyx that was convinced she was twelve, then the Nyx who couldn't stop having a laughing-crying fit. "Kind of? Tobi said—" She cut off, realizing Tobi wasn't among the others, and a quick check of the Station's senses showed he wasn't on the grounds.

He had to be exhausted—he was just a kid, no matter how powerful a network he was tapped into—so she didn't blame him for bailing the moment she was up and running on her own. She just hoped he wasn't—

"He is fine," Griff said. "Only tired. The Warlock insisted he return home now that he had done what he could."

"Right, of course. I should go see her." She wanted to make sure Earth Between's Warlock understood that Nyx didn't view Tobi as her personal fix-all-problems healer on-call, and that she was grateful for his assistance.

She knew Ankira struggled with how much to let Tobi do. He *had* to work, because the magic was in him and it was his calling and if he *didn't* use it that would be as detrimental to him as being worked constantly. But Ankira had to balance that with the recognition that, no matter how old he seemed when the

Congregation spoke through him, he was still an eight-year-old who didn't understand his own limits.

Nyx didn't want to add to either of their difficulties.

Her stomach chose that moment to give an embarrassingly loud, painful growl.

"Yeah, you aren't going anywhere except the kitchen," Seth said. "Tobi gave you some kind of vitamin-mineral infusion thing, but you haven't eaten actual food in almost a week."

"And while you are in the kitchen, you can explain what happened," Evra added.

Recognizing defeat, Nyx went where instructed. Once given an americano, she told Griff, Morgen, and Evra what she'd already told Seth. By the time she was done, she'd finished the beverage, and the caffeine was making her vaguely nauseous. Probably on account of the whole not-having-eaten-for-five-days thing. Seth was putting the finishing touches on some kind of pureed soup that probably contained at least one of every vegetable known to man, but would likely taste so good she wouldn't notice.

"So what are you going to do?" Evra asked.

Seth plunked a bowl in front of Nyx and slipped onto an empty seat.

"I don't know." She stirred her spoon through the soup. "Do what Tobi suggested, I guess. Try to recreate the Hiding. If I can make my own, then I can take it apart little by little."

It would still take her years to get everything back, if she ever did, but at least she would be in control. At least she wouldn't be likely to go insane.

"Is that really what you want?" Evra asked.

"No. Of course it's not what I want. But I don't seem to have another option."

3

Nyx stuck it out in the kitchen long enough to convince everyone that she was fine. Then she left on the excuse that she needed to check on the mass murderer in her basement. She really did want to make sure Kaliaris hadn't killed Laiveran sometime in the five days Nyx had been unconscious, but she was doing it right this moment because she couldn't take another concerned, sidelong glance from any of her friends.

They'd been very careful to make those sidelong glances when they thought she wasn't looking, and she appreciated that they cared, but she couldn't handle a single minute more of being subtly surveyed like she was a bomb that might start ticking at any moment.

She slipped into the Arrival Room. At her request, the portal floor shifted pathways, so that it led to the Station's Heart instead of to the ley lines.

Her first journey into the Heart had been a panicked free fall that Kaliaris had done nothing to mitigate. In fact, she was relatively certain they'd made it as unpleasant of a journey as possible. But Kaliaris was warming up to her, and her descent this time was gentle. She'd never had occasion to jump out of a plane, but she imagined her current downward pace was similar to falling once you'd pulled the cord on a parachute.

Complete blackness surrounded her and she breathed it in, her lungs adjusting to the otherness that was the "air" inside the Station's Heart. Her mind strayed as she descended, something about the full absence of light and the weightless way her body floated putting her in a reflective state.

She couldn't ignore what it was she passed through, what her Station truly was: the soul of a planet. The remnant of a being too immense to truly comprehend. A being that had watched everything it loved die, then watched as others of its kind endured the same fate. A being that had then found their essence stretched and stitched onto another of their kind, forced to live as a parasite on the back of a different world.

<You are morose this visit.>

Her feet touched down on the thick mat of vines that covered the floor of the Station's Heart. Soft light illuminated the space.

"I'm keeping a person in chains. I'm allowed to be morose." She still wasn't comfortable with the fact she had a man in a cage. At least, she assumed he was in a cage. She couldn't see Laiveran. She couldn't feel him either. Within the Heart, Kaliaris' senses were more *Kaliaris*, more incomprehensible, and her connection to them didn't compensate enough for those differences to let her interpret them.

The Heart was the one place within the Station she couldn't sense. So the fact she couldn't locate Laiveran disturbed her more than it might have if she could feel his whereabouts. Especially considering that humane conditions of imprisonment were unlikely to be at the forefront of Kaliaris' concerns.

She couldn't blame her Station for that—Laiveran was responsible for Kaliaris' current condition—but it was hard to keep that in the forefront of her mind when she remembered the man himself. Because the man himself was broken, and it was difficult for her not to pity him. She had been faced with the reality of him as he was now—a haunted individual in agony—

while the deaths of the planets he'd destroyed were a mere story to her.

Knowing the story to be true didn't make it easier to comprehend. Didn't make it easier to fathom how he could be so blinded by desperation that he could believe his actions had been acceptable. That he could actually have created an object capable of destroying worlds.

The object in question, which hung even now around her neck, pulsed angrily against her skin. The Harvester disliked its nearness to Laiveran…and she very much suspected it wished to draw Kaliaris' soul back into its depths.

The vines around her rustled as Kaliaris thought. <You feel sorrow for Laiveran because you could imagine yourself in his condition.>

She shook her head. "I feel sorrow for him because he doesn't think what he's done is wrong." When Laiveran had stood unfettered in this room, Kaliaris' soul in his clutches, he had been almost sane. Calm. In that clarity he had explained to her, with the earnest sincerity of the devout, why she shouldn't judge him for his actions.

It would have been easier if he'd simply been a terrible person. If he'd believed he was forever destroying untold numbers of people. But he believed he could go back, that the energy drawn from the planets could actually spin time in reverse, and every planet he destroyed wouldn't actually be gone. To him, maybe the councilors were the ones truly responsible for the billions of people who had died on the planets he'd harvested. In his mind, the councilors had prevented him from carrying out his plan, thus making a return to a time when those planets hadn't died impossible.

Nyx didn't know if she believed that he could actually do it. On the one hand, time wasn't always as linear as people liked to believe. On the other, she didn't think that meant the universe could actually be returned to a previous state. But even if Laiveran *could* do it, she doubted the return to a past time would restore every planet he'd harvested without consequence.

It was too…neat. Too much the story someone told themselves to alleviate their own guilt. Nothing was ever as cut-and-dry as people wanted it to be. Actions had consequences. If someone gathered an unimaginable amount of power and energy to expend on a purpose, she didn't think that power and energy would simply re-manifest after the fact. It would have been spent, and spent things could never be returned in exactly the same condition as before.

The Harvester pulsed against her chest, as if in agreement. Or hunger. She wasn't sure which. She *was* sure she would prefer not to have it in close proximity to Laiveran any longer than necessary. "Where is he?"

The vines to Nyx's right rustled, shifting. Laiveran rose up through them, like a corpse surfacing from the mire.

Nyx's stomach turned. Small cuts littered Laiveran's face and hands, the skin around his wrists rubbed raw from where Kaliaris had bound them with a set of suppressing cuffs dredged up from the Station's Den. According to Griff, that particular pair was a recalled model that caused extreme irritation.

She understood the need for them—they were the only thing that kept Laiveran from accessing his magic and subjugating Kaliaris' will to his own—but she wanted a model that wouldn't physically damage him. Unfortunately, suppressing cuffs were only available to specific classifications of Enforcers, and no one was lining up to sell her a set.

She'd been having Kaliaris treat the wounds, but it looked like they might have stopped doing so during her five-day stretch of unconsciousness. She took another step forward and Laiveran noticed her. He immediately started babbling, incoherent nonsense pouring out of his mouth, one word atop another. It was too fast, too jumbled, for her to make anything out.

She glared at the center of the room, where the pedestal that was the truest Heart of the Station rested. "You promised you wouldn't keep him like this." She'd visited the Heart in the days after Laiveran's initial capture, before she'd gotten lost inside her own mind. She'd seen his condition for all of five seconds before she and Kaliaris had had a heavily-worded discussion about humane living conditions.

Apparently, Kaliaris had forgotten that discussion.

<He deserves worse.>

"Maybe. But I won't help you if you keep doing this."

<You will. You care for Griff too much. You have made promises to the councilor.>

It was the same argument they'd had before. "I won't be *able* to help you if you keep doing this. What's the point in letting him live if he's too traumatized to help us?"

Laiveran was still talking and straining toward her, familiar madness burning in his eyes. Nyx fought her rising gorge, relatively certain Kaliaris wouldn't appreciate it if she threw up in their Heart.

<You might recall that I wanted to kill him.>

"And you might recall that he's your only hope of getting what you want."

<Very well.> Kaliaris relented with an easiness that made Nyx wonder why they'd had to have the argument again at all.

A side area of the room came into view. Nyx was never clear, in the Heart, precisely how things worked. It wasn't like the Station above, where she could see things changing as they did so. Here, it was as if things simply manifested. So she wasn't sure if this new area of the room had always been there and was now suddenly visible, or if it had only just been created.

Regardless, a cell made of vines was now before her, containing basic amenities like a shower and a toilet and a bed. Those things felt out of place here, in Kaliaris' inner sanctum. But so long as they were willing to have them here, Nyx wouldn't push to move Laiveran to any other area of the Station.

This was the safest place for him, given that it was the only area of the Station the All Council couldn't force entry to. So long as Laiveran was here, and bound with the cuffs, he couldn't get out and no one could get to him.

Kaliaris transferred Laiveran to the inside of the cell.

<It shall be as you wish, for now. Though I am growing forgetful, as the centuries pass me by. You ought to check on him frequently, to be certain I do not regress where his care is concerned.> The way Kaliaris said it…she suddenly knew why they'd had this argument again. Why Kaliaris had done what they had to Laiveran.

It wasn't that they were angry—though she had no doubt they *were*—it was that they were lonely. Kaliaris was connected to her and Griff, and so could feel and experience what happened within the rest of the Station. But the way the Council had bound them to their location meant they couldn't act without some direction from Nyx or Griff.

Only within the Heart did they have true agency. Only within the Heart could Nyx hear their voice and talk to them. Kaliaris wanted her to be worried about Laiveran's condition, wanted her to feel the need to check on him, so she would have to come visit them.

This desire for her company was a vast improvement from feeling like Kaliaris held nothing but contempt for her, but she wished they weren't using another individual's physical well-being to coerce her into it. They could have just *asked* her to visit. But they either didn't realize that, or were too proud to actually do it.

"I'll check on him daily," she promised. "So don't even think about burying him under the vines again." She traversed the room until she stood by the cell. "Laiveran?"

His head turned toward her at the sound of his name, but there was no recognition behind his eyes, and he never stopped spitting out his stream of incoherent words, barely pausing to draw breath. She settled onto the floor, cross-legged, and waited.

Fifteen minutes ticked by, then thirty, then two hours. Laiveran's movements eventually became less erratic, his words less frantic, but the most response she got from her attempts to engage with him was a single, "Nyaera?" Then he squinted at her, realized she wasn't his dead wife, and returned to his rambling. Another hour of waiting did nothing.

Watching him, she couldn't help but wonder if that would be her, soon. If she was unable to fix her memory problem, would she end up wandering this Station like a half-present wraith, rarely aware of what time period it was and what she was doing? If that became her fate, what would it do to Kaliaris and Griff?

She brushed the thought away and stood, stretching, something in her upper back popping and releasing a knot of tension. "*Please* don't bury him again," she begged Kaliaris. "If you keep setting him back he'll never be rational." It was also unspeakably cruel, but she already knew that line of reasoning would get her nowhere with Kaliaris.

The vines around her rustled in assent.

"Beam me up?" she asked.

<Which of the stars is that, again? The one with the wars?>

"No, it's Trek," she said. "Star Trek." Sight was one of those senses Kaliaris only had through her or Griff, and thus far they'd been even less impressed by movies than their Avatar, and that was saying something.

Black mist curled around her legs, lifting her. She was floating a foot above the ground when her upward momentum paused and Kaliaris said, <Should you become lost in yourself, Nyx Fortuna, and should the Council threaten to take you from us, we will hide you here, in our Heart. We will protect you, until you come back to yourself. And we will protect your family as well.>

Tears pricked unexpectedly at the backs of her eyes. "Thank you."

The mist pushed, and she rose again.

She didn't know how realistic Kaliaris' plan was. If the

Council tried to replace her and Kaliaris rebelled, she didn't know that the Council wouldn't simply destroy the Station. After all, Earth Between's Station was one they had basically invented as a test run for the ability to create Stations at all. She'd heard it joked about more than once that Earth Between was, by most of the universe's standards, a backwater place to disappear to.

But it meant everything to her that Kaliaris would try.

4

Nyx spent the next week burying herself in the equally difficult problems that were Laiveran and her memories. And getting precisely nowhere with either of them.

Instead of getting better, Laiveran was regressing. She'd gone from trying to get him to talk, to feeling successful if she got him to eat. He didn't seem capable of focusing long enough to remember he had a physical body that needed feeding.

Had his temporary near-sanity when he'd held control of Kaliaris' soul been *because* of his contact with it? Was a soul connection of some kind like an essential nutrient for him? Or had his brief lucidity been born from his focus on finding Nyaera, and his belief that he was close to doing so?

She had tried and failed to find the answer to those questions. There were no histories available to Nyx on the subject because, as far as the known universe was aware, Laiveran's people had never existed. She'd hoped Griff might know, but he hadn't. Laiveran's belief that identical twins were, more or less, abominations, had led him to extend his dislike of Jevryn to the man dating him. As a result, Griff had had little occasion to learn about Laiveran's race in any depth.

With no better options, she'd started visiting twice a day,

hoping more human contact would help him. It was all she knew to do, for now, and it was one failure to distract her from another.

Her attempts to recreate the Hiding her mother had placed over her memories was proving equally frustrating. Nyx wasn't even resolved to taking that course of action yet, but she wanted to have it if no other solution presented itself. Unfortunately, as things were going, she wasn't going to have it.

Whatever else Elena Fortuna might have been, she was a master of her craft, with a wealth of experience Nyx either didn't have or couldn't remember having. No matter how many times she entered that place inside of her where her mother's Hiding had been, careful so as not to inadvertently trip onto a memory fragment, she couldn't understand what her mother had done. It was an ordinary Hiding, a net of magic like any her mother might make, and yet…it wasn't.

Nyx tried to Hide a single sphere of memory, but her promise to keep it Hidden fizzled out before it even came to life. She knew that childlike approach to Hidden magic had its limitations. Sometimes, a lack of skill or interference from other magic would prevent a promise from taking hold.

The only question was, did she lack the skill or magic necessary to hold something as complex as the net of her memories, or was something else preventing her magic from doing its job? Was the residue of her mother's magic interfering with her attempts to replicate the original Hiding?

The only way to eliminate the residue theory would be to Hide a memory that was in its proper place, one settled back into the puzzle board. She was reluctant to try it. For one, she had very few pieces to try from—she wasn't touching the gleaming whole, unscarred swathe of her post-eighteen memories for anything—and of the scattered pieces on the rest of the board…

She didn't know what they were. Which ones were which. Now that they'd been fitted back where they belonged, they weren't like videos she could pluck out and watch. She didn't know what she was willing to lose again. And if she *did* Hide one, since it was a part of her, would she remember doing it? What if she could never find it again? What if keeping all her old memories from crashing back into her mind and shattering it meant never having any hope of reclaiming them?

The tug of the Station's portal pulled her out of her worries—and yet another failed attempt at sussing out precisely what her mother had done—and she was grateful for the excuse to quit. She rubbed her temples as she walked to the Arrival Room, Griff joining her en route.

"Any idea what this is about?" she asked.

He shook his head.

The portal's activity didn't have the urgent feel of an unexpected traveler, and even if someone had paid to book a last-minute trip, she should have been notified if that was the case.

They walked into the Arrival Room right as a large box rose between the posts that formed the hexagonal portal. Ley dust crumbled off, revealing a large chest. It was a steamer-style trunk, black with silver designs etched onto it.

The portal floor re-solidified beneath the trunk, no individual following it through. That alone told her it had come from a member of the All Council—they were the only ones who could send unattended items through the lines to the Stations—but if she'd needed further proof, the large *JM* painted in the center would have given it.

JM could only stand for one thing: Jevryn A-Morridahn. When she squinted, the letters gave her the same double-vision she got when her translator was interpreting written language. Briefly, she dropped out of that network of spells, so she could see the letters as they actually were.

They transformed into a script that looked like Cyrillic and hieratic had had a love child, and they appeared to be part of a house crest. The letters arched above a silver skull. When she focused on it, hairline fractures spiderwebbed across the skull, then fused back together, leaving it whole once more. Another set of script rested beneath the skull, which her translator converted to: *Never broken.*

As family mottos went, she supposed it could be worse.

Something about the trunk itself bothered her—the smooth black material it was carved from felt familiar—but she couldn't put her finger on why. She grabbed one of the silver handles on the end and dragged it off the portal floor, grunting with the effort. Damn thing was heavy.

She dropped it and dusted off her hands, looking at Griff. "Well? You want to open it? You want me to throw it in the Den and pretend we never got it? Or send it back? I can send it back. I mean, I don't know where *to* send it, or how much intergalactic shipping costs on something this heavy, but—"

"I do not believe it is for me."

Nyx frowned. "Who else would it be for?"

Griff reached out, his talon hooking a tag that dangled from the opposite handle Nyx had grabbed. Her name was written on it.

She glared at it. "This had better be a very large Temerex care package or I'm sending it back, intergalactic shipping fees be damned." She undid the silver latches on the trunk's front and lifted the lid.

It was...sort of a Temerex care package. At least, the left half of the trunk was. The largest items were a slim black saddle with a matching pad. Next came a bag containing an assortment of bottles and soft cloths, along with a book on scale care. The last thing in that section was a journal in neat, handwritten script. A brief perusal showed it was a record of Temerex's medical history and a list of feeding guidelines.

As Nyx flipped through it, a page fell out. She picked it up, the paper thick between her fingers, and turned it over to find a picture of baby Temerex. She was unable to stop the *Aww* that came out of her mouth at seeing the unicorn-dragon as a foal. Her scales had been a lighter red as a baby, her horn more of a cute stub-spiral than the wicked implement of goring death it was today.

"I'm going to copy this, blow it up, and frame it." Maybe display it above the fireplace in the library. She tucked it carefully back into the pages of the notebook and turned her attention to the other half of the trunk.

Removable trays layered that portion, and she'd barely gone through the items on the uppermost one before she had to stop. "Okay, that I get"—she pointed at the Temerex-related side—"but this I don't. Why is he sending me all this stuff?"

There were two books of the forbidden-knowledge variety—both of them primers on portal magic and its workings—and a thin pamphlet that looked suspiciously like the user manual to her mercury boots. Well, at least he'd accepted that he wasn't getting the boots back.

There was so *much* stuff filling the right side of the chest that she hesitated to look through it all. "Well?" she asked, when Griff didn't answer. "You know him better than anyone, so what is he doing?"

Griff's beak opened, clicked shut. He ducked his head. "You did promise to attempt a nearly impossible feat. One he would like to see accomplished. He could simply be trying to aid you in that endeavor."

Nyx tossed the manual on the boots back into the trunk and crossed her arms. "But you don't think that's what he's doing."

"I think he *is* trying to help you. As for his motives for doing so...I cannot say."

"It sounds like you have a theory," she pressed.

Griff only shook his head. "One based on emotion and little fact."

Nyx sighed and let it go. When he put it like that, there was no need to push. Because, put like that, Jevryn had every reason in the world to aid her. He did want her to succeed, because her success meant Griff's freedom. He would want her to trust him —maybe even to like him—because Griff cared for her.

That, and if Jevryn had *any* modicum of decency, maybe he was feeling the teensiest bit guilty for dropping Nyx here as a baby with only her mother's tender mercies to rely on.

"I guess there's no need to look a gift trunk in the mouth." She closed the lid and had the Station send it up to her room. She could finish looking through everything later. As for right now, she had someone to check up on.

She made her way to the Station's guest wing and knocked on Liya's door. No one answered. Nyx hesitated a moment, then did a surface layer connection to Kaliaris' senses in Liya's room. As a general rule, Nyx stayed out of individual quarters now that she'd mastered enough control of the Station to do so.

She would personally find it creepy to know she was living in a building where someone had unmitigated spying rights on her—even if visual sight wasn't included, since Kaliaris had never had eyes—and was surprised her friends had just accepted that she wouldn't invade their privacy unless it was an emergency. Her surprise wasn't because she was untrustworthy, but because she didn't know if she could trust anyone else that way. Which probably said something about her, but she didn't care to parse out what that something was right now.

She connected to Liya's room just enough to sense that the girl was inside, lying on the bed, and didn't appear to be in distress. "Liya?"

The form on the bed stilled, like she was trying to keep even the sound of her breathing from exiting the room. Nyx respected that Liya didn't want to talk to her and broke her connection to the room, changing course for the Station's cafe.

It had picked up a brisker business now that Kalvar had taken back over most of the shifts, but it was empty at the moment except for her Tiagren barista. He gave her a broad smile, black stripes prominent against his skin. She was glad he'd stopped feeling like he needed to hide them.

"Hey, Nyx."

"Hey yourself." She hopped onto one of the barstools.

"You want something?"

"Sure. You pick." She didn't need anything—having a coffee shop literally at her disposal at all hours of the day and night was turning out to be a fast-track for shooting her caffeine consumption into the stratosphere—but she figured she was only young once and she might as well enjoy it while it lasted.

Not that her body was aging while she lived within the Station. Yet another thing she preferred not to think about most days. It wasn't that she was unhappy with the prospect of extended youth, precisely. It was that, having lived so much of her life completely alone or almost completely alone, she knew how devastating loneliness could be.

The people who were here with her now—they wouldn't always be. Griff, yes. Seth...maybe. But everyone else? They would reasonably want to go live their own lives—lives that would involve jobs and homes and families that couldn't be conducted or created within the small world of her Station. It was a *way*station for a reason. It was never intended to be a permanent dwelling.

Kalvar placed a mug in front of her. She sniffed it, not recognizing the scent. "What is this?"

"Latte with crushed talshia berry."

She took a cautious sip. It tasted like a lavender plant had mated with a blueberry. "It's...interesting," she said diplomatically.

He snorted. "You hate it. But you should know I sold ten of those this morning at a twenty-percent markup. It's not my fault your base Human subgroup Boring tastebuds are unrefined."

"*My* tastebuds are unrefined? You're the one who doesn't like gumbo."

Kalvar's face took on a pinched expression. "It's weird. And slimy."

"It is not slimy. Okra is not slimy when immersed in that much soup base. It becomes a thickening agent, that's the whole point."

"It's slimy," he insisted.

"You're weird," she shot back lamely. She tried the drink again, decided she still didn't like it, but was polite enough not to scrunch her face up at it despite his denigration of her favorite food. "Speaking of weird, I haven't seen Liya since I came back from the Land of Broken Memories. She doing okay?"

Kalvar's face went a little more neutral, a little harder to read. "She's...processing."

"It might be helpful if I had some idea of what she was processing."

Kalvar didn't answer.

"I'm beginning to think everyone in this Station, including myself, has a communication problem."

"If she needs to leave, I'll—"

"She doesn't need to leave. I told you she could stay as long as she needed to, and I meant it. But I get concerned when someone doesn't leave their room for five days." She knew Kalvar had brought Liya food, and even if he hadn't Kaliaris would send it up. Liya had her own bathroom. All her physical needs were met and it was literally impossible for her to be locked inside her room given that the Station was the Station, so her isolation was self-imposed, but that didn't mean she was *okay*.

Nyx didn't know anything about Liya, save that the girl looked like she wanted to run away, and fast, any time anyone save Kalvar looked at her for longer than three seconds. "Can you tell me anything without violating her privacy?"

"She's...dealing with some medical stuff."

"Is she okay? Does she need a doctor?"

"She's fine. She's in a recovery period physically, and emotionally she's just..."

"Processing," Nyx finished for him. "Okay. I'll back off. But please let her know she doesn't have to stay in her room all the time? There's no need to be afraid of us. And if she just doesn't want to see us, which is fine, I can have the Station add on a private exit from her room. I don't want her to feel trapped."

He nodded. "I'll tell her."

"How are you doing?"

The slightest stiffening of his shoulders, so minuscule she wouldn't have noticed it if she wasn't looking for it. "I'm good."

Again, she didn't push. The kid had his pride. She took her undrinkable beverage with her to her room—really, diplomacy had its virtues, and she could pretend to not dislike something as vehemently as she did—and set it on her nightstand before turning her attention to the black trunk now taking up a large chunk of her room.

"Okay, let's see what a councilor has to offer." She lifted out the top tray and placed it on the floor. Settling cross-legged next to it, she pulled out the remaining objects and placed them around her.

Mostly books—some histories that probably didn't exist outside of the All Council's hands anymore, since they looked like they detailed the rise of the connected universe and the conflict with the Minethrans—but there was also what looked like a softbound journal with twin quills on the front, and a plain box.

The box had a note on the front that read, "Arradin expressed you had concerns over the side effects of the first generation model." She pried the lid off to find a pair of shiny black suppressing cuffs.

Huh. So Griff and Jevryn were talking. That was interesting.

A knock sounded on her door. She put the lid back on the box and yelled, "Come in."

The door opened and Evra entered, her blonde hair in its typical plait down her back. "You're late," she said without preamble.

Nyx looked up. "Late for what?"

"Cardio."

Nyx groaned. "I don't remember signing up for cardio."

"Remember yesterday, when I said that you spent too long unconscious, only being kept in decent shape by medical magic, and you should expend some actual physical effort?"

"Uh-huh."

"You agreed that cardio was a good idea."

"I remember grunting in response to your obvious attempts to convince me that cardio was a good idea."

Evra waved a hand. "It is the same thing."

"It's really not."

Evra crossed her arms. "You will come running with me."

Nyx sighed. "Fine, but only because you asked so politely." And because she *had* spent five days unconscious and, despite the week that had passed between then and now, her body still felt sluggish and unused.

She started packing all of the stuff back into the chest.

"What is all of this?" Evra asked, stepping forward to survey the items.

"Jevryn's attempt to convince me that he's one of the good guys and just wants to be helpful." She repacked everything and was putting the last item—the softbound journal—into the trunk when Evra stopped her.

"May I see that?"

Nyx shrugged and handed the journal to her. The Amazon's long fingers stroked across the cover. She turned it over in her hands before finally opening it, inhaling sharply. "Do you know what this is?"

"I'm guessing if I did, I would be as excited as you are."

"It's a companion journal. They are made in pairs. Whatever is written in the one journal is transmitted to the other, no matter how far apart the two are. It is an instant means of communication to whoever holds the twin."

Nyx remembered reading something about them a few months ago. Evra sounded so impressed that Nyx wondered if it was time to tell her about cell phones and text messaging. Of course, cell phones required cell towers and networks and couldn't reach across space and time to another planet, so maybe the companion journals *were* impressive after all.

"Who has its twin?" Evra asked, handing it back.

Nyx read the text on the front page and snorted. "Jevryn, obviously. You couldn't tell by his message?"

Evra shook her head. "Their writings are only legible to their owners. So you, and Jevryn. What does it say?"

"Just Jevryn being Jevryn." The script on the first cream-colored page read:

> This is more efficient than shouting down a ring. I will check it in the evenings, unless you give me reason to do so more frequently. I will expect you to do the same.

Translation, he expected her to be at his beck and call each and every day. So much for feeling like she had some breathing room to make progress on the Harvester problem before she had to report to him on it.

Then again, what was he going to do if she didn't check the magic journal every night? Write her a sternly-worded reprimand in all caps?

"Yeah, I'm just going to put this back in the box." She tossed it into the trunk and closed the lid.

"Should you not take this a little more seriously?"

"Nope. I learned at a young age to distrust authority. I intend to continue distrusting it until forced to do otherwise."

Evra stared at the trunk, a frown worrying her brow. Nyx clapped her on the shoulder and steered her out of the room. "Come on, cardio waits for no one."

If she let Evra think about it any longer, the Amazon would probably force Nyx to write back. As far as Nyx was concerned, as long as she didn't write back, she could reasonably pretend she hadn't opened the journal and had no idea what it was.

5

Nyx returned from her run sweaty, thirsty, and annoyed by how much better she felt. That new and improved mood took an immediate hit when she saw who was waiting for her in the cafe.

Ankira and Tobi sat at the bar, the former with a glass of water, the latter with his usual mug of hot chocolate that was mostly whipped cream. He looked up when she entered, a big smile on his face.

Nyx's own expression must have given away how she felt, because his smile faltered, uncertainty in his eyes. Nyx mentally kicked herself. Tobi was far more used to being punished for what he could do than being appreciated for it, and she didn't want him to start thinking *she* didn't appreciate him.

She did. If he was also currently a reminder that her mental health was fragile and mostly out of her control, well, that wasn't his fault and he didn't need to see it.

"Hey, Doc," she said brightly.

Tobi's uncertainty disappeared at her greeting, and he gave her a shy smile that was all eight-year-old, even though the Congregation lurked in his eyes. He'd insisted that Ankira bring him to the Station every day to check on the deterioration in

Nyx's mind—and no, putting it like that didn't make her break out in hives *at all*—but he'd been reluctant to tell her anything concrete, saying he needed more time.

On his first visit, Nyx had called him "Doc" and, after explaining the nickname—it didn't translate so well—he'd decided he liked it.

"Am I due for my regular checkup?" she asked.

"Yes," he answered, voice serious. "We'll need the exam room."

The "exam room" was actually Morgen's meditation room, and infinitely more comfortable than a sterile room with a plastic bed and removable paper lining. But since Tobi had no idea what a typical US doctor's office exam room looked like, he'd taken her joke that the meditation room was the exam room literally, and she hadn't seen any point in disillusioning him.

She led him there now, settling onto one of the many floor cushions as he and Ankira did the same. The Warlock was uncharacteristically quiet, having said nothing more to Nyx than a routine greeting.

"Ready?" Tobi asked.

"Ready as I'll ever be." She took a deep breath and, at the gentle tap of Tobi's magic, let him into her mind.

A soft mental tug from Tobi drew Nyx out of the interior of her mind. She settled back into her body, blinking as she re-oriented herself in the room. A glance at her watch showed an hour had passed, though it felt like she'd sat down mere seconds ago.

She forced herself to affect an easy, non-serious tone. "What's the verdict, Doc?"

His little face was grave as he considered her question, and when he looked over his shoulder at Ankira his voice was all Congregation. "I would like to speak to her alone."

The Warlock clearly didn't like the idea. In this room and in this moment, she was a mother first, and it didn't matter to her that something ancient beyond reason was looking out through her son's eyes, she felt the need to protect him.

"It's okay," Nyx told Tobi. "Whatever you need to tell me, I don't mind if she hears."

Ankira shot her a wordless look of thanks. Nyx just nodded. Ankira had never pried, but after Tobi's first foray into Nyx's mind, she'd obviously figured out what Nyx was. Tobi was too young to understand that in explaining what was wrong with Nyx, he'd also made it clear to anyone who knew anything about the Hidden that that was what she was.

"The good news," Tobi said, "is that the smaller, more easily assimilable pieces of your memories will fall first. They required less magical structure to hold them in place to begin with, so there is less of its skeleton to hold them now."

Right. Less skeleton equaled quicker deterioration. She'd already noticed as much, arrested here and there on occasion by some poignant flash of memory, sometimes something so small it was less a memory and more a random emotion. It was always followed by the feeling of something missing inside her being made whole, of a slender internal cut healed over. "And the bad news?"

"While the bulk of your memories are not entirely uniform in size, they all fall within a narrow spectrum of size, and therefore required a narrow spectrum of magical structure to hold them in place."

Nyx's stomach sank. "So I'm going to have lots of them crashing into me at the same time."

Tobi nodded. "Yes. Or close enough to the same time that it won't make any material difference. We can't predict how you will respond to these influxes. If you simply become lost in a memory, remaining within it until able to reincorporate it, that would be disruptive to your life but might protect you from mental damage. But if your mind attempts to drag you into multiple memory spheres at the same time...we simply don't know what the effects will be. This is nothing we have ever encountered before."

Nyx nodded, feeling a little numb. "How long do you think I have before that starts happening?"

"It's difficult to say. Two weeks? Perhaps three? Once it begins, the rate of failure will only increase. If you have two days between a large memory fall and the next, after you might only have one. Then less. Does that make sense?"

"Yeah." Once the ride started, it would pick up speed until its inevitable crash landing. "Thank you. I appreciate everything you've done for me." She started to rise but Tobi reached out, drawing her back down.

"We said that we couldn't heal this for you, and we can't. But there might be someone who can." Hope was a quickened heartbeat in Nyx's chest. Tobi hesitated, and she had a feeling this was the part the Congregation had thought she might want privacy for. "We calculated the rate of decay several days ago. We have continued coming back to study the structure of the magical net that once held your memories. We believe—though we cannot be certain—that it was built in sequence.

"Think of it like knitting a hat from a pattern. As such, if someone knows the pattern, if they *built* the pattern, they might be able to recognize it in the pieces that are left, pieces that are attached to memory fragments. And if they can, then they would know where your memories belong based on their placement in the net fragments. With their assistance, you should be able to guide the memories into place with minimal repercussions."

Her earlier hope dimmed.

"We are sorry," Tobi said. "We weren't certain if it would be cruel to tell you, given..." He trailed off.

She choked down the anger that was rising in the wake of hope. It wasn't Tobi she was angry at. "Given that if someone did this to me, they're unlikely to want to help me fix it?" She stood and made herself smile. "I'm glad you told me. Thank you for coming, and for everything you've done for me."

Tobi nodded. The Congregation left his eyes and he was just a kid again, young and with that insecure look he got on his face after every single one of these sessions, because he still wasn't used to not being treated with contempt for doing good things.

Nyx opened her arms. "Hug?" she offered.

That shy smile returned and he came over to hug her. She squeezed him back, ruffling his hair, and dutifully pretended she didn't notice Ankira's eyes brightening.

"Did you give Kade my letter?" Tobi asked, his voice muffled where his face pressed into her shirt. He could finally pronounce Kaden's full name, but he still tended to drop the *N* out of habit. And he still hero-worshipped the guy.

"Morgen sent it," she told him. To Maruca, who'd enigmatically said she'd get it to him. "But we're not sure exactly where he is, so it might be a while before he can respond."

"Okay." Tobi let her go and stepped back. "Is he gone helping other people like he helped me?"

Nyx had absolutely no idea what Kaden Moor was doing, and she wanted to keep it that way. He'd left with Jevryn, and the councilor's morals didn't quite line up with Nyx's. But an eight-year-old didn't need to know any of that. "I don't know. but I'm sure that whatever he's doing, it's important. He'll write you back when he gets the chance."

She didn't doubt he would. After they'd come back from Arkadia, before the kids had gone to live with Ankira and Diana, Kaden used to wake up in the middle of the night, sometimes several times, to go check on them.

"Tobi, would you mind waiting outside?" Ankira said. "I'd like to speak with the Guardian for a moment."

The Guardian. Not Nyx. It set a certain tone, and indecision marred the Warlock's face. As if she had thought long and hard about what she wanted to say, but now that the time had come to say it, she was having second thoughts.

"That bad?" Nyx asked.

"I respect you. More than that, I like you. You brought me my children and you have always been kind. Furthermore, I am uniquely situated to understand how difficult your current predicament is."

"But?"

Ankira grimaced. "But as a citizen of Earth Between, I have to state the obvious. If you are unable to stop the progression of your condition, you are unlikely to be able to perform the duties of the Guardian role. You should consider stepping down and allowing a new Guardian to take your place, before you are no longer able to make the decision."

The words stung. Perhaps more so because of the preparatory statement Ankira had led with before saying them. It wasn't that they didn't make sense—to someone who couldn't know that Nyx *couldn't* step down, not with the way she was now tied to the Station, to Griff, it was a logical thing to point out—it was that she thought of Ankira as a friend. And as a friend, she might have hoped for something a little less cold.

Ankira didn't stop there. "We may be a small community here, but the Station is important to our daily lives. We rely on the goods that are transported through it."

Nyx wasn't unaware of this fact. Since Earth Between saw so little tourism, no small number of her regular Arrivals were merchants and their wares. It was a fact she turned over and over in her mind every time she remembered her promise to Kaliaris: to undo what had been done to her Station. To all the Stations.

Which would mean there wouldn't *be* any Stations left. The fallout from that…it would be like halting all travel between every country on Earth without preparation. The planets the Stations connected—like the countries on Earth—were too reliant on each other to suddenly halt all exchanges of goods without repercussions, some of which would be catastrophic.

"If you are unable to handle Arrivals and furthermore

unaware of the fact that you are not doing so, it could take time for the Council to become aware of the situation and replace you. If it takes them six months to resolve the problem, it won't mean anything to them. We aren't an important outpost. But it will cost a great deal to the people who live here."

"You don't need to worry about it coming to that," Nyx made herself say.

Ankira gave her a smile that was both sad and resolved. "See that it doesn't."

Something in her words, her voice, made Nyx's spine stiffen. If Nyx didn't give Ankira a solution before the Warlock thought Nyx posed a problem to Earth Between, would she petition the Council about her?

Ankira had no idea how bad that would be. If they had a reason to look at Nyx again, if they discovered how her bond with the Station had altered, how she'd altered *Griff's* bond...she didn't think even Jevryn's help would be enough to protect her.

She opened her mouth to say something—anything—to convince Ankira she didn't need to make that choice, when the door opened, admitting Griff.

"I am sorry to interrupt, but we've had a request for an unscheduled Arrival. It's a high priority request, and I gather from the urgency that the travelers may be in some distress."

"I'll be right there." The high priority travelers would be stuck in the ley line, waiting, until she opened the portal. Griff's altered bond with the Station meant he could open it as well, but for obvious reasons they were keeping that fact to themselves. She looked to Ankira. "Please don't make any hasty decisions. You have my word that Earth Between won't suffer for my condition."

If Nyx lost her grip on reality, Griff could handle the influx of travelers with Seth glamouring him to look like her. But again, not something she could tell Ankira.

Nyx headed for the Arrival room. She'd never had a high priority Arrival request. Plenty of unplanned Departures came through—Earth Between wasn't for everyone, and some tourists got bored enough in the first few days of a planned vacation that they decided to hightail it for more interesting destinations—but never any unplanned Arrivals.

She had a mild sense of foreboding as she strode into the Arrival Room. The six posts that formed the hexagonal landing space were already humming with activity, the silver spheres atop them spinning. The movement indicated her travelers already waited on the other side of that cosmic floor.

Who needed to get to *Earth* so quickly that they paid the outrageous fees to do so unplanned? She wondered if Griff was right, and the travelers were in distress. Except she couldn't imagine a single kind of distress that was better served by getting on a ley line instead of finding the nearest medical professional.

She waited with uneasy anticipation as the floor began to shift and swirl. The surface of the landing zone broke as two heads surfaced, then two forms, the smaller of them looking as if it was trying to keep the larger one upright.

The ley dust crumbled off. The smaller person—a Tiagren woman with straight black hair and prominent stripes on her tan skin—Nyx didn't recognize. But the other...

"Lord Beauregard?" Morgen's uncle had departed Earth months ago, and Morgen hadn't heard a single word from him. Nyx knew, because she pestered Morgen about him constantly, wanting to dive into the man's wealth of knowledge on the Kumir. Or, at least, what she presumed was a wealth of knowledge since he'd made hunting the Kumir his life's passion.

And now here he was, in her Station, barely standing. He took a step forward and went down. The woman tried to hold him up but he was taller, wider, and heavier, and she wasn't built with Evra's muscle. She crashed to her knees with him.

"Griff," Nyx yelled, "get Morgen." The command was unnecessary, as Griff was already flying from the room.

She rushed to Beauregard's side. "What happened?" she asked the woman. "Where is he hurt?"

"Knife wound to the stomach."

Nyx blinked. If he'd taken a knife wound, where was all the blood?

"Anything else?" she asked as a first-aid kid bubbled up through the floor, the Station responding to her silent request. She flung it open, hastily pulling on a pair of latex gloves and grabbing several packages of gauze.

She pulled Beauregard's hands from his wounds and lifted his shirt. His abdomen was wrapped in a tight bandage that felt like wax to her touch, as if it had melded to his skin. She tried to peel the edge of it back but the woman slurred, "Don't. Regen kit—" The woman broke off, swaying, which was when Nyx realized she had blood dripping from her scalp. The woman had a head wound, and likely a concussion to go with it. She blinked, as if willing herself to remain conscious, and finished, "Malfunctioned."

Nyx assumed she meant the Enforcer regen kits, but she had no idea what a malfunction of one of them meant for Beauregard's injury. At that moment Morgen rushed into the room, Seth and Evra in tow.

Seth's gaze snapped to the woman, his voice filled with incredulity. "Reyva?"

The woman smiled and said,"Hey, Hawthorne," before promptly losing her battle with consciousness.

Evra caught her as she fell, keeping her head from hitting the ground. "What happened?"

Nyx returned to the problem of Beauregard. "I don't know. She said Beauregard took a knife wound. I don't know how long ago and when I tried to remove his bandaging, she told me not to because the regen kit had malfunctioned."

Morgen cursed. "Is the Warlock still here?" His voice was clipped, eyes worried as he catalogued his uncle's condition.

"Yes," the Warlock answered for herself as Tobi practically

dragged her into the room. His hand was clenched in Ankira's, his face taking on the kind of carefully impassive expression a child shouldn't be able to manage.

Nyx couldn't help but wonder if it came from his time on Arkadia, or if it was the Congregation's influence. Either way, Ankira noticed. Her free hand squeezed his shoulder. "You do not have to do this, sweetheart."

He straightened his shoulders and dropped her hand. "I do. He won't live if I don't." His eyes drifted to the woman—what had Seth called her? Reyva?—and said, "She has more time." He knelt in between Nyx and Morgen. Ankira followed, her hands placed firmly on his shoulders, her eyes resigned.

Tobi gently moved Nyx's hands off Beauregard's stomach, replacing them with his own.

"Just like we practiced," Ankira told him, her voice soothing. "It doesn't control you, you control it."

Nyx wondered at the Warlock's new concern, the guiding tone. She hadn't been worried while Tobi worked on Nyx. But maybe that was because she knew there was nothing Tobi could heal inside Nyx, and therefore nothing to cause him a massive expenditure of effort, while Beauregard had an assortment of wounds ranging from the shallow to the critical.

Tobi's eyes glazed over. As magic flowed from his hands, the Warlock began carefully peeling the bandage from the wound. Skin came away with the waxy material, as if the bandage had chemically bonded to it. Blood poured as she pulled. But the bleeding stopped almost as fast as it began, Tobi's magic suffusing Beauregard's skin, knitting it back together.

The wound closed fully over and Tobi hovered there, his hands shaking a little, as if he struggled to be both here and wherever the *there* was that the Congregation existed. The pull to that collective appeared to be gripping him stronger than it had when he'd worked with Nyx.

"Good," the Warlock murmured soothingly, "keep control. Move to the next one. But at *your* pace."

Tobi managed a small nod and turned to Reyva, his hand brushing over the head wound. Nyx felt his magic working at something that was deeper than skin-level, before moving up to the surface, the visible cut closing over. His hands reached for the other small slashes and bruises on Reyva's arms, but Ankira caught his wrists.

"Are any of the other wounds life-threatening?" she asked him.

"No, but I can—"

"Then let it go, like we practiced. You've done enough."

Clearly straining against the impulse to keep healing, Tobi finally gave another small nod and took a deep breath. "Thank you for your help," he said, and it took Nyx a moment to realize he was talking to the Congregation that drove him to keep healing. "But my need of you is over." His voice sounded small in the Arrival Room, as he spoke to something ancient and far bigger than himself, but he was firm, for all that.

To Nyx, Tobi said, "They'll be okay. And it's safe to move them. But they're going to sleep for a few hours."

"Thank you." Morgen held out his hand to Tobi, who took it with a grave little handshake.

For ease of conveyance, Nyx had the Station add on two rooms adjacent to the Arrival Room to house Beauregard and Reyva until they woke. Evra and Morgen carried Beauregard. Seth picked up Reyva and followed.

As they left, Ankira quietly suggested Tobi go out front to check on the two Gliblin birds they'd ridden to the Station. Mention of the birds brought a happy smile to his face and he ran out, Congregation and life-threatening wounds forgotten for now.

Nyx turned to Ankira. "I'm sorry.

Surprise flickered across the Warlock's face. "For what? You didn't summon Lord Beauregard and his injuries here, nor did you force Tobi to heal him. It was out of your control."

Nyx's next words were out of her mouth before she could

stop them. "You seem to want to hold me accountable for other things that are outside of my control."

Ankira drew back. "That's different," she said stiffly.

"Is it?"

"Yes. I'm sorry for it, but I am not wrong."

"Ankira…" She used the Warlock's name because the woman had given so few people in Earth Between permission to use it. "You know me. I care about the people here too, and I promise this won't affect them. I just need a little time."

"Time," Ankira said softly, "is exactly what you do not have." She walked out as Seth was coming back in.

He narrowed his eyes at the Warlock's retreating figure. "What was that about?"

6

Nyx wanted to say nothing. She wanted to pretend this wasn't happening to her. But apparently there wasn't enough time for her to have the luxury of faking normal, even for a few more days. "Turns out my prognosis is worse than we thought."

"What do you mean?" Griff asked, drawing closer.

"I mean I'm a memory avalanche waiting to happen. Once the bigger memories start hitting, Tobi thinks they'll *all* start hitting. I've got maybe three weeks before I don't remember what age I am.

"The Warlock is concerned about how the people of Earth Between will be affected by this. For instance, if I can't receive any incoming goods shipments because I can't remember I'm twenty-six instead of six. She wants me to resign because she doesn't think the Council will be very speedy in sorting out the mess if I go off the rails."

"And if you don't?" Seth's voice had an edge to it she'd rarely heard. He was clearly tense from Reyva's arrival and looking for something else to be riled up about to take his mind off it.

"She heavily implied she would make the request to the Council for me."

A muscle feathered in his jaw and he turned, heading for the Station door.

She sighed. "Where are you going?"

"To talk to her."

"You know, shockingly I did try that."

"You did," he called back. "I didn't."

"Stubborn ass," she muttered.

"Should one of us go after him?" Griff asked.

Nyx shook her head. "There's no reasoning with him when he gets that tone." Something niggled at the back of her mind, like a loose tooth she wanted to worry with her tongue.

"Are you certain?"

"Yeah, trust me. There was this time he—" She broke off, frowning. The memory was there, right on the tip of her tongue, but she couldn't quite catch it. The niggling sensation intensified, then something broke free, and she was falling into it.

<hr>

"**N**yx?"

A large eagle's eye blinked in Nyx's face. She took a step back. Griff had been poodle-sized and fifteen feet away, but now he was buffalo-sized and in her face. How had he gotten there? She'd been thinking about Seth, and—oh.

A memory sliver. Something small enough she'd experienced it as a remembered event rather than thinking she was still in that point in time. "How long was I out?"

"Only a minute," Griff said cautiously. "But you were unresponsive."

"So I didn't do anything weird?"

He shook his head, shrinking to his previous size. "No. It was as if you had fallen asleep standing up, with your eyes open. You showed no recognition of me when I stepped in front of you. Are you certain you're alright?"

She had a feeling she was going to be hearing that question a lot over the next few days. "I'm fine. I'm not confused. It was a small memory." He opened his beak, but she pushed forward. "We should check on Reyva and Beauregard."

She didn't want to talk about her "condition" anymore. Not right now. She'd always needed time for bad news to settle. To know her true emotional reaction to something, she usually needed around forty-eight hours to process it. As Ankira had said, time was exactly what Nyx didn't have right now, but she at least needed a few hours. Surely she could afford to take them.

And Beauregard's return—his and Reyva's injuries and current status—was a tangible problem she could dedicate herself to. She popped into Reyva's room first. The woman was still out, her breathing steady, so Nyx moved on to Beauregard's, Griff following her in.

Morgen sat in a chair beside the bed Beauregard lay on. Morgen had removed his uncle's torn clothing and replaced it with loose-fitting clothes the Station had provided.

With those practical things taken care of, he didn't appear to know what to do with himself. He was bent forward, forearms resting on his thighs, hands loosely clasped, a pensive expression on his face.

"Knock knock," she said softly.

"Hey, little Guardian." He didn't look away from the bed.

"Where's Evra?"

"Went to get some salve she swears by for the small cuts Tobi didn't heal." His voice lacked its usual warmth and charm, the words coming out in an empty, mechanical beat.

"He'll be okay. Tobi's never wrong about this stuff."

Morgen nodded but didn't say anything else.

"Do you know who the woman is? Reyva?"

He shook his head. "Didn't Seth say?"

"He'd have to be here to say." At that, Morgen did look at

her. She shrugged. "He got some news he didn't want to hear. He'll be back once he's processed it. What's your excuse?"

"For what?"

"The anger oozing out of your pores." She'd been around him long enough to tell the difference between his worry and his anger. Earlier, in the Arrival Room, he'd been worried. Now that it had sunk in that Beauregard would be fine, concern had given way to a quiet fury.

Morgen's clasped hands tightened. "If Tobi had not, by pure chance, been here, Uncle Beau would be dead. Along with that poor woman he no doubt roped into his schemes like the rest of his followers.

"Aside from the Moors and my mother, Beau's my only remaining family. And when he left four months ago, he couldn't even be bothered to tell me he was leaving, much less where he was going. You know how I learned? I went to see him and found out from the castle guards."

Nyx didn't know what to say, how to help. Her only close relationships before she'd come to the Station had included Seth, her mother, and Viktor. She wasn't entirely sure the last two even counted.

"Wherever he was—I'm sure he had a good reason. I'm sure it was important."

Morgen gave a dry laugh. "Oh, I'm sure. His damn crusade is *always* more important than everything and everyone else."

Evra slipped into the room, a jar in her hands. She walked around the opposite side of the bed from Morgen, a careful quiet in her movements as she started applying the salve, like she didn't want to interrupt Morgen's train of thought. But when he didn't continue talking, she asked quietly, "When did it start?"

"Before I was born. He tried to give it up once, when I was five. He lived with us for a year. Getting him there took Mum years of insisting his attempts to heal his grief obviously weren't working, and he needed to come home.

"I heard that reasoning later, of course. I was too young to really get it then, but I remember how he was when he came to us. Barely ate anything, slept all the time. Mum used to make me knock at his room and ask him to do things with me—draw or play or help me with chores or whatever.

"I didn't understand until later it was because it's a lot harder to say no to a kid who's too young to grasp depression. Especially hard to say no when that kid's half-Siren. It took six months before he stopped acting like a zombie, and by the time another six had passed, it was like I had an actual uncle.

"Then the Kumir came for him." He paused, a phantom of a smile on his face. "He's not paranoid, you know? They really *are* out to get him. They broke into the house in the middle of the night. They came to my room first. I still remember those dead eyes staring into mine before they turned and walked out because I wasn't what they wanted.

"Mum and Uncle Beau took them all out. She screamed at me to stay in my room, but I came out anyway. They were all dead between his room and the hallway and he was just kneeling there, in all that blood, crying.

"Then he stood up, looked at my mother and said, 'It won't stop until I make it stop.' He walked out and I didn't see him more than a handful of days a year in the next decade. By then the Kumir had a reputation across all the planets and he'd built himself an army of devoted grief-stricken idiots. Every single one of them just as happy as him to turn their backs on their remaining family in favor of a vendetta in memory of the family they'd lost.

"You know Mum almost died a few years ago? A rare bacterial infection the healers almost failed to identify. He didn't even come home then. Because he had 'a lead.' Sent a damn bouquet of flowers and you know what she told me? 'He's doing what he has to, son.' Well, fuck that.

"When I asked him to come to Earth Between when I knew I might need a place to disappear to here, I'm surprised he did it. I thought maybe he was changing a little. Thought maybe if I spent some time with him, I'd finally understand.

"But I still don't understand. And he still isn't talking. He's going to disappear one day and we'll never know if he's dead or worse, and for what? A lifetime of service to a dead woman's memory."

The room settled into silence, nothing but the quiet sounds of breathing and the rustle of Griff's feathers as he shifted. Then the sound of Evra clicking the cap back on the jar of salve and setting it aside.

"Sometimes," Evra said softly, "people don't know how to let a thing go. Sometimes, once they've followed a thing for too long, if they let it go they'll crumble. Because it has become their foundation, and if you remove it there is nothing left to hold them up.

"And sometimes"—she crossed to the other side of the bed and knelt beside Morgen, taking his clenched hands in hers—"they do have their reasons. Your mother seems to think Beauregard has his."

In response to the look he gave her she said, "I'm not saying that makes them right. I am only saying that sometimes we need to recognize when we want more from people than they are capable of giving."

Nyx slipped out of the room as unobtrusively as she could, Griff on her heels. It felt like the conversation was heading into deeply personal territory, and she didn't feel like she had any part in it.

She checked in on Reyva again, but the woman was still out, and since Seth hadn't come back, Nyx still had no idea who Reyva was. Or rather, she had no idea who she *actually* was. Nyx had gone looking for her and Beauregard's papers, intending to finish their Arrival check-in to the Station. But Beauregard's papers hadn't had his name or his face on them, and since Cordaline Ander was a name that in no way shortened to Reyva, Nyx was guessing the woman's papers weren't hers either. The picture on them looked similar enough to her, sans tiger stripes, but Cordaline's race was listed as Anduvian, not Tiagren.

Nyx entered her room, gaze landing on the black trunk Jevryn had sent. She already had a chest at the end of her bed that she didn't want to give up, so she'd shifted a section of the wall, forming a recessed nook for the new one.

On impulse, she took out the companion journal. Of all the people she knew, Jevryn was the one most likely to know where her mother was. Since she now had a pressing need to see her mother, maybe she could pretend she'd just discovered the journal and ease into asking him for help?

Three new sentences had appeared below his original message. Judging by the gradually crankier tone of each one, she was guessing they'd all been written on different days.

> How is Temerex faring?

> If you do not wish to speak of Temerex, how is your work with Laiveran coming along?

> It is a simple task to check a notebook and reply.

She could practically hear the irritation in the last one. She wondered how many centuries it had been since someone had failed to follow Jevryn's orders to the letter.

She found a pen, hesitating over her word choice before deciding it didn't matter. She was never going to impress him. He'd either help her or he wouldn't.

> I don't perform tasks well on command, even simple ones. You gave up the right to ask about Temerex when you dumped her here.

She waited. It was evening. Assuming that when he'd said they should both check it in the evening he intended to do her the courtesy of meaning *Earth* evening, there was a chance he might write back.

She continued waiting. Was it better or worse that a companion journal didn't have blinking ellipses to let her know if Jevryn was composing a response?

Leaving the notebook open on the bed, she pulled out one of the books he'd sent on portal magic and started reading. She wasn't petty enough to turn down freely given forbidden knowledge just because it had come from him.

An hour and a half went by before movement in her peripheral vision caught her eye. She traded the book for the journal, following the words as they appeared on the page.

> Am I to assume, then, that since you have deigned to reply you intend to ask something of me?

So much for subtlety.

> Yes.

His reply spread across the page in fast, short strokes.

> I have already done much on your behalf with little return. Have you learned anything of note from Laiveran?

> Nothing yet.

She almost asked Jevryn about the potential for Laiveran to need a soul connection, but decided to push in the direction of her own personal needs first.

> If you want me to get anything out of Laiveran, I'm going to need a favor.

Ten minutes went by without a reply. "Ten bucks says he's forming the most eloquent version of 'Do you know who I am?' to ever grace the physical page," she said aloud.

She'd started saying things aloud a lot in the last few days. At first, she'd thought she was developing a habit of talking to herself. But the more she did it, the more she realized it was because she could feel someone listening: Kaliaris.

Yes, the Station could feel everything that went on within its walls. But nothing was ever directed *to* them because, prior to Nyx, no one save Griff had realized there was a *they* that existed.

So she'd started talking, directing her thoughts to the Station. Deep within, she felt a faraway rustle of vines as Kaliaris perked up, a sliver of their attention diverting to her.

Jevryn's reply began,

> You are young—

"Ooh, he's about to explain the facts of life to me." Another rustle of vines that was almost a chuckle.

> —so I will do you the courtesy of imparting knowledge you have perhaps not yet had the time to acquire. You may feel that because I have been lenient with you in the past, because I have come to your aid in the past, that I am here to be commanded at your whim. I am not.

"Wait for it," she told Kaliaris.

> I have lived dozens of your mortal lifespans. I have seen civilizations rise and fall. I have traveled to more planets than you will ever know even existed, and I have lost more than you could ever hope to gain.
>
> Do not presume to threaten me. You have no idea who you are dealing with.

"Aaand there it is." She slow-clapped for Kaliaris' benefit and was pretty sure she got an actual laugh this time. She couldn't hear their voice outside of the Station's Heart, but she was getting better at interpreting that sense of rustling vines she felt through their bond.

She lifted her pen.

I would never presume to threaten you.

She was almost feeling petulant enough to add, *Oh Great One,* but refrained. He was right about one thing—she *did* fail to take him as seriously as she should. And she wasn't entirely sure why.

But since we are working together toward a common goal, I feel obligated to let you know that, unless you can help me out, I might be as insane as Laiveran in a few weeks and therefore not much use to you.

He responded with a single demand.

Explain.

She gave him a brief recap of her current scenario, as factually and unemotionally as she could.

I must apologize. This might not have happened had I taken more care with your mother's…situation.

She snorted.

Maybe consider that the next time you decide to drop a woman with a newborn in the middle of nowhere.

Had I not dropped her there, I would have strangled her and you would have died for lack of a mother.

Cold text wasn't good at conveying emotion, but she didn't get the impression Jevryn was joking. The finality in his words got to her in a way his do-you-know-who-I-am speech hadn't. It wasn't that she bore her mother any particular loyalty. She didn't. Nor was it that the idea of never being born bothered her, because if she'd never been born, there would be no *her* to be bothered.

No, it was the way he threw it out so casually, as if people were nothing to him. Maybe they weren't. After someone had lived so long…did they even view themselves as a person anymore?

She pressed her pen to the page and wrote back.

Can you find my mother and bring her to Earth's Station? Without strangling her? She's the only guarantee I have of fixing this.

Precisely how much time do you have?

Best-case scenario? Three Earth weeks.

I will handle it.

Can you find her that soon?

Finding her is not the issue.

What is?

Extricating her from her current location without drawing attention.

Where is she?

That is not your concern. As I have said, I will handle it. In the meantime, I would appreciate it if you would check the book in the evenings.

"Yes, fine, I'll check it," she muttered, flipping the book closed. Raising her voice, she said, "You might as well come in."

The door opened, revealing nothing. But through Kaliaris she felt Seth standing there, the same way she'd felt him walk into the Station five minutes ago, pausing for a moment to look into Reyva's room before coming up the stairs.

"It's creepy the way you do that," he said, dropping the illusion. He leaned against the doorjamb, his hands shoved into his pockets.

"You're just upset because you still can't trick the Station's senses."

"I'm doing everything right. Sight, hearing, touch—I should be beyond notice. When are you going to tell me why I'm not?"

She shrugged. "Whenever I figure it out? I don't really know."

"But if you had to guess?" His voice was a little too monotone, and it was that more than anything else that made her answer rather than ask about Reyva.

"You've listed the senses of the universe's races. Human, general mammalian, reptilian, avian—we all have some version of sight, hearing, and touch. Kaliaris…isn't any of those things. They feel. They sense, they hear. They see through my eyes and Griff's.

"But they were a planet. I don't know if either of us can comprehend the immensity of a being like that. I don't know if you could ever understand their senses enough to trick them. Or at least, I think to do it, you would have to trick the *entirety* of the Station. Not just make them think you aren't where you are right now, but that you aren't anywhere on the grounds.

"You're good. I don't know if you're *that* good." He frowned, but she knew it wasn't at what she'd told him. Not really. "So how'd your talk go? I give you a ten out of ten on storming out of the Station, by the way. Very dramatic."

"Thanks," he said drily. A half-smile curved his lips, then

died. "The Warlock told me what Tobi said. About your mother being able to fix this."

Nyx leaned back against the bed pillows, crossing her arms. "Yeah, well, *I* would have told you if you hadn't left."

"Sorry." He looked away from her. "You don't need to worry anymore. The Warlock won't go to the Council."

Nyx raised an eyebrow. "Yeah? How did you manage that?"

"I told her that if you get lost and you can't come back, I'll take the Guardianship."

That hit Nyx with a barrage of conflicting emotions, so what came out of her mouth next was what *didn't* matter. "That won't be necessary. Even if I'm…lost, Griff can handle the Arrivals now."

"She doesn't know that."

"That isn't even how Guardianships work, you can't just *take* it."

"Again, she doesn't know that."

"I would never ask you to do that for me, even if you could."

"I know. But if you needed me to, and I could, then I would."

She knew it, even if she hated it a little because she was sick of him being tethered to places because of her. She knew he didn't mean it like that, that he didn't see it that way. But she did.

Seth continued, "We have to find your mother. I know we don't have any good leads, but I—"

"We don't have to find her. Jevryn already knows where she is."

He stiffened. "When were you going to tell me that?"

"Literally right now. I've known for all of five minutes, by the way, so thanks for biting my head off over it."

"Five minutes? At the risk of sounding patronizing, I don't see Jevryn here." Nyx tossed the companion journal at him. He stared. "What is this?"

"It's the companion journal Jevryn sent me."

He whistled. "And what prompted that gift?"

"He wanted progress reports on my attempts to liberate his ex. Since I can't help him if I can't remember who I am, I told him it was in his best interests to find my mother."

Seth's frown returned. He dropped the journal onto the foot of her bed. "So where is she?"

"His Immortal Awesomeness didn't see fit to tell me."

Seth raised an eyebrow. "Tell me you're feeling bitter about it without telling me you're feeling bitter."

"My mind's about to shatter and my best course of action is to rely on a guy I'm pretty sure cares about *nothing* in this universe apart from Griff, so excuse me if I feel like I have the right to be bitter about it!" And now she was yelling. Perfect.

"Hey." Seth stepped close, wrapped his arms around her, and pulled her in. "Shit, I'm sorry."

She buried her face in his neck, breathing in the familiar scent of him, and said what she'd been trying not to admit, even to herself. "I'm scared, Seth."

He squeezed her tighter. "Me too."

"Stay with me tonight." They hadn't slept in the same bed together since the Shadow Market. It was weird. Not because she didn't understand the mechanics of "taking it slow" but because they'd rarely *not* slept in the same bed. It was a habit developed long before they'd ever started having sex.

She missed his presence, his company. Missed the sound of his breathing and the feel of his heartbeat.

"I don't think I should."

"Just *stay*. I'm not going to jump you in your sleep."

He exhaled heavily. "That's not what I'm worried about."

"Yeah, it is, though I don't really understand why. You're going to give me a fucking complex."

"I just wanted you to remember, first." He shook his head. "I didn't mind waiting, and now…"

"And now I might go crazy at any minute," she finished. That could be problematic, she supposed. If they were in the middle of…things, and her brain suddenly short-circuited.

"Please don't joke about that after what you just said."

"It's not a joke, it's a factual statement." She sighed. "If you want space from me, that's fine. But you need to tell me you want it because I don't know where the lines are. Near as I can tell we never had any before."

Far from sounding relieved, his next words were grumpier than ever. "I don't want space." He let her go and began unlacing his shoes.

"What are you doing?"

"Staying." He finished with the laces, kicked the shoes off, closed the door, and flopped onto her bed. "Happy?"

"How could I not be, with such cheery company?"

He rubbed at his eyebrow with his middle finger.

"Very mature." She dropped onto her usual side of the bed. He was practically hugging the edge of the mattress on his. "Are you actually going to stay all the way over there? I seem to recall you bragging about your cuddling abilities back when I barely remembered who you were."

He glared at her.

"Come on." She batted her eyelashes at him. "I promise I'll still respect you in the morning."

"You're a pain in the ass," he grumbled. But he turned onto his side and pulled her against him.

"Yeah, well, you're a jerk," she shot back. The words came out muffled against his shirt.

"I know it. Try not to drool on me in your sleep."

"You know what? I take it back. I don't want to cuddle anymore." She put her hands on his chest and pushed away from him. He pulled her back in.

"Too late. You made your choices, now you have to live with them."

"Story of my life."

"Yeah." His hand stroked up her back absently. "Mine too."

"So..." she began.

The corner of his mouth tilted up, like he already knew what she was leading into. "Yes?"

"You and Reyva had a thing, huh?"

"Why, Nyxi, are you jealous?" His eyes were practically dancing with laughter.

She scoffed. "As if."

His grin widened. "Oh, you definitely are. Or maybe 'possessive' is the better term for it. You do get practically feral when other people touch your things."

"You aren't a possession."

"Mmm. But I'm yours." He kissed the tip of her nose. "And maybe I like it when you're possessive."

She rolled her eyes. "If you're envisioning Reyva and me having a cat fight over you, just let me know when you'd like me to punch the sense back into you."

"Please, why aspire so low as a cat fight when I could go straight for lingerie pillow fight?"

She punched him in the stomach. It was a half-hearted punch and he was braced for it before she ever moved, so he barely even grunted.

"For the record," she said, "even though you and Kaden were dicks to each other—"

"Because he's a dick."

"—I'm not going to do the same to Reyva. She seems nice. I'm just curious."

"She seems nice," he repeated. "Did you glean that from the expression on her face in the twenty seconds you saw her before she passed out, or do people with head wounds automatically qualify as nice?"

"Remind me why I like you?"

"Hell if I know." He kissed her again. "But to answer your question, yeah, Reyva and I had 'a thing.' We worked together for a couple years in the Market. Sometimes neither of us felt like being lonely. It was never serious."

She should probably leave it there, but she'd never been good at leaving things alone. "Why not?"

He shrugged. "I always knew I was missing something. Maybe I didn't know what it was, but I knew it wasn't her."

She sighed. "You can be really sweet when you're not even trying."

"Don't you forget it either." He winced as soon as the words were out of his mouth, as if just realizing that she was, quite possibly, very soon to forget it. Softly, he added, "Please."

"I'll try." It was the only promise she could make and have any hope of keeping.

7

The twinge that woke Nyx was soft and gentle, an internal tug from the Station. It took her a groggy moment to identify what it was for, until her sleep-addled brain remembered she'd put sensors on Beauregard's and Reyva's doors that would wake her if either of them left their rooms.

She stabbed at the light-up button on her watch. The briefly-illuminated numbers informed her it was oh-four-thirty. A good hour-and-a-half earlier than she preferred to be awake.

She bit back a groan and slid out of bed carefully, her gaze trained on Seth. He *looked* as if he slept like the dead, but he had a tendency to wake at the slightest sound from her. She made it out of the room without disturbing him, pausing in the hallway long enough to change from sleep attire into jeans and a t-shirt.

She wasn't entirely sure why she hadn't wanted to wake him. At least, she wasn't sure if it was because this portion of what she had to do was Guardian business, and therefore not really any of his, or if it was because part of her wanted to talk to Reyva without him there.

Despite his teasing last night, she wasn't jealous. She trusted him too much for jealousy. It was more…curiosity. And, okay, maybe it was a *little* possessiveness.

He was hers. He'd always *been* hers, and if things had been different, he might never have stopped being hers. Now she had this period where he hadn't been, and she was curious about the woman who'd stepped into her place, if only for a short while. She wondered if Seth had felt like this about Kaden—this sense of not knowing *how* to feel.

She was happy he hadn't been alone. Part of her thought that maybe if he could be happy with someone a little less screwed-up than her, someone who wasn't tied to a Station, embroiled in things way over her head, and about to lose her mind, then maybe he should be.

Maybe Reyva was better for him than she was. Maybe—

She shook her head. Maybe she needed to ingest actual caffeine before she did any more philosophical introspecting about her relationship. Especially if she was spiraling into trying to determine if a woman she didn't even know was better for her boyfriend than she was.

Downstairs, Reyva was awake and looking generally unhappy. Probably because the Station was keeping her confined to her room and the cafe. Naturally, she was looking for a way out.

Nyx found her crouched in front of the door that let onto the front porch, obviously trying to pick the lock. Reyva didn't have metal picks, or any physical tools Nyx could see, but the intent pouring off her magic was clearly meant to make the door's lock release.

"It's not going to open," Nyx said.

Reyva jerked upright, turning, her light brown eyes angry.

"I did try explaining that," Griff said from his perch on the back of one of the barstools. He was in his non-threatening housecat size again.

Reyva ignored him, focusing on Nyx. "You have no right to hold me here."

"I do, actually." Nyx kept her voice mild. "Given the unusual circumstances of your Arrival, you and Beauregard were put under a security lockdown for your protection." Just not an official one, as Nyx didn't want anything recorded that might bring attention to her Station.

"We don't need protection. If you've checked us in, we're free to go."

"About that. Your papers aren't yours, and neither are his." Reyva opened her mouth and Nyx held up her hand. "Before you even try talking your way out of that one, your papers list you as Anduvian."

Reyva didn't look particularly thrilled at that reminder. "Where is Lord Beauregard?"

"Still asleep."

"I want to see him."

Suspecting the woman wouldn't tell her anything until she had, Nyx showed her Beauregard's room.

"Why isn't he awake?"

"Because he had a gut wound a few hours ago and I hear that level of magical healing really takes it out of a guy." She closed the door and led Reyva back to the cafe. "Care to tell me what happened?"

Reyva shook her head, as if it had been a legitimate question as opposed to a polite demand for answers, and she was free to refuse a response.

Nyx started over. "You're Reyva, right?"

Reyva's eyes narrowed, neither confirming nor denying, before she seemed to remember who had let her name slip. "I want to talk to Seth."

"He'll be down shortly." Because he was the kind of insanity that woke up at five in the morning for *fun*. As soon as he did, and realized Nyx had gotten out of bed before him, he'd know something was up.

Reyva opened her mouth, no doubt to protest, when Kalvar walked in. He was bleary-eyed and so out of it he didn't seem to notice that the lights were on and people were there until he nearly ran into Nyx.

"You're awake." His tone conveyed the depth of his confusion. "Is the world ending?"

"Ha. Ha." Nyx's aversion to mornings was well-documented. Her Station's inhabitants all had a tendency to rise obnoxiously early, and someone inevitably always wanted something from her first thing in the morning.

After being rudely awakened one-too-many times, she'd removed all access to her room for a week. Now everyone knew that she woke up at oh-six-hundred, and that if anyone knocked on her door before oh-six-thirty for anything less than the end of the world, there would be something more immediate than hell to pay as the price.

Nyx gripped Kalvar's shoulders and pointed him in the direction of Reyva. "We have guests."

Kalvar took this in with all the reactivity of the uncaffeinated. Which was to say, none at all. He managed a half-wave before trying to walk around Nyx to the espresso machine.

"Uh-uh." She blocked him. "You aren't going anywhere near machinery in your condition."

"But I need coffee," he whined.

"I'll make it."

"Making the coffee is my job."

"Then I'll give you a raise if you sit down and let me do it."

"Sold." He dropped heavily onto the chair two seats down from Reyva.

The other Tiagren looked even more unhappy than she had a moment ago, her voice low when she spoke. "Are you required to work here?"

Kalvar, whose head was resting on his arms, cracked one eye open. "I didn't mean sold as in, like, actually sold."

"Indentured servitude is hardly kinder."

"Not doing that either. Appreciate the concern. Honestly, I do. But I'm good. I like it here. Plus, I just got my eighth raise in the last two months."

Griff cleared his throat. "Eight, Nyx, truly?"

She shrugged. "It's not my money, so as far as I'm concerned he can have a raise every week."

"There *is* a budget ceiling."

"Oh. Well in that case, he can have a raise every week until we hit the budget ceiling," she corrected. She finished the two drinks she was making, plunking one down in front of Kalvar, the other in front of Reyva. "I made you what he gets, so if you don't like it, you know who to blame."

Kalvar liked caramel macchiatos that replaced the traditional crosshatch layer of caramel, which was meant to rest on top of the latte foam, with what amounted to a solid inch of caramel that dropped straight to the bottom.

Reyva stared at the drink, then at Nyx. "Who *are* you?"

"Nyxi?" Seth walked in, looking fresh and alert like he always did at this ungodly hour. He also looked annoyed.

"Morning," she answered cheerfully. Too cheerfully, because that undercurrent in his voice had said he was maybe just the teensiest bit irritated that she hadn't woken him up.

"Your name is…Nyxi?" Reyva rolled the two syllables around like they felt odd on her tongue.

Kalvar choked on his coffee, laughing. "Her name's Nyx. Seth's the only one who gets to call her Nyxi. I tried it as a joke once and she switched all the coffee in the Station out with decaf. It was an unjust punishment, if you ask me."

Nyx crossed her arms. "It was entirely just." When Seth called her Nyxi, it felt natural. When anyone else did, it was weird. "You needed a caffeine detox anyway."

Seth was notably not amused by any of this, which meant he was definitely annoyed she hadn't woken him up.

Reyva's eyebrows crept steadily toward her hairline. "The company you keep these days is a little odd, Hawthorne."

He snorted. "And yours is a little dangerous. I didn't think you were dumb enough to actually join Beauregard's crusade."

Reyva stiffened. "At least I'm not still wasting my time in the Shadow Market. Which is what I heard you were doing until Bryn finally ran you out a few months ago."

"No one ran me out of anywhere." Seth stalked behind the counter and started making coffee.

Reyva rolled her eyes. "I should have guessed your obsession with this planet would drive you here. Tell me, what are the Kumir sightings like in Earth Between?"

"Surprisingly more frequent than you'd think." He finished the two drinks he was making and turned, handing one to Nyx.

Good. He wasn't *that* annoyed with her if he'd made her coffee.

Kalvar's gaze was bouncing between Seth and Reyva, clearly waiting for their next words, his attention riveted like their interchange was more gripping than the final season of *Pretty Little Liars*.

A throat cleared in the hallway entrance. Beauregard was awake, and he had Morgen and Evra in tow. Now, if Nyx could only convince Liya to leave her room, they could have all of the Station's occupants shoved into the same small space.

Except, of course, the cafe wasn't that small anymore. The Station had subtly expanded the room and the bar to make space for the new arrivals.

"Lord Beauregard." Reyva didn't actually stand and bow, but she looked like she wanted to. "How are you?"

"Surprisingly uninjured." He looked questioningly at Nyx.

"Not my secret to tell." Ankira wanted Toby's gift kept under wraps for good reason. Several good reasons. If everyone in Earth Between knew he existed, they'd be banging down her door every time someone had the sniffles. Ankira was teaching the kid he had the right to set boundaries, but it wasn't instinctual for him, and he was too young to be asked to do it all the time, besides.

Then there was the question of what happened when there was something he *couldn't* fix, whether it was something outside of his abilities, or because he wasn't there at the exact moment someone needed him, or because he was too tired from fixing too many things already. Whatever the reason, someone would blame him for it. He'd blame himself for it.

He didn't deserve any of that. He deserved what every kid did—a safe, loving home with enough time to grow into himself without being pushed to give too much too early. He'd already had that stolen from him once. Nyx wasn't going to let it be taken away again over something as unimportant as Beauregard's curiosity.

He took it in stride. "Please send along my thanks to whomever is deserving of it."

She nodded. That she could do.

"Then could we discuss the matter of you letting us leave?" Reyva suggested.

"Perhaps somewhere a little more private?" Beauregard added.

"I'm not going anywhere," Morgen said.

Beauregard sighed. "I expected as much."

Evra said, "I will be staying too."

Beauregard didn't look pleased at that. "The last time we spoke, I recall you had rather strong opinions regarding what should and should not be said about our governing body. I'm not sure I trust you with the contents of the conversation we are about to have."

Evra didn't budge. "I find myself up to the hilt in illegalities these days. I hardly think talk of one more will matter."

"Even so."

Morgen stepped in. "She's my girlfriend, Uncle Beau. I won't lie to her. She can stay, or I can tell her everything later."

Beauregard muttered something under his breath about young love, then said, "And the other three?"

"What I know, Griff knows," Nyx said.

Reyva cleared her throat and nodded at Seth. "This is Seth Hawthorne."

"Ah," Beauregard said, looking at Seth like he was a particularly advantageous chess piece he'd been hoping to acquire. Nyx didn't like it. "If you wouldn't mind staying, then?"

Seth narrowed his eyes at Reyva. Nyx knew that look. It was his what-have-you-gotten-me-into look. "I'd be delighted," he said.

That left all eyes in the room on Kalvar. He stood with an exaggerated flourish. "I'd like to say I want to stay, but the truth is, I don't. I think I'm giving up the mercenary life. Might go for something nice and boring like academy." His face fell and he said, "Or, you know, something."

With a pang, Nyx realized that if he really did want to go for higher education, he couldn't. Because his last known location was the Arkadian prison planet and he couldn't enroll in *anything* legally, just like he couldn't travel via any method other than portal stones.

She watched him go, wondering how she was supposed to balance how much resentment she had in her heart for the All Council with how much she desperately needed Jevryn's help.

8

"Are you sure this area is secure enough?" Beauregard asked.

Nyx nodded. "I have no Arrivals or Departures today. The doors are locked."

Beauregard cast a glance at Reyva. Her lips thinned. "Their locks are good. I didn't have time to get through them."

The response, along with Beauregard's nod of acceptance, pretty much cemented Nyx's belief that Reyva was some kind of magical lock-picker. Which she supposed would be a useful skill if Reyva had spent any length of time in the Shadow Market.

"So," Nyx said conversationally, "what brings you to my Station half-dead with a false identity?"

Morgen raised his hand. "I have a guess. Would it be the one group of people you've spent the last thirty years pissing off? Auburn-haired assassins about yea tall"—he held up a hand to indicate how high—"eerily identical?"

Beauregard sighed, looking bone-weary and older than she remembered. The appearance of added years was in the weight of grief in his eyes, in the exhaustion pouring off him that wasn't physical. "I hate to disappoint you, but no, I was not run through by a Kumir."

"So your condition had nothing to do with them, then?"

Beauregard didn't answer.

"That's what I thought. When are you going to finally let this obsession go?"

"When it's finished."

Morgen made a disgusted sound low in this throat. "Then I'll be burying you sooner rather than later. And then I'll have to watch my mother cry her heart out because her baby brother's dead, and she never saw him while he was alive because he cared more about a dead woman's memory than he did his own family."

The lines around Beauregard's lips tightened. "We have had this argument before. I have no interest in renewing it in public. But I will tell you that either the Kumir will be gone within the next two weeks, or yes, you *will* be burying me."

Predictably, Morgen didn't look happy.

"What do you mean they'll be gone?" Seth asked, stepping closer to the counter that separated him and Nyx from the rest of the group.

Reyva cast a questioning glance at Beauregard. When he nodded, she said, "We found out where the Kumir come from. We located the source."

"You're certain?" There was an edge to Seth's voice. This was what he'd spent seven years in the Shadow Market looking for. Because every time he'd tried to ride the ley lines, the Kumir had followed him.

He couldn't say for certain why, but the only thing that made sense was his connection to Nyx. And the only way anyone would know Seth was connected to her was if they knew that his father, Viktor, had been connected to Elena Fortuna. And the only one who *should* have known that was Jevryn.

And since Jevryn had always known where to find Elena if he wanted to, that meant someone else was behind this. Most likely another councilor. Most likely the one who had wanted the Harvester in the first place: Alastair.

But they needed proof, because there was nothing that said Alastair was working alone, or that there couldn't be someone else attempting to achieve the same goal. Finding the Kumir—who had first hunted the Hidden to near extinction—was their best chance of determining who had started this mess.

"We're certain," Reyva told Seth. "We can finally do it. Stop them." Her eyes were shining with that kind of feverish light that comes on when a previously unattainable goal has suddenly come into reach. "But we need your help to do it. And for your"—her eyes flicked to Nyx, as if unsure what to call her—"Guardian to check us into the Station."

Seth gave Nyx a look that said, *You didn't tell them?* She shrugged. He rolled his eyes and said, "She's not *my* Guardian, so if you want her to check you in, you should be directing your convincing arguments in this direction." He tapped Nyx's temple. "I'm her boyfriend, not her boss."

Reyva winced. "Right." She looked at Nyx. "Sorry. I don't suppose you also happen to have a long-standing grudge against the Kumir?"

"Sure. Doesn't everyone?"

Beauregard looked at her. "You did not seem to have any knowledge of who the Kumir were when you ran a contingent of them onto my grounds six months ago."

"I didn't. Then I found out they killed most of my family."

It was true, even if the knowledge felt distant to her because she'd never thought of herself as having family outside of her mother. If she could tell them who that family was, they would have zero doubts about her enthusiasm for getting rid of the Kumir. But she wasn't about to announce she was Hidden to the only two people in the room who didn't already know it.

"I see." Beauregard was looking between her and Seth, a new calculation taking place behind his eyes. "And if I can convince you that I *can* end the Kumir, once and for all, will you agree to check Reyva and I in?"

"Yes."

If he was surprised by her easy agreement, he didn't remark on it. "The Kumir originate from the planet Nethrayne."

Morgen groaned. Nyx looked to Griff—she hadn't heard of the planet, but there were enough of them that she still hadn't memorized all the names, and she'd only sent or received travelers from less than half of them—but he shook his head.

"Uncle Beau, please tell me you did not get stabbed while infiltrating Nethrayne."

"I cannot say that without telling falsehoods."

Griff rustled his wings. "There is no planet Nethrayne listed in the Archives."

Nyx heard what he didn't say, which was that *he* didn't know about Nethrayne. Which meant it wasn't a planet name he recognized from his time before he'd become the Station's Avatar.

"That's because no one's supposed to know about it," Morgen said. "Or its twelve sister planets. One for every councilor. They're all hubs for research, manufacturing, weapons development, or some combination of all three. Not even the councilors know the location of *every* planet. They each know three—their own, and two others.

"It's a kind of built-in failsafe to keep any one councilor from gaining too much power, while ensuring none of the planets is lost should one of the councilors die." He looked at Beauregard. "I'm not saying it isn't as secure of a base location as you could hope to get for something like the Kumir, but what makes you so sure that's where they are?"

For a moment, Beauregard's blank expression made Nyx certain he wasn't going to tell them. Or that he was going to lie.

In the end, he opened with something that wasn't even an answer. "You know I lost my wife to this."

Morgen's temper—which was still so odd to see, given he rarely showed it—snapped. "Everyone in the damn universe knows you lost your wife to this. But you know what the funny thing about that is? You never *had* a wife.

"There's no record of you ever being married. You've never

said her name. *Mom's* never said her name. Mom wasn't at your wedding, either, and I haven't been able to track down anyone who was. There isn't a single picture of you with a woman anywhere. Not in our house, and not in your rooms in your castle."

"You searched my rooms?"

Morgen gave him a look. "I *am* your nephew, give me some credit. There's no trace of your supposed wife anywhere. For all you've done in her memory, you'd think you'd have a damn shrine to the woman."

"I don't need a shrine to remember she existed."

Nyx cut in before this could devolve into a family squabble. "I take it your wife has something to do with why you're convinced the Kumir originate on Nethrayne?"

"She was…involved, in a manner of speaking, with their creation. Her involvement wasn't voluntary, and she did everything she could to prevent the end result, yet here we are.

"Because of her connection, I became aware of a medical compound necessary for the continual creation of the Kumir. I have tracked the shipment of it to Nethrayne."

"It took you thirty years to track down a compound shipment?" Seth asked.

"Yes. It is not one that is produced on a commercial scale. It isn't bought or sold outside of this one specific purpose, and it doesn't even have a registered name. I had a single sample my wife had procured, from which I had to identify all of the ingredients that went into its making.

"There are over three-hundred of them. The first four scientists I hired to attempt it were killed. Then I was hunted so ruthlessly by the Kumir that I had little time to do anything but survive. By the time I gained some measure of peace, no one was foolish enough to work with me."

"So how did you get the sample analyzed?" Nyx asked.

"He told a sixteen-year-old kid it couldn't be done," Morgen said. He had a sour expression on his face, like he'd just put everything together. "I can't believe I spent a year of my life on part of your crusade."

"Four scientists died just for *looking* at this sample and then you gave it to your sixteen-year-old nephew?" Nyx asked.

"Thank you," Morgen told her. "It's good to know someone is outraged on my behalf."

"Would you like me to yell at him as well?" Evra asked.

Morgen gave her the world's most adoring smile. "Would you?"

Evra just shook her head, but the corner of her lip was tugging up. It was nice to see them happy.

Beauregard said, "I was very careful to ensure Morgen did not add to nor search any public archives while he worked. He was perfectly safe."

"Perfectly safe," Morgen agreed. "Except for that part where I blew up half the lab because your sample contained tilithium, which is extremely volatile when not bound to karbenyx."

"I paid for all the damages."

"Yes, but money can't fix the heart attack you nearly gave my mother."

Reyva cleared her throat. "Not to be insensitive, but we are in a time crunch."

Beauregard's face fell. "Indeed. To answer your original question, Seth, yes. It took me a very long time to both identify the compound and the place where it is produced, and track the shipments of it to Nethrayne. It is transported there by an extremely expensive, highly selective private courier service known as Chameleon.

"Reyva and I were able to take the place of two of Chameleon's transport messengers and surveil Nethrayne. But the messengers are only allowed to deliver the cargo as far as the interior of the city's first level. When we attempted to move deeper into Nethrayne during yesterday's delivery, it quickly became clear that the illusion magic we possessed was insufficient for overcoming the city's security. We ran into difficulties and barely managed to leave Nethrayne without compromising our identities within Chameleon."

Nyx stared at him. "You took an abdominal wound, I'm assuming on Nethrayne, and you—what? Slapped a Bandaid on it and delayed actual medical care so you wouldn't compromise a stolen identity? Reyva had a head wound, for stars' sake, you could both be dead."

Morgen waved a hand theatrically. "Welcome to the Uncle Beau Show. Nothing comes before the sake of the crusade."

Beauregard shot him a look that was either regret, guilt, exhaustion, or some combination of all three. "My decisions may appear extreme to you, but Reyva and I both agreed to take the risk. Getting to Nethrayne is nearly impossible. Only a small subset of the population even knows its name.

"There are no portal stones one can purchase to it. A ley line trip to it cannot be booked without an identity that has the proper clearance because, as I'm sure you have already realized, not even the Guardians know its location.

"It is the combination of the Guardian's seal on an identification paper with verified access that triggers the ley line to open a path to the planet. There is no way to trace the route. Were our identities compromised, our access would be disabled.

"Furthermore, Chameleon itself would likely be put under review, if the company's access wasn't outright suspended, and the increase in scrutiny would make our goal all but impossible. The risk was worth taking."

He turned all of his attention on Nyx. "I am hoping the risk of coming *here* was worth taking. If you do not approve our Arrival, that fact will be noted on our records, and this opportunity will close.

"You have seen what the Kumir can do. Ask yourself if the universe wouldn't be a better place without them in it, and then ask yourself if you want to stand in the way of what may well be the only chance of destroying them."

It was a careful manipulation. A subtle implication that she would be partly responsible for any future atrocities the Kumir committed if she didn't help him in this matter. He'd no doubt chosen it because he remembered the reaction she'd had to her first brush with the Kumir. Her guilt over leading them onto his property, resulting in the deaths of two of his guards.

But however masterful the manipulation, it was pointless. She opened one of the kitchen drawers, withdrew Reyva and Beauregard's identification papers, and tossed them onto the counter. "I checked you both in yesterday. I just wanted to know what I was dealing with."

Beauregard gave her a look that said he was reprising his opinion of her. She wondered if that opinion was going in a positive or negative direction.

"So anyway, what do you want with Seth? You lose your Illusionist on the ley trip here?"

"No." Reyva was quiet long enough Nyx wasn't sure if she'd speak again. When she did, she sounded resigned. "We ran out of one-shot glamours."

The look on Seth's face was nothing short of professional horror. "You tried to infiltrate a council-run planet using second-rate off-the-shelf bottle illusions? Are you insane?"

"They were *your* second-rate off-the-shelf bottle illusions, so it should have been fine. It *would* have been fine if we hadn't run out."

Seth's eyes narrowed. "What do you mean they were mine?"

Reyva swallowed, guilt creeping into her eyes.

Seth exhaled heavily. "So it *was* you who stole the shipment I made for Andrin. Holy fucking stars, Reyva, he almost took my fucking head off over that."

"You're too good to get your head taken off by the likes of him, and I needed it more."

"Why would you—" He broke off, his gaze flicking to Beauregard. Then he laughed. "You bought your way into his little private army with *my* magic?"

"He takes everyone, you don't have to buy your way in. I told you that."

"He doesn't take everyone, actually. And, so, what? You bought your way onto this specific mission, then?"

She looked away, which was answer enough.

"Did it ever occur to you that you could have just *asked* me for what you needed? Instead of nearly getting me decapitated and leaving me wondering why the only person who could have stolen that shipment from me would have?"

Reyva's eyes flashed. "I did ask. I asked you to come with me. But no, you couldn't be bothered to answer to anyone's authority but your own, because you don't understand what it's like to lose something to the Kumir."

"They hunted me everywhere I went, I think I know what it's like."

She laughed. "So you lost easy freedom of movement? I lost *everything*. My family, my friends, my employer, my home. But you could never understand that because you've never had anything it would hurt to lose."

Seth jerked back.

"Shit. I didn't mean—"

"Yeah," he cut in, "you did." He turned his attention on Beauregard. "You want my help?"

"I need *an* Illusionist. Are you as good as Reyva says?"

"You've been spending a fortune's worth of my glamours like pennies for the last few months, so you tell me."

"I have no proof you made those."

Nyx couldn't tell if Beauregard really thought there was a chance Seth had been passing some other Illusionist's work off as his own, or if he just wanted to push Seth to see what he would do.

Seth crossed his arms, and somewhere between the start of the movement and the finish, he wasn't Seth anymore, but Beauregard. Taller, larger, taking up all the space around him, his face a mirror of the other man's stern but otherwise implacable expression.

"How am I doing?" Seth asked in Beauregard's voice.

Beauregard leaned forward. "You can mimic voice and tone, too. What else?"

"Pretty much anything you want," he said, but he was answering in Morgen's voice now, wearing Morgen's face.

"I don't stand like that," Morgen objected.

"You do," Nyx and Evra chorused in unison.

"And biological markers in ward systems?" Beauregard asked.

Seth's jaw clenched and he shot Reyva a look that made her drop her gaze. So the answer was yes, he could mimic them, and no, he didn't appreciate that she'd told someone that. "You have possibly the best wardbreaker in the verse sitting right there." He pointed at Reyva. "What do you need to trick a bio marker for?"

"Given what we encountered on our brief foray deeper into the city, I believe the sheer number of security points between us and the Kumir will make it impossible for one individual to handle them alone. If we are to have any chance of success, I need two of Reyva. Or in this case, one of her and the next best thing: you. So can you do it?"

"With that kind of praise?" Seth shrugged. "Sure. If I have access to the person the bio markers are made from."

"Show me." Beauregard pulled a chain from beneath his shirt. The predominant item on it was a large, silver oval locket, but it also held several smaller items, like you might find on an Earth charm bracelet.

He unhooked one of the tokens—a flat amber disc—and placed it on the counter. "This contains access to my personal archives. Open it."

"What marker is it tied to?"

Beauregard didn't answer.

"Right." Seth became a mirror of Beauregard in a blink. He

only tried a fingerprint and holding it up to his eye once before he asked, in Beauregard's voice, "Blood, saliva, or breath? And yes, I can try all of them but I don't like dealing in bodily fluids before breakfast unless it's absolutely necessary."

"Breath."

"You *would* be that paranoid."

Nyx supposed it *was* the one access marker that couldn't be obtained from Beauregard's dead body, so…

Seth held out his hand to Beauregard, a thin sheen of magic coating his palm. "Exhale." Beauregard did. Seth wrinkled his nose—it was beyond strange to see such a Seth expression when he was wearing Beauregard's face—eyes closing as he lost himself in his magic. Fifteen seconds later, he opened his eyes and huffed out a breath onto the amber disc.

An array of hologram options popped up, connected like little planets on a solar system model. Seth poked one at random and the map disappeared, replaced by a new one, presumably related to the option he'd chosen. She was looking at the magical version of a computer system file storage, complete with folders and subfolders.

Nyx looked at Griff. "Why do Beauregard's archives look like Windows 11 and the Station's are like a card catalog?"

"What do eleven windows have to do with an archive system?" Reyva asked.

"You become accustomed to her strange Earth references with time," Evra said sagely. "I believe in this instance she is referring to a technological means of storing information."

Nyx beamed at her. "You *do* listen when I talk."

Griff said, "Individuals purchase whichever archive storage system they prefer. The Station's conform to a version they believe the Guardian will find most pleasing. You have an overwhelming fondness for physical books, hence the library model. It can, of course, be changed if you prefer."

Nyx shook her head. "Library model is fine. I was just curious."

Seth poked at another subfolder in Beauregard's archives. "Am I being graded on my ability to find specific information, too, or is opening them good enough?"

"Your demonstration has been sufficient, thank you." Beauregard held out his hand and Seth dumped the archive disc onto it, the folders winking out as it fell. "I suppose the remaining question is, will you come with us?"

Seth dropped his illusion, shrinking down to his natural appearance. "I don't know. I came to you for information once and you wouldn't even talk to me. I'd like to know why."

"I am not entirely certain you want that answer."

"I am."

"It was because of your father."

A muscle in Seth's jaw ticked. "What about him?"

"We were in the Enforcer ranks at the same time, though not in the same division. I didn't know him personally, but I knew of him. He was pulled for a special assignment around the time the Kumir became active, and he was never heard from again."

"You think my *dad* had something to do with the Kumir's creation?"

"The timing is right."

The Kumir had become active when they performed their first feat—namely, obliterating the Hidden families. Nyx had always wondered how Viktor ended up with her mother. She supposed she had her answer now. He'd been pulled for special assignment, in conjunction with the rise of the Kumir, in order to *protect* the remaining Hidden.

"My dad may have been the world's shittiest father, but he didn't have anything to do with the Kumir."

"How can you be certain?"

"Because he would have had to—" He snapped his mouth shut, looking to Nyx.

This was uncharted territory for both of them. They'd never been in a position to talk about Viktor and Elena to anyone who didn't already know what Nyx was. But no one outside that small circle of people knew Elena Fortuna had come to Earth, so admitting to growing up here with Viktor wasn't going to tell Beauregard anything except that Seth's father—and therefore Seth—wasn't involved with the Kumir.

"Because he would have had to leave my mother's side for more than five seconds," Nyx said, completing Seth's sentence for him. "And that was something Viktor pretty much never did."

Reyva looked between them with something akin to horror. "You're related?"

"No!" They both shouted in near-perfect tandem.

"My mother was pregnant by someone else when Viktor met her," Nyx said. "And Seth came along two years before that. Anyway, point being, Viktor definitely wasn't in collusion with whoever created the Kumir."

Beauregard didn't look convinced. "If that is true, then why does his official record list him as missing? Why has no one heard from him in almost three decades?"

Seth shrugged. "Not like he ever explained anything to me."

"I would like to speak with him."

"Join the club."

"Meaning?"

Nyx put her hand on Seth's arm. He had that look that said he was about to say something particularly unpleasant, and while she didn't blame him, he didn't always think rationally where Viktor was concerned.

There *was* that time he'd snapped at his father and—

The tiniest sliver of memory fell loose in Nyx's mind.

9

Nyx blinked. Seth's hands cupped her face, his dark eyes a mere two inches from her own.

"Hey," he said. "You back?"

She bit back a groan. She'd just had a memory lapse in front of everyone. Perfect. "Yeah. I'm back."

Seth nodded and let her go.

"Is she okay?" Reyva asked.

"She is perfectly well," Griff answered. "As you may have heard, the Station suffered an unfortunate outbreak of Centerian Hyplexia a few months ago due to an unvaccinated traveler. Approximately one percent of individuals who contract the virus experience lingering side effects, including brief moments of immobility."

Nyx had no idea if that was true, but Griff delivered it with such assuredness that she doubted Beauregard or Reyva would be looking it up later to confirm the validity.

"At least I'm in the one percent of something, right?" she joked. She turned back to Beauregard like nothing was wrong. "About your question. My mother ditched me pretty much the moment I could take care of myself. Viktor left with her. We haven't heard from them in years."

"I see." To Seth he said, "Will you come with us, then?"

Nyx recognized the look on Seth's face. She'd lost count of the times she'd seen it over the years. It was the one he got when what he wanted to do conflicted with what she *could* do, so he wasn't going to do the thing he wanted because he wasn't willing to leave her out.

"Could I talk to you?" she asked him. "Alone?" At his nod, she told Beauregard, "He'll give you an answer in a minute."

She pulled Seth into the library and had barely closed the door behind them when he pulled her in and kissed her. Long and slow, the kind of kiss he'd been avoiding in his determination to "take things slow" until her memories came back.

"What was that for?" she asked when they broke apart.

"Me. I really didn't like seeing you like that." He gave her a crooked half-smile. "I have a lot of trauma about you being unconscious. There was the time your mom stole all your memories, the time Kaliaris and Griff put you under after your fight with Laiveran, the time you disappeared in your head for five days trying to get your memories back, the time—"

"I think I get the idea." She cut him off before he could decide to recite every instance of her being unconscious that he could remember. Because knowing Seth, he would, and knowing her, there were probably a lot of instances to recite.

He grinned. "If you didn't want me to make out with you, what did you drag me in here for?"

"To stop you from telling them no when you want to tell them yes." At the look he gave her, she laughed. "I know you as well as you know me. Maybe I don't remember it all, but I can still read you like a book. You were wearing your martyr face."

"My martyr face?" he repeated.

She nodded. "The one you wear every time you want to do something but I can't, so you valiantly determine you aren't going to do it. You should go. We both know the Kumir aren't going to stop hunting you, because whatever councilor is in charge of them"—and the Kumir being on a council-run planet just proved that one or more of them *was* behind the assassins— "clearly knows your father was pulled for that 'special assignment' to protect the Hidden.

"They're looking for me through you and they aren't going to stop until they find us. Getting rid of them won't solve everything but it will make things more difficult for the opposing side."

The look on his face said she wasn't telling him anything he didn't already know. "You could come," he said softly.

The beginnings of panic swept through her at the words. *You could come.* Like it was easy, like it was nothing, like it was just running to the grocery store.

But it wasn't. She'd treated it that cavalierly twice—when she'd gone to Arkadia for Kaden, then to the Shadow Market for Seth—but she couldn't anymore. Not now that Laiveran had shown her just how easy it was for her to be taken. To end up somewhere no one would ever find her. Somewhere she had only come back from because of a genetically inherited magical ability, a whole lot of luck, and her friends' mercifully stubborn unwillingness to let her disappear.

She wasn't kidding herself that she could be that lucky twice. She was out of portal magic. Jevryn hadn't taken back the bracelets he'd given her on Amentia Furor, but she'd realized after he left that he'd siphoned all the remaining portal magic from the one that had still had some.

She didn't have the means to bring herself home, and even if she did, all the instruction Jevryn had given her on using portal magic had been about using it planet-side. He hadn't taught her how to read the constellation map that appeared when she possessed enough magic to reach another planet. He hadn't taught her how to search for Earth in that sea and find it.

"Nyx?"

She had to say something. Anything that didn't let Seth know how nausea-inducing the idea of leaving Earth had become. She hadn't even been able to bring herself to leave the Station.

Because she was safe here, the Station's dominance too powerful to allow anyone to portal into or out of it.

It felt like weakness and she didn't want to show it, now more than ever, so she settled on the unobjectionable reason why she should stay right where she was. "You know I can't go. Too many people already know I can leave the Station when Guardians aren't supposed to. But at least I trust all of them."

Well, she trusted most of them, and trusted that the rest had good reasons to keep the information to themselves. "But even if we ignored that, I'm a liability at best right now and you know it. I just zoned out in front of everyone. That's only going to keep happening, and it's only going to keep getting worse.

"What are we supposed to do if we're in a delicate situation and I suddenly think I'm five?" Though Tobi had, thank the stars, said it was unlikely she would remain in any very young mental state for too long.

Memories from that long ago tended to be vague in the extreme, more collections of feelings and learned traits than specific events. He'd said it should make those earlier ones easier to reabsorb and place. That, and the disconnect between a mind that young being stuck in an adult body should also make her snap out of the state sooner.

It was a relief to know she probably wouldn't end up crying in a corner clutching a blanket for days on end, but it didn't make what she'd said about being a liability any less true.

"I can cover you," he said stubbornly.

"While you're busy spinning illusions for everyone else? Didn't you tell me in the Shadow Market that you couldn't make us both invisible at the same time?"

He gave her a look that said she really ought to know better, and furthermore had insulted him. "I was ninety-nine percent tapped out in the Shadow Market. I'd just pulled off a major job, and then I was constantly masking because you had Bryn's people looking everywhere for me. I was running on fumes."

She threw her hands up. "Okay, fine, you're the best Illusionist ever. You still aren't omniscient, and you'll have a *lot* of better uses for your magic than me." Which he already knew. "What's the real problem?"

He looked away, a muscle feathering in his jaw. Finally, he looked back. "How am I supposed to leave you right now? How can you *ask me* to leave you right now?"

"Seth…" She didn't know what to say. Or rather, she did, but she didn't know how to say it.

"I wasn't there for you when it mattered. And now it matters again and you're telling me to leave." There was an unspoken question there, a thin layer of hurt in the words.

"I'm not trying to punish you," she said softly.

"Then what?"

She exhaled and just said it. "Tobi said I reach for memories instinctively. When I want to know something, or remember something, my brain reaches for the piece, and now that the Hiding's gone, those pieces are available. Every time something triggers me to want to remember, I speed up my path to a gloriously fucked-up brain. And you're what triggers me."

He stiffened.

"You're almost the entirety of the parts of my life I've forgotten. Everything you do has me reaching for memories. Yesterday, it was you storming out of the Station that had me barreling back down Memory Lane. Just now, it was because I was thinking about the way you always react to your father. I can't stop myself from reaching for the past when you're constantly here reminding me of it."

"So I'm the thing that's making you sick," he said bitterly.

"That's not fair." At least, she hadn't meant it that way.

He gave a short laugh. "Nothing about this is fair. Nothing about *us* is ever fair."

The words hit harder because they were so unexpected. "I… didn't realize you felt that way."

"I don't." He sighed, pulling her in and dropping his forehead against hers. "But then sometimes I do."

She shut her eyes. "I know we're messed up. But I don't want to be messed up with anyone but you."

He squeezed her tighter. "Neither do I. What am I supposed to do if you're not here when I come back? What if the next few days is all we have, and we don't really have them at all because apparently I shouldn't be around you?"

Her throat tightened. "I'll be here. At least, some version of me will. Maybe it won't be the one you want, if Jevryn can't get my mother here in time. Maybe it will take me years to come back to the version you want. But we have time.

"Inside the Station…it's not like ten or twenty years will mean we've wasted half our lives. It's just…stasis, while we're here. Suspension." She swallowed. "If I get lost for a while, will you wait for me to come back?"

"Of course I will. If it takes a hundred years this time, I'll wait."

Maybe a better person would have said that if it came to a hundred years, he should go. But she wasn't a better person. "Good."

There were words hovering between them. Words she couldn't remember if they'd ever said before or if they'd just always felt, and that had been enough. But she didn't want to say them now, either. Not out of sadness and desperation.

"For the record," he whispered, "there is no version of you I don't want."

And because there wasn't much else to do with a statement like that, she kissed him.

When they broke apart, he said, "So I guess we get to find out what 'giving each other space' feels like."

"Probably a lot like the last seven years."

"Then it's going to suck," he predicted.

———

They walked back into the kitchen. Everyone was still there, waiting, giving Nyx the weird feeling that time had stalled while they were gone. It reminded her of that philosophical idea that things quit existing when you weren't around to observe them. Like now that she'd returned to the room, everyone had suddenly popped back into existence, exactly as she'd left them.

The problem with having a brain that frequently thought strange things was that she couldn't tell if this weird thought was just her being *her*, or if it was some sign of her worsening mental fragility.

Seth looked at Beauregard. "Prove to me this isn't a suicide mission, and I'm in."

"We have four days until Reyva and I's team is scheduled to make another shipment. That should be adequate time to walk you through Nethrayne's layout and devise a method of approach we can all agree has a reasonable chance of success."

Seth nodded.

To Nyx, Beauregard said, "We will, however, require a base of operations."

She raised an eyebrow. "You have a very nice castle and a standing private army and you want to hide out in my Station?"

"Yes."

"Why?"

"Because every member of that private standing army is going to want to come, and this is not the kind of endeavor won with overwhelming force. The risk of any member of that guard learning of this and ruining it is one I will not take."

"Then why do you *have* a private army?"

"Why else?" Morgen said. "The Kumir wouldn't stop coming after him, so he needed something impressive enough to put between himself and the rest of the world. It was never about giving them vengeance. It was about buying himself enough protection that the Kumir backed off." Morgen looked at Reyva. "You'd do well to remember that."

She shrugged. "I'm not confused about why I'm here."

"Unfortunately, neither am I. Congratulations, Uncle Beau, you just added a half-Siren to your plan."

"No. Your mother will never forgive me if anything happens to you."

"Mum's forgiveness is the least of your problems. I'm coming whether you like it or not."

"And how are you going to manage that if I do not agree?"

Morgen looked at Seth. Then Morgen disappeared. He reappeared a couple seconds later behind Beauregard. "Surprise," he said.

To his credit, Beauregard only *barely* jumped.

Morgen said, "It will be easier for all of us if you simply factor me in."

"Or I could write your mother and tell her of the foolishness you plan on engaging in."

"I'll just tell her I'm doing what I have to do. It's the excuse she gives for you every time you fail to be there for her when she needs you."

Beauregard flinched. The reaction was so subtle Nyx almost missed it, but it was there. "Very well. Come, then. But think about what it will do to her to lose her only son and her only brother at the same time, and try not to die."

Morgen clapped a hand to his heart. "Your words of encouragement will inspire me."

"Is there anyone *else* I need to factor in?" Beauregard clearly meant it as a rhetorical question. He shouldn't have tempted fate.

"Me," Evra said. "And before you object, know that you would be foolish to do so. You may have Reyva's ability for breaking through magical security systems, but my mother runs one of the top ten private security firms in the verse. I can account for the human element."

Beauregard wiped his hand over his face. "Very well. Chameleon runs six-man messenger crews. At the rate we're going, we might as well replace the entire team." He looked to Seth. "Can you manage that many?"

"It would be easiest if I can pre-make glamours for the rest of you and handle the detailed elements on the go. Get me physical profiles on the team members we're replacing and I'll get started."

Beauregard withdrew a different archive disc than the one Seth had opened earlier and placed it on the counter. "You'll find the profiles on here, along with the layout of Nethrayne. You three"—he pointed to Seth, Evra, and Morgen—"familiarize yourselves with it. Reyva can answer any questions you have.

"I will spend the day reviewing potential candidates to replace the final transport messenger from the castle guard and bring back a list of options. We'll decide together who we feel would fit best into the group.

"I don't want surprises and I don't want issues. So whatever's between you two"—he pointed between Seth and Reyva—"work it out before I get back."

"This is the other reason he has an army," Morgen said, in a faux-whisper guaranteed to carry to Beauregard's ears as he exited the Station. "Otherwise he'd never get to fulfill his calling as an authoritarian warlord." The door slammed shut and Morgen looked at Seth. "On a more serious note, you sure you want to do this with…everything going on?" He cast the world's least-subtle glance at Nyx.

Evra clapped her hand on his shoulder. Heavily. "This is the part where you stay out of other people's business."

He gave her a wide-eyed, innocent look. "Why would I want to do that?"

"Because it's polite."

"I never thought I'd see the day you would be the one lecturing anyone on politeness."

"I do have manners. I just don't care to use them for most people."

Morgen snorted. But he didn't drop the original subject. "Not to be maudlin, but the council planets are no joke. None of them are planets that have ever been naturally capable of sustaining life.

"I got assigned to three different high-risk transports in my time with the Enforcers, and every single planet looked like it had been chosen specifically for its inhospitable nature. They're just singular city outposts on otherwise barren worlds.

"We get caught? There is nowhere to run to. This is the one we might not come back from."

Nyx didn't like the sound of that at all. Not when she wouldn't be going too, when their coming back or not would be completely out of her hands. She was reassuring herself, more than anyone else, when she said, "Seth has like eight-billion portal stones that all come right back here. You can each take enough to bring all of Nethrayne home with you. Just because no one has a rock to spell to portal *there* doesn't mean you can't portal out."

"No," Morgen said slowly, "but they might have a way of tracking it. It *is* a council planet after all. We could lead them here."

"Then lead them here." Nyx crossed her arms. "Let me be perfectly clear. If any one of you is in imminent danger, break the damn rock. I don't care if you know for certain every single councilor will follow you here, you come home. Got it?" She didn't have a plan for how she would deal with attracting the attention of the very people she didn't want to interact with, but if it was her friends' lives or that inevitability coming due sooner than expected, she'd find a way to deal.

"Yes, General?" Morgen offered.

Reyva was staring at her with an odd kind of fascination. "You're some kind of crazy, you know that?"

"Several different kinds, actually, with a new one coming due any day." Oh, good, she was babbling now.

"Right." Reyva drew the word out. To Seth, she said, "Can I talk to you?"

"Sure."

"Outside of the Station?" That request indicated she had some idea of the awareness Stations possessed—or at least that their Avatars possessed—and that was…interesting.

Seth held his hand out toward the front door. "Let's go for a walk."

They were barely gone before Morgen said, "Did you guys figure out who she is?" He was obviously asking Evra, since Nyx didn't know who anyone in the verse was, but it was nice to be included, even if only for politeness.

"No. She looks familiar. I would swear I've seen her somewhere, but I cannot place it."

"She's NuReyva Duraven."

Evra frowned, then her eyes widened. "No."

"Oh, yes."

Nyx raised her hand. "What does it mean to be NuReyva Duraven?"

Morgen answered. "Seth said she's possibly the best wardbreaker in the verse? There's no 'possibly' about it. She was a prodigy from age five. She went to the best magical academies on scholarship. When she was close to graduation, every security conglomerate wanted to hire her. She was every Tiagren kid's idol because she was so good that no one dared to comment on what she was.

"She had a lot of offers to pick over when she graduated. Which she did at thirteen. She went with Medean Services, because they were at the top of the market and they offered her a pay package that was double the next highest offer. They signed her into an exclusive contract for seven years. You know what they did with her?"

Nyx shook her head.

"Nothing. It's not unusual for those contracts to be commission-based off work performed, which this one was. They didn't give her any work. She was stuck in a contract making no money and she couldn't work anywhere else because of the exclusivity clause in it.

"She was supposed to be able to lift her family out of poverty and instead she was stuck for seven years."

"Why would they do that?" Nyx asked.

"Medean Services is owned and operated by the Medean family. Prior to NuReyva's genius coming to attention, Julianus Medean, the son of the company's owner, was widely accepted to be the best wardbreaker on record. He didn't like being upstaged by a kid of what he viewed to be inferior breeding.

"He wanted to erase her. The non-compete in her contract forbid her from talking about her work at Medean in any capacity. Which meant she couldn't even talk about the fact that she *wasn't* working.

"He spent the entirety of her contract spreading rumors that the reason no one had gotten a new ward system of surpassing brilliance from Duraven's employment was because she was a fraud. In short, he ruined her so that no one would want her once her contract was up."

"But," Evra said, taking up the thread of the story, "he miscalculated. He'd been working on a new system, one that was supposed to be completely impervious to even the best wardbreakers. He planned its unveiling to coincide with the end of her contract. So that in case what he'd already done wasn't enough, he had the new system to draw attention."

"What did she do?" Nyx asked. Because she was certain that, with seven years of what must have been unmitigated rage, Reyva had done *something*.

Evra smiled. "She walked into the unveiling demonstration and cracked his precious new system in less than five minutes. Then she told the room, filled with every influential person in the industry, that *that's* what she could do when she hadn't been allowed to touch a system in years.

"Everyone wanted her after that. She went to work for a small firm no one had ever heard of, who couldn't pay her half of what she was worth. But they didn't lock her into a contract and they provided her family with a place to live.

"Within three years, Reyva had them dominating the market, and Medean Services was facing decline from public backlash." Evra's voice grew somber. "Then the Kumir took out her company, her family, and burned all of the buildings to the ground."

Nyx remembered the pain in Reyva's voice when she'd said she'd lost everything. "She escaped somehow?"

"No. They left her alive, because that's what they were ordered to do. So it would hurt her."

"That's sick."

"Yes. She disappeared after that. It's been years since anyone's heard from her. Well," Evra added, "except for Seth, apparently."

"He said they worked together on and off for a few years," Nyx said in response to Evra's unasked question. "They were both in the Market for the same reason, after all."

But Reyva's reason to go after the Kumir was a *lot* more personal—a lot more raw—than Seth's. As was Beauregard's. "About what I said, about expecting you guys to bail and come home if it gets too dangerous? I don't expect much sense out of Beauregard and Reyva on what counts as 'too dangerous.' So I'm counting on you two, okay? If everything goes to hell, promise me you'll bring everyone home?"

"You have my word," Evra said. She never gave her word lightly.

"As you have mine, little Guardian."

That was all she could ask for.

10

G riff waited until Morgen and Evra left to say, "You dislike staying behind."

"Of course I dislike staying behind." Disliked it almost as much as she was terrified of actually leaving Earth again.

"You also dislike that Seth is going."

"That too." She wasn't nearly as calm about anyone going on this adventure as she was pretending. In less than a week pretty much everyone she loved, with the exception of Griff and Temerex, was going to waltz off to a council-run planet to take out an entire race of assassins.

It sounded like a lot of crazy when she thought about it like that, and she hadn't missed that Beauregard had evaded, in all his talk of medical compounds, telling them anything about what the Kumir actually were. The part of her that liked puzzles, that liked trying to figure out the unspoken parts behind the words people actually said, suspected Beauregard's long-standing feud with the Kumir had something more complex behind it than them killing his wife.

Not that that wasn't reason enough—Laiveran, deep in the Station's heart, was proof enough of what lost love could drive some people to, but Beauregard wasn't Laiveran. Perhaps some of what he had done skirted the black-and-white of morality and lingered in the gray, but she didn't think he would ever hurt anyone innocent in his quest. But she suspected he would—and probably already had—hurt himself a great deal.

"If you did not wish Seth to go," Griff said, "why did you not ask him to stay?"

Nyx raised an eyebrow. "Are you listening in on my private conversations?"

"Of course not."

"Then maybe I did ask him."

Grif shook his head. "If you'd asked him to stay, he would have."

She blew out a breath. "And that's exactly why I asked him to go."

"Ah."

"He *wanted* to go. And I'm sick of always being the thing holding him back. But I'm worried."

"He has been in difficult situations before. As have Morgen and Evra. As have you."

Her stomach clenched at the reminder. "I know."

But this was different. Because they were going to a *councilor's* planet. If they got caught… Well, as Morgen had said, this was the one they might not come back from.

The urge to run upstairs to her companion journal and ask Jevryn which councilor Nethrayne belonged to was strong. But she had a feeling she knew precisely what his view on this expedition would be, regardless of which councilor ran Nethrayne, and she didn't think tipping him off to what was about to occur was a very smart decision.

Not to mention she was coming to the uncomfortable conclusion that she was using Jevryn A-Morridahn as a crutch. It was easy to see why it was happening. Every time she'd needed something and contacted him, he'd delivered. He was the heaviest hitter she had access to, and that made it sorely tempting to ask him to solve every problem that came up because, so far, he'd been amenable to doing so.

She'd never before had the luxury of being able to offer said problems up to someone older and theoretically wiser. Someone who had the experience, means, and willingness to handle them. It said a lot about her childhood—and the lack of adult care in it —that it relieved her so much to have even the possibility of Jevryn to rely on.

Shit. Jevryn. Griff. Jevryn *here*, around Griff. "I have to tell you something."

"That is a phrase usually followed by unwanted information, is it not?"

"I asked Jevryn to find my mother."

"I understand Tobi said that was your best chance of resolving your difficulties." He stretched his wings and resettled them, something she'd come to learn meant he was uncomfortable.

"I guess he knows where she is, but it might take him time to retrieve her. I don't even know if he plans on being the one who brings her here, but I could ask him to send her with someone else."

Griff shook his head. "Truly, it is fine. In all honesty, it is your mother I am less excited to meet. How are *you* handling that?"

"By not thinking about it." She'd dealt with Tobi's news, and her request of Jevryn, by treating them like steps of a procedure that had to be completed. Items on a to-do list to be checked off and not lingered over. Because as long as she thought about them that way, she didn't have to think about the fact that if everything went the way she needed it to, she was going to be standing in the same room as Elena Fortuna very soon.

"I don't want to see her," she admitted.

Griff fluttered to her side, bumping her shoulder with his beak in silent support.

"I hate that I need her. For anything. She was never...I don't think she was ever kind. Or if she was, it's tucked away in some memory I don't have access to right now, and that's her fault." Nyx's fingers clenched around the mug in her hands. "I don't understand why she had me."

Contraception was easy in the magical world, as was abortion, and near as she could tell, her mother wouldn't have had moral oppositions to either. Nyx had spent time researching what publicly-available information there was on the Hidden. Had even found her mother's family tree, the public one of which notably didn't include Nyx.

Morgen had told her the Hidden spawned from only five families who had initially held the talent, and that was true. But Hidden abilities were fully dominant. So long as one parent was Hidden, those abilities transferred to their child no matter what magical abilities the other parent did or did not possess and pass on.

It was how the Hidden ranks had swelled from five families to hundreds. But despite the fact that *all* Hidden could trace their way back to the founders, like most things, some lines were considered purer than others. Specifically those that kept the name of one of the original founders. Like Fortuna.

Her mother, according to Nyx's research, had basically grown up Hidden royalty. The youngest of three siblings in a family whose net worth was staggering. It explained a lot about Elena. She'd likely grown up believing the world was hers for the taking, only to have the silver spoon ripped out of her mouth by the annihilation of her people.

In Nyx's more charitable moments, she tried to remember that it was probably scary to be nineteen, hunted, pregnant, and hung out to dry somewhere like Earth. Except she kept coming back to the pregnancy thing and why Elena had bothered.

Was it out of some sense of duty to carry on the Hidden line? Had Nyx been the result of a love match and her father had died tragically along with Elena's—*Nyx's*—family? Records didn't show that her mother had married, but maybe there had been someone special?

It was a nice daydream to think she'd been the result of love. And maybe, if she had any sense that her mother had ever once looked at her with anything but contempt, she could believe it. Nyx didn't look like her mother, which meant that unless her physical features came from a generational skip, she looked like her father. And given the way she *did* remember Elena looking at her, Nyx got the impression Elena absolutely hated the man she'd produced Nyx with.

That didn't leave a lot of good options.

"Perhaps," Griff said, "this is one of those things best not dwelled upon until it comes to pass."

"Easier said than done."

"If it helps, remember that *she* is being brought *here*. In your past interactions, she held all the power. You were a child, with no resources and no connections.

"Here, you are as close to a god as it is possible for mortals to be. Even if the rest of your friends have not returned by the time she arrives, you will have me. You will have Kaliaris, who has accepted you, now. Neither of us will leave you defenseless. She will have no freedom within these walls save that which you grant her."

It should have made Nyx feel better. Stronger. But all she kept coming back to was a single fear buried deep beneath the others. "What if she won't help me? What if I can't trust her enough to let her?"

She remembered the certainty that, as she'd been cutting through the Hiding surrounding her memories, her mother had been laughing.

Griff waited several breaths to answer. "If Jevryn has agreed to bring her, then she will help. He is…an unyielding man. Few refuse him for long."

Her lips twitched. "Did you?"

"Longer than most. But he can be patient, when he's certain of an outcome. And he was certain of me."

"Can I ask how you met?" She had always been intensely

curious of other people's relationships. In Dead Earth, she'd never had the opportunity to form any of her own, so she'd watched people all the time. They'd never noticed, and she hadn't had much of anything better to do.

Griff and Jevryn's relationship fascinated her. To some degree it was because of the weight of history behind it—centuries spanned and yet they were still connected, for better or worse. But most of it was because she cared about Griff. Jevryn's reintroduction into his life—bringing back the memories and identity Griff had chosen to shove down and forget in order to endure his existence as the Station's Avatar—had brought first anger and sadness.

Now, she wasn't entirely sure what his feelings were. But she wanted to believe that at their dawn, Griff and Jevryn had been happy. Because she wanted *Griff* to have been happy.

He was silent so long that she said, "You don't have to answer if you don't want to."

"No, I don't mind. Merely thinking of how to begin. I will have to talk around the mechanisms involved in how we met, but since you already know them, it shouldn't be an issue for you to infer what I mean."

"Meaning you can't say the *P* word?" She understood why Kiev had bound Griff with magic that forbade him from speaking about portaling, as it had existed in his youth, but it irked her that Griff had to talk around his own history.

"Indeed," Griff said. "I suppose you might say fate threw Jevryn and I together. You know that I chose my current form because of the wings?"

Nyx nodded.

"I am denied from taking any form with a base Human component. But originally, I looked no different from Earth humans, with a notable exception." He shook his feathers.

"No way. Like an angel?"

"Your Earth concept of angels is very strange to me."

"Do you have a picture?"

"I do have one." He didn't immediately manifest it, and she cursed herself for a curiosity that often failed to consider how her requests might hurt. But he pulled it up a second later and she thought his hesitation hadn't been at seeing himself as he once was, but because Jevryn was in the picture with him.

She'd thought Jevryn was tall, but Griff—Arradin—had been a couple inches taller. He stood behind the councilor, his hands on Jevryn's waist, his skin a warm brown against Jevryn's more neutral olive tone. He wore glasses identical in design to the small ones now perched on his beak, his eyes the same brilliant gold, a perfect match to his hair.

Splayed out to either side, stretching six feet in span, were shining, golden wings. Oddly, that wasn't the thing Nyx found most arresting about the photo. It was how ordinary Jevryn looked. His expression still held the cool arrogance she'd come to expect from the councilor, but he looked more...human. He looked happy.

This picture didn't show councilor Jevryn A-Morridahn. It simply showed a man, one slightly younger than she was now. A man who hadn't yet had everything he loved ripped away from him.

No, she realized, it held *two* men who had not yet experienced that. The difference made by the centuries that had passed was that Jevryn had hardened to the point nothing could damage him, while Griff had made himself pliant. They had both, she thought, done what they had to in order to survive. They'd just done so differently.

She wondered which way she would go. If she found herself in this Station, centuries passing while she tried to solve the problem of the Harvester. If she found herself alone in those centuries, would she become as difficult to break as stone, or would she turn as malleable as water?

Carefully, she handed the picture back to Griff. It disappeared, and he shook out his feathers. "Now, I think I was telling you a story, unless you do not wish to hear it anymore?"

"I'm all ears."

"It wasn't terribly romantic. I was flying. He fell out of the sky a few feet above me."

"He portaled into midair?"

Griff's head gave an odd jerk that told her he'd tried to nod, and been halted by magic. He sighed. "That was in the early days of Jevryn's…extracurricular travels," he said, choosing his words carefully. "No one engaging in such travel at the time had a great deal of experience. Jevryn probably had the most natural aptitude of any of the original explorers, and it gave him an invincibility complex.

"The moment he found somewhere new, he went without thought to the consequences. It just so happened that traveling to my home was the first time he did so and found himself a few hundred feet above the ground. He crushed my right wing when he fell into me, which sent us both into a tailspin. Before I could try to pull up, injured wing or no, he panicked and returned to his home. Since we were a little entangled at the time, he took me with him."

Nyx tried to imagine what it would be like to be minding your own business only to have someone appear out of literal thin air and then transport you to somewhere utterly foreign. "Did you lose it?"

"In a manner of speaking. I thought I had been, to use your Earth phrase, abducted by aliens."

"You kind of had been," she pointed out. "Wait, could you even talk to him? Did they have the translator spells back then?"

"No." He canted his head. "I believe I can actually speak about this without issue. At that stage, they had a standard plan for approaching newly-found indigenous peoples. One that usually involved someone very good with languages. Which Jevryn is not.

"Unfortunately, neither am I. Once I stopped trying to kill him, we each worked out enough words and phrases for rudimentary communication. Eventually, I picked up enough to build a spell that would work out the rest of it."

Had he just said what she thought he'd just said? "You created the first translator spell? On a whim?"

"I would call it a necessity more than a whim. You have no idea how cranky Jevryn can be when he can't get a point across. He is extremely short-tempered. In truth, my initial opinion of him was that he was very pretty but not particularly bright."

Nyx barely managed not to choke on thin air at that description of Jevryn. "How long did it take you?"

"A few hours, once I got Jevryn to sit down and feed the magic enough words to go off."

"A few hours," she repeated. "You invented a translator spell from scratch in a few hours?"

"A rudimentary one, yes. Adaptive magics were my specialty. Give something enough form and intent, and it can learn with very little structured guidance. Once the core language commonalities were input, it mostly ran itself."

Sure. He'd just invented the magical version of AI learning because he hadn't liked dealing with Jevryn's crankiness. No wonder Griff liked having Morgen in the Station. The two of them were on the same intellectual level several floors above everyone else.

"Of course," Griff continued, "as I said, it was rudimentary. There were a few…misunderstandings in translation during the initial weeks. In retrospect, they are hilarious, though I can't say either of us felt that way about them at the time."

"Do you still make stuff like that? Adaptive spells?" She regretted it the second she asked.

Griff's face fell, all amusement fading. "No. As I told you before, my bond to the Station is quite different from the Guardian bond, both as it was for you initially, and as you have changed it. My inborn talents are locked to me now."

She wanted to say that she was sorry, but sometimes she felt like all she did was apologize to him. She wanted to promise that she would fix it, but she'd already promised to try, and she still didn't know if she could succeed. And she knew he was doing his best not to get his hopes up about it in case she never did.

He stretched his wings and changed the subject. "I believe I will go check on Temerex."

"Have you had any luck communicating with her?" Nyx had finally convinced Morgen and the others that she could do it by having Temerex perform a series of tasks, but none of the others had been able to achieve similar results.

"No," Griff said. "I am not sure where that connection stems from. Would you like me to try something new?"

"No, it's okay. Tell her hi for me." He left, and she thought of the companion journal upstairs. She supposed, now that she was talking to Jevryn, she could just ask him about Temerex's communication ability. Of course, whether he'd give her an answer was anyone's guess.

Alone, she closed her eyes and sank into the Station's senses. Maybe she was being paranoid, but with the addition of Beauregard and Reyva to the Station's inhabitants, along with whatever third person they selected from the castle guard, she wanted to section off what she thought of as the private areas of the Station from the public.

Her consciousness felt like roots spilling through the walls and floors as she tugged and tucked and rearranged, like playing Tetris with an infinitely malleable substance. First, she pulled everyone's rooms except Liya's into the back half of the building. The library, along with all its doors to places like the Den and Morgen's laboratory, went next.

In the front half of the building, what she now thought of as the public area, she left the Arrival Room, the cafe, the gym, and a suite of guest rooms for Beauregard, Reyva, and the potential new addition.

She added a smaller replica of the library, along with a few rooms for studying and lounging while she was at it, and called it good. The only connection between the public and private halves of the Station was a small section of wall along the back hallway. It was indistinguishable from the rest of the wall, but would allow those with the proper clearance, so to speak, to pass through.

She shifted Liya's room to an exterior corner of the building. It was technically in the public section, but came with a private entrance no one would be likely to stumble upon. Liya so rarely came into the rest of the Station that she probably wouldn't even notice the difference. Even so, Nyx drew up a rudimentary map of the changes and sent it to Liya's room, along with a note informing her that the Station would be hosting Beauregard and two of his guests for a few days.

She sent other copies of the maps to Evra and Morgen, and one to Seth's room as well. With nothing else to do, she made her daily visit to the Station's Heart. But while Kaliaris was obviously pleased to see her, the visit itself was no more fruitful than any of her others had been. Laiveran was as unreachable as ever.

She had Kaliaris gently restrain him, so she could snap on the new suppressing cuffs Jevryn had sent and remove the old ones, but he barely seemed to notice. She stayed for two hours anyway, talking to him—and Kaliaris—and hoping for a response or an opening that she didn't get. Defeated, she let Kaliaris send her back up to the rest of the Station.

She needed to try something new—she just didn't know what that something new was. She stood for a moment in the portal room, unsure of where to go. Seth and Reyva had returned. They were with Morgen and Evra in the new planning room she'd added on, seated around a table, no doubt looking over the information in the archive disc Beauregard had left them.

She thought about joining them, but she wasn't sure what the point would be. She wasn't going on this trip. She wasn't part of the team. And if she wasn't part of the team, she would only be in the way.

Trying and failing not to feel sorry for herself, she trudged outside to Temerex's stall. The unicorn-dragon trotted up to her, tossing her head and pawing excitedly.

Nyx scratched behind her ear. "I made you something. You want to see it?"

Not waiting for an answer, she stretched out her hand, the landscape changing, branching dirt paths sprouting between the trees. The paths were lined with targets—fake soldiers on equally fake horses. In some areas logs hung suspended above the path, ready to knock from their horse any rider who failed to duck as they passed that portion. In other areas the ground dropped into deep pits anywhere from two to six feet wide.

Temerex came to excited alertness, head up and ears pricked as she surveyed this new delight. Once the mare had climbed partly out of the depression Jevryn's abandonment had left her in, she had started sending Nyx images of what amounted to an obstacle course for practicing ridden warfare. She seemed to think this was her purpose in life and that it was Nyx's duty, as her human, to facilitate that purpose.

"What do you say? Want to give it a go?" She sent Temerex an image of Nyx astride her as they ran through the course. Temerex whinnied and sent the image back.

"Okay then." Nyx picked out her hooves, wiped down her scales with one of the cloths Jevryn had sent, and tacked her up. In place of the wool or synthetic saddle blanket typical of western-style horse tack, Temerex's saddle had an underside clearly meant to prevent chafing against her scales, while still providing the requisite padding to prevent muscle soreness.

Her bridle was more of a fancy padded halter, with reins attached to the small ring on the underside. No bit. Was that because she didn't need it, or because her mouth couldn't accommodate one? Horses had a natural gap between their teeth, called the "bars" of their mouth, where the bit rested. Nyx wondered if Tem—whose teeth were very much sharp and pointed like the kelpies of fae lore—even had that gap.

Not that she had any intention of sticking her hand in

Temerex's mouth to find out. She'd ridden with only a halter plenty of times, especially on her old mare, Belle, who—

Nyx tossed the lead rope over Belle's neck, catching the loose end and threading it through the halter ring under her chin, tying a knot to make a quick set of looped reins.

She placed her left hand against the mare's withers, took two quick steps and vaulted onto Belle's back in a move she'd practiced until she could do it in her sleep.

She gathered the reins and set off, a soft squeeze of her legs and a kissing sound all it took to move Belle smoothly from walk to canter, skipping the trot Nyx found so onerous bareback.

She lost herself in the smooth glide of the horse beneath her, and the wind in her hair, and for a moment she pretended she was someone— anyone—else. That the world was a different, nicer place, and she a different, more exciting person.

Maybe she was a warrior, on one of the far-off planets Viktor sometimes told her about when Nyx's mother wasn't around to tell him not to. Maybe she was the best warrior, with the fastest horse, and because she was the best, her father was proud of her.

She urged Belle faster, galloping down the narrow path through the woods, and let herself believe the water streaming down her face was from the wind in her eyes. And she let herself pretend that she was that other Nyx, one who had a father who looked like her.

A father who would never let her grow up in isolation, her only company a boy whose existence was a misery because of her. A father she could pretend was out there, looking for her even now.

Maybe her mother had stolen her away from him. Maybe he had wanted her, and he missed her, and loved her, and someday soon he would find her. And when he did, she wouldn't be a disappointment to him like she was to Elena. She would show him that she could be strong. That she could be quick and clever, and she would never be any trouble.

And when he came for her and took her away from this place, he would let her bring Seth with them, because Viktor wouldn't care, or probably even notice, if Seth was gone.

Her heart beat with the borrowed happiness of a future she desperately wanted to believe could come to pass. But her eyes streamed water because she was getting older, and the more she grew, the less likely that future seemed.

She was already ten. If her father wanted her, hadn't he had enough time to find her?

The misplaced sliver fell back into place in Nyx's mind, filling in a small crack, and she jolted back to the present.

Temerex had grabbed hold of Nyx's shirt with her mouth and was tugging on it, clearly concerned. The sound of tearing fabric rent the air as the unicorn-dragon's sharp teeth tore an irregular circle clean out of the shirt.

"Thanks for that," Nyx said drily.

Temerex bobbed her head, tongue lolling out as she tried to drop the fabric now sticking to it. Nyx grabbed hold of a corner and pulled it free.

"We do the obstacle course on one condition—I freeze, you freeze." She sent Temerex an image of Nyx going suddenly rigid on her back, trying to convey what that might feel like for Temerex, and coupling it with the image of Temerex coming to a gradual halt. If the mare just stopped dead from a gallop, Nyx would come right off for sure.

She'd probably come off anyway, but the course was designed to be as forgiving as possible. If she fell off, the ground would react in an absorbent, cushioning manner. If she failed to duck one of the logs, it would burst into powder on impact.

She couldn't ask for much more. She strapped on a practice sword and a belt pouch filled with throwing darts, and mounted. She rode the perimeter path that skirted the actual course first, easing Temerex through walk, trot, and canter to warm up her back, until the mare practically dance with impatience beneath her.

"Okay girl," she murmured, "let's see what you can do."

Temerex *moved*, and Nyx suddenly understood why the saddle had so damn deep of a seat. She failed to hit most of her targets on the first run-through, everything a blur as Temerex shot past it all. But Nyx didn't have it in her to rein Tem in, letting her have her fun.

Though she nearly did come off when Temerex's fun included coming to an unexpected sliding stop, then pivoting on her forehand and double-barrel kicking one of the faux-horses in the chest. Fake horse and rider fell to the ground, and Tem took off like a shot for the end of the course.

The automatic scoring system Nyx had rigged declared that she'd hit approximately fifty percent of the targets. Of those, she'd only hit the ideal target area, or bullseye, forty percent of the time.

Temerex sent Nyx an image of Jevryn, the councilor wearing an expression of extreme disappointment. Couldn't the unicorn-dragon at least use an image of Griff looking disappointed to convey her displeasure with Nyx's abysmal performance? Jevryn A-Morridahn's disappointed looks were a little too severe.

Besides, "You can't possibly read a scoreboard." And while she didn't actually think the unicorn-dragon *could*, she didn't doubt she had felt uncoordinated on top of her. "You had your fun with the speed demon routine, let's do it again a little slower."

Temerex huffed out a breath and trotted back to the start of the course, clearly resigned to being held to a more inferior standard than she was accustomed to. They ran the course again, and then a third and fourth time, until Nyx's arms and shoulders were too heavy to swing the sword anymore, her core screaming in outrage, and her thigh muscles informing her that maybe she *used* to ride a horse every day, but seven years had passed between then and now, and good luck walking tomorrow.

But all of the physical exertion quieted her mind, and she was *almost* too tired to think for the next couple of hours.

That evening, she climbed into bed with the companion journal and one of the books Jevryn had sent her on portal magic. In the first one she dutifully wrote:

Checking in for the evening. Are you happy?

Jevryn's near-instant reply was a single word.

Ecstatic.

She could practically hear the sarcasm.

Do you have her?

If I had her, I would be at your Station.

Which answered the question of whether he intended to deliver Nyx's mother himself.

Where is she that a councilor can't just walk in and get her?

Somewhere prominent enough that if I "walk in and get her" it will draw attention. You are unknown. Your mother is not. Though she is presumed dead, bringing notice to her could dispel that presumption quite easily.

Be patient.

Patience was never one of my virtues.

Obviously.

Is your condition worsening?

Her *condition*. That was one way to put it, she supposed.

I'd say it's progressing on schedule.

This is hardly the time for levity.

I don't know what you want me to tell you.

I would like for you to take the situation seriously.

It's my mind that's about to resemble the inside of a pinball machine. I take it very seriously.

What is a pinball machine?

Forget it.

She was having trouble figuring out why she was so touchy. Maybe it was the clinical way he'd approached everything. Or the fact he'd decided to lecture her on how she should be feeling.

I am merely attempting to ascertain the time left to me to accomplish a delicate task that you have placed upon me with little warning. There are risks I might or might not take depending on the direness of your condition.

Nyx blew out a breath.

I haven't had a major episode yet. If I don't check in with you one night, it's safe to say I'm in the middle of one.

Apprise me of any such event the moment you are able.

The sentence had a feeling of finality to it, as if he was finished discussing things for the evening.

Are you still there?

Nothing.

When you see this, two questions:

1. How does Temerex's communication work?

2. Does Laiveran need some kind of soul connection to maintain his grip on reality? And if he does, how do I fix that without putting someone in danger?

She left it open, so she'd see if he happened to answer, then started in on the portal magic book. She kept nodding off, on account of it being the most dryly academic thing she'd ever read. The author either enjoyed writing in such a way as to sound esoterically intellectual while being entirely incomprehensible, or it wasn't translating efficiently into English via the translator spells.

Knowing her luck, it was both.

She fell asleep again, startling awake when the book fell onto the floor with a loud *thunk*.

"Okay," she muttered, retrieving the book and stumbling, barely awake, back to Jevryn's trunk, "I give up on this one."

She tossed it inside and pulled out the other one he'd sent. It was a soft, leather-bound tome titled *Portal Magic: Its Uses and Limitations*. It had sounded more academic than the other one, which had been simply titled *A Guide to Portal Magic*. If this one was worse, she was *not* starting it tonight.

She flipped to the first page, hoping the opening paragraph would give her a better idea of whether or not it was more readable. Tucked inside the front cover was a piece of paper with Jevryn's now-familiar elegant scrawl.

I recommend starting with this one. I included the other because it

has a few useful insights, but it gives one a splitting headache to
read.

"You couldn't have put that note on the *outside* of the book?" she grumbled. She tucked the piece of paper into the back pages for later use as a bookmark, then froze when she saw the title page.

The exterior hadn't listed an author, but here it was, printed in looping scrawl. *Portal Magic: Its Uses and Limitations by Arradin Thesrani.* She almost called for Griff—he'd always had a scholarly manner so it didn't surprise her he'd written a book—but then she flipped the page and saw the dedication.

For Jevryn, who quite literally fell into my life and turned it upside down. You surprise me every day. I hope I do the nature of your ability justice.

She stared at the book. It had occurred to her earlier, as Griff told her how he'd met Jevryn, that her Avatar probably knew more about how portal magic worked than anyone in the universe save the councilors. Yet another reason to hate Kiev was that Nyx would much rather have Griff teach her about her magic than Jevryn. Except Griff couldn't, because he couldn't talk about it.

But this…this was like having him teach her. Because as she flipped to the first page and started reading, she could hear his voice in the words, and it was almost like he was talking to her.

11

Nyx woke to a crick in her neck and a numb left ass cheek. She supposed it was the expected price to be paid for falling asleep while sitting on the floor and leaning against a gigantic luggage trunk. She stood and stretched, a satisfying series of cracks going up her back.

A piece of paper on the floor in front of her door caught her attention. She hobbled over, skin tingling with pins and needles as her butt woke up, and retrieved the paper.

Seth's sharp hand had scrawled five words:

I was right. Space sucks.

She smiled and grabbed a notebook.

I imagine it feels the same way about you.

She tore out the page, dropped it on the floor, and sent it through the Station to the nightstand in Seth's room. She felt him pick it up.

A minute went by before a new piece of paper dropped onto

his nightstand. She pulled it through and unfolded it. A universal note worth roughly five US dollars fell out.

> I try to reward art in its nascent stages but I wouldn't try stand-up any time soon.

She rolled her eyes. Another piece of paper dropped onto the nightstand.

> You're cute when you roll your eyes.

> I hate you.

> It's that cheerful affection that has me missing you already. So how do we do this?

> Do what?

> Avoid each other. Do I get the public areas in the morning, you in the afternoon? Who gets predominant visitation rights on our friends?

She rolled her eyes again.

> You may not know this, but I'm kind of part of a sentient building that knows where you are at all times. I think I can manage to avoid you. And I don't think any of you are going to have much free time anyway, what with having an infiltration to plan.

> Fine. I'll keep myself busy. But I'll be thinking of you.

She didn't write back. Because thinking of him was exactly what she was supposed to be trying *not* to do.

She tucked the notes into her nightstand drawer. She grabbed the companion journal to put away as well, and saw Jevryn had written back.

> Laiveran's people were not particularly forthcoming about the specific nature of their abilities. Most of us were not, at that time. I can tell you that he never traveled alone, and claimed to be able to touch the souls of animals. He was very fond of—what do you call them on Earth? Ah, yes. Cats. You might consider getting him a cat, and seeing if there is any improvement.

"Get him a cat?" she repeated aloud. "That's your brilliant advice?" He also, she noted, hadn't responded to the question about Temerex.

She considered his suggestion. She considered it during her morning shower, while she was getting dressed, while she ate breakfast, and then let it hover in the back of her mind while she sent off the two Departures that had been scheduled for that morning. She watched the last one disappear into the ley lines, the floor re-solidifying behind him. The spinning orbs atop the hexagonal posts wound down, slower and slower until they stilled.

She stared at the floor that could be either the entrance to the ley lines or to the Station's Heart, depending on what Kaliaris wanted. She thought of Laiveran down there, alone, his only company a being that hated him immensely.

Would it hurt anything to get him a cat? There was an animal shelter a few doors down from Ankira's shop.

Fuck. "Me, my bleeding heart, and Jevryn's bad advice," she muttered. It sounded like a country song.

She walked out of the building toward Wayfarer's Way. She was thirty paces from the border that demarcated the Station's grounds from the rest of Earth Between when her breathing kicked up. At twenty paces, she started sweating. Fifteen paces and her steps slowed, her heart rate so rapid her pulse beat like drums in her ears.

Everything was fine. How many times had she gone into

Earth Between since she'd come here? Dozens. Things had only gone wrong once, and the person responsible for those things was currently under her control.

She clenched her fists, hands shaky, and kept going. Ten paces. Her whole body was trembling now. Five paces and she was so light-headed it felt like her spirit was trying to detach from her body.

At the border, she halted, staring at the path that led to Earth Between proper. She stretched out her hand, fingers whispering through the invisible wall, reaching air that wasn't the Station's.

Nausea roiled in her stomach and she snatched her hand back.

This wasn't logical. She was fine. If she went into Earth Between she would *be* fine. No one was waiting to snatch her. She was being ridiculous.

But the longer she stood by the border the dizzier she became, until her vision blurred and she found herself turning, sprinting for the Station building. She didn't stop running until she was in her bathroom, stripping off her clothes and letting the ice-cold spray of the shower shock her out of her spiral.

She stayed until she was shivering from cold instead of fear. When she finally shut the water off and climbed out, she pointedly didn't look in the mirror.

It would be better next time, she promised herself. She just wasn't ready yet. Between her own problems, and Seth and the others about to leave, it was just too much right now. She didn't have to push this. And no one needed to know.

She pulled on her comfort clothes, loose gray sweatpants and a black tank top so soft it felt like a cloud. Then she went to the library, where Griff was sprawled out on a plush rug, a book held delicately in one talon.

He looked up as she walked in. "Are you alright?"

"Fine!" She winced at the excessive enthusiasm in her voice and toned it down. "Uh, listen, do you think you could get Seth to glamour you so you can go to the animal shelter by the Warlock's shop and get me a cat?"

Griff closed his book with studious precision and rose to a sitting position, giving her his undivided attention, concern worrying the corners of his eyes. "Have you had a more severe memory lapse?"

"What? No. I just—Jevryn said I should get Laiveran a cat." At the deepening worry on Griff's face, she forced herself to take a deep breath, slow down, and give a proper explanation. Once she had, she added, "I'd go, but given the whole memory thing right now it's maybe not the best idea. You know?"

He studied her, as if looking for what she wasn't saying. If he found it, he mercifully didn't comment. "Very well. I will get you a cat."

"Thank you." She threw her arms around his neck and hugged him, showing far more gratitude than was warranted by him agreeing to run what amounted to an errand for her. Again, he thankfully said nothing.

<hr>

A shrieking yowl split the library air, jolting Nyx out of her favorite papasan chair. Griff walked in. A fabric carrier with a fortified bottom dangled from his left hand, held as far away from his body as he could manage.

The outraged yowl sounded again, the sides of the carrier bulging in sequence, as if a bowling ball were being thrown around inside it like a pinball in a machine.

"I am not entirely certain it is safe to put down," Griff confessed.

"What is it?" Nyx caught only a blur of gray as the carrier lurched again.

"This is Her Majesty, the Queen of Wrath. However, as her full name is somewhat tedious, I am informed she is more frequently referred to as Fangs." He held the carrier out to Nyx. "She is your cat."

Nyx accepted the carrier, cradling it to her stomach rather than holding it by the strap. The furious motion stilled, replaced by a low, warning growl. "Umm, I wasn't aware we were trying to assassinate Laiveran via cat."

"She was the only cat available at the shelter, and there was no other species remotely similar. And...I confess I felt poorly for her. Shelter staff said she had been there for almost a year, with no progress on her socialization."

Nyx craned her neck, trying to peer through the mesh side of the carrier to get a glimpse of the creature she was still not convinced was a cat. The growl turned into a cry that more befitted a mountain lion, and there was a blur of gray as a paw lashed at her.

She jerked back. The paw slammed into the carrier, claws digging through the mesh, white tips appearing on the outside. "Well," she crooned at the creature, "with a sunny disposition like that, how could you *not* socialize well?"

Her baby talk elicited another low growl from within the carrier, but the cat didn't launch itself at her again. It did leave its claws dug into the cloth side.

"Her food and other necessities are outside the door," Griff said, casually backing towards said door, "so I'll just leave you to it." He turned and fled, leaving Nyx alone with the Queen of Wrath.

"Coward!" she called after him. She looked down at the growling bundle in her arms. "Alright, Your Majesty. Let's get you settled."

<What have you brought into my sanctum?> Kaliaris demanded, as soon as Nyx landed in the Heart.

"This is Fangs. Fangs is a cat." She explained why she'd brought the feline.

<You wish me to allow the beast to live *here*?> They sounded outraged enough, but the rustle of vines in the room spoke more of interest than irritation.

"Yes. I hope it will help with our cause, but I have conditions. Serious conditions."

<Such as?>

"However unpleasant of a cat Fangs may be"—a fresh cry of indignation split the air—"she deserves safety and comfort. Cats have needs. Like daylight. While she's here, you need to simulate daylight for at least twelve hours. She'll need things to climb, soft places to sleep, and somewhere she feels like she can hide.

"I've brought you her food, a cat bed, some toys, and her litter box."

<Litter box?>

Nyx explained that too. "It'll need to be cleaned frequently. I'll come down and do it, but if something happens to me, you're going to have to take over. Can you do that?"

She expected them to argue, but they just said, <As you insist. Anything else?>

"Yes, and this is the most important one. She has to be safe. I don't think Laiveran will harm her. As far as I know, he's never shown violence as an impulse, only as a means to an end, but if he makes *any* move to hurt her, I expect you to protect her. Can you promise me that?"

<You have my word.>

"Thank you."

<Let us see the beast, then.>

Nyx crouched, hesitating. "I'm also not sure this is the best environment for a cat. If she shows any indicators of stress, I'll have to move her out."

Kaliaris bristled. <Are you suggesting I am incapable of providing a decent home for this feline?>

"No, I—"

<Because it certainly sounds as if you are. Let this Fangs roam free. I assure you I am capable of seeing to her happiness.>

She supposed if Kaliaris got attached to Fangs, that could only be a good thing. She opened the carrier door and sprang back. Fangs crept out slowly, fur sticking up in a ridge down her spine, tail puffed.

She was massive, with tufted ears and paws. Nyx was pretty sure she was looking at a Maine coon. Even though everything she knew about the breed said they were sweet, affectionate cats. Maybe the Queen of Wrath had Seen Things and therefore developed a poor attitude towards life.

"How did you wind up in Earth Between, girl?"

Fangs whipped her head around to look at Nyx. She hissed, revealing the very large incisors for which she had presumably been nicknamed. Laiveran, who had been quietly slouched in a corner of his cell this whole time, was drawn by the sound.

His gaze landed on Fangs, his face showing the first hint of interest in anything that Nyx had seen since she'd started visiting him. He crouched, extending his hand in invitation.

Fangs threw another disdainful hiss at Nyx, lifted her tail in the air, and nimbly leapt her way over criss-crossing vines to sniff Laiveran's hand. Apparently finding him to her satisfaction, she rubbed her face across his fingers, a loud purr replacing her earlier yowling.

Well, there was no accounting for taste. Since there wasn't much else for her to do, she left the mass murderer and the angry feline to bond.

12

Nyx had thought having Fangs to check in on would keep her mind off everything else, but two such wellness checks the next day proved that Fangs was happier without her. On her first visit, the cat had been curled up in Laiveran's lap, and promptly sprang to her feet to hiss upon Nyx's arrival. The second time, she'd been athletically bouncing from vine to vine on some sort of cat jungle-gym Kaliaris had built for her.

Fangs was happy. She still hated Nyx, but Nyx could live with that. And the cat's presence *did* seem to be having a positive effect on Laiveran. Not enough for Nyx to get any information out of him, but she was hopeful that in a few days or weeks, she might.

But since that day wasn't today, that left her without much to distract. She made it halfway through the day before she decided that, surely, a Seth in a room full of other people was a Seth unlikely to trigger a memory fragment, and she could pop in to the planning room for a brief check-in. Evra and Morgen had been sequestered in there with Seth and Reyva ever since yesterday, and Nyx missed everyone.

She walked in to find them all gathered around a 3D model of a… Well, it looked like a space station.

Except no one in the connected magical universe traveled by strapping themselves into spaceships, so this thing that *looked* like a space station was presumably not floating out in the nothingness of space anchored only by some planet's gravity.

Actually, the more she looked at it, the *less* it looked like a space station, despite the black metal industrial feel of it. "Why does that look like someone made Darth Vader's dream wedding cake and put it in a pool of blood?"

Seth laughed. He laughed so hard he snorted the water he'd been drinking directly onto the 3D model. Which it turned out was actually a magical projection instead of a model, so the water went through it and landed on Morgen's shirt.

Evra looked confused, but she thumped Seth "helpfully" on the back, perhaps with a little too much enthusiasm. Beauregard looked annoyed at the interruption, and Morgen was busy wiping water off his shirt with a towel Griff summoned for him.

Reyva raised her hand. "What is Darth Vader and why is it funny?"

"It's a long explanation," Nyx said. "And it isn't that funny."

Reyva raised her eyebrows in skepticism and pointed at where Seth was still laughing.

Nyx shrugged. "He's an easy target." Another *itch* in the back of her mind. She shut it out fiercely because she didn't want to leave, even if she knew she should.

"*Darth Vader's wedding cake,*" Seth said, after he finally sucked in a decent lungful of air, "is the only city on Nethrayne. For all intents and purposes, it *is* Nethrayne. The rest of the planet is covered in lava."

"Lava? The blood lake represents a lava ocean?"

"Yep." Seth drew the word out, making a popping sound when he hit the *P*.

She had a lot of questions. The first one that came out was, "So how hot is it?"

Morgen answered. "The planet's surface is approximately twenty-one hundred universal degrees."

"Around fifty-four-hundred degrees Fahrenheit," Seth converted.

"Fifty-four-*hundred*? How did anyone survive *finding* the place?" Much less building a city on it that was protected from constant heat that extreme.

Griff opened his beak, then paused, as if waiting for something to happen. When nothing did, he said, "I believe I can actually answer that. After a few unsavory accidents, the individuals who now form the Council developed insulating atmospheric spells capable of withstanding even the most extreme of environments. At least for long enough to abandon ship, so to speak, if needed."

Nyx remembered trying to exit the prison on Lehine and hearing a disembodied voice saying, "No insulating atmospheric spells detected."

"And one of the councilors thought it would be a good idea to build a city on a lava ocean?" She had no idea what an insulating atmospheric spell looked like—or if it even looked like anything at all—but her imagination was putting people inside of big clear bubbles. She then envisioned them floating in molten red depths while they built support beams that somehow didn't melt in extreme heat, all so a councilor could have a city in one of the least hospitable environments imaginable.

No, no, and also, *hell no*.

"How else would they feel important?" Reyva asked.

"As I was saying," Beauregard said, with the air of a combat general who'd been interrupted one-too-many times and someone was going to have to pay for it, "Nethrayne's Station is here." He indicated the place on the model. It was a small circle connected to the large wedding cake structure by a thin bridge.

It gave Nyx flashbacks to crossing a certain bridge over death sand to get to the Keeper's spire in the Shadow Market. Everyone liked their death moats. Except this wasn't a death moat, it was a death ocean that covered an entire planet.

Delightful.

"The Station is merely the first point of security. Once we pass inspection there—"

Nyx quit listening as her attention was drawn by footsteps on the Station's front grounds. *Familiar* footsteps.

Except she was having a hard time figuring out *why* these familiar footsteps were here. "Morgen, did you invite anyone else on this quest?" she asked. She winced when she realized she'd talked right over Beauregard.

Morgen looked up. "No. Why?"

"Nothing. I'll be right back." She turned and strode out.

Maybe she was wrong. The one sense she didn't really have through the Station was sight. She couldn't look at the front grounds like she had a security camera on it. Instead, what she memorized through the Station was patterns. Each person's weight, the length of their stride, the way their feet landed. How lightly or heavily they trod. And while *she* wasn't always the best at doing that, Kaliaris was, and she had Kaliaris' awareness of their inhabitants.

For instance, she knew the person currently in the cafe was Kalvar, because his step length was approximately twenty-nine inches, his boots had a smooth grip sole that gave a particular feel to the Station's floor when they landed, and she could hear him whistling.

Shit. *Kalvar* was in the cafe. In the event Nyx wasn't wrong about who was at her doorstep, she broke into a jog. She skidded into the cafe a few seconds later, startling Kalvar. "Hey, could you run down to the cellar? I think I forgot to do inventory on the Ganvaila milk. We have that group coming in from there tomorrow."

Kalvar gave her a concerned look. "Nyx," he said, drawing her name out slowly. "We don't have a Ganvaila group coming. Is this memory thing already getting to you?" He placed a hand over his heart. "It's me. Remember? Kalvar. Your favorite employee."

"There's nothing wrong with my brain function," she

snapped. The footsteps were almost at the front door. "I just really need that inventory done. Like right now."

"Since when do we do inventory?"

The front door opened and Maruca Moor walked in. Her gaze met Kalvar's and she froze.

"Oh," Kalvar said flatly, "*that* inventory. The very important inventory I definitely make a top priority every week. I'll go do that right now."

He pulled the barista's towel hanging from his back pocket, dropped it on the counter, and walked out without a single acknowledgment in Maruca's direction.

Which left Nyx with one Moor sibling whose red hair looked like it might burst into actual flames if given the opportunity. Nyx couldn't quite bring herself to say anything welcoming, considering the last time she'd seen Maruca, the woman had punched her. In the face. While essentially blaming her for absolutely everything wrong with her and her brother's lives.

Okay, yes, it *had* been right after Kaden had nearly been cut in half by a rapidly closing magical doorway, which might or might not have been Nyx's fault. So she gave Maruca some leeway for that, but she certainly hadn't expected her to ever show up at the Station again. At least, not without a hefty advance warning.

Maruca's gaze, which had followed Kalvar down the hall-way, snapped back to Nyx. The woman's green eyes, so like Kaden's, were lacking their usual brimming dislike. She didn't snap out a cutting remark. She didn't gloss over Nyx as if she wasn't there and demand to see Morgen, who she'd probably come here to see.

No, Maruca opened her mouth and…hesitated. Maruca Moor didn't hesitate. She made the world bow before her out of habit, and if it turned out the world hadn't *needed* to bow, she would generously allow it to rise.

Before she figured out whatever it was she wanted to say, Morgen, Seth, and Evra walked in.

"Ruca?" Morgen said. "What are you doing here?"

Relief eased the rigid stiffness of Maruca's posture, as if now that Morgen was here, she was freed from whatever she'd been about to say to Nyx. "Mom sent me."

"Why?"

"Because you sent her a letter that said, and I quote, 'Dear Mother, I love you very much. You are the best mother a man could ever hope to have. I hope you know how much I appreciate you.'"

"It's important to appreciate people."

"It is the kind of letter you send someone when you're about to do something monumentally stupid. She sent me to talk you out of whatever the monumentally stupid thing is or, if I cannot, to go along and keep you alive."

Beauregard, apparently tired of being left to an audience of one, came in with Reyva on his heels.

Maruca broke into a smile. "Uncle Beau?"

"Little Ruca."

Nyx had to do a double-take as Maruca laughed—yes, the flame-haired witch was actually capable of *happy* laughter—and flung herself into Beauregard's open arms.

Uncle Beau? *Little* Ruca? Nyx had the very vague knowledge that Morgen's mom had taken Kaden and Maruca in after their parents died, but she wasn't sure how old they'd been at the time, or how much they'd integrated into his family. Or maybe it wasn't just *his* family anymore. Judging by the way Beauregard squeezed Maruca in a bear hug and twirled her in a circle like she was five, maybe it was just *their* family now.

Reyva came up beside Nyx. "I didn't realize there was a family reunion going on."

Evra claimed the spot on Nyx's other side and said, seriously, "I do not believe it to be a formal reunion."

Reyva laughed. "It was a joke, Ev."

Evra shivered. "Do not call me that."

"Are you going to throw me in a midden heap like last time?"

Evra cursed. "I knew you looked familiar. So *that's* where I've seen you before."

Nyx looked at Evra. "You threw a complete stranger in a midden heap for calling you Ev?"

"It is a hideous abbreviation of a name short enough that it should require no abbreviation."

"Still seems harsh."

"There were extenuating factors involved."

"I kissed her girlfriend," Reyva admitted.

"You kissed Bryn Morrigan?" Nyx whisper-shrieked. "When she was with Evra?"

"I didn't know she had a girlfriend and I needed to distract her."

Beauregard's booming voice stole Nyx's attention back from this fascinating glimpse into the Keeper of Shadows' past. "You are not going." His joviality had given way to a stern, absolutely-not expression.

"Morgen is going," Maruca pointed out.

"Morgen is a—" Beauregard bit off his sentence.

Maruca crossed her arms, literal flames of blue energy magic flickering in her eyes. "Please," she purred, "go ahead and finish that sentence. Morgen can go because he is a…?"

Beauregard wisely declined to finish it.

"A half-Siren?" Maruca suggested. "A former Enforcer? Because I am a full energy mage *and* a former Enforcer. I *know* you weren't about to suggest he can go because he's a man?"

Morgen clapped Beauregard on the shoulder. "Dug your own grave on that one."

"You can't go because your mother will kill me," Beauregard said, in an obvious attempt at recovery.

Maruca snorted. "Mom trusts me to keep you two alive. Which I will do, because I will be going."

"We already need someone else," Morgen pointed out. "And she knows how to work with me and Evra."

Nyx could practically see the internal debate play out on Beauregard's face. The strategic side of him recognized Maruca was an asset, while the familial side didn't want to put either Maruca or Morgen in danger.

"It isn't up for discussion," Maruca said flatly. "I'm going, so there's no need for you to have a moral crisis over it."

Beauregard dragged a hand across his face. "You both got your mother's stubborn streak." Which Nyx supposed was a testament to both nature and nurture. "Very well."

"Wonderful," Maruca said. "Where are we going and why?"

"To Nethrayne," Morgen said. "To end the Kumir."

Maruca blew out a breath. "Of course we are."

13

"Are we boring you, Hawthorne?" Reyva's voice snapped across the planning room.

Point of fact, they *were* boring him. But even in his currently bad mood, he had enough sense not to respond with a flippant, *Yes.* "Not all of us have to sit on the edge of our seats and say, 'Yes, Lord Beauregard,' at every opportunity to prove we're paying attention."

It was a good thing he'd never had to attend the kind of school where students were expected to listen to lectures and then turn in essays parroting back what their professors wanted to hear. He'd have failed miserably.

So what if, in terms of the US education system, he was the equivalent of a twenty-eight year-old who'd never even attended kindergarten? Nyx was the only one his father had bothered to fill out the homeschooling paperwork on. Not that it mattered. Seth wasn't dumb. He could read and write and do math and everything else that went along with an education. He just didn't have the piece of paper that would prove it and allow him to get a respectable job.

Fortunately he'd never had much interest in being respectable.

Reyva, on the other hand, had always struck him as a front-row student. He might have met her in the Shadow Market, but it had been obvious from the get-go that she didn't belong there. Oh, she was tough enough to handle it, but she'd always looked like she'd rather be performing an assigned task and being patted on the back for doing it well.

Hazards of being a child prodigy, he supposed. Maybe if adults had *oohed* and *ahhed* over *his* magic potential from the second he first used it, he would have found he was eager to work hard and prove them all right, too.

Then again, probably not.

Reyva gave him a look that could have scorched metal. "If you're paying attention, then what were we just going over?"

"Plan Z for what happens if we get caught at one of the checkpoints. Which is pointless. If we do get caught and Plans A through Y have failed, Z probably will too. By that point, I guarantee you all the plans will be shot to hell, and we'll be making it up as we go."

"We need to be prepared for every contingency."

"We *are* prepared. We've been beating this plan to death for days. It's dead. Hell, it's past dead and it's moved on to the afterlife. You know what the plan boils down to at this point? You and me doing really good magic, and them"—he pointed at Beauregard, Morgen, Evra and Maruca—"killing anything that gets in the way."

"I do good magic too," Morgen and Maruca objected in unison.

Another time, Seth would have found that funny. They were so obviously siblings it kind of made him wish he'd had a little brother or sister of his own. But he couldn't find the humor right now.

And when Seth couldn't find the humor, things were bad. He looked at Morgen and Maruca. "We do good magic and we kill things. We all agree that's the plan?"

"In a nutshell," Morgen agreed.

"Then let's call it a night. It's late and we have an early start. I for one would rather no one cut off my arm tomorrow because they're sleep-deprived and their sword-hand is twitchy."

No one voiced an objection, and by the time Beauregard gave a curt nod Seth was already pushing his chair back and heading for the door.

Out. He needed out.

He slipped through the public library and out the French doors onto the back porch. He let out a breath when he found it empty. No small part of him had thought Nyx would be here. It was the perfect kind of night for her—a touch colder than most people liked, not even a hint of a breeze, and the stars shining bright for days.

Maybe she had been here, and he'd run her off by coming out. He couldn't know, could he? She was the one who could mark everyone's whereabouts as easily as she drew breath. She was the one who could rearrange the Station in a blink, so seamlessly the rest of them wouldn't even notice it had happened.

He leaned against one of the porch's wooden support beams and stared out at the space where he'd been planning to make a garden. He hadn't gotten past drawing the plans for it before Nyx had fallen into her memory coma and he'd forgotten all about it.

When he'd been planning it, he'd been excited—he'd liked the idea, and he'd thought she would like it, too. A living maze, something he'd made because he could and not because he had to. Something that didn't have to serve a function other than to be enjoyed.

Because he'd felt like they finally had a sliver of the peace they'd been chasing their entire lives. Like even though there were things they needed to deal with, they could afford to take a moment to breathe and just be people.

He should have known better. Should have known he'd end up feeling now like he had then, promising her everything would be fine and only having the faintest hope of delivering on that promise.

Footsteps sounded behind him and he didn't need eyes in the back of his head to know they were Reyva's.

"You didn't have to bite my head off in there," she said, resting her forearms on the railing next to him. She waited, until it became obvious he wasn't going to answer. "You're not the only one worried about how this is going to go, you know. And it doesn't fill me with confidence that you don't seem to have your head on straight."

"There's nothing wrong with my head."

She snorted. "You look like a kicked puppy any time Nyx's name gets brought up, and I haven't seen the two of you together since I first got here. If you've got relationship issues, sort them out before we leave."

"My relationship's fine." If you counted a lifetime of everything being fucked six ways from Sunday as *fine.* "But if you want to talk about personal problems likely to get us killed, let's talk about Beauregard."

A strangled noise came out of her throat. "I'm not involved with Beauregard."

"No shit. I'm talking about his wife. The one his life's work is supposedly all about. The one there's apparently no evidence ever existed. Morgen's pushed him but he won't say anything else about it."

"Did you ever think maybe that's because she's dead and it's a sore subject for him? For stars' sake, he's spent most of his life trying to avenge her."

That was exactly the problem. "And you don't think that's a little weird? That he's never once quit yet he won't even tell us his wife's name?"

Reyva's eyes flashed. "What exactly are you suggesting?"

"Just that I find it hard to trust someone when I don't trust their motivations. If you know anything—"

"I know what everyone knows," she snapped. "And just

because you don't understand the kind of commitment that drives him doesn't mean it isn't valid." She shoved off the railing and started walking back inside.

Good. He wasn't in the mood to talk.

She stopped and threw back, "You know, when I saw her—saw you *with* her—I thought you finally cared about something. But you're just the same as always. Fun to be around but nothing to count on."

You don't know me. The words hovered on the tip of his tongue, but he didn't say them. He just gave her the smile that said he didn't care about anything in the world, the one that infuriated most people. It had the desired effect and she left, shaking her head.

She might not know him—he'd never let her—but she was right about one thing: he *was* just the same as ever. Just as stupidly in love with Nyx as he'd always been, not under-standing how he still had what he did, and terrified he was going to lose it.

He went inside, up the spiral staircase to Nyx's room. Her door was closed. He stood outside it, wanting to knock. Wanting that night back when she'd asked him to stay and he had, and for that short time everything had felt normal again. Right.

There was nothing normal about the fact he couldn't even knock on her door. Nothing right about the certainty that going to her now was the most selfish thing he could possibly do.

He brushed his hand across the wood grain of her door and then he turned and walked away, before selfishness could get the better of him.

14

The one person Nyx wanted most right now was the last person she should be around.

The small memory slivers were crashing into her with increasing frequency, even when she prevented herself from actively reaching for them. The magic skeleton in her brain was decaying, and a quick glance at the asteroid field in her mind had shown she didn't have too many of the small bits left.

Seeing Seth was a bad idea. Which was why she'd left the back porch when she'd felt him heading in that direction. And when Reyva had followed him out, Nyx had heroically avoided listening in on the conversation, and furthermore restrained herself from summoning a thunderstorm. It wasn't Reyva's fault she could talk to Seth without risking her sanity.

But superhuman restraint didn't come naturally to Nyx, and she might have required the liberal application of a tequila sunrise in order to keep from either talking to Seth or playing at being the god of thunder. Then, because she'd forgotten how much she liked tequila sunrises, she'd gotten halfway through a second one by the time Seth came up to lurk outside her bedroom door.

It was a pathetic state of affairs when she found lurking

sweet. She almost said to hell with it and dragged him inside. But even if she could control her end of things and *he* didn't trigger a memory event, she was likely to have one in front of him anyway, if he stayed long enough. And she didn't want him to know how frequent they were. How bad she was getting.

And if, when he put his hand on her door she put hers to the side opposite, well, it wasn't like anyone knew that but her. She downed the rest of drink number two as he walked away, and really wished Evra were available for a girls' night. Even if Evra's version of a girls' night consisted of things like cleaning weaponry and drinking alcohol that tasted like lighter fluid.

But the Amazon had disappeared into Morgen's room, and Nyx wasn't going to knock on his door and interrupt activities likely of the in-case-we-die-tomorrow variety just because she was miserable and wanted someone to distract her. Besides, it wasn't like Griff and Temerex were going to let her drink alone.

She returned to the back porch, apologizing to Temerex for rudely shunting her into her stall earlier. Since Jevryn had said Temerex was one-of-a-kind, Nyx hadn't needed Reyva seeing Tem and getting curious. After much apologizing and treat-giving on Nyx's end, Temerex huffed out a breath and magnanimously offered her neck for scratches.

"I see you have been forgiven," Griff said, ambling over to them.

"For the moment." She went to the outdoor bar she'd added to the back porch at Morgen's insistence. She pulled out the tequila, orange juice, and grenadine, made two new drinks and handed one to Griff.

He sniffed it curiously. "What is this?"

"Tequila sunrise. Unless you have personal objections to alcohol, you're morally obligated to drink it with me while I languish in self-pity."

Griff lifted the glass in her direction. "Never let it be said that I allowed you to languish in solitude." He tipped the glass carefully up to his beak, then tilted his head back, swallowing, a contemplative expression on his face. "Oh. That is surprisingly good."

"The best," Nyx agreed. She'd asked him once if he was forced to have an eagle's tastebuds in his current incarnation and was relieved to learn that, while he couldn't take a base Human form, he *could* keep the tastebuds he'd had in his original body.

A series of unpleasant prickles ran through her—or, rather, through the Station—and she groaned. "She's at it *again*?"

"It appears so," Griff said, resigned.

Reyva was prodding at the entrance to the private areas of the Station. Her rooms were up front with Beauregard's, but the wardbreaker clearly hadn't failed to notice that the Station's other inhabitants disappeared to parts unknown every night. She'd also traced those disappearances to the one section of wall that, though it included no obvious door, gave access to the other parts of the Station to those allowed such access.

Reyva had been pushing at that hidden door every night since her arrival. She hadn't asked a single person about it, but it was clearly driving her up the wall that she couldn't get through it.

Nyx supposed if *she* was the best wardbreaker in the verse, a magical lock she couldn't override would get under her skin, too. Despite the unpleasant feeling Reyva's magical lock-picking attempts caused, Nyx had let her tinker to her heart's content, because she wasn't worried about her getting through.

That willingness to let tinkerers tinker disappeared when Reyva sent a sharp jolt of *something* into the wall that made both Nyx and Griff jump like they'd been shocked by a livewire. A slight rumble shook the ground as Nyx let Kaliaris express their displeasure through their bond.

Kaliaris had been doing things like that a lot more, lately. Though Griff and Nyx were the conduits by which the Station was physically changed, their recognition of Kaliaris' personhood allowed the Station some small measure of direct expression through them.

Reyva lifted her hand, and Nyx felt the same charge in the air she'd felt right before Reyva zinged them all.

"Damn it." Nyx polished off her third tequila sunrise—poor life choice, she knew—and shifted the Station's structure in a blink, layering her current location over the floor above Reyva. Then she took the floor away and dropped down, catching Reyva's hand before the other woman could put it to the hidden doorway.

It wasn't *quite* portaling, but it had the same surprise effect of startling the woman. Her claws slashed out of her fingertips, bouncing harmlessly off the thin layer of hardened air Nyx coated her skin in.

"Chill out," Nyx said. Okay, the third drink had definitely pushed her a little closer to the drunk side if she was telling someone to *chill out*.

"I wasn't doing anything," Reyva said.

Nyx snorted, letting go of her wrist. "I really hope you lie better than that if you get caught on Nethrayne, otherwise you're all doomed."

Reyva didn't seem to know what to say to that, and stood there bravely as if waiting for punishment.

Nyx waved her hand at the hidden door. "It's fine, I get it, professional curiosity and all. That's why I didn't say anything the last three nights you've gone poking at it. But whatever you just did hurt, so please stop doing it."

"You...felt that?"

Nyx shrugged. "Me and a few others. Anyway, I can save you the trouble and tell you you're not getting through."

"I can get through *any* lock or ward," Reyva insisted.

"Probably," Nyx agreed. "But you aren't getting through this, so save your magic for when it matters and get some rest. You're taking almost everyone I love in the world with you tomorrow and I'd rather you weren't sleep deprived." She turned away.

"Why aren't you talking to him?"

Nyx groaned and turned back. "We're really doing this?"

Reyva shrugged. "It's messing with his head and our entire plan hinges on him."

Nyx doubted that was the whole reason, but Reyva didn't seem hostile, just genuinely curious, so Nyx tried to come up with some kind of answer to give her.

"You know how I'm sick?"

A hesitant nod.

"You might say he exacerbates the condition."

Reyva frowned. "It's impossible for a *person* to exacerbate the lingering side effects of a virus."

It was Nyx's turn to shrug. "It's the explanation I've got." She should have walked away then. She started to, and if she'd been sober, she would have. But since she wasn't, and since Reyva seemed as fanatical as Beauregard about this mission… "You know how I said almost everyone I care about is going with you? Well I don't know what I'm going to do if they don't come home, so just…bring them all back, okay?

"I know you've lost a lot and I probably can't understand what that's like, but I don't want to either. If it comes down to getting what you want or making it back out? The living are always more important than the dead. And that includes you, too."

It took Reyva a few seconds to respond, and when she did, it was soft, barely spoken. "I don't plan on dying. He'll come back."

Nyx blew out a breath. "You worked with him, right?"

Reyva nodded.

"Then you know he can do brilliant things. But what you might not know is that sometimes he does *stupidly* brilliant things." Especially when he was trying to protect people. "Try not to let him do the stupid ones."

She just needed Reyva to agree, and maybe the other woman sensed that, because all she said was, "I'll try."

Nyx nodded. And because it was the only kind of thanks she could offer, she stretched her hand to the wall and made a portion of it disappear. Reyva's magic surged out, trying to follow what had happened. She let out a growl of frustration. "Why can't I figure it out?"

Nyx smiled. "Because it isn't a ward *or* a lock, so it's immune to your charms." Idly, she wondered what the difference was between what Reyva was trying to do, as a wardbreaker, and what the Opener of Doors did. The latter had opened the path to the ley lines on Arkadia, so whatever magic it utilized clearly had some effect on the Stations.

A shame she couldn't just send that item with Seth tomorrow. Unfortunately, while the Council accepted that they couldn't remove items from the Stations' Dens, and while they theoretically believed the Opener of Doors had never left hers, they had nonetheless decided leaving it accessible was a future risk they preferred not to take.

She'd discovered, in her time doing a thorough inventory of the Den, that they had locked it inside a box of pure magic. Griff had taken one look at it and informed her, in no uncertain terms, that she was never to go near it. When she'd pushed, he'd informed her it was Kiev's magic—the same death magic Jevryn possessed—that had built it, and that it would take a hundred deaths to open it.

Upon learning that, she'd had the Station place it in an out-of-the-way corner of the Den, and made double-sure to lock the room when she wasn't using it.

Reyva's nose crinkled as she mulled over what Nyx had told her, a frown worrying between her brows. "What do you mean it's not a ward or a lock? Then what is it?"

Nyx stepped through the opening. Right before it closed up behind her, she said, "My secret to keep."

It was hardly the first one she'd ever kept. She *liked* secrets. Liked finding them. Liked knowing them. Liked keeping them.

Something shifted in her mind as she thought it, wobbling back and forth. She had just enough warning, just enough presence of mind about how different this time was going to be, to tug on the Station and draw herself up to her room.

She sealed her doors and windows, locked herself inside, and dropped to the floor just as the loose memory island came tumbling down.

A t first, Nyx thought she was having a weird dream, because the room she was in definitely wasn't her own. It was three or four times as big as hers, and didn't contain the small stack of books Viktor had brought her from Dead Earth, even though his bringing them irritated her mother.

Though honestly, after what Nyx had just done, Elena was so angry with *her* that she'd probably forget to be mad at Viktor over something as silly as books.

All Nyx had wanted was to know where her mom went when she left them. Because Elena Fortuna was keeping secrets and Nyx wanted to know what they were. So she'd followed her, using the tricks Viktor had taught her that she still wasn't very good at, but she was good enough to escape Elena's notice.

Good enough to follow her to a car and hop into the trunk without being seen. She'd regretted it, because they'd driven a *long* time, and when they'd finally stopped, she'd discovered she didn't know enough about cars, because she couldn't get the trunk to open again.

And when the car drove on a few minutes later, she'd been afraid maybe it wasn't her mother driving anymore. When the car came to its third stop and *stayed* stopped, she'd no longer cared if she got caught or not. She'd taken the little knife from her boot and cut her way through the back seat.

Here, her memory was a little fuzzy. That was strange, because it had only just happened, but all she could really remember was emerging onto a street and seeing her mother inside a diner, sitting across from a man.

A man whose face she couldn't remember. She remembered his hair, though. Dark and black like hers, and maybe that's why she'd…

Embarrassment made her stomach hurt as she remembered how excited she'd felt when she'd seen him. How *sure* she'd been.

How she'd run into the diner, right up to them both, her shirt sweaty and her hair stuck against her face from hiding in the hot trunk of the car, and said, "Daddy?"

Because that's what the kids in the books called their fathers. And if she couldn't remember the man's face, he *must* have looked like her, because she'd been so certain—that it was him, and that if he saw her, if he knew she was here, he would want to take her with him.

But that…hadn't happened. She couldn't remember exactly what *had* happened, the same way she couldn't remember his face. Couldn't remember if he'd said anything, just that somehow she was back in the car with her mother, driving off, and that once they were a few blocks away Elena had hit the brakes so hard that Nyx slammed into the dash because she wasn't wearing a seatbelt.

Remembered that she'd barely climbed back into the seat before her mother slapped her, hard, and told her that if she ever said anything about this, to anyone, Elena would send Seth away and Nyx would never see him again.

She'd cried after that. Huge, wracking sobs that made her sides hurt and snot run out her nose while her mother screamed at her to shut up, just *shut up and stop crying.* But that made her cry harder, which made her mother angrier.

Nyx reached up to touch the side of her face, expecting to feel a bruise. Her cheek felt fine, which wasn't right, because that had only happened a couple days ago…hadn't it? But as she prodded her cheek, searching for the pain she was certain she should feel, she realized something far more disturbing.

Her face didn't feel right. It was too big, just like the fingers she probed it with were too long. Her entire body was too big. She stumbled to her feet, looking for a mirror and not finding one. But it almost didn't matter because she was way, way too tall.

Her heart jumped into her throat, beat faster when the careful circle she spun revealed another terrifying fact. This room she didn't recognize had no doors. No windows. No way *out*.

She looked down at her hands, her body, again. Could it be an illusion? Could the whole room be an illusion? Except...the biggest thing she'd ever seen Seth glamour was Belle.

He was better than he used to be, but he could still only do little stuff, and he never did magic to scare her. At least, not past silly little jump scares. Mostly he just tried to make her laugh, or trick her so she lost in their sparring matches.

This didn't feel like something he'd do. But as she walked along the perimeter of the wall, feeling for any cracks or seams that might indicate a door, she *wanted* it to be him doing this. Because if it was, then there was a way out.

"Seth?" she called. "Are you there?"

No answer.

"If you're there, please say something. I'm scared."

Nothing. No sounds of another presence, just empty, isolated existence.

She panicked fully after that, searching the room for any clue to where she was or what she should do. She emptied the chest of drawers, bothered that she could reach the top one and see into it without standing on a stool, because her body was *too tall*.

The chest of drawers held nothing but clothes, the chest at the end of the bed nothing but blankets and pillows. She dumped everything out of them anyway, hoping for something useful before moving on to the large black trunk that occupied a recess in the wall.

She flung it open, taking the items out one by one. They were mostly books on magic, and with each one she withdrew, she calmed a little. Each one felt like it was reminding her of something, some knowledge that would make everything around her make sense.

Knowledge of magic beyond the things her mother taught her and the things she and Seth figured out on their own. Because…because she *wasn't* eight years old anymore, was she?

Nyx came back to herself shakily, the vivid feeling of being a child again slowly receding. It was a strange experience, re-entering her actual present. Like she'd been asleep for a few days, or lost so deep in daydreaming that her concept of how much time had passed was fuzzy. A glance at her watch showed it had been less than an hour.

Her room was a mess. She remembered everything she'd done when locked in that memory island, but despite the events having just occurred, they felt far older.

But…her father. She'd thought she'd seen her father. Had she had a good reason for thinking that, or had it just been a child's hope? It looked like the meeting had taken place in Dead Earth. She had no reason to think the man was anything special.

Having the same hair color wasn't exactly a smoking gun proving lineage, even if she could see why the kid version of herself might have thought so. But…it was strange, how faded her memory of the man was, how she couldn't remember what had happened between running up to him and her mother driving them away.

As if that part had been stolen from her. The thought that maybe her mother had started messing with her memories long before she'd left her in Tempe sent chills down Nyx's spine.

Was the part she couldn't remember another thing that had been Hidden from her? And if it was, why not take the entire memory? And why couldn't Nyx recall it now, when as far as she knew, she'd broken all of her mother's Hidings on her? When it came to memories, did Hiding a thing twice destroy it?

She shook her head. She was probably reading too much into it. That the man had been important to Elena in some way, Nyx had no doubt. She wouldn't have gone to the trouble to drive so far, or been so angry with Nyx for following, if he hadn't been. But there were many reasons a man could be important to Elena, many reasons Elena might want Nyx to forget meeting him, other than the thought that maybe Nyx actually *had* met her father.

The man, whoever he was, had probably told her, in response to her question, that no, he wasn't her father. Remembering how certain she'd felt, Nyx had no doubt that denial would have devastated her. Perhaps enough to block it all from her memory herself.

Sometimes there were simple answers to things. It didn't have to be all magic and sinister parental agendas all the time.

At least, that's what she told herself as she climbed into bed, exhaustion begging her to leave off cleaning the mess she'd made of her room until the following morning.

But she couldn't quite shake the feeling that she was lying to herself. That her inability to remember something days after it had happened had an unpleasant explanation.

That maybe, just maybe, she *had* once met her father. And what a disappointment she must have been, that he'd never looked for her again.

15

The smell of coffee woke Nyx the next morning, and she cautiously cracked one eye open. Steam rose from a pretty green ceramic mug, a black kitten painted on its side.

The kitten looked cheerful. The griffin sitting by her bedside, who had transformed from housecat size to small pony size, brown fur and feathers gone to black, and spectacles nowhere in sight, looked significantly less cheerful.

"Morning?" she offered, sitting up and reaching for the coffee mug. The rich aroma was practically intoxicating.

Griff's tail thunked heavily on the floor in response.

She took a fortifying drink, set the mug back down, and focused on Griff. "You're upset with me. Do you want to tell me what I did?"

"You shut me out."

She frowned. "I did what?"

"Last night. You appeared to be in some distress and you removed the entryways to your room. Have I done something to make you feel that you cannot trust me?"

"No. I wasn't keeping you out, Griff. I was keeping myself in." She went on to explain, watching his expression of restrained hurt turn to one of worry. But there was a part of this she didn't understand. "Couldn't you just make a new door if you were concerned?"

"I did not try. It seemed to me that your intent was to keep me out, though I understand the error in that thought now. I had no desire to override your wishes.

"As to whether I *could* have overridden them…I am not sure. I am still discovering the ways in which your bond to the Station has altered the functions here. It allows you to control things within the Station, as I do, but you and I have never attempted to control the same thing at the same time, nor have we ever had opposing purposes.

"If it came down to us giving Kaliaris contradictory orders, I believe it would be much like when we wrested control of Kaliaris back from Laiveran."

Laiveran's control of the Station had come from his command of souls and his understanding of the Station's construction. She and Griff had overcome him by will and determination. Which meant— "If I really lose it, can you contain me?"

His answer was long in coming, and it wasn't the one she wanted. "I don't know."

***

That *I don't know* lingered in Nyx's thoughts as she showered and got ready for the day. Or, more accurately, as she avoided leaving her room before she absolutely had to.

She pretty much absolutely had to, now. The Departure for Beauregard and his crew was scheduled for nine, and it was eight-thirty. She felt them all downstairs, gathered in the cafe for one last caffeine rally.

But even though she needed to go, she hesitated. What if she had a memory lapse again? There had to be some way to get through to her younger selves when she was having episodes, didn't there? She'd watched a movie once where a guy with short-term memory loss had tattooed information on himself. Could something like that work for her?

Figuring it didn't hurt to try, she grabbed a fine-tipped black marker and uncapped it. The tip hovered over the skin of her inner forearm while she tried to decide what to write. Something succinct that got the point across.

Elena Hid your memories. This will pass. Trust the griffin.

It was as succinct as she could manage, and maybe it wouldn't work, but it was as good a first attempt as any. She swiped her palm over her skin, Hiding the message. Surely her magic covering it would add a little extra credence to the message.

With no remaining excuses to linger, she went to the cafe, pausing in the doorway. No one had noticed her yet, and she watched them quietly. It was hard to let them go. Harder still to not have any control over what was to come. To not be a part of it or even know what was going on. To simply wait here, in the dark, hoping they would all come home safe.

Her gaze lingered on Seth and her heart squeezed. She'd told him to go. She knew she *couldn't* go. But no matter how irrational, it still felt like being abandoned. Knowing that her being left behind had absolutely nothing to do with her being *unwanted* didn't change her emotional reaction.

It didn't change that her life right now was a parallel of the one it had been in her childhood. Seth had always been able to leave their patch of Earth Between whenever he'd wanted. Because as long as it was just him, Viktor didn't bother searching for him.

Even knowing that, he hadn't gone off by himself often. Usually only when the tension hit a breaking point, and then he always came back soon. And he always brought something for her—some wild story or trinket or book or something to try to make up for how shitty their lives were, and the fact that she was the one tethering them to that misery.

She'd never understood why he kept coming back. He hadn't

had to. If he'd been willing to leave her, they'd both known he could get far enough away that by the time Viktor decided to track him, it would take too long to be worth the effort. Not when it drove Viktor half-crazy being away from Elena.

Nyx had loved Seth for coming back, just as she'd envied him the freedom to leave. The same freedom he now had that she once again didn't. She was tied to the Station by bond and circumstance the same way she'd been tied to Elena by necessity and Viktor.

Sena's voice floated into her mind. *Even a haven, if you are given no choice in staying, will eventually become a prison.*

Nyx had been held in Montana by blood and youth, been bound to Tempe by magic, and was now tied to this Station by her own impulsive choices. Was she ever going to know what it was like to *not* be trapped?

Seth shifted in his seat, his gaze catching on her as he moved. He took one look at her face and moved out of his chair and across the room. His hands gripped her waist and lifted, holding her aloft long enough to carry her the ten steps that took them through the library door. He shut it behind them and set her down.

"I'm sorry," he said.

"For what?"

"This." His mouth met hers and every emotion she'd shoved into a box the last few days came pouring out. She wrapped her arms around his neck as his hands threaded into her hair. She met and returned every brush of his lips, every stroke of his tongue, and didn't care if it sent her into a memory island. It would be worth it.

He was as familiar beneath her hands as he was foreign. Familiar in the lifetime of memories that her body knew but her mind didn't. Foreign in the changes wrought by the seven intervening years between then and now that they would never get back.

She lost herself in both, and pretended it didn't have to end.

But everything ended, eventually, and she was out of breath when they broke apart.

He cupped her face in his hands, thumbs brushing across her cheeks. As usual, he knew exactly what she was thinking. "You know I'd rather be going with you. I'd *always* rather be going with you."

"I know." That made it worse, somehow.

"I won't stay gone long."

"I know."

"I'll bring you something back."

That got her to laugh. "What are you going to bring back from a councilor's secret city? Somehow I doubt they have a gift shop selling *I Heart Nethrayne* t-shirts."

He shrugged. "Classified documents? Escaped mad-scientist's project? Photograph of me making a peace sign in front of the Darth Vader wedding cake?"

"You're taking a camera?"

"No, but I will if you want me to."

"I just want you to come back. If you die, I'll never forgive you."

"I'm too cocky to die."

"I'm serious. If you die, I'll become the first portal witch in history to make a portal to the afterlife just so I can come kick your ass." Maybe she could put that idea in Laiveran's head— *Laiveran, there's no need to turn back time, just create a portal to the Other Side.*

Of course, she'd have to believe in an Other Side to be convincing on that front, so maybe not.

"I'll tell you a secret." He leaned in and whispered in her ear. "Not going to die."

But she wouldn't know he was alive, would she? Not until he came back, and there was no timeline for when she could expect him to return. It wasn't as if she had a way to feel if his heart stopped beating.

Unless…unless she did. "Can I Hide something? Something you have?"

His eyes softened. "Because it would let you find me like you did on Amentia Furor?"

She nodded. She'd found him on Amentia Furor because he'd held the Harvester, and her magic had been wrapped around it.

"That…won't tell you if I'm alive."

Simply giving him something she'd Hidden wouldn't. Even Hiding something on him—a lock of his hair, his tattoo—wouldn't either. Unless his body was incinerated, those things would still be around after his death to be Hidden. She needed to Hide something that required his life, the way her mother would have known Nyx was alive because to Hide her memories required her to be alive to *have* those memories.

She placed her hand over Seth's chest. "If I Hide your heartbeat, I'll know."

The left corner of his mouth curved up. "If you steal my heart do you think it'll kill me?"

"You know I never Hide anything from *you*." He was her constant, built-in exception. Even when she'd Hidden the Harvester when she couldn't remember him, her magic had remembered that exception.

But it posed an interesting question, one she'd never considered before. If someone couldn't feel their heart beating, if their brain thought it *wasn't*…would that kill a person?

She didn't want to know, had no intention of Hiding someone's heartbeat from them to find out if it would send them into cardiac arrest.

Seth's hand covered hers. "Then Hide away."

She did, feeling the thump of his heart beneath her palm, weaving strands of magic around and around, until that heartbeat existed only for her and for him. And then, romantic as that was, she considered that if he ended up knocked out, anyone searching him for a pulse wouldn't find one. If they didn't notice he was breathing, they might think he was dead. So she built a few more exceptions into that cloak of Hiding.

"All done," she said softly. This time, when she met his gaze, his eyes were entirely too serious.

"Nyx…" He only ever called her *Nyx* instead of *Nyxi* when things were bad. He swallowed. "You know that I—"

She clapped a hand over his mouth so fast she surprised both of them. "Don't even think about saying that shit to me right now. Save it for when you come back."

He gently peeled her hand off. "But you know, right?"

"I know. And…you know. Right?"

"Yeah," he said hoarsely. "I know."

———

G riff met them in the cafe, still in his large form from that morning, and walked them to the portal room. One by one, Nyx's friends changed, Seth's illusions transforming them from the people she recognized into their aliases. He glamoured himself last, dark black hair and bronze skin giving way to the grayish, mottled skin of a Quindellen. Sharp, serrated teeth replaced his own, pupils shrinking to vertical slits.

He lost two inches of height, the breadth of his shoulders dwindling, his waist tapering away to almost nothing. She *knew* he wasn't physically shapeshifting and it was still creepy to watch.

The Arrival Room's orbs spun atop their posts, and Beauregard stepped onto the ley line platform, sinking down. Evra went next, then Morgen, then Maruca. Reyva followed the redhead, casting a single glance back over her shoulder before the ley mist swallowed her.

Seth held Nyx's gaze, those eerie reptilian pupils unblinking as he walked backwards onto the platform. And then the ley mist was crawling up his body too, dragging him down until he was gone.

Slowly, the orbs stopped spinning. The deep thrum of the portal eased, softened, went quiet, and the swirling cosmic floor went solid and gleaming as glass. She leaned against Griff's broad shoulder and he stretched out his wing, settling it around her like a cloak.

"Is it too soon to say I miss them?" she asked.

"If it is, then it is too soon for me, as well."

The Station felt wrongly quiet. Liya was, as usual, in her room. Temerex was asleep in her stall. Kalvar had gone into Earth Between, likely so he could avoid Maruca's departure.

The Station was calm, as it never was when the others were here. Even in the middle of the night, someone was doing something. She didn't like the stillness, the emptiness. It reminded her of the time when she was seven, and she'd woken up one morning and couldn't find anyone. She'd gone from room to room in the small house, then out to the barn, then the garden, but no matter where she looked, she couldn't find anyone.

There had been no note in the kitchen, no indication of where anyone was or when they would be back. She'd settled on the front porch, waiting for someone, *anyone*, to come home as the sun crept higher in the sky and then started its descent again, and at the end of the day…

She frowned. What had happened at the end of the day? She'd waited on the porch for hours, and—

The last bit of scaffolding holding that chunk of memories in place gave way, and Nyx fell into it.

16

After her experience the previous night, Nyx had expected every future memory event to be one in which she thought herself a younger age. But this one proved to be only another sliver—a larger one than most, but still only something she relived as opposed to something that caused her to lose her current identity.

As she came back to herself, the chunk of memory settled into her mind, like a puzzle piece clicking satisfyingly into place. Griff said she'd only been out for about five minutes. His great golden eyes were concerned, but he didn't ask her if she was alright, for which she was grateful.

She wasn't alright, and he knew that. Knew how asking would make her feel—like she'd failed somehow, even if she knew there was nothing she could do to prevent what was happening.

Should she be relieved or worried that things weren't progressing as linearly as the Congregation had predicted? They'd thought she would run entirely out of the small memories before falling into the larger ones, but this experience proved that guess hadn't been entirely accurate.

On the one hand, maybe that meant she would have a little

more reprieve from the worst of the effects. On the other hand, if they'd been wrong about this, had they also been wrong about how much time she had left?

She pressed her hands to her stomach, trying to quiet the anxious fluttering that had taken up residence there. She was glad the others hadn't seen the event last night, or this one. She didn't know Maruca, Reyva, or Beauregard well enough to experience that kind of vulnerability around them.

And as much as the Station felt too large without her friends here, she didn't want them as witnesses to this either. If Morgen and Evra pitied her, she wouldn't be able to handle it. As for Seth...he would blame himself. She understood why, and she understood where that tendency to self-blame came from, but she didn't have the emotional bandwidth to deal with what was happening to her *and* try to bring him up from the dark place he would go into if he saw her like this.

Griff knew how to let her be. She supposed he'd fallen apart enough times in his long life to both understand what she was going through, and also understand that she didn't need twenty questions. To understand that mounting an inquisition into her experience wouldn't prevent it from happening again.

Instead, he gave her something she'd desperately needed, even if she hadn't realized it.

"You're taking the day off," he informed her.

"But—"

"No objections. Put on comfortable clothing and meet me in the theater room. Unless of course," he continued, "you do not *want* me to finally watch the ego and bias film."

"*Pride and Prejudice,*" she corrected automatically. Titles were one of those things she'd discovered translator spells tended to jumble up.

Griff still wasn't a big fan of movies. Maybe because most of them contained a good deal of technology, and things like cars and computers and—okay, yes, televisions—were still strange to him. And not in a way he liked.

So it meant a lot that he was voluntarily sitting down to a pastime he still considered inferior to plays. According to him, the fact that a film played precisely the same every single time—whereas no production of a play was ever an exact replica of a previous one—meant it lacked originality.

"You really don't have to watch TV with me," she said, unable to quash her natural habit of pushing away the thing she wanted when someone offered it to her. It was an irritating habit to have discovered she had, and probably stemmed from that deep-seated fear of abandonment in her. As if actually doing something she wanted, something as simple as watching a film other people didn't want to watch, would be the silly stupid thing that made everyone not want to be around her anymore.

Griff tilted his head at her in that manner that conveyed the reproach of a single eyebrow raise. "This is the film that always makes you feel happy when you are sad, yes?"

She'd said that. And he'd remembered. "Yes."

"Then we are watching it."

She didn't argue any further. She changed and went to the theater room, rearranging the Station until the room had a hallway connecting to Temerex's stall. As soon as she sent the mare a mental image of the television and the new hallway, Temerex came running.

Literally. She cantered into the room, skidding to a fast halt that had her hind legs sliding under her, butt hitting the floor. She sat there like a dog, reptilian eyes bright and interested, and her long tongue came out to lick Nyx's cheek.

"Thank you for that," Nyx deadpanned, wiping unicorn-dragon slobber off her face. She scratched the fine scales behind Temerex's ears, her voice slipping into a coo. "Some elegant, vicious killing machine you are."

The unicorn-dragon was, in fact, a vicious killer when the occasion called for it, and her tendency to impersonate a goofy labrador when not engaged in said vicious killing kind of made her all the more frightening.

Not that Nyx minded the puppy-dog act. It was a lot better than the dejected Temerex who would hardly eat because Jevryn had left her here. Remembering that was a surefire way to get Nyx's temper up, so she shoved the thought away before she could accidentally send any stray images of Jevryn to the mare.

She'd done that twice, and Temerex had gotten *so* excited before she realized Nyx had simply been thinking about the councilor, and he wasn't actually here.

Fuck.

Jevryn.

She needed to write him and tell him what had happened. She'd forgotten to write at all last night, so she was probably going to get an earful—was it an eyeful, when written?—about that, and he'd need to take it into consideration where her mother was concerned.

But she could do that…later.

Griff came in, a large bowl of popcorn clutched to him with one talon while he walked along on his two hind paws and the other talon. He could walk upright on his hind paws alone if he absolutely needed to, but found it, to use his own words, "Undignified."

Temerex's nostrils flared and she scrambled to her hooves, shaking like a dog and sending a few loose scales flying. Her attention fixated on the bowl of popcorn, and she let out a nicker of interest.

"No popcorn for you," Nyx said. Temerex nickered again. "You remember what happened last time. They got stuck in your throat and you coughed for an hour." Nyx sent a mental picture of the event in question. Though Temerex's digestion wasn't equine—she was omnivorous and could eat almost anything without ill effect—she nonetheless shared the equine inability to vomit. Which meant when something got stuck in her throat— like, say, an entire bowl of popcorn she'd been told explicitly *not* to eat—her only recourse to get it out was to either cough it up or swallow it down.

After Temerex had run around coughing like she had pneumonia for forty minutes, Nyx had finally convinced her to drink a gallon of water. Once she was out of the woods, the unicorn-dragon had proceeded to give Nyx big betrayed eyes, as if she were somehow responsible for the mare eating the popcorn she'd been told not to have.

Temerex's betrayed look was very similar to her I'm-so-sad-don't-you-love-me-enough-to-let-me-try-popcorn-again look.

"No popcorn," Nyx said firmly.

Temerex blew out a long breath and sulkily went to lie down on the bed of warm rocks that appeared in front of the couch. Nyx and Griff settled onto the couch and started the movie, which Nyx had difficulty following because every time she reached for a handful of popcorn, Temerex sent her an image of gray skies that gave Nyx a sense of endless despair.

Nyx pulled up a bowl of Temerex's favorite qualtez fish, recognizing it was the only thing that would buy her any measure of peace. The mare took to it with gusto, slurping the fish into her mouth and chomping them with her very pointed, very non-horse-like teeth.

Nyx relaxed, letting the movie draw her into another world. By the time Elizabeth Bennett's looks were being casually insulted at the ball, Temerex had finished eating. She stretched out on her side with a groan, leaving Nyx to watch the film sans mental images of despair.

Nyx settled against Griff's side, letting herself get lost in the story and forget her problems for a couple of hours.

By the time evening came, Nyx had taken Griff through a marathon of Jane Austen film adaptations. They were only a distraction, and if she'd felt better while she watched them, now that they were over she was once again acutely aware of the Station's near-emptiness as she returned to her room.

Only the thread of her magic, stretching across space and time to another planet, reassured her. If she focused hard enough, she could feel that heartbeat her magic Hid. The strong, steady surety of it.

In her room, she was almost relieved to be greeted with the mess she'd left from last night. It gave her something to focus on. She gathered all the contents of Jevryn's trunk and sorted them into organized piles. But as she went to place the first item back inside, she noticed something she hadn't when the trunk had been filled.

Namely that its dimensions didn't entirely add up. The bottom of the trunk should be a couple inches lower. It *could* simply be a design choice. Or, the part of her that loved secrets whispered, it could be that the trunk had a false bottom. She ran her fingers over the interior, looking for a seam or any indication that there was a piece that might lift out and reveal something below.

When she found none, she turned her attention to the outside, subjecting the lower exterior portion of the trunk to the same thorough inspection she'd given the interior. Her fingers found the faintest depression. A small decorative skull was in that hollow, and she pushed on it.

Sharp pain pierced her middle finger. She jerked it back, blood welling at its tip. She grabbed a tissue and pressed it to her finger, glaring at the small silver skull. The damn thing had bitten her, and now it was drinking her blood. Or at least, the bright red that had stained the skeletal mouth was disappearing, as if being ingested.

A second passed, then two, then three. Then, as if it had tested her and found her acceptable, a soft snick announced the unlocking of a shallow drawer. Still glaring at it, Nyx gripped the drawer and pulled it out.

She let out a low whistle and promptly forgot she was mad about being bit. The entire drawer was laid out like the interior of a jewelry box, and it was filled with accessories—rings, bracelets, armbands, earrings. But the jewelry itself wasn't the kind encrusted with gemstones and designed for ornamentation. No, it was made for something far more precious to her.

To a one, the base of every piece was built in black thalacite. And through the clear extyll portions glowed the sweet, intense blue of portal magic.

A piece of paper with Jevryn's handwriting rested in the center.

It is my sincerest hope that you do not find this compartment until I tell you of it, given what happened the last time you had access to any quantity of portal magic.

However, in the event you do find it, I beg of you to exercise caution. Do read the books I sent, and do not experiment before you have a firm sense of portal magic theory in place.

I do vaguely remember how impossible the call is not to answer when it is first discovered, if the magic is readily available. But keep your practicing planet-side, for now.

And you would do well to work on your efficiency which, while quite good for someone with practically no training, is nonetheless still atrocious.

Do not portal off this planet unless I am present to assist you.

Nyx ran her fingers over the drawer's contents, the pull of the portal magic muted, since it hid within the thalacite. Still, she wondered that she hadn't felt it at all before now...until she finally realized why the trunk itself had seemed so strange to her upon its arrival: it was *built* from thalacite. The half-inch thick walls would have acted as a superb insulating layer to keep any portal witch from feeling the magic stored within.

Her fingers twitched and she reached for a bracelet. She wanted them badly. Wanted to place every single bit of jewelry on her body, until she was so gaudily decorated she looked like a six-year-old playing dress-up with costume jewelry.

You shouldn't. Not with how screwed up you are right now.

But she needed the magic. That twisting place inside her that panicked every time she even thought of leaving the Station *needed* it. She hadn't bargained with Kaliaris for the limited freedom she had only to be too afraid to use it.

This magic was safety. It was control. It was the knowledge that she could never be lost entirely again.

She curled her fingers around the bracelet and clasped it on her wrist. It settled against her skin like a promise, cool and potent and beautiful.

Take it off, the logical side of her whispered. But was it really logical to leave this resource out of her reach? Did she really think her younger self could access it when it had taken Jevryn's coaching for her to be able to coax the magic from the thalacite the first time?

It might call to her, sure, but she wouldn't be able to withdraw it—much less use it—without her present-day memories. Reassured, she slipped another five bracelets onto her wrist, stacking them like bangles. She surveyed the array of small hoop earrings. Did Jevryn have eight billion ear piercings she'd never noticed before? More importantly, just how efficient was he with portal magic if the tiny amount held in those earrings was actually useful to him?

She could probably make an on-planet line-of-sight portal with one, but that was it. Maybe that's what they were for?

Her own ears weren't pierced—after Seth had talked her into piercing his left lobe when he was fifteen, she'd promptly decided not to have that experience herself—so she passed them over. The bracelets were enough. More than enough. But she found herself reaching for the lone necklace in the set, a choker with a thick pendant that would rest in the hollow of her throat.

She put it on and her hand slid down to close in a fist around the pendant, the soft pulse of magic within whispering, *Safe, safe, safe.*

Maybe she was being paranoid. But this was the only guarantee that if something happened to her again, if anyone *took* her again, she could come home.

She passed her fingers over each piece, strands of Hidden magic coming more easily and pliably to her fingers than ever before. She didn't like to think about what that ease implied regarding her memories. She wove the power instinctively, covering each piece of portal jewelry she wore, Hiding them from sight.

Then she repacked Jevryn's trunk, replacing the secret drawer, and did what she probably should have done the moment she'd gotten the thing. She Hid it in its entirety, then slid it into its recess and walled it over.

She was ready to fall into bed when she remembered she hadn't written Jevryn yesterday or today. The companion journal contained three lines from the councilor.

You have not checked in this evening.

I thought we were past your flippant shirking of responsibilities.

I am growing concerned.

She wrote out a quick summary of yesterday and today's slips and waited. Part of her hoped for one of the cursory "I understand" responses he'd been giving the last few days. But most of her hoped for something completely out of character from Jevryn—reassurance. Because if someone who had lived that long could be reassuring, it would have to mean something, right?

I will accelerate my timetable.

That response was only reassuring in that it meant her mother should be here faster. His next words were entirely unrelated, and took her mind off her issues.

> In other concerns, could you explain to me why yet another raise request has been sent in for your Station's barista?

> What is a barista?

> There have been enough requests that it has been flagged as potential fraud.

Count on financial auditing to be the one consistent thing in the universe.

> It's not fraud. Baristas are extremely important. You get my Station's accounting reports?

> The Station of Earth is one of the many placed under my oversight. So, yes, I receive the accounting reports.

> And you bother to look at them?

> I bother to look at everything relating to your Station.

> For which you should be grateful, as it keeps individuals such as auditors from arriving in your portal bay when your memory is in the delicate condition it is currently in.

She was glad her lack of sincerity couldn't be detected via the written word when she gave her one-word reply.

> Sorry.

> Please refrain from giving your barista any more raises for at least six months.

> I'll do my best.

> I am being quite serious.

And quite easy to tease.

So am I. He's a very good barista.

Is there a particular reason you are intent on
trying my patience?

Is there a particular reason you're part of a
governing body that lets kids get abducted to
prison planets? A governing body that then
doesn't do anything about it, so said kids
spend their formative years in a very bad place
and come out on the other side with no legal
means of getting a job and a lot of trauma, so
they end up working as my barista when what
they really want is to go back to school?

The page darkened suddenly at the edges, as if flames were
licking at the corners. The blackness crept over the page, swallowing the ink, before the paper turned brittle and crinkled
into ash.

Oookay. Clearly, Jevryn A-Morridahn's long years in the
universe had bestowed upon him the ability to handle criticism
with grace.

She swept the disintegrated page remnants off the book, then
blew the dust stragglers away as writing appeared on the next
page.

If I send the boy enough money to attend
academy will you cease giving him raises?

You can't buy yourself out of this situation.
How's he supposed to attend academy when
his identity is flagged as supposed-to-be-on-
Arkadia?

The Station had managed to churn out false identification
papers for the escaped slaves from the Shadow Market, but they
were only capable of passing the kind of cursory-level test most
employers and landlords gave. They were not good enough to

gain passage through the Stations or to apply to institutions of higher education.

A single black dot appeared on the page, growing wider in circumference, as if Jevryn had placed the tip of a pen down and the ink was continuing to bleed through.

> Send me the boy's information and I will fix it.

Nyx blinked and wrote back.

> Seriously?

> If that is what it takes, then yes.

She bit her lower lip.

> What if it takes two other names, too?

In the pause that followed, she could practically see him pinching the bridge of his nose.

> Precisely how many children did you return from Arkadia with?

The question sent a sharp pang of sorrow through her, and she penned her next words angrily, without thought.

> Two less than I should have, thanks to your brother.

He didn't apologize, and that was probably for the best.

> Send me the other names as well.

And if her heart hurt, remembering two giggling Luminescent girls who would never get to grow up, the pain eased a fraction at the hope that Tobi, Lauralyn, and Kalvar might get the clean slate they deserved. It wasn't that Tobi and Lauralyn couldn't have lives here without new identities, it was that she knew exactly how they were likely to feel, growing up without even the possibility of getting out: trapped.

No one deserved to feel that way. If they grew up and never wanted to leave, if Earth Between was where they felt they belonged, then that was wonderful. But it should be their choice.

The same way Kalvar deserved the choice to do anything he wanted, wherever he wanted, without having to acquire his means of travel through the Shadow Market, or his employment under-the-table. She wanted for him—for all of them—the opportunities she'd never had.

She didn't even care if that opportunity came from a man who was, at least in part, responsible for the system that had gotten them into this situation in the first place. She couldn't change how they'd ended up where they had, but she had no qualms about using Jevryn to change their futures.

He was, after all, using *her* to get what *he* wanted.

17

Nethrayne was a city of rings.

Five rings, stacked atop each other, formed the different levels, while the levels themselves were broken into sectors. Seth thought the sectors were like the growth rings of a tree, each one smaller than the last as they worked further toward the center.

The first level was the largest, comprised of eighteen sectors, the outer of which had a five-mile circumference. They'd had to walk half of that circumference to reach the single entry point to the next sector, passing a dozen checkpoints on the way there. It continued like that all the way to the heart of the first level, because Nethrayne was intentionally designed to be as inconvenient to navigate as possible.

Crossing from one sector to the next could only be accomplished via each sector's single door, which was never conveniently located next to the one from the previous sector. It meant covering an exhaustive amount of ground, and by the time they'd reached the elevator, Seth had felt like a little metal ball in one of those spherical puzzle maze games he'd once shoplifted for Nyx when they were kids. The kind where you kept twisting and turning the thing, trying to get the ball to fall through the right openings to reach the center, and if you screwed it up the ball went tumbling all the way back to the start.

At least on the base level, the Chameleon team they'd impersonated had the appropriate clearance to deliver their cargo to the innermost sector, where the elevator to the second level waited. Once they reached it, they handed off the shipment of compound to a local security team, and that was when the work really began.

Morgen slipped into Siren-talk, encouraging the other team to linger long enough for Seth to copy the lead's bio markers to access the second level. Then Seth made half-a-dozen new glamours as they moved to that level, catching up to the internal team that had taken control of the shipment.

Beauregard was relentless in his determination to never lose sight of it. Seth thought his insistence on that was pointless. They didn't *need* to follow the shipment to know where they would find the Kumir. Given the city's layout, the most secure location was the fifth and final floor, and he highly doubted anything on Nethrayne was worth protecting more than the Kumir. Keeping the security team in sight only meant rushing, which meant a higher magic spend. But Seth's opinion had been overruled by their dictator-in-charge.

The second floor was smaller than the first—each subsequent one was, giving the city the wedding-cake structure Nyx had pointed out—but it was still a lot of ground to cover, and it was packed with people. The more people, the more minds he had to glamour against.

By the time they reached the elevator that led to the third floor—naturally, it was located on the exterior of level two—he was feeling the strain. He hadn't been this exhausted, hadn't stretched his magic this much for this long, since his first year in the Market. Even Amentia Furor hadn't drained him like this. There, he'd been glamouring against animal minds, which was infinitely easier than glamouring against sapient minds. He'd also only been glamouring himself for most of his time on

Amentia Furor. He'd had so much practice working illusion on himself that it was practically as easy as breathing.

Here, he was covering five other people and switching out their glamours with dizzying frequency. Not to mention the more specialized illusion he needed to trick the bio markers at the security checkpoints was draining his magic like a hole in a water bucket.

They'd planned for him to handle the checkpoints as long as possible, conserving Reyva's magic. Common sense dictated that it was better to save her for the cases where they couldn't find someone with the proper clearance for Seth to mimic, or for the more complex systems they were likely to encounter the higher they ascended within the city.

They were halfway through the third level, working toward the interior elevator, when he handed the checkpoints over to her. He wasn't at his limit yet, but it didn't matter. There was no way they were making it all the way to the top floor without a rest. But since Beauregard hadn't been willing to hear that the three times Seth had brought it up, he chose to conserve his dwindling magic and let Reyva take the lead.

He dropped to the back of their unit, shooting Morgen a pointed glance as he did, and his friend joined him a few minutes later.

"He's pushing us too hard," Seth said, pointing out the obvious.

Morgen had been Siren-talking everything in sight at the checkpoints, capturing people's attention and making it easier for Seth's glamours to take hold. That expenditure showed in the roughness of his usually-smooth voice. "I know."

"There's no point in following the shipment. There's only one place it could be going."

Morgen exhaled softly and repeated, "I know."

"Can't you talk some sense into him?" Seth put a subtle emphasis on the word *talk*.

Morgen shook his head. "Uncle Beau has a high resistance to mental magic."

There went one good idea down the drain. "We can't count on Reyva to pull the plug. She won't stop, even when she knows she should."

Maruca, who'd been in the middle of their little pack with Evra, dropped back in between him and Morgen. "Talking about anything fun?"

Seth shrugged. "Just the probability that Beau and Reyva are going to get us all killed out of sheer stubbornness."

"And here I thought I was the only one who'd noticed you're sweating a lake and Reyva's burning through magic like fire through a dead forest."

"You can't see that I'm sweating." Glamoured, he looked fresh as a damn daisy.

"No, but I can guess. The energy in your aura has been steadily diminishing to the point that typically precedes physical collapse, and Reyva is approaching the same thing at a faster rate than you did."

Fucking energy mages. Now he had to add *find a way to glamour an aura I can't see* to his list of Illusionist Life Goals.

"How many more checkpoints do you think she has in her?" Morgen asked.

Maruca tilted her head, considering. "Six, conservatively? Seven or eight if someone doesn't mind hauling her dead weight around after she blacks out."

Ahead, Evra made an irritated hand gesture at them behind her back. Seth didn't know if it was a movement meant only to express her irritation, or if it was part of a sign language he wasn't fluent in, but he was absolutely certain it meant, "Someone better fill me in on what you're talking about in the next thirty seconds, or else."

He shot Morgen a look. "You thinking what I'm thinking?"

"Planned failure?"

Seth nodded.

"When?" Maruca asked.

"Once we hit the residential sector." On every prior level, the residential had been located in the middle rings, sandwiched between the recreation sector and the higher-security work sectors. If the pattern held, Reyva should have enough magic to get them there. "Once we're past the first checkpoint into residential, I'll let the glamour slip. I'll keep faces blurred, but it'll draw notice. Should cause enough of a distraction that we'll lose the transport team and have no reason to keep pushing tonight."

Maruca nodded. "I'll inform Evra."

One hour later they were holed up in an efficiency apartment barely large enough for all of them to squeeze into. Evra and Beauregard were bleeding from a few shallow cuts. Reyva was so burned out on magic she was clinging to consciousness solely through stubborn effort. Morgen had overexerted himself to the extent he apparently couldn't speak words of any kind for at least an hour, according to Maruca.

As for Maruca herself, Seth had witnessed her take out the main power to the entire sector, lighting up like an electric Christmas tree as she did. The subsequent plunge into darkness had lasted for all of one-point-five seconds before the backup power restored the lights, but that had been all the time he needed to make his little group disappear.

And now he was fucking spent. The inside of his body had the scraped-raw feeling that came from bleeding glamour like it was an infinite resource. Each pump of his heart felt like it pushed acid through his veins instead of blood, and he was going to wake up tomorrow with the mother of all headaches.

Though he wasn't certain if that inevitability would be because of too much magic use, or because of Beauregard's booming voice. The man could have made himself heard over a battlefield without much effort, so his words were currently taking up all the space in this tiny apartment.

"What happened out there?"

From her spot on the small bed in the corner, Reyva winced. Whether from the volume, or from having to live through the horror of disappointing her idol, Seth couldn't tell.

"Told you we were pushing too hard." He gave up his valiant effort to remain standing and slid down the wall until his butt hit the floor. His left knee knocked into Evra as he did—seriously no room in this place—and he muttered an apology that the Amazon waved off. He was sandwiched between her on one side and Maruca on the other. Morgen had the arguably roomy post on the threshold of the bathroom door, and Beauregard had the undisputed best location in the small kitchen. There still wasn't more than five feet of space between any of them.

"Convenient you were so exhausted that your glamours slipped directly before the guards, and yet you managed enough illusion to get us all here."

"If by convenient you mean that one of us had the sense to force a rest before we actually got into a situation we couldn't get out of, then yeah. Convenient."

"We lost the transport."

Seth had the mental energy to come up with the intelligent response of, "So what?"

Beauregard took the three steps necessary to get in Seth's face, his voice lowered to a dangerous level. "So what?" he repeated. "So *what?* You may treat life like a game, Hawthorne, but I do not. You have no idea the injustices that will continue to be perpetrated if we fail."

This felt suspiciously like the way Seth's old man used to get in his face. At least, the way Viktor used to before he got so far gone on Elena he quit caring altogether. He didn't appreciate it from Beauregard any more than he'd appreciated it from his father. "You're the only one treating life like it's expendable. The people in this room aren't resources you can exhaust and replace when we keel over, so I suggest you take two steps back and remember that all of *us*"—he twirled his finger in a circle, encompassing the room—"are the only reason you've gotten as far as you have.

"And if I have 'no idea' of the consequences of failure, that's only because you aren't talking. So how about it? What's the real story behind your wife and the Kumir? What is it you aren't telling us?"

Beauregard's face went blank, but not before Seth saw the flash of raw emotion in his eyes. Decades of pain and longing and futility. But he was as silent on the subject as ever.

Seth leaned forward. "You don't want me to push you on that? You don't want me to sit my ass in this room and refuse to go on until you talk, or to decide I want to take this"—he pulled a portal stone to Earth from his pocket—"and go home? Then when any of us tells you we're tapped out, we're fucking tapped out. Got it?"

The tension in the room was thick enough to smother a fire. Beauregard glanced at the faces around the room, as if just noticing that everyone was practically dead on their feet. "Is this the collective opinion?"

Morgen didn't have his voice back. Reyva was listing slightly, eyelids fluttering as she fought to stay awake. Maruca opened her mouth but shut it, clearly having trouble deciding whether she should be responding in the capacity of Beauregard's niece or as a member of the unit.

Fortunately, there was Evra. "No team can function well when they are exhausted, and ignoring limitations doesn't make them go away. It is obvious where the transport was heading. We will be much better equipped to make our way to the top level once we've rested."

And eaten, which was another thing they hadn't had time to do. They'd be stuck on protein bars tonight, because Seth didn't have the energy to glamour even himself to go out and purchase anything. This apartment might have a kitchen, but they'd chosen it because the entire strip down this corridor had been emptied for renovations.

Beauregard gave a sharp nod and stood. "We'll continue in the morning then." He retreated to the kitchen.

Seth dug a protein bar out of his pocket and ate it with all the enthusiasm he'd have if it was cardboard. He'd never really liked the things, but Nyx ate them like candy. Thinking of her was why he'd packed the damned vanilla-almond flavored ones she liked instead of the slightly-less-disgusting peanut-butter-chocolate ones.

Nyx.

He pressed the heel of his palm to his heart, as if it would let him feel the magic he knew was there, tying a part of him to her. It felt unfair that she had a way of knowing he was fine, and he didn't have the same where she was concerned.

Was she doing better, now that he was gone? And wasn't it just the story of his fucking life that she should be better off without him? Some part of him had always felt like, once they got away from Viktor and Elena, out into the real world, all he'd do was hold her back. He'd never known if it was true, or if that was just the messed-up load of shit he carried around because of the messed-up way they'd grown up.

The isolation from her the last few days hadn't helped. Isolation never helped anything, in his experience. Isolation was where the quiet fears, the ones that normally had the decency to slumber in dirty cobweb-covered corners of your mind, stretched spindly legs and crept out into the twilight. And when you were alone, you were never certain if they were real or simply apparitions.

Would her life be better off without him in it? He dug his heel harder into his chest. He didn't know the answer. All he knew was that he didn't get to make the decision for her. He didn't get to cop out like that, to leave just because it was messy and he was afraid it wouldn't work out the way he wanted it to.

Because life *was* the mess. That was a lesson he'd learned

over and over and over again, and he could focus on how much it sucked or he could find the things he loved in between it all, the wildflowers growing between cracks in ugly concrete, and he could hold onto them.

He could hold on to *her*.

He crumpled the protein wrapper into a ball and shoved it into his pocket. He wasn't dying here. He wasn't letting Beauregard get them all killed because the mania that drove him had risen so close to the surface that it was practically all that was left.

If Seth had to butt heads with stubborn fanaticism until it gave way, he would. Because he was finishing this, and he was going *home*.

Whatever it took.

18

The Queen of Wrath was good for Laiveran. For Kaliaris, too, if the way they'd rearranged their Heart to cater to the feline's comfort was any indication. She now had multiple cat towers constructed of interwoven vines and containing small cubby holes to disappear into, and a large square space in the corner—the Heart hadn't even *had* corners before—was now a sand-layered self-cleaning litter box.

As for the queen herself, she accepted these concessions to her comfort and happiness as her due, and any fears Nyx had harbored that she would be distressed living down here had been thoroughly put to rest. Her Majesty also still disliked Nyx with a passion, hissing as soon as the Guardian approached. She eyed the brightly-colored box in Nyx's hands with the deepest of suspicion, yowling as she twined in and out of Laiveran's legs.

Laiveran bent to give the cat a soothing stroke down her back. "There there, sweet girl, all is well." It was the first coherent sentence Nyx had heard him utter since she'd wrested control of the Station back from him.

But though his words to the cat were calm and sure, the look in his eyes was anything but. Wariness and confusion lurked in his irises, and the open vulnerability there made Nyx feel like she was the monster in this situation. She couldn't tell if he recognized her, and asking didn't seem like a good idea.

She smiled, like everything was normal, and held up the box. "I thought we might play a game today."

Some of the wariness left Laiveran's eyes, replaced with interest. "A game?"

This suggestion had come from Griff, who'd said Laiveran had always traveled with a deck of cards, and that his favorite method of making friends with new people had been to learn their games.

Since she'd talked Kaliaris into making Laiveran an actual room, rather than a cell with basic amenities, she had a table to place the board game on. The tabletop was blue glass, reflecting the room's odd angles. The walls sloped inward as they rose, and the burnt orange color of them felt like an odd choice to her.

But the space seemed familiar to Laiveran. He took the seat across from her, and Fangs leapt onto his lap, turning two circles before curling into a ball. The cat purred loudly and periodically shot Nyx warning glares, as if daring her to come closer. Nyx stayed on her side of the table, laid out the setup for *Rivals for Catan*, and then proceeded to explain how the game was played.

Laiveran listened with avid interest, idly stroking Fangs— who purred louder—and interrupting every now and again with questions of how this or that rule mechanism worked. Soon enough they settled into the game, and for the first half-hour, he was almost normal. His tendency to ramble was still there, but it was kept to barely audible mumbles clearly not intended for Nyx.

Scowling down at the cards in front of him, long fingers sorting and counting the little plastic resources for the game, he didn't *seem* like a mass murderer. Not that she had a lot—or any—experience with other people who bore that label. But what she was faced with right now was frightening. Not because *he* was frightening, but because he was so very ordinary in the moment. He was a walking, talking reminder that people were just…people. That every one of them was capable of terrible things, and some of them chose to act upon those things.

She didn't know if it was compassion, cowardice, or sheer inexperience that made her decide not to ask him anything today. She told herself that this—what she was doing—was building a baseline for future encounters. That next time, she would find a way to bring up the Harvester. There were plenty of boardgames that spanned galaxies. She could pick one— maybe one Laiveran would be less terrible at than he was at *Catan*—and use the setting to segue into the Harvester.

Having made the decision not to push anything today, she'd just relaxed when Laiveran's mood shifted without warning. He swiped his hand across the board, scattering the cards and pieces. The Queen of Wrath startled at the noise, jumping off Laiveran's lap with an angry yowl.

Laiveran didn't seem to notice her leave. He crossed his arms, a scowl darkening his brow. "This is a foolish game, Nyaera, I do not know why you insist on playing it."

Nyx opened her mouth to gently tell him that she wasn't his dead wife, realized that would be about the stupidest thing she could do, and shut it. If he was in some sort of confused reality in his head where he thought she was someone he trusted…well, she hadn't intended to push for information today, but maybe she should. Maybe she could use this.

She was afraid to talk, though, afraid that her voice would be enough to pull him out of the illusion. So she smiled and started pulling the cards and game pieces toward her, sorting them back into the box.

He made a discontented noise in his throat. "Still not talking, I see. I cannot tell if you come to me like this out of pity, or merely to torment me. If you do not speak to me because you wish me that pain, or because you cannot speak in your condition." He rubbed wearily at his eyes. "I cannot tell if you even know you are here. Your soul, my heart. Every day I feel it shredded further. And every day it shreds mine with it. There's hardly any left of it now. I wonder that you can manifest at all."

Nyx froze, her hands on the last set of cards. She understood how he might see *any* woman and have his brain trick him into believing that woman his lost wife. When he had kept her on Lehine, he'd been consistently confused about *when* in time he was.

But his talk about Nyaera's soul, as if he still felt it—that was the gift of his people. To see into those souls, to feel them, and to some measure, control them. It was why his people didn't often survive the death of a bonded lover—because their souls were connected on such an intimate level that they couldn't withstand the separation.

Laiveran had *felt* his wife's soul. Felt it when she became trapped in an endless loop of portals on Amentia Furor, felt it as she died. He'd told Nyx that Nyaera was dead. But he was talking now as if he *still* felt the woman's soul.

How could he be mistaken about that?

No matter what age or memory set Nyx was in, she would always feel the connection to any Hiding she had active. Even in Dead Earth, when she'd had no memory of her self, of magic, she'd felt the pull to the Harvester she'd promised to Hide. She hadn't known what that pull was, hadn't understood just how dangerous it could be, but she'd known. Been unable to leave the Harvester behind. She could never be mistaken about it.

She doubted Laiveran's magic was any different. Doubted that he could say now that he felt Nyaera's soul in the present, and be wrong. But that would mean…that would mean Nyaera was, in some sense, *alive*. Or at least that her soul still existed.

Every day I feel it shredded further. Was Nyaera still trapped, her soul being picked apart with each new portal loop she fell through, like threads on a sweater wearing slowly away with each wash? And if any part of her still felt, still endured that endless deconstruction that had been going on for centuries, how much torment did she have left to endure? How much longer would it continue?

No wonder Laiveran was mad. No wonder he'd gone to such lengths to attempt to end that suffering. No wonder he refused to back down.

"I wish…" His voice overflowed with that endless sorrow. "I wish you would give me some sign. Some hope. I am doing everything I can."

Steeling herself—and trusting Kaliaris to get her out of the situation if it went sideways—Nyx took a chance. She slid her hand across the table and covered Laiveran's.

He shuddered and closed his eyes. Tears leaked out the corners, drawing wet lines down his cheeks, and Nyx experienced a moment of pure self-loathing for her deceit.

He'd done monstrous things. If it was her standing between him and the annihilation of another planet, she wouldn't hesitate to kill him. She could do what had to be done, when push came to shove. She'd discovered that, with the Kumir.

But torture did not sit well with her. And while she might not be pulling his fingernails off one by one, she had no doubt that what she was doing to him now was a different kind of torture. Maybe even a worse kind.

She was giving him hope—hope that Nyaera was with him, that his wife understood, that she accepted and forgave—and as soon as this illusion broke and he understood that none of those things had been real, Nyx would be wrenching that hope from him.

And it would hurt all the more in the end, for having had the false hope in the first place.

"Thank you." His voice was thick with the tears running down his face. "I'm almost there. I've finalized the binding process. Once Gharew solves the issue with the metal expansion, the Devourer will be mine. I will succeed. I will free you."

He turned his hand over beneath hers and froze. "Your skin

—" His eyes snapped open, recognition and anger blazing in their depths. "*You.*"

The wall behind Nyx disappeared. Kaliaris' vines shot around her waist, yanking her to safety as more sprouted from the floor. They bound Laiveran's wrists and ankles, preventing him from following.

Laiveran's room began to melt away.

"Don't," Nyx said. "Let him have it." *Let him have some comfort, some…peace.*

<He does not deserve it.>

"Maybe not. But I'm not some underworld god, to weigh his heart and his deeds and choose his punishment. I can't hold him here in darkness. I won't."

<*You* are not required to.>

"I won't let you, either."

The rustling of vines whispered through the Heart like a sigh. <You are too soft for what you have promised to do.>

"I can do what I have to."

<Are you so certain? You forget that a part of you now lives in me.> The pedestal in the center of the room began to glow, and she saw the space where one of her chaos thorns rested. <You were not made for the difficult choices.>

"I wasn't *made* for anything. It's a damn room, let him have it."

<Or?>

"Does everything have to be a bargain or a threat with you?" She'd thought Kaliaris was starting to like her. "Well fine. Here's one. Let him have the room or I won't be talking to you anymore. I'll block out your senses every second they aren't necessary, and I won't come down here to visit."

<You need to speak with him.>

"He gave me a name. I'm sure that can keep me busy for a while."

<Do you honestly believe that I would miss you?>

"Yes, Kaliaris, I think you would miss me. Maybe I'm not the company you would have chosen, but I am the company you have."

<So you will not leave in darkness a man who has destroyed so much, who has caused irrevocable pain, but you would threaten me with that very punishment? I, who have done no wrong to you?>

Nyx slumped. "No. Of course I won't."

A rustle of laughter through the vines. <You *are* too soft, capitulating with such ease.>

What did they want from her?

<But very well. He may have his room.>

"Thank you." She thought to leave, and no sooner had the thought occurred than she was floating up, away from the Heart.

Kaliaris' satisfaction followed her. <I think it is worse for him, like this. That room reminds him of her.>

On that note, Nyx was expelled onto the portal room floor, exhaling the last cloud of black mist from her lungs. "Seriously, K?" The floor rippled beneath her, as if Kaliaris laughed.

She shook her head and shoved to her feet, angry, unsure if her Station was serious about the room being a greater punishment than the cell Laiveran had been in before. Kaliaris was probably just screwing with her. Trying to make her feel guilty for getting what she'd asked for.

She had to comfort herself with the knowledge that, in the end, if Laiveran *was* tormented every moment by his wife's memory, Nyx didn't think that was honestly the result of a room. Where his thoughts went wasn't something she could control, and his guilt and his shame weren't her responsibilities.

His sanitary, decent living conditions *were*. And she'd seen to them, so Kaliaris could fuck right off with the mind games.

She looked down, as if she could see through the floor to Kaliaris' Heart, and said, "For the record, this isn't a punishment. This is because you were an ass and I don't want to talk to you right now."

She blocked the Station's senses.

It hurt. Not a physical pain, but she'd gotten so used to feeling the Station that it was like losing sight, touch, and sound on one half of her body. She frowned as she walked, realizing she hadn't felt with the Station's senses any of the times she'd been pulled onto a different memory island.

On the one hand, that was probably a good thing. Being five or ten or fifteen in a foreign place with no idea of how she'd gotten there while *also* feeling herself on her floor along with all the other people in the Station—she didn't want to know what kind of reaction she would have to that.

But it didn't answer the question of *why* she didn't feel the Station when on those islands. Her connection to Kaliaris wasn't mental, it was magical—and potentially physical, given that she didn't fully understand what the chaos thorns *were*.

Which, now that she thought about it, was probably something she should ask Kaliaris to explain. It hadn't really come up, since they'd staunchly ignored her after the initial bonding, and now that they had finally started talking to her again, she'd been a little distracted with Laiveran and her own issues.

And now that Kaliaris *was* talking to her again, it hadn't occurred to her to ask, because she realized she hadn't been having problems. The thorns had started to feel like just another part of her, like a tattoo or a piercing. While the Meerkin had told her she could learn to control the effects of the thorns, and she had done so with some success, this felt like more.

She remembered her first visit to Kaliaris' Heart, when she'd given them the thorn and *felt* that overabundance of rage leave her, as if Kaliaris had taken it. Remembered how Kaliaris had calmed afterwards, as if what they had taken had an opposite effect on them than it did on her. As if it was something they'd *needed*.

Given what she now knew about what the Stations and the ley lines were, maybe the chaos pockets, as Morgen had called them, *were* something Kaliaris needed. And maybe, now that

Kaliaris had accepted her, they were somehow mitigating the thorns' effects.

She would ask them tomorrow. After she'd had time to cool off.

Right now, she had a name to research.

19

Nyx was passing through the library on her way to the Den, intent on searching through the Station's Archives for mention of anyone named Gharew, when she fell out of touch with reality again. One moment her gaze was snagging on a copy of Madeleine L'Engle's *A Wrinkle in Time*, followed by a sudden flash of Viktor's scarred hands presenting her with a battered secondhand copy of that same book, and then she was crashing headlong into the eleven-year-old version of herself.

Nyx stared down at a copy of *A Wrinkle in Time*. It wasn't hers. The copy Viktor had brought her was soft and worn, with a centaur flying across a sort of nightmarish background. The copy she held now was so pretty it hurt. The pages were crisp, the cover glossy, the art a kind of picture-frame made of people and buildings that framed stars floating in empty space.

She'd only just noticed that the hands holding the book—her hands—were bigger than they should be when she saw the words on her arm. They were black and a little smeared, as if written with an old marker and then brushed before they were dry.

Elena Hid your memories. This will pass. Trust the griffin.

Nyx rolled her eyes. Seth must be really, *really* bored right now. Looking around at the cozy library that surrounded her, she realized he also must have gone to a bookstore last week when he'd snuck off to Dead Earth. His illusions were always getting better, and he'd made her a fake world once before, but it had had nothing on *this.*

The place was awesome. Bookshelves towered around her, made of glossy, black-lacquered wood and filled with books. She expected to only find the titles in her room, the rest of the spines empty, but she was surprised that a closer inspection showed they all had names and authors inscribed on the spines. Had he memorized the whole damn bookstore to recreate this, or was he just making the titles up?

She trailed her too-big fingers across the spines—what was up with that, anyway?—smiling as she read. If even half of these books actually existed, and she could have them, she might actually forget for more than a few hours that her life sucked.

"Nyx?"

She turned toward the speaker. "Oh, wow." Even her voice sounded off—more adult—but she didn't care too much about Seth's weird decision to make illusion-her older. Because standing in the doorway was a griffin. Like an *actual* griffin. He was smaller than she'd expected, maybe six feet in total height, and— "You're wearing *glasses.*"

The griffin sat, tilting his head slightly. "I frequently am."

"This is so cool!" She ran to him, tripping over her feet because they weren't quite where she expected them to be, and brushed her hand down his left wing. He even *felt* real, feathers soft and silky beneath her palm. "How are you making it this real?"

"This—ah, I see. Nyx, dear, how old are you?"

She laughed. "Did you do all this because you forgot when

my birthday is? Again?" When the griffin hesitated, she patted his shoulder. "It's next month, but can I keep this illusion for a bit anyway?"

"Of course," the griffin said gently, and he sounded so *un-Seth*-like that for a minute she wondered if this wasn't an illusion, and those words written on her arm were actually telling the truth.

But she just had, as her mother would say, an overactive imagination and an importance complex. She wanted to be someone special. Because if she was special, then someone important would eventually come looking for her. That was how it always worked in the books.

She really wanted someone—anyone—to be looking for her. Except that wasn't true either. She didn't want just anyone. She wanted her dad. Late at night, when she couldn't sleep and she'd already re-read every book she owned four times, she imagined what he might be like.

Strong, obviously, but powerful too. He would be important, and he would have been looking for her her whole life, but she was hard to find because no one in the universe bothered coming to Earth. And when he finally *did* find her, he'd tell her how sorry he was that he hadn't found her sooner, and to pack her bags and Seth's too, because he was taking them away. And even her mother wouldn't try to stop him because Elena, who wasn't afraid of anything, would be afraid of him.

"Would you like to read for a while?" The griffin asked. Looking at him, at the softness in his eyes and the gentleness in his voice that felt so real, like he was an actual person, she added one more thing her father would be: kind.

She shook her head in response to the reading question. It wasn't like Seth could fabricate an entire book in this illusory world, and she didn't want the fiction broken. "Tell me a story instead?"

"What kind of story?"

She looked around the room, so cozy and inviting, so everything she wanted. "Tell me about this place. What's my story? Why am I here? Who are you?"

"You're a Guardian," he said. "The Guardian of this Station. I am its Avatar, and your friend."

He continued, telling her how she'd come to be here, and she was easily lost in the vivid story he told. Hot cocoa appeared on the side table next to the couch, and she curled up with it while he talked about the Waystations she'd only ever heard Viktor mention in passing. There were a lot more embellishments in the griffin's version, wild claims about nexuses in time and bonds and old magic.

She liked this version better, listening until, lulled by the griffin's soft, melodic voice, she fell asleep.

W hen Nyx woke she was herself again, and Griff was still there, settled on the floor in front of the couch, keeping watch. He'd talked to her for hours, telling her the story of her life since she'd met him like it was a storybook, for a version of herself who was a lonely, mostly-forgotten kid who just wanted someone to love her.

Her heart squeezed and she wanted to cry, and she didn't know if that was because she'd just been thrust back into the bitter solitude of her childhood, or if it was because even the adult her had difficulty believing someone actually cared about her.

"How are you feeling?" Griff rose to a sitting position.

"Like a Station Guardian who had another tangle with a memory island." Impulsively, she leaned forward and hugged him, careful not to squeeze too hard and pull out any of his feathers. "Thank you," she whispered. "No one ever told me stories as a kid."

His wings curved around her, returning the hug. "I never had children of my own to tell any to. You were a sweet kid."

Her answering laugh was a little shaky. "Wouldn't it be nice if all my memory slips were that easy?" Nice, but unlikely. She extricated herself, wiping at eyes that were definitely having an allergic reaction to something, because no way was she crying.

Sensing her discomfort, Griff changed the subject. "Before this event, you had asked me to meet you in the Den?"

She'd all but forgotten that. Being so recently in a younger timeframe, what had happened right before with Laiveran—mere hours ago—now felt years distanced. Not in the past, but in the forward, which was difficult to explain the feeling of, even to herself. Stranger was the way she now had a childhood memory that felt like it had *just* happened. Because she'd made a new memory, just now, as a younger version of herself.

It was…weird. Beyond weird. So she did what she had gotten good at doing with *beyond weird* things and ignored it.

"Laiveran had a moment where he thought I was Nyaera's soul or something. I think he was talking about almost having the Harvester finished, and he mentioned someone named Gharew. Does that name mean anything to you?"

"Gharew," Griff repeated. "It sounds familiar, but I cannot place why."

"Well, it's probably been about nine centuries since you would have heard it, so I'm not shocked. Does the name sound like it belongs to any particular species?"

He shook his head. Again, Nyx wasn't surprised. Gharew was all of two syllables, easily pronounced by anyone with base Human vocal cords. Was it asking too much for the Harvester's creator to have had a name like Tlik-Varthume-Medahl of the Harvadean Medahls?

She didn't even have a last name to go on. She gave Griff a bright, sunny smile. "Join me in a long day of scouring the Archives?"

The long day of scouring the Station's Archives was just that: long. In addition, it was also fruitless. Gharew, it turned out, was a popular enough name across several species, as both a first and last name. The Archives catalogued over sixty-million instances of its use. Which she figured made it the universe equivalent of John or Michael as found in the United States.

The Archives, though capable of essentially searching with filters in place, weren't much more help because she didn't know what filters to use. She'd already filtered by a time-span of two-hundred years around the time she thought the Harvester had been made, but she didn't have much else to go on. She'd sorted by metal-workers and individuals with magical talents, but that had still left her with a list of Gharews in the millions.

Without more to go on, she didn't know what to do. Maybe Jevryn would remember the name, where Griff couldn't? If everything went well, he'd be here soon enough, and she could ask him. Until then, she'd keep visiting Laiveran and looking through the Station's Archives, hoping inspiration would give her the precisely correct filter she needed to find the right Gharew in a sea of millions.

But it turned out that future plan was wishful thinking. As she walked back to her bedroom that night, it was a stray thought about the wall color, of all things, that sent her spiraling down into another memory island.

For the next seven days, she wasn't much of her present self at all.

20

From the companion journals of Nyx Fortuna and Jevryn A-Morridahn

Nyx, the day after Seth's departure:

Two episodes today. Six hours apart. First lasted thirty minutes, the second forty-five.

Nyx, Day Two:

One episode. Two hours.

Nyx, Day Three:

Five episodes. No regularity in time between. Shortest five minutes, longest four hours.

Nyx, Day Three, Second Entry:

It would be really great if you could give me
some update. Or, you know, respond at all.

Jevryn, Day Four:

I am altering my plans based on your most
recent update.

Jevryn, Day Five:

Are things worsening?

Jevryn, Day Six:

I must express the hope that you are indulging
in a childish tantrum of ignoring me for my
previous silence as opposed to the alternative.

Nyx, Day Seven:

Sorry to disappoint you, but no childish tantrum
here. The predictions on how this might go
were both correct and incorrect. I spent one
day jumping in and out of ages so fast I
couldn't understand anything.

I spent the next two thinking I was thirteen.
Finally woke up as myself this morning.

Griff says it wasn't pretty. Not to be overly
dramatic, but you might want to get on those
alternate plans.

Jevryn:

Expect my arrival in two days' time.

21

Being stuck between the proverbial rock and a hard place was one of Seth Hawthorne's least favorite places to be. Being stuck there with a yawning chasm below him and a ceiling of loose spikes above, waiting to fall, was even lower on his list.

He—and everyone with him—was stuck in the latter place right now. They had now spent an entire Earth week on Nethrayne, with the bulk of their activity occurring in the early half. There had been the first day, where they'd nearly gotten themselves caught or killed from Beauregard's insistence on pushing themselves to their limits.

The second day they'd spent recuperating magic so that on day three they could make their way from the third level to the fourth. Day four had been spent exploring the fourth level and locating the door that led to the fifth—and uppermost—level.

That was where things had gotten sticky. Because no matter what Seth or Reyva tried, they couldn't get through that door. They'd been at it for three days straight now. They'd zeroed in on the one scientist who lived on the fourth floor and had regular access to the fifth, and Seth had mimicked everything about him.

It was the most detailed illusory clone he'd ever made, and it had done fuck-all to get them through. It was like the door wasn't even scanning for bio markers—or like the door somehow *knew* his bio markers were fake when no other alarm system had ever pegged the falsehood.

Reyva was similarly frustrated. The woman who'd broken the world's most premier alarm system in less than five minutes had gotten nowhere on this. She was currently pacing in the living area of the suite they'd borrowed—owners conveniently off-planet—while Beauregard drilled the two of them for the eight-billionth time.

"I'm telling you," she said, Tiagren claws breaking from the tips of her fingers in frustration, "it's like it isn't even an alarm system. It's as impenetrable as that damn door on Earth's Station."

Seth straightened. "What do you mean? What door?"

Reyva flicked a lock of hair over her shoulder in irritation. "The one you all disappeared through every night to reach the Station's private quarters. The door your girlfriend oh-so-help-fully told me wasn't bound by a lock *or* a ward, so I was never getting through it. What does that even mean? If it's not a lock or a ward, what's holding it?"

"Shit." Seth dropped onto one of the living area couches. What was the one thing his illusion magic still couldn't fool, the one thing he'd asked Nyx how to get past, and she hadn't really had an answer?

The Station.

"'Shit', as in, you know what the door is?" Reyva asked.

"'Shit', as in, I *think* I know what the door is, and if I'm right, we're fucked in more ways than one." He dug one of the Earth portal stones from his pocket and crumbled it. Nothing. Abso-fucking-lutely *nothing*.

He watched as everyone around him took in the nothing happening.

"What does that mean?" Reyva asked. "Why isn't the portal stone working?"

He looked at Morgen and shook his head. As far as he knew, most people didn't understand that portal stones wouldn't work within a Station's confines. After all, if someone was going to the trouble to use a portal stone in the first place, it was because they either couldn't travel via a Station, or didn't want their movements tracked through one.

"It means," he said slowly, "that unless I can figure out how to do something I've been trying and failing to do for months, we aren't getting through that door."

How did he trick a Station's senses?

Nyx, saying, *They were a planet. I don't know if you could ever understand their senses enough* to *trick them.*

"And the portal stones?" Maruca asked.

"Won't work here." Maybe they would work somewhere else? At an earlier point on Nethrayne? He didn't think the entire city was the Station. Why bother with all the ordinary wards and alarms they'd gone through, if that was the case? But it seemed that parts of Nethrayne were also parts of the Station —and maybe there were tendrils of the Station throughout all of it, just enough to insert the level of dominance needed to prevent the ability to portal in or out. Just the kind of protection a councilor would want, when they'd know that every *other* councilor would otherwise have the ability to come or go at will.

"If we cannot leave," Beauregard said, "then our only option is to go forward." He didn't exactly sound heartbroken about their being stuck here. But then again, he clearly intended to reach the Kumir or die trying. Man didn't seem big on third options. "We keep at the door until someone tries something that works."

Seth didn't bother telling him that nothing was going to work. The only person who had a chance in hell of getting them through that door was Nyx.

And she wasn't here.

22

Two days was not, in theory, a long time to wait for Jevryn. But in the finicky way of time, it was all about perception, and Nyx's perception was shot.

She spent the morning after his last journal entry feeling scattered and out-of-sorts. She wandered into rooms and stood there staring, having no idea why she'd gone in to this one or that one. It wasn't that she wasn't cognizant of her surroundings, it was that she was incapable of focusing. On *anything*.

She felt at some turns shaky, at others lethargic, like her blood sugar was off or her blood pressure was low, except there was no way to fix it because neither of those two things was what was actually wrong with her.

The only time she felt at all normal these days was when she slipped into a memory island. At least when that happened, she was only ever concerned with two things: where was she, and where was Seth?

Sometimes the message she'd written on her arm helped, and sometimes it didn't. If it made her think Seth was playing a joke on her, it put her at ease. If it made her think someone was trying to trick her, she went into a state of heightened paranoia.

She'd tried other similar things—a notebook with a lengthier explanation written to herself, some photos of her and Griff and present-day Seth—but they had the same end result as the words on her arm: she either thought it was Seth, or she thought it was someone bad. And she couldn't come up with a foolproof way to make herself reliably think the former.

The unreliability meant that even when she was soundly in the mental space of Present Day Her, she was constantly waiting for the other shoe to drop. Like she was doing right now. Because despite her dire warning to Jevryn, she'd been herself all morning, and instead of being comforted by the fact, all it did was make her worry about how much worse the next episode was going to be.

She tried to take advantage of the reprieve. To read or work. To spend time with Griff and Kalvar and Temerex.

Except Griff and Kalvar couldn't hide their concern, now that they'd been subjected to an entire week of her shifting in and out of different ages—in effect, in and out of different identities, because each age of her was slightly different, if slightly the same—and being around them was stressful, even if they didn't mean it to be.

She understood. They wanted to help. They wanted to *do* something that could help, but there wasn't anything to be done, and so they were constantly scurrying underfoot, offering her this or that creature comfort. While she appreciated the sentiment and what they wanted to do for her, their eagerness to help filled her with a sense of overwhelming guilt.

She couldn't *be* helped, so she was going to let them down. No matter what they did, she was going to fall into another memory island and put them both through the same explanations and worries they'd gone through so many times by now.

She was a broken record, stuck on repeat.

So, no. She didn't *relax* in her temporary reprieve. She worried. She tried to fill her time with reading, except her brain couldn't even focus on fiction, much less on the academic texts on portal magic. There was no work for her to do. No Arrivals or

Departures, though it was doubtful Griff would have let her receive them even if they were scheduled. No one from Earth Between had come up to visit the cafe or bookstore, though again, it was unlikely she would have been allowed near the espresso machine even if someone showed up. Kalvar had been monitoring the storefronts with a determined persistence, as if convinced she needed to be kept away from them at all costs.

Which, in all fairness to him, she probably did. The last thing she needed to do was reveal her condition to anyone who might wander in from Earth Between. She'd spent the first half of the day with Temerex, but Temerex *really* wanted to run the obstacle course again, and Nyx's communication with her wasn't good enough to explain why that was a really bad idea. No matter how softly the ground might catch her, or how easily the hanging logs would explode into powder upon contact, getting on a half-ton animal when her memory-lapses were so frequent now was a really stupid idea.

Since she'd failed at communicating the why behind her refusal, Temerex thought Nyx was angry with her, and started sulking. With nowhere else to go, Nyx was in her room, trying yet again to read the same sentence in *Portal Magic: Its Uses and Limitations.*

The section was on anchoring. Apparently, portal witches were good at using anchors for known locales. Jevryn's home, where he'd opened a portal to when they'd been on Amentia Furor and casually made her a sandwich from his kitchen, was likely one such anchor.

She wondered, idly, if the Hiding she'd placed on Seth could act as an anchor. If *any* Hiding she did could act as an anchor. It would be highly convenient. And it made a sort of sense, that she should be connected to her works. She knew her mother had still been connected to her, through the active Hiding that had been keeping her memories from her. She'd *felt* Elena behind that working.

And Nyx herself had been able to find Seth on Amentia Furor

because he'd held the Harvester she'd Hidden. So she likely had an easier chance at anchoring than any other portal witch. At least, she had an easier chance at making an abundance of anchors than any other portal witch did.

Because her anchors would be made with her own magic rather than a locator spell, she could tap into them more quickly, could make them on the fly, whenever necessary. She liked the idea—that she could never lose anything, or become lost in turn.

Being taken to Lehine by Laiveran, and then lost on Amentia Furor, had irrevocably shifted something in her. The knowledge that she could become lost, somewhere so far from home that she might never have *any* hope of returning, that she might die alone and lost and with no control over her situation—she woke up a lot of nights, thinking about that.

It was why she was currently decked out in the portal magic jewelry she'd Hidden from public sight. She wore each piece like a talisman of protection. Even if the books hadn't told her enough yet to let her understand the planetary maps she'd drawn up instinctively on Lehine, or how to sort through the points on them and find which one was the one she wanted. Even if she understood that, until she became more efficient with her use of portal magic, she might yet find herself somewhere too far away to return home.

But the anchors—they acted as a type of shortcut. She didn't need the map if she had an anchor. And depending on how strong the anchor was, she might be able to go somewhere she otherwise wouldn't have enough magic or experience to reach.

She didn't fully grasp the theory behind it, both because of the difficulty she was having focusing on the sentence, and because Griff's brain—if his writing of this book was any indication—clearly worked in ways hers did not. She'd always been better at learning by practical experience than she had been by reading theory and attempting to interpret it.

Still, if anything was going to give her a reprieve from the anxiety constantly clutching at her chest, making her feel like she both couldn't breathe and was maybe also on the verge of having a heart attack, maybe this was it. While she'd Hidden one thing inside the Station—the trunk Jevryn had sent—anchors inside the Station wouldn't help.

She would be able to feel them if she was gone, but she wouldn't be able to reach them because the Station's dominance was so strong no one could portal in or out of it. She was assuming even the councilors couldn't manage it because, if they could, they wouldn't travel to the Stations via the ley lines. And she supposed they didn't need to, since they clearly had control over access to those ley lines in some other manner.

Kaliaris couldn't deny them entrance via the lines, though they could fight the small control the councilors had over the Station, as they'd done when they kept Jevryn out of their Heart when the councilor had very much wanted to enter it.

So, no, an anchor *inside* the Station wouldn't help her if she ever became lost again. But an anchor just outside the Station's territory? That would work.

It was one small thing she could do to take back a measure of control. Stars knew she didn't have any over anything else happening in her life right now. Still, she let Griff know what she was doing, so he could follow her out to the Station's perimeter in case she happened to have an episode while there. He could keep her from wandering off.

They walked in silence to the Station's boundary, Temerex falling in step beside them. Nyx wished she could ask Griff about the anchors, to find out if she was understanding them correctly. But while he might not be able to talk to her about them, she figured if he thought it was dangerous for her to make one, he would tell her not to. He didn't have to talk about portal magic to tell her not to do something.

She stopped half-a-dozen feet from the Station's border. Griff had written in his book that most portal witches, bereft of any secondary magical abilities, purchased locator spells that were attuned to them to use as anchors. He hadn't stated whether the object they attached the spells *to* held any significance. Whether it mattered or not what it was.

But just in case it did, she held a throwing star in her left hand. It might look like any other, but it wasn't. Seth had made it, the cut and weight and feel of it precise. She cradled it in her palm, working her Hiding over it. When it was finished, she took a proper grip on it and let it fly. It spun past the Station's border, embedding itself in one of the many trees that lined the area.

Checking, she tugged on that thin thread of magic that ran from her to the star, satisfied with the connection, the weight, between her and it. Hopefully, it would be enough to find her way back here, if she ever got lost again.

She turned and Griff turned with her. They'd gone maybe fifteen steps when another memory island shook loose without warning, and she was falling.

23

Nyx froze, taking stock of her surroundings. Her extremely *unfamiliar* surroundings. She knew every inch of the woods that surrounded the little clearing her home nestled in. The clearing she stood in now was not that clearing, and the woods that surrounded it were not her woods.

A building loomed ahead, but though it was roughly cabin-esque in architecture, it certainly wasn't the small dwelling she called home, nor was it the barn. Two creatures, which must have been walking beside her but which had gotten a few paces ahead of her before noticing her halt, were like nothing she had ever seen.

One she could name from the mythology books Seth had brought back for her on one of his many unauthorized trips into Dead Earth. It had the head, neck, and front talons of an eagle, and the body of a lion: a griffin.

As for the other...the other she had no name for. It had an equine body but no fur. Instead, small scarlet scales covered its hide, and a spiral horn jutted from its forehead. It was like some kind of reptilian unicorn, both terrifying and mesmerizing, and Nyx was certain she had never seen anything like it in her life.

The two creatures stared at her. Nyx swallowed. Was this

another one of Viktor's tests? One of her mother's? Was this Seth playing a practical joke on her?

She threw the last idea out immediately. She'd made some rules in the last year where his illusions were concerned. Never the entirety of the environment. Never anything while she was asleep, making her wake into something she didn't recognize. And if she ever *asked* if something was him, he had to end it, right then.

So even though she knew this *shouldn't* be him, it was so weird and fantastical and out of place that she asked it anyway. "Seth?" She spoke quietly, too quietly for the words to travel, because if this *was* Seth, he would hear. "Is this you?"

No answer from an unseen Seth, but the two monstrous figures turned toward her. The reptilian unicorn snorted, and for some reason Nyx couldn't fathom, an image of a storm-cloud-filled sky came into her mind, along with a feeling of intense uncertainty.

The griffin spoke, like they didn't have an eagle's beak and an eagle's tongue, and so they could speak perfectly good English if they wanted to, thank you very much.

"Nyx? Are you feeling…unwell?" The voice was a low tenor, obviously male.

He knew her name. Why did he know her name? And why did he ask if she was feeling unwell in a manner that suggested he thought she was a wild animal to be treated with caution?

She forced herself to answer, Viktor's training urging her to respond with something vague and innocuous while she assessed the situation. "I'm fine. Just a little out of sorts."

She wasn't restrained. She was outside. That could be good or bad. Either she wasn't being held captive by these creatures, or she was, and they were so confident in their ability to keep her here that they didn't feel the need for restraints or confinement.

"How out of sorts?" the griffin asked. Despite his massive

size, he felt…safe. Nyx recoiled from the feeling. He wasn't safe. She didn't know him.

More importantly…were griffins real? She'd read about them in her mythology books and loved the idea of them, but she'd never quite worked up the nerve to ask Viktor if they existed. She'd been too afraid of having yet another dream ruined, of hearing him inform her, in that patient but impersonal and emotionless way he did almost everything, that they were not.

She might be on the fence about griffins, but she was relatively certain that scaled unicorns did *not* exist. Which meant the griffin probably didn't either, and what she was seeing wasn't real. Either it was an illusion, made by someone other than Seth, or she was hallucinating and seeing the people before her as something other than what they actually were.

The latter seemed more likely. She'd fallen for Seth's illusions so many times she'd become fairly adept at seeing her way out of them, and since none of her usual tricks—like looking out the corner of her eye or squinting like she was trying to bring things into focus—was working, she was pretty certain it wasn't illusion.

That left the likelihood that she'd been drugged, via either magical or non-magical substances. There were plenty of both. It would also explain why she wasn't restrained. Her captors expected her to come along docilely. Likely because they wanted something from her.

Hadn't her mother constantly been warning her that if anyone discovered what she was, it would end poorly for her? Had she finally made a mistake? She…couldn't remember what she'd done last. She and Seth had been planning to leave—they were always planning to leave, but it was different this time. They had a chance this time, they just had to wait a little longer.

But he'd been taking her into Dead Earth more often. Had someone found her? Come looking for her mother and found her instead? It seemed so unlikely, of all the planets in the universe, for someone to track their way to Earth, then actually find the middle-of-nowhere place they lived. That was *why* they lived there, wasn't it?

"Nyx?" the griffin asked, snapping her back to the situation in front of her. "Are you about to have an episode?"

What the hell was an episode? Was that something they'd trained into her, for when the drugs were about to wear off? "No," she said, hoping the words didn't come out too fast. Hoping she didn't sound panicked. "No. I think I'm just"—what would be believable?—"tired."

The griffins eyes softened, and Nyx had to remind herself that this being—why were the drugs making her see a griffin?—was likely her captor. She ought to feel no sympathy or trust toward him, nor guilt at lying to him.

"It has been an eventful few days," he said, as if her excuse made perfect sense. "Come inside. I think Seth left some gumbo in the freezer. We can heat it up."

"Will he be joining us?" She knew the question was a mistake the second it left her mouth, knew from the look in the griffin's eyes that Seth wasn't here, and she was supposed to know that.

The griffin tilted his head at an odd angle. "What is my name?" he asked quietly. "What is her name?" A tilt of his head at the scaled unicorn.

Nyx forced a laugh. It sounded brittle, but she hoped that was only because she knew what her laugh *should* sound like, and not because it sounded like an obviously fake laugh in general. "Why would you ask me that? You're being weird."

The griffin's voice dropped to that measured tone people took when they were trying to placate someone. "Nyx, look at your arm."

And give him a chance to attack while she was distracted? She didn't think so. "Look," she said, carefully taking a step back while keeping her eyes on him. "You're being kind of strange. And I really think I should just get home."

She backed away. One step. Two. Three. On the next step her back slammed into something hard, knocking the breath from her lungs. When she turned, nothing was there. Nothing visible, anyway. When she stretched out her hand, trying to find what she'd hit, her palm pressed against clear air like it was solid metal.

"You won't remember this," the griffin said, stopping parallel to her but several feet away, "but I am your friend. We've been through this several times already. I know you must be feeling scared. You have no idea where you are, and you are likely suspicious that I am not what I appear.

"But I assure you, everything is going to be alright. If you would look at your right arm, I think you would—"

She turned and shoved at the invisible wall. Her first instinct had been to run and see if she could make it into the building, but there was no point in running when the two quadrupeds would easily overtake her. Besides, it was probably *their* building.

Her better option was to get to the forest and hope she could lose them there. But she needed to be able to get there. Her shove against the invisible wall did nothing. The griffin did not attempt to physically restrain her, which meant he thought he didn't need to.

"You cannot leave," he said. His voice was still gentle. Soothing. "And this will be much easier if you simply calm down and let me explain."

You cannot leave. Story of her fucking life.

Well, not this time. She didn't know where she was, but she wasn't staying. Not when all the plans she and Seth had made were finally going to come true. He was *so* close to perfecting the masking method that would keep Viktor from following them. Another week, maybe two, and she was certain he'd have it.

Then they'd be free. They'd have a new life, a *real* life. She was not going to lose that, not now. So she didn't dwell on the fact that she had no idea how she'd gotten here, or that she couldn't specifically remember the last time she'd seen Seth.

Seth. He was her priority. *Finding him* was her priority. It made her plan simple, really. Step one: escape. Step two: find Seth.

She took a deep breath and turned to the griffin, one hand still resting on the invisible wall. "Okay then, explain." Better to have him occupied thinking she wanted to be persuaded while her mind ran through her options.

She'd barely calculated the likelihood that she could subdue the two unknown individuals—practically non-existent—when something tugged at her. A Hiding. Not the one for whatever was hanging around her neck, but one that was close, maybe twenty or thirty feet away. On the *other* side of the invisible wall.

The Hiding was fresh, only a few minutes old. That she couldn't remember making it only further confirmed that whoever the griffin was, however soothingly and convincingly he was talking in words that she was purposefully not listening to, she couldn't trust him.

He'd had her Hide something for him—why else would they be out here?—and then he'd done something to make her forget. But the fact the Hidden object was over there meant there was a way to get past the wall.

The Hiding tugged on her like an anchor and she reached, stretching mental fingers toward it. As she did, as her magic reached back, something *else* twinged inside her. The hardness of the wall beneath her fingers softened. It hardened again almost immediately, but it *had* softened.

She gauged the griffin's reaction but he didn't seem to have noticed the small lapse in the wall's rigidity, caught up in the lecture he spoke in calm-the-wild-beastie tones. Repeating what she had done before, she sought her Hiding. This time, when it reached back for her and that other feeling inside her woke, she latched onto it.

Sensation poured through her in a dizzying rush, the feeling of boots and paws and hooves upon her, of roots growing through her and worms burrowing into her like…like she *was* the land.

What the hell kind of drugs did they have her on?

That panicked need to get out, get *away*, surged through her. The wall beneath her hand vanished and she went tumbling through it. She didn't pause to contemplate how her success had happened. She just ran.

Behind her the griffin shouted and the unicorn let out a distressed whinny. She didn't look over her shoulder to see if they were following—she could hear that they were—nor did she stop when the ground began trying to trap her. It grew vines first, but she could *feel* them, and she told herself that this—the invisible wall, and now the vines—was only in her head, some result of her undoubtedly altered mental state.

She'd gotten through the wall because her subconscious had found a way to work around it, to feel like she *was* the land and had some control over it. So she went with that delusion. She told herself the vines were *hers* to command, and she commanded them to let her go.

When they did, it added fuel to the fire of her confidence. So when next her feet tried to sink into the ground, she imagined it solid beneath the soles of her boots and it became so. When it felt like the air was hardening, she imagined it pliant.

For a few steps it was like running through thickened sludge, but she pushed through, until she took a step and all those extra sensations vanished. She was no longer the dirt and the roots and the trees and the air but just…Nyx.

Her relief lasted a mere fraction of a second before panic took its place. She had the overwhelming sense that she shouldn't have left. That something terrible would happen to her out here, and if she just returned to where she'd been, she would be safe.

She fought past her racing heart and looked back over her shoulder. The griffin and the unicorn had halted at the exact place where, when she'd crossed, she'd stopped being every-thing and started being herself again.

The unicorn pawed at the ground, sparks flying each time her hoof struck. The griffin was still calling for her, pleading and frantic, and she faltered. She skidded to a halt and, for a moment, she swayed back in that direction.

Safe, something within her whispered. *Go back, and you'll be safe. Anything could happen to you out here.*

"Nyx, please," the griffin begged. His concern seemed so genuine, like she was making a terrible mistake. "Come back. Everything will be fine."

And she understood. He couldn't follow. It didn't look like the unicorn could, either. Some kind of...locational magic, then. The griffin and the unicorn were caught in it, and within the boundaries where the magic roamed, it had affected Nyx as well.

This panic she was feeling, the terror of leaving—that had to be part of the magic, meant to keep her there, to draw her back if she escaped. She wouldn't go back but...was she wrong about the griffin and the unicorn? Were they perhaps not her captors, but captives as well?

She took another step away from them, all too aware of that urgent push inside her to return. The griffin wasn't *acting* like a captive. He wasn't asking her to get him out too, or telling her to go find help. He was only trying to convince her to come back within the boundaries of his confinement.

Still, something about those big golden eyes, the pain in them... She had to ask. "Do you need help? I'm not going back in there," she warned, when it looked like he was going to take the question as an invitation to once again try and persuade her, "but if you need help..." She trailed off because...what? If he needed help, what was she going to do?

She didn't even know where she was. It looked like Earth, but it wasn't unreasonable that some planets might. And even if this *was* Earth, where on Earth was she? Where was Seth?

The griffin still hadn't answered her question, like he was trying to decide which answer was the best one to give. His hesitation made her decide that she wouldn't let him give one.

"Look, if you're trapped I—I'm really sorry. And I'll find a way to help you. I just have to find Seth first." The griffin had mentioned him, so she must have talked about him to them. Maybe he'd even been here at some point, from the way the griffin had acted, but Seth clearly wasn't here now. All she had to do was find him, and everything would be fine.

As soon as she had the thought she felt it. A Hiding tied to a familiar feeling—the steady *thump thump* of Seth's heart. Why would she Hide his heartbeat? She was almost too relieved to care, except that he felt so very, very far away. She poured magic into the Hiding, strengthening it, a thin string becoming a rope, one she could grab onto and tug, trying to gain a sense for how far away the thing tied to the other end was.

She must have tugged too hard because the heartbeat on the other end skipped, like he'd felt it. A beat later it smoothed back into slow, steady regularity, the way it felt when she had her head on his chest and he was already asleep.

She kept the connection between them strong and glowing. She just needed a direction to head in, but when she spun a slow circle, searching for the *ping* that would tell her she was facing the right way, there was nothing.

He was *somewhere*, and she was connected to him, which meant she should be able to find him. She *had* to find him. It was an urgent, insistent desperation inside her and—and that's when the Hidden bracelets running up her arms began to glow, magic spilling out of them in answer to her need, half-a-dozen blue streams coalescing into a single sphere before her.

"No!" the griffin shouted.

Nyx barely heard him. She was transfixed by the magic. Technically, she understood that it must be answering to her—magic didn't function without a directive—that somehow, she had called it forth from the bracelets she'd Hidden. Bracelets she didn't remember Hiding.

But it didn't feel like she was in control. She was transfixed, hypnotized, because though it made no sense, though she'd never heard of this kind of magic before, some innate part of her knew what this had to be. Some kind of transportation magic.

She'd needed to find Seth. She had a tether to him. And when her need had surfaced, this magic had answered.

It stretched into an oval as tall as she was and only a fraction wider. The space between it was hazy, half-opaque, but through it she saw a familiar form. Bronze skin, black hair fallen over his eyes as he slept. Something about him was different, something she couldn't put her finger on through the muddied image, but it was him. Her Hiding, snapping with sudden vibrancy, screamed that he was *right there*, a handful of feet all that separated them. She could just make out the tattoo on his naked chest, the one that was a twin to her own.

The edges of the oval wobbled, the space between growing more opaque, an instability that spoke of imminent collapse. She pushed her will at the magic, hoping that it *was* a will-based magic. For one second, two, the edges stabilized. But it was as if something on the other side fought her. Like she was an intruder it was trying to push out. Like she was trespassing on territory claimed by another.

The oval shrank, the top and bottom moving toward each other, until all she could hold in place was a sphere that hovered at torso level. She was losing it. Losing Seth.

No. Desperation surged anew and a fresh wave of magic poured from something—a necklace—around her throat. The fresh burst of magic locked the edges in place, the center growing clearer. The moment it was perfectly clear, like she was looking through a window from one place into another, she backed up two steps, got a running start, and dove through.

She felt the magic collapse, the window shrinking as that unseen opposing force struggled to keep her out. She jerked her knees to her chest, pulling her feet clear just as she lost her hold on the magic.

She landed gracelessly on the bed, half on the mattress, half on top of Seth. He woke in a blink. She didn't even get his name out before he'd flipped her onto her back, pinning her arms and legs.

When had he gotten that fast?

"Hey," she said quickly, because Seth and sharp objects were never far from each other, and he didn't seem fully awake yet.

He blinked at her in the dim light, shock washing over his face, like she was the last person he'd ever expected to see. "Nyxi?"

She didn't get to formulate a response before the door burst open behind them.

24

Nyx only caught a glimpse of the woman who charged into the room—warm brown skin with black stripes like a tiger's, long fingers lengthened into wickedly sharp black claws —before Seth turned his head and bit off, "Get the fuck out, Reyva."

Nyx tried to peer around him but Seth shifted, blocking her view, as if he didn't want her to see the woman. Or as if he didn't want the woman to see *her*.

"Shit. I heard a disturbance. I didn't think…" She trailed off, and though Nyx couldn't see her, she could practically *hear* the blush in her voice. Then something like anger or disappointment edged out the embarrassment. "Are you insane? This is hardly the time for that. Not to mention you have a sick girlfriend at home. What the fuck are you doing?"

"I'm not sic—" Was all Nyx got out before Seth clapped his hand over her mouth. But it was too late. Instead of leaving, the woman edged around him. She was pretty, somewhere in her early twenties, probably.

Reyva's eyes widened. "Is that…*Nyx*?"

Nyx struggled to sit up. Seth kept her pinned, like he was afraid she was going to run out the door if given freedom of movement, like a puppy taking the first chance at escape. She glared at him. "Let me up."

"Not happening." He practically growled the words at her. If it was anyone else, she'd say he sounded like she'd caused him a massive inconvenience by showing up right now, and he was really wishing he could undo it. But when Seth sounded like that, it meant one thing: internally, he was freaking out.

Which, okay, she had literally appeared out of thin air and landed on top of him. It was admittedly weird, but that didn't seem to be what was concerning him. What seemed to be concerning him was the woman in the room. The woman who kept edging closer, as if she wasn't certain of what she was seeing.

"It *is* you. How did you get here? How did—" She cut off, waving her hand. "Never mind, I don't care. Well, I do, but I'll care later. Right now, I need you to come with me."

Nyx had thought she couldn't have any less of an idea of what was going on after running from a griffin and a unicorn and stepping through a magic circle. Apparently, she'd been wrong. "I'm sorry, what?"

"I need you to come with me. The door at the Station? The one I couldn't get through because you said it wasn't secured by a ward *or* a lock? I'm stuck on the same thing here." The woman —Reyva, Seth had called her—sounded like this should all make perfect sense to Nyx.

"I have no idea what you're talking about." *And I have no idea who you are.* But she didn't add that because…well, because.

"You weren't *that* drunk," Reyva said. "And don't worry, I won't repeat the rest of the conversation in the present company."

Seth answered, which was probably good because Nyx had no clue what to say. "I need to talk to Nyx alone." When Reyva didn't move, he added, "That means you need to leave."

Reyva gave him a look like he'd suggested two plus two did not equal four. "I get that you have been parted from her for a whole seven days and that must be a hardship, but the bigger hardship is us stuck here uselessly cooling our heels. So hand her over. We have enough time before morning for her to look at the door and hopefully solve all our problems." She shifted her gaze to Nyx. "Can you talk some sense into him, please?"

"I..." What was she supposed to say? Her frustration found an outlet in her physical predicament. Namely, being trapped under Seth. "Could you *please* let me up?" She wriggled one arm free of his hold and put her palm on his chest, shoving him.

He moved all of a centimeter because she had no leverage. But that touch, the feel of his skin—and the scar beneath it—finally clicked into place that thing she thought had been different about him but couldn't put her finger on.

He was Seth but he was...different. He shouldn't have that scar, or the two others she spotted, one on his shoulder, one across his abdomen. He was a little broader in the shoulders, more muscled, and when she looked at his face...

It was so obvious she couldn't believe she'd missed it until now. He wasn't nineteen.

"Seth," she said carefully, "how old are you?"

He didn't look surprised by the question. He didn't answer, either, sitting back and finally allowing her up. His hand remained circled around her wrist, like he was still afraid she was a flight risk.

You have a sick girlfriend at home.

"Am I—" She swallowed. "*Am* I sick?"

Was that why she couldn't remember how she'd gotten where she'd been? When the griffin had said that Seth had left food for her in the fridge...had she been convalescing in some kind of home for people suffering from magical ailments, and Seth dropped by to visit on occasion?

True panic rose in her chest. She could handle potentially having been held somewhere against her will. She could handle people trying to use her for her power. She'd been told to prepare for those things her entire life.

What she couldn't handle was the idea that her own mind might betray her. That she might be in a state where she couldn't accurately interpret what was going on. A state so bad that Seth had…what? Left her somewhere to be cared for by others?

What could be so bad that he couldn't handle being around it? Was she violent?

No, it couldn't be that bad. Otherwise this Reyva would have been worried by Nyx's presence, instead of wanting Nyx to help her.

But Seth still wasn't saying anything.

"Seth? Please talk to me."

More people spilled through the doorway before he could answer, four of them in total. A white woman with plaited blonde hair who was built like a heavyweight boxer, standing next to a Black man of medium build, his hair in long, sleek braids. An absolute mountain of a man stood behind them, his skin a touch darker than the first man's, his hair cropped short. The woman next to him, pale skin and flame red hair, looked practically diminutive at his side.

All four of the newcomers stared at Nyx like she was a corpse that had suddenly come back to life.

The Black man with the long hair looked at her and said, hesitantly, "Little Guardian?" He had a pretty voice, smooth and melodious, and she tried to focus on that instead of the fact that he obviously expected her to know him.

She didn't know him, and she didn't have to think very hard to be sure of that. She didn't know *anyone*. Just her mom. Viktor. Seth. The man who ran the arcade in the closest town to them and always let them stay to closing, even when they didn't have any money. She was pretty sure he thought they were homeless, but he never treated them as if they were. With pity or scorn. He just gave them a place to be on the rare occasions they snuck out.

If anything was going to drive her crazy, wouldn't it have been that? The fact she knew precisely four people in the universe she could attach a name and a face to? The rest were just people, seen in passing, to be studied in order to mimic behavior when necessary.

She'd read enough books and watched enough kids in Dead Earth to know that it wasn't supposed to be that way. Seventeen-year-olds were supposed to have friends. To at least know people. But then…she looked at definitely *not* nineteen-year-old Seth. At the fact everyone else in the room, people who knew him, people who acted as if they knew her, were all older as well.

She studied Seth. Because even obviously older, even with fingers a little more callused than she remembered, he was still *him*. He was still the person she trusted most and that wouldn't have changed…would it?

The mountain posing as a man fixed her with a direct stare. "How did you get here?"

Nyx didn't answer. She couldn't. It felt like things were piling on top of each other in her mind. The strange place she'd been. The magic she'd used to get here. Seth being older.

Too many people around, all focused on *her*. She'd never been the center of so much attention and she didn't like it. She wanted to hide. Something trembled and it felt like the trembling thing was inside her head. Like she stood beneath a field of floating debris and it was about to come crashing down on her.

She shuddered, her eyes going out of focus. Seth gripped her chin, fingers digging in hard enough to get her attention, and forced her eyes back to his. "*Don't,*" he said. "Wherever you are, whenever you are, *stay there.*"

"That doesn't make any sense." Except it did. On some level she didn't fully comprehend, it did. She shuddered again but it was smaller, and that shakiness in her head was quieter.

She glanced at the others. "Who are they?"

The blonde cursed.

Seth turned on them, moving in front of Nyx, as if blocking her view of them would help. And…it kind of did. "Get out. I need to talk to her."

The mountain began, "Not without some explanation for—"

"Yes," the man with the world's best voice interrupted him, "without that. You don't understand what's going on here."

"Which is precisely the—"

"*Please*, Uncle Beau?"

Beau hesitated. "Half an hour, Hawthorne." Then he nodded at Reyva, who cast a final confused glance at Nyx before following him and the others out of the room.

As soon as they were gone, Seth rounded on her. "What's the last thing you remember? The last *normal* thing you remember?"

The request planted her even more firmly in that *whenever* she currently was, the inside of her mind finally feeling stable again. She searched her memory, before the griffin and the unicorn.

"I…don't know, exactly?" Was that just the day-to-day of life blurring together? It was easy for that to happen, the way they lived. Sometimes she felt like entire months ran together, an unending string of pointlessness. So she thought back to the last big thing that had happened. "We took that trip to Washington. Like we always talked about. It was maybe a week ago?" She touched her fingertips to the faint lines at the corners of his eyes. "Except I'm guessing it…wasn't really a week ago, was it?"

She looked around at the room. She'd never seen it before, and it was hardly to Seth's taste, either. The walls were a vibrant orange overlaid with gold that managed to be pretty rather than garish. Contrasted with the dark brown floor, it gave her the impression of flames licking up from firewood. Hanging plants dripped from the ceiling.

The bed was low to the ground and covered in a plush, forest-green duvet threaded through with gold. A dozen matching pillows, obviously meant to be on the bed, had been tossed carelessly onto the floor beside it. Seth hated extra pillows. He might be staying here, but it was obviously temporary.

She clutched one of the discarded pillows to her stomach and sat on the bed. She was so tired, and she wondered when she'd last slept. Or if whatever was happening to her was simply taking an extra toll on her body.

Seth still hadn't offered her an explanation, and she looked at him expectantly.

He swallowed. "I don't know how to tell you this."

She clutched the pillow tighter. "Then just tell me. Whatever's going on can't be as bad as what I'm coming up with in my head."

Nyx said that what Seth had to tell her couldn't be worse than what her imagination could conjure, but that was only because the Nyx she was right now, for all she'd seen seventeen years of Elena Fortuna's fickle brand of cruelty, hadn't yet been abandoned by her in the worst way possible. Hadn't yet been abandoned by *him*.

Seth didn't know how to tell her that. He didn't *want* to tell her that. Seeing her like this—looking at him like there was nothing complicated between them, like he could never do anything worse to her than be annoying—was a double kick to the gut.

"Are you sure you want to know?" he asked softly. "You don't have to. This—all of this—it will pass soon enough, and it won't matter."

She gave him that look she'd mastered when she was seven, the one that said *You're joking, right?* and also said *Tell me what I want to know right now, or I'll fill your toothpaste tube with mayonnaise again.*

"How old are you?" she asked again.

That one was easier to answer than what would come after. "Twenty-eight."

She opened her mouth, shut it, her eyes going distant like they did when she was coming to terms with something she didn't want to come to terms with. Finally she looked at him again. "I've lost eight *years* of my life?"

"Not exactly." He lifted her right wrist, turning it to show her the message she'd written on her inner forearm. The one that, in typical Nyx fashion, she hadn't noticed yet. She'd always paid attention to everything around her before she ever paid attention to herself.

She read the simple words over and over again. "The griffin kept trying to get me to look at my arm." She blew out a breath. "I thought he was trying to distract me from getting away."

"You were with Griff when this happened?" How had she come here if she'd been inside the Station? And how badly was Griff losing his mind worrying over her right now?

Her brow creased in a frown. "The griffin's name is Griff?"

A smile teased at his lips. "You're the one who named him."

"And he just went with it?"

"I think he finds it endearing."

She took her arm back, clutched the pillow tighter to her stomach. "This is crazy."

"Yeah, well, not as crazy as this." He stopped putting it off and just told her. Haltingly and scattered at first, then finding his stride. And he could see by the way her face shut down that he'd been right. No wild theory running through her head was as bad as: *Your mother Hid your own identity from you. She dumped you in Dead Earth and then I forgot you and now your brain is on a collision course with itself.*

He didn't tell her that he'd had a choice in leaving her. What good would it do? She needed to know what was happening to her, but right now, he was the only person on this planet she remembered that she could trust. And judging by the expression on her face, he didn't know if even that was enough.

N yx fiddled with the bracelets on her arms, trying to take it all in. Especially the part where she knew Seth wasn't telling her something. It was the inflection in his voice, the slight hesitation before he'd explained that he'd forgotten her, too, before the Hiding had begun to fail and he'd come back.

She didn't ask. She wasn't sure she could handle anything more. What her mother had done to her—it had happened years ago, but to her, it felt like something that was *going* to happen. Like he was telling her the future, except she was sitting in the future and it was actually the present, and it was fucking confusing.

As for the rest of what he'd told her, about where they were and why they were here, about how *she* had to have gotten here…that didn't feel real at all. Her mother used to tell her bedtime stories about the Kumir—well, Nyx pretended they were bedtime stories, because it was the closest Elena Fortuna had ever come to doing something motherly—and that's what the Kumir had always felt like to Nyx: fiction.

She knew Elena was terrified of them, had seen it in the way her mother would pale before she caught herself and became angry instead. It was the telling of those stories, that slight slip of reaction, that had made Nyx wonder if maybe her mother was angry all the time because the alternative was being frightened all the time.

And now Seth was telling her that, not only did the Kumir exist, but Nyx had had multiple tangles with them. Moreover, he'd been *trying* to find them, and now she'd followed him to a planet far from home. One she wasn't supposed to be on because her memory complications could easily get them all killed.

None of it felt real. It felt like a nightmare and she wanted to wake up. She wanted Seth to stop giving her that hesitant look, like he was waiting for her to snap.

He clasped his hands together. "Can you…say something?"

She laughed. Or she thought she did. It didn't sound right

when it came out. And she knew she was supposed to be an adult now, but she didn't feel like one, and she didn't remember the experiences that had taken her to adulthood, so the one thing she couldn't get her mind off of was a ruined adolescent hope.

"It was supposed to get better," she whispered.

He didn't answer. Just watched her quietly, like he knew what she meant, what she felt, and he didn't have an answer for her.

"It was supposed to get better," she repeated. "My life. Your life. *Our* lives." Her breaths turned shallow, coming closer together. "We were going to leave and things were going to be better. We were going to be happy."

The words sounded so stupid. So childish and stupid, and her breaths were coming too fast because no matter how hard she tried, she'd never been able to hold back from crying. And stars, how she'd wanted to be able to. So she'd never have to see that sneer on her mother's face again, never have to hear her say, "Go ahead and cry your heart out. Run to that boy and cry. Let him hold you and tell you everything will be fine. He'll tire of it soon enough."

Seth reached for her. "It's okay. Everything's going to be—"

"Fine?" She laughed through those stupid, stupid tears that still wouldn't stop. "What about this is fine? Nothing got better. Everything got worse." She looked at him and asked the question she didn't want to. "Are we even... We didn't remember each other for seven years. Are you and I still...?" She couldn't finish the question.

He responded by tugging her onto his lap and squeezing her so tight she could barely breathe. She didn't relax. She couldn't. Because he hadn't answered. When he finally did, it wasn't what she wanted to hear.

"We're figuring it out."

From the other side of the door, Reyva called, "Beauregard says you've got five minutes, Hawthorne."

Nyx straightened, wiping her eyes. It was going to be

obvious she'd been crying, and she hated that, but she couldn't do anything about it. She couldn't change what had already happened.

She'd learned, in a life that had so much time for nothing but thinking, that focusing on a task was the best way to stop herself from thinking too much. If her day didn't have enough tasks, she made up new ones and convinced herself they were important and had to get done, because the alternative was slow insanity.

Right now, she didn't have to make up a task. There was a readymade one waiting for her on this planet, and the woman on the other side of the door already wanted her help with it.

"Why does Reyva think I can help her unlock a door?"

25

While Seth explained her "condition" to the others' satisfaction, Evra helped Nyx attach names to the faces in the room, since she was apparently already fully aware of Nyx's problems.

"And how do I know these people?" she asked.

Evra pointed at herself. "Best friend." Pointed at Morgen. "Friend." Pointed at Maruca, hesitated, and said, "Acquaintance." Pointed at Reyva. "Seth's former work partner." Pointed at Beauregard. "You and I once lead a group of Kumir onto his private property."

"We did what?"

"It was your idea. I wanted to run back to the Station but your cardio wasn't up to the task. I've been trying to rectify that physical weakness but you whine incessantly about being made to run."

"That...sounds like me," Nyx admitted. She much preferred horseback riding through the woods to running through the woods.

Seth finished his explanation, and Reyva's incredulous voice filled the room. "Let me get this straight. Her memory is fractured and she's randomly falling into pieces of it?"

"So I'm told," Nyx said. She'd never been good at being talked around like she wasn't in the room. She'd been happy to let Seth do the explaining about her memory, since at this point he probably understood it better than she did, but if that bit was done, she intended to be a part of the rest of the conversation.

"And you believe you are seventeen?"

Nyx tried not to bristle. "Look, I logically understand that I'm not, but yeah, that's all I know right now." She still might not have believed it if she hadn't tried to think back to an earlier point in her life—some memory of being five or twelve or any other age—and been unable to do it. And then felt her mind shaking and worked very hard to focus on being seventeen, so she didn't fall into another time.

"So you don't remember me? You don't remember the door?"

"Umm...no?"

Reyva turned on Seth. "How long until she's the Nyx I met again?"

"I don't know. It's not exactly on a schedule."

"Earlier, you stopped her from sliding out of this point. Why?"

"Why?" Seth echoed. "Did you listen to a word I said earlier? Because if she stops being rooted in her current age, there's no telling if she'll slide into the present or into a different point in the past. Because the more she does this, the less likely it is we can fix it, and you may not care about her sanity but I do."

Reyva reddened. "I didn't mean—It's not that I don't *care*, I just..."

"You just care about getting through that fucking door more. Yeah. I got that."

"Maybe," Morgen interrupted, "we should focus on the thing *this* Nyx can do? Like potentially get us out of here?"

Seth looked at her. "You sure about this?"

He was asking if she was sure about letting Beauregard, Maruca, and Reyva know that she was a portal witch. Which was, apparently, how she'd gotten here. The problem with her making this decision was that Seth could explain the dangers behind opening up the circle of people who knew that particular secret all he wanted to, but she wasn't the one it was going to affect. The results of the decision would be on that future Nyx, not her. She was a temporary incarnation, a fleeting moment in time, born less than two hours ago and destined to die in a few more.

"I'm not sure about anything. Maybe you three"—she pointed at Seth, Evra, and Morgen—"should take a vote."

No one answered.

"I'm being serious. You understand the dangers. I don't. You know them"—she indicated the three currently out of the loop—"I don't. You know the me that's going to be affected by this. I don't. Are you following the general direction I'm going with this?"

Morgen looked at Seth. "There's only one way she got here, mate, and everybody's going to come to the same conclusion. We may as well lay it out right."

"I agree," Evra said.

Seth's shoulders slumped a fraction, and when he spoke it sounded like he'd just bitten into something bitter. "She's a portal witch. She portaled here."

"The portal stones are not working." Beauregard's voice held an edge of suspicion. "I've seen them fail in this location, and unless my own kin have lied to me, they didn't work when you slipped back down to the lower levels to try, either."

"No one lied to you. Portal stones and portal witches aren't the same thing."

Morgen stepped in. "Take everything you think you know about portal magic and throw it out the window." Excitement buzzed beneath his voice. "We thought something within Nethrayne was negating any magic that attempted to exit the boundaries of the city, but what if what we actually have is an issue of competing dominance?"

Maruca frowned. "Like within the Stations?"

"*Exactly* like within the Stations. What if Nethrayne *is* the Station?"

"The entire city?" Maruca said. "It's not feasible. Given what we know about the Stations and their effects on individual longevity, I can't see the Council leaving anyone here longterm, were that the case."

Nyx really wished she had any idea what they were talking about.

"Not the entire city. Just pieces of it. Like the skeleton of the city, its support beams. Just enough to mean the usual suspects" —he took a stone out of his pocket and waved it back and forth —"don't work, but the *unusual* suspects"—he indicated Nyx— "can overcome it with the proper motivation."

Maruca was shaking her head. "You are smart, little brother, but this... The Stations are *buildings*. If the ley lines within them give them some measure of dominance, that is tied to the ley line entrance, four floors beneath us."

"Morgen's right," Seth said. Every pair of eyes in the room went to him.

Reyva's voice turned hard. "This is what you meant yesterday when you said we were fucked? You've known since then that we were in a Station and you didn't feel the need to mention it to anyone?"

"Because it didn't matter. We were stuck here, and either I could finally figure out how to make an illusion that would fool a Station, or I couldn't. You didn't need to know what it was."

"That wasn't your call to make."

"Quiet," Beauregard ordered. "While I dislike you keeping this knowledge to yourself, it is beside the point now. If the door is a part of the Station here, then we have everything we need to get through it right there." He pointed at Nyx.

So she was a resource on a game board now. Wonderful.

"No." Seth's voice was that particular calm it got when he'd made up his mind and no one was changing it. "She doesn't even remember the Station."

"Then we wait for her to remember," Reyva said.

"And if she stops being herself while we're walking around in public? She'll panic."

"Then you can cover it."

"And what if I can't? I completely tapped out after we got here. I've barely regenerated half my full capacity and—"

"Then we wait a few days for you to recharge. It's not that difficult, Hawthorne."

"I am *not* losing her here."

Nyx faded into the background while they all rushed to talk over each other at once. Beauregard and Reyva were debating with Seth the logistics of his magical range, and pointing out *Can't someone just grab the amnesiac girl if she goes crazy and runs off*. Morgen was enthusiastically trying to convince Maruca and Evra of something regarding portal magic.

An hour went by while they settled into what they probably called planning, but which sounded to Nyx more like talking in circles. She tried to include herself—looking at layouts of the city with them, their location within it, and the location of the final door that Reyva was pushing hard to take Nyx to—but she never really had anything to say.

She followed the flow of the conversation just fine. She understood what they were talking about when they weighed the risks and benefits of trotting her out to said door to see if she could open it. But she wasn't *part* of the conversation. They talked around her like she was...well, like she was the kid she felt like right now.

Eventually, she slipped away with an excuse about being hungry. She *was* hungry, but she hardly recognized any of the food in the kitchen. Variants of the base Human group mostly had the same tolerances for food, but mostly wasn't completely. Some variants ate things that were toxic to some other variants, so she didn't know what was safe.

Viktor had taught her the fundamentals of foraging for food in the wilderness she'd grown up in, but she hadn't exactly had textbook resources for foraging on other planets. There wasn't much point when she didn't have an encyclopedic memory capable of memorizing the basics for over a hundred other planets, all of which would have different biomes and the different plants and animals that went with them.

She'd just let out a soft growl of frustration when Seth slipped into the kitchen. He reached around her into the spelled cold box, extracted a container and handed it to her. "I made it this morning."

She took it on reflex, but it sparked something angry in her. "I don't need you to do everything for me."

Like she was a kid and he wasn't so he had to take care of her. She knew it wasn't what he'd meant by it, but the fact that she felt so young and he looked so much older and she *did* actually need help figuring out something as basic as what to eat rubbed her the wrong way.

"I know."

The calm response also irritated her. Because she'd always had the tendency to bottle up emotions until they came bursting free, and ninety-nine times out of a hundred, he was still calm as a clear sky when she went off.

"I can take care of myself."

"I know." A hint of a smile at the corner of his lips, like he'd forgotten she could be this way, and he found it cute. She didn't want him to find her cute. At least, not like this.

It sent a pulse of anger through her, and that pulse wasn't metaphorical. It felt like something rippling through her veins.

"Well, that hasn't happened in a while." He caught her hand, holding it up so she saw the lines of black running beneath her skin like veins.

She almost dropped the container of food. He extracted it from her, saying, "Just being cautious. Last time this happened, you shattered my favorite mug."

"What *is* happening?"

"You're pissed off."

She glared at him. "No shit. I meant this." She waved her hand, indicating the black lines beneath the skin.

"I know what you meant. Let's just say you came back from your first intergalactic trip with a souvenir." He brushed his fingertips across her cheek, and when she realized it wasn't only her skin he was touching, she jerked her own hand up.

Cool stone greeted her fingertips, little pieces embedded into her skin, starting in the center of her cheek and spiraling out. "I want a mirror," she gritted out. So far, every time she'd stated that, someone found a reason to distract her. Like she'd be so horrified at seeing what she looked like that the world would end or something.

But this time he just took her to one, and her face really didn't look that much different to her save for the spiky black thorns in it. He told her how she'd gotten them and about the effect they had on her.

"They make me angry?"

"Heighten emotion, from what I understand." He grinned at her. "You just have a violent streak most people don't see. It's buried underneath the innocent face."

She rolled her eyes. "And you didn't think to mention I might have a higher propensity toward violent outbursts? Or did you just think this version of me wouldn't be around long enough for it to be worth it to explain?"

"I kind of just forgot. I'm used to seeing them now and, like I said, this hasn't happened in a while. You met someone else who had the same thing happen to them. They said you could learn to control it, and I think you did, but I also think maybe the Station was mitigating their effect on you."

"Seth?" Reyva called from the main room. "Can you come look at this?"

"Does she need *you* specifically?" Nyx grumbled. She might not have been around here long, but it wasn't that difficult to interpret the way Reyva looked at Seth. Or the way she'd looked at finding Nyx here, even if she'd covered it over with enthusiasm for the mystical door problem Other Nyx was supposed to be able to solve.

"I don't have to go."

Sure. Then he would be playing nursemaid to poor, sick Nyx who couldn't even remember her own age or where she was. She'd never particularly liked being taken care of. When her mother took care of her, Elena did it resentfully. When Viktor took care of her it was because it was a task her mother wanted him to do and he—there was something wrong with Viktor's devotion to Elena Fortuna. Something unnatural.

It wasn't a surprise Nyx had never wanted the care either of them had to give. As for when Seth did it, well, she didn't mind that so much except that it never felt like a choice. Someone had to take care of them both and he was the older one, so he'd figured out the things that needed doing and he'd done them.

He'd always done it of his own accord, but she wasn't clueless. She'd felt, at times, the resentment underneath some of that, even if that resentment was never really directed at her, but just at their situation.

"Go on," she said. "I'm going to eat."

He hesitated. "Maybe you shouldn't be alone."

Her shoulders stiffened. "There's one door out of this place and you'll all be between me and it. I'll be fine."

She retrieved the food container, found what looked like a more slender version of a spork to go with it, and left before Seth could overthink it.

26

The domicile they were staying in belonged to someone named Hyalene Vori. As one of Nethrayne's most valuable scientists, Vori and her family were allowed the luxury of one two-week, off-planet vacation every three-point-five Earth years, and Seth's hacking of this level's directory archives had shown they were currently on it.

Apparently there'd been two other individuals also off-planet, but Vori was the only one with a home that had enough room for all of them. *More* than enough room. The scientist lived here with her three wives, two husbands, and their six children. She was apparently paid very well because everyone had their own room, and plenty of shared spaces. In addition to the common room, where Seth and the others were currently gathered, there was also a swimming pool, a library, two rooms that looked like offices, the kitchen, a dining area, and the indoor garden Nyx was currently entering.

And by entering, she meant descending the short six-foot ladder into. It was a sunken garden, the plants filling a circular room as big as the entire cabin she'd grown up in, and it was brimming with life. Everywhere she looked was a riot of color and, near as she could tell, color was the only metric by which the plants had been chosen. They clustered together in sections divided by those colors—all blue or purple, orange or green, white or yellow.

Through the snowy white fronds of what looked like stubby, bleached-out palm trees, she caught a vivid glow of orange-red. She walked toward it, brushing the fronds aside to find a thick glass window. It was an exterior window that looked out onto the planet beyond.

Morgen had told her Nethrayne had a surface covered in a lava ocean, but she hadn't quite been prepared to look out a window and see it. Building a city here was clearly taking paranoia to new heights. The sheer magical expenditure necessary to insulate the city against the extreme surface temperatures, to keep the support structures of the city from melting and collapsing... She sincerely hoped whoever was in charge of making sure that magic kept working was doing their job.

She let the fronds go and returned to the small pond in the center of the room. Brightly colored fish darted around in the clear water. She took off her boots and socks, rolled up her jeans, and slid her feet into the water.

Yes, she was taking a chance that the fish didn't have piranha-like tendencies, but she figured no house that had six children under the age of twelve would have dangerous fish without safety measures in place. It didn't matter how well you warned the children, it just wasn't a risk parents took. At least, it wasn't a risk parents in the books she read would take. Elena would probably toss her right in.

Nyx pulled the lid off the container of food and decided she was being uncharitable. Elena wouldn't throw her into a lake of piranhas. And if Nyx were to fall into one, while Elena might not rescue her personally, she *would* send Viktor or Seth to do it.

Nyx just didn't know why. The woman was stubbornly dedicated to Nyx's continued existence while to all appearances being thoroughly irritated by that existence.

She sighed, dug her spork into the container's contents, and took a bite. An explosion of flavor hit her tongue. The base of the dish was a grain with a smooth, nutty flavor, tossed together with vegetables and spices. She had no idea what any of it was, but it was delicious and she finished off the container in under ten minutes.

Pleasantly full, she leaned back on her elbows, kicking her feet slowly in the water, and that was how Maruca found her. The redhead descended the ladder, eyed Nyx, then rolled up the bottoms of her own pants and sank her feet in alongside her.

They sat like that for a few minutes, silent, the comforting scent of earth and green growing things around them. The scents might be comforting, but the silence wasn't. It wasn't precisely *un*comfortable either, it was just…awkward.

Nyx couldn't get a handle on Maruca. She understood everyone else and how she related to them. Beauregard was here on a mission and that was his primary focus. He related to Nyx in a way that was mostly concerned with how her presence helped or hindered his chosen path. Reyva was similar, if a little more wary.

Being around Evra and Morgen was like…well, like being around close friends. Which Nyx took as a good sign since that's what they were supposed to be. Seth had been a little more vague as to how Nyx knew Maruca, where "a little more" meant he'd told her the woman's name, that she was Morgen's adopted sister, and that she was here to support both him and her uncle.

Since Nyx doubted the woman had happened upon Nyx just now by accident—it was really easy to see from above that Nyx was in here—she figured Maruca wanted something. The easiest way to get at that something—and to learn more about Maruca —was to make an obviously false assumption and see how she responded.

"So," Nyx ventured. "We're friends?"

Maruca let out a startled laugh. "No. No, we're definitely not friends." She cast her a sidelong glance. "The last time we saw each other, I hit you. Really hard."

Nyx looked for some indication that Maruca was messing with her, but she didn't find one. Maruca struck her as that kind of person who was bluntly honest, to the extent that people found her rude. The kind of person who didn't seem to have any empathy but that was only because they didn't express empathy in the way most people expected.

So Maruca had hit her. That was interesting. "Did I deserve it?"

Maruca had a look in her eyes like she was about to snap back something unflattering, checked herself, and said, "I thought you did, at the time."

"And now?"

"Now… Now I find my life isn't as black-and-white as I wanted it to be." She leaned forward, forearms resting on her thighs, hands clasped together as she stared into the water. "I always thought life was a simple matter of making the right choices. If you made them, no one ever got hurt. Or if they got hurt, it wasn't your fault because you had done everything right, and no one could point to your actions and say, 'There, that's where you went wrong.'

"And then—" She shook her head. "Then my neat and orderly life got thrown into chaos. I made what I thought were the right choices and everything still went to shit. But then it all had to go a step more sideways and shove in my face that sometimes there isn't a *good* choice, just the best choice you can make at the time. And sometimes that choice still sucks."

Nyx couldn't help but be a little transfixed by this glimpse into inner turmoil. Because she'd had so few relationships of any kind, she'd always been fascinated by other people's lives. When she'd first started sneaking out into Dead Earth, she'd been so overwhelmed by the sheer number of people that she'd Hidden herself, finding it easier to explore this new world when no one else could notice her. It had become a habit, after a while, to simply observe other people without any emotion attached.

Maruca talking was a little like that now, like a story that hadn't been finished yet, and Nyx couldn't help but wonder, "What choice did you make?"

Pale fingers clenched tight and went even paler, the knuckles white. "I broke a kid's heart because I didn't know any other way to save him. Didn't know any other way to get him away from *me* before I ruined his entire life." She looked up suddenly, like she'd forgotten who she was talking to. "Are you going to remember this conversation when you're back to yourself again?"

Nyx could lie, but she was terrible at it. "Yep."

"Fuck." Maruca watched the brightly colored fish dart around beneath the water's surface. "You don't have any reason to do me a favor, but you like Kalvar, so do him one. Don't tell him anything I just said."

She didn't have any idea who Kalvar was, but what could it hurt? "Okay."

Maruca shook her head, something like disgust on her face. "See, that's why I have so much trouble with you. You're so *nice.*"

"I'm not always." She could be ugly, but she fought those urges. She was all too acutely aware that her mother's constant anger lived in her, too, and she didn't want to be like Elena Fortuna. So that anger stayed leashed and she tried to think through her responses to everything from every point of view before she made them. She didn't always succeed and sometimes that anger, so long repressed, snapped out of her when she least wanted it to, at the only person she had to vent it on.

Maruca studied her, like she was sussing all that out. "No. I don't suppose anyone is."

"If it helps, that probably means you aren't all that mean."

Maruca snorted. "Maybe. You know, I came back to Earth—to your Station—to make sure the men in my family didn't get themselves killed, but it was an excuse, too. I wanted to apologize to you, but I didn't know how." She gave a humorless smile. "So, naturally, I didn't actually do it."

"Why do we dislike each other?"

Maruca sighed. "I take it Seth didn't tell you about Kaden?"

Nyx shook her head.

"Of course he didn't. Kaden is my little brother."

"How much younger?"

Maruca smiled. "Seventeen minutes and forty-three seconds, and I never let him forget it." The smile faded. "Our parents died when we were five. At least, we assume that's what happened. They left for work one day and they never came home. We hid it from everyone for a while, afraid we'd be separated, and I made him a promise: that no matter what happened, I would never leave him alone.

"We were the only family each other had. Even when we finally got caught out and Morgen's mother took us in, even once there wasn't a reason to be afraid anymore, we still were. Or at least, *I* was.

"And I'd found a purpose in that darkness of us being alone. An identity, I guess. I was Kaden's big sister. It was my job to protect him. So even once we were safe, I didn't know how to let go of that. Or maybe I didn't want to. Maybe both.

"It was easy to add Morgen to the mix, a second little brother to look after. They'll tell you it was all their idea, but I'm the one who convinced them to join the Enforcers. If you sign up as a unit they'll let you stay together, so long as all of you pass the requisite training. I could keep on playing my self-assigned role.

"Then something happened. Something that wasn't anyone's fault, just Kaden and Morgen being in the wrong place at the wrong time, and Kaden had to disappear for a while. I expected him to reach out to me when it was safe. I guess…I don't know, I guess I expected him to still need me.

"But he *didn't* need me anymore. He didn't reach out. He'd outgrown the roles of our childhood and I hadn't, because as long as I hid in that, I didn't have to think too hard about anything else. I didn't have to think too hard about *my* life.

"I didn't see him for three years, and when we did reconnect, it was because he'd landed in a pretty bad place and I went after him. Long story short, when I finally met you? I was pissed off about pretty much everything in my life. And then I found out that two out of those three years Kaden was gone, he spent with you. I guess you seemed like a nice target for every unpleasant feeling I was having.

"Kaden was…he'd been through a lot and it had lingering effects, and I blamed you for it when it wasn't your fault. I'm sorry for that."

Nyx's exhausted, overworked brain was scrambling to put everything Maruca had said together. "What do you mean?"

"Just what I said. I'm sorry. I never gave you the benefit of the doubt on anything. It was easier to hate you. I guess it would mean more if I was saying it to the version of you that remembers the complete bitch I was, but…" She shrugged. "This you is easier to apologize to."

"No—I mean, thanks for the apology, I think, for whatever you did that I don't remember, but what do you mean your brother spent two years with me?"

"Oh." Maruca's nose wrinkled. "That. You dated my brother."

Denial rose swiftly. "That's not— I mean, I wouldn't have— Seth and I…" She trailed off.

Maruca took one look at her face and snorted. "Relax. I don't think it can reasonably be called cheating if you didn't remember Seth existed."

"Yeah." Nyx was still having trouble with it though. Not the part where she'd had another relationship, though that didn't quite feel real to her, but the part where she'd been left alone to have it in the first place.

Earlier, she'd been caught up in the loss of what Seth had told her. The loss of herself, of her memories, of *him*. Now she found herself stuck on the *why*.

Why take her identity? Why abandon her? Why *any* of it?

Had her mother told her the answer to those questions before she'd ripped everything away?

Nyx was searching for the answer, reaching before she realized what she was doing, and too many things were shaking free at her touch. Buried things, eager to rise to the surface, pelting into her like hail, and there was no way to avoid it. She crashed into them, one after the other after the other, her mind a kaleidoscope of cascading timelines.

Nyx huddled in a formless place, shaking and exhausted. She felt the press of forces on every side, weighty spheres dragging at her, pulling her in opposite directions.

She couldn't remember how she'd gotten here. She couldn't remember where *here* even was, or what the spheres pressing in on her were. Each one felt different and yet familiar, promising that if she simply chose the right one, the spinning in her head would finally stop.

Half a dozen spheres swam toward her. She shrank away from them, as if touching one would start a domino effect and send her spiraling again. Another pressed at her back, this one more familiar than the rest. Recent, like she'd chosen it before.

The six spheres at her front pushed closer and she shuddered. Better the devil she knew, even if she didn't know *what* she knew. She kicked back, plunging into the sphere behind her—

—and came to on the cold floor of the kitchen, Seth's hands cradling her face.

"Nyx?" There was panic in his eyes.

"It's okay. I'm okay." She slumped against the wall behind her, not certain if the words were true. The wall shifted. It was also lumpy. She tilted her head back and found herself looking up the length of a long, muscled body. "Oh," she said weakly. "Hey Evra."

The blonde Amazon frowned at her. That seemed to be par for the course, near as Nyx could tell. It was almost like frowning was an affectionate gesture, coming from her.

"How did I get here? The last thing I remember was talking to Maruca in the garden."

Seth's hands, still framing her face, tightened. "You're in the same memory island you were in earlier? Seventeen? You remember coming here?"

"Falling onto your bed and getting told my life's all fucked up? Yeah, I remember." Seth shared a look with Morgen, and neither of them appeared happy. "What, is it not supposed to work like that?"

"No," Seth said. "It's not supposed to work like that. Once you've been at one time period it's supposed to go back where it belongs."

She decided not to tell him that it felt like, not only had this one not gone back where it belonged, but inhabiting this particular island felt like sitting in the eye of a storm. "This is what I get for wanting to be special," she mumbled.

"What's that?" Evra said.

"Nothing." She shoved to her feet and would have promptly fallen back down if Seth hadn't caught her. She focused very hard on staying upright and forming words. "I think I'm tired. Can we go to bed?"

Her eyelids fluttered shut, and it was everything she could do to force them back open. Seth dipped, one arm slipping beneath her legs as he hoisted her up.

"I hate being carried." The words were even more mumbled than her last ones. She was so tired she could barely think.

"Deal with it." Seth hauled her into his room, kicked the door shut, and deposited her onto the bed, wrapping himself around her. "Try not to fall into a bunch of different times again. You kept us all on our toes for the last two hours."

"Don't remember that," she said sleepily.

"I know." His arms tightened around her, and he pressed a kiss to her hair. "You scared the shit out of me, Nyxi."

Sorry. The word was on the tip of her tongue, but she was too tired to get it out, falling blissfully into sleep.

She woke again sometime later, still feeling seventeen, and still locked in Seth's arms. Only now she was terrified, too. Terrified of those hours she'd lost between talking to Maruca and coming back to herself on the kitchen floor, of every other aspect of her life she couldn't remember.

The only thing she could remember, the only thing that was constant, and safe, was Seth. She turned in the circle of his arms and he jolted awake, that now-familiar worry in his eyes.

She didn't want him to worry about her. *She* didn't want to be worried. She wanted the world to stop for a few minutes, a few hours. She wanted to forget the world existed and that everything was wrong.

And there was only one thing that had ever made that happen. She pressed her mouth to Seth's, drinking in his lips, the taste of him, so familiar and yet so different. He kissed her back and the world blurred, and she was sinking into that perfect place where only they existed and nothing else mattered.

She hitched her leg over his hip and deepened the kiss, her tongue sliding into his mouth and—

—and then his hands were on her waist, holding her back instead of pulling her into him. "Nyxi, we have to stop."

"Why?" He'd said things were complicated, but this part of them had never been complicated.

"I'm twenty-eight," he said gently.

"Which means I'm twenty-six."

"Your body's twenty-six. But right now you're seventeen."

She closed her eyes, not wanting to admit that he had a point. So she admitted something else instead. "I'm scared."

"So am I."

"I'm scared, and I *miss you.*" It was a feeling she'd never had before. He'd never been far enough away *to* miss, and her memory might be saying she was seventeen and had never been without him, but the rest of her felt an aching emptiness inside, as if her body remembered the years he said they'd been parted even when she didn't.

"I miss you too, baby." He pressed a kiss to her forehead, and said the same thing he always did on nights when she couldn't settle, lying awake wrapped in more anxiety than she could hold. "Go to sleep, Nyxi darling. It could all be different in the morning."

She guessed those words had finally proved true. It was all different, now. She just didn't remember how it had gotten that way.

27

Nyx woke in a cage. A warm, Seth-shaped cage, the bars of which consisted of his leg thrown over hers, foot dug under her calf, his arm tucked so tight around her ribs it was a miracle she could breathe.

Her head hurt, like a hangover, dehydration, and caffeine withdrawal had all conspired to form one ultimate headache. She also had that muzzy, enervated feeling weighing her body down, as if her limbs belonged to a robot running low on battery power, and if she tried to move she would only succeed in doing so in jerky, stumbling lurches.

For once in her life, she'd *like* to say she didn't remember what had happened, or how she'd ended up being held under arm and leg. But now that she was back to her Present Day Self, she remembered just fine. Crashing through dozens of small, mostly-broken memory islands before hopping back into the one of her seventeen-year-old self that she'd already inhabited.

It bothered her that going into it once hadn't put it neatly back into the puzzle board in her mind. It bothered her that she could still feel it, like a sore tooth waiting to push free. The same way she could feel some of the others she'd passed through last night.

As if she hadn't stayed in any of them long enough to settle them back into her mind, and since the skeleton of her mother's dead magic no longer held them they were simply orbiting around her, waiting, held at bay by nothing more than her remaining determination to stay in a single state of mind. She wondered how long it would take for mental exhaustion to kick in and her to end up in another state like last night, flitting between ages.

But as much as feeling the loose pieces worried her, they also gave her some hope. After all, Tobi had said the mind wasn't the body. The Congregation had given her their best guess on what would happen in her mind—how and when it would happen— but they could be wrong. They already had been wrong, on some things. So maybe they were also wrong about her losing it alto- gether, about her not having any control over how this happened.

She'd already proved she had *some,* when Seth had told her to stay where she was yesterday, and she'd managed to do it. So maybe…

She sighed. Seth came awake at the small noise, limbs clamping more firmly around her.

"Not that I'm really complaining, but you can stop imperson- ating a boa constrictor, if you want. You have Present Day Me, for however long that lasts."

He nuzzled the side of her neck. "Don't take this question the wrong way, but can you prove it?"

"I have a mass murderer locked in the Station's basement." He hadn't mentioned that particular tidbit to any of her incarna- tions. There really hadn't been any point in going into that much detail with someone who wouldn't be around that long.

"That'll do it. Though I'm not sure how Kaliaris would feel about you calling their Heart a basement."

"You've never been there. It was exceptionally basement-like before the Queen of Wrath moved in, all dark and dank and vine-filled. Very creepy."

"I think you're confusing basements with cellars."

"Pretty sure I'm not."

"Some people have really nice basements."

"Spent a lot of time I don't know about in basements?"

He tickled her in lieu of an answer. She was extremely ticklish, and the move resulted in her making an undignified sound probably best classified as a squeal, though she didn't want to admit it. By the way it brought two sets of footsteps pounding and throwing open the door, you would have thought she'd screamed like an actress in a horror film.

At seeing her laughing, Morgen and Evra both looked embarrassed. Okay, no, only Morgen looked embarrassed. Nyx didn't think Evra knew the meaning of the expression as it might relate to the Amazon's own face.

"We're fine," Nyx said. "I am neither being murdered nor am I murdering Seth."

"I'm delighted to hear that," Morgen said. "Which Nyx do I have the pleasure of addressing this morning?"

"The one who built you your very own mad scientist's lab."

Evra let out a breath of relief. "Finally."

"Real sorry I couldn't make an earlier appearance, but, you know"—Nyx indicated her head—"it's a little confusing up here."

"How long are you likely to be here?"

"No idea. So we should probably come up with a plan before I disappear again." Seth's grip on her tightened, but he didn't say anything. "Since the portal stones aren't working, Beauregard said that after getting to the Kumir, your best plan was to make your way back to the Station, right?"

Morgen and Evra shared a look. "Right."

"I'm guessing that look you just gave each other is because you know trying to get back to the Station is a stupid idea? Even if you make it, which is a big if considering the hell that is going to break loose if you succeed in taking out the Kumir, you can't compel the Station Guardian here to let you leave.

"You've been here too long to return under your false identities, and your real ones aren't cleared for Departure."

"We're aware of that. We just don't have a better plan. Or rather, I have a single hastily thrown-together plan that has a low chance of success."

Nyx made a go-on gesture.

"While the portal stones have been unable to open a portal in any of the areas we've been on Nethrayne, they have come closer to it in some places rather than others. This would make sense if my theory about the Station forming the framework of the city is correct. Which means—"

"You might be able to find a part of the city where the Station's dominance is weak enough for a portal stone to work."

"Yes."

"How many do you have left?" Nyx asked.

"Fifteen," Seth answered. "It's not a lot, but…" He shrugged, as if to say, "Better than nothing."

"I…might have a better idea. Do you know why the portal stones work?" She was talking mostly to Morgen, because he was her magic theory expert. At the shake of his head she said, "It's because they're anchor points."

"Anchor points?"

"Yeah. Jevryn sent me a book. Anyway, an anchor point can be used as a kind of shortcut, which cuts down on the amount of magic needed to reach that place. It also means that if a portal witch gets lost somewhere, an anchor point can act as an easy way to return to a known location. A lot of portal witches use locator spells tied between them and a chosen location, but it can be any magic that's tied to you and another place." She cleared her throat and glanced at Seth. "Or another person."

He raised his eyebrows. "You made me into an anchor point?"

"Not intentionally, but yeah."

Evra frowned. "How?"

"I Hid part of him."

Morgen coughed. "Little Guardian, remind me to never make you angry."

Heat rose in her cheeks. "I didn't Hide *that*. Get your mind out of the gutter. Geez."

"Then what did you Hide?"

"Something else. Something that's none of your business."

"You realize that only makes it sound even dirtier, right?"

Nyx grabbed one of the bed's fluffy pillows and flung it at him. "His heartbeat, okay? I Hid his damn heartbeat so I'd know he was alive."

Morgen caught the pillow. "Oh. I can't make fun of you for that."

Nyx glared. "Point being, I think I was able to get here because I had that anchor point. With the amount of portal magic I had and that connection, along with the likelihood that there are only tendrils of the Station in this area, it gave me enough to fight its dominance long enough to get through."

"But if the portal stones are also anchor points," Morgen said, catching on to where she was going with this, "why can't they overcome the Station's dominance in the same way?"

"Because they aren't very *good* anchors. The Council wanted to seed an idea that would give the portal witches left in the universe an outlet for their abilities, without ever letting them realize there was more to what they could do. Using a rock from another planet is an easy anchor, because it's a piece of that planet, so it's tied to it. But the best anchors aren't *from* the place you want to go, they're actually *at* the place you want to go. Like Seth was here."

"Like," she continued, "the anchor point I have on Earth, just outside the Station."

"I like where you're going with this, little Guardian, but didn't you say it took almost all of the portal magic you had to get here?"

"It did," she agreed. "But I do have *some* left. More importantly, I have fifteen other anchor points to Earth."

"Ohhhh," he said, drawing the word out.

"Oh, what?" Evra asked.

"She can break the portal stones as a starting point for opening the connection to *her* anchor point, using the portal magic she has left to hold the way open. In theory, if she breaks the portal stones in succession, while holding the connection with some of her own magic, each anchor point should amplify the one before it. The abundance of anchors might allow her to hold the portal open without the same amount of magic she needed to get here."

"Then do it." Seth dug a handful of stones from his pocket and held them out.

She didn't take them. "Are you coming with me? Are you *all* coming with me?"

Seth and Evra didn't answer. Morgen said, "Uncle Beau won't leave. And if he's not leaving, Ruca and Reyva won't either."

She sighed. "And you're not leaving without them, and Evra's not leaving without you, and Seth's not leaving without both of you. Do you need a Magic 8 Ball to know I'm also not leaving without all of you?"

"Magic 8 Ball?" Evra repeated. She had that look on her face that said she knew this was an Earth thing, but knowing that didn't help her understand it in any way.

"I'll buy you one when we get home."

"Which will be now," Seth said, "because if you can go right now, then you are."

She shook her head.

"What happened to understanding you're a liability in your current condition?" He said it harshly, and even knowing that he did it on purpose, that he was trying to hurt her so she *would* go, it still cut.

"That was before I was your only good chance at getting home. I'm not going without you, and you can't make me, so get over it."

He cursed and shoved the portal stones back into his pocket. "You're as stubborn as that damn mule we had."

"Sadie had her priorities right."

"Doesn't mean you do."

"Just because they're not *your* priorities doesn't mean they're wrong. Now do you want to tell me what the plan is and show me to the door Reyva can't crack, or do you want to argue about it until I have another brain quake and I'm a younger even more stubborn version of myself who doesn't remember how to use portal magic?"

"Fine," he gritted out.

She responded with excessive cheerfulness. "Great."

Evra broke the tension with, "Brain quake?"

Nyx shrugged. "The word seemed suitable."

28

Nyx held a mental map of Nethrayne in her head as they exited Vori's suite of rooms and entered the main hallway of this level. Nethrayne had five levels, large rings with primary halls cutting like ringed arteries through them. It felt very much like she thought being inside a space station, or an underground city, would.

Because of the extreme exterior temperatures, not a single window or door physically opened to the planet's atmosphere. Presumably, every exterior surface was coated in the insulating atmospheric spells that kept the heat from melting every piece of metal the city was built with. This was not the kind of place where fleeing the building in the event of an emergency was an option.

Each ring, or level, was divided into three parts. The work and residential sectors, which were self-explanatory, and the recreational sector, which housed shops, restaurants, and whatever entertainment could be had. The one and only pathway to the level above, where they would find the Kumir, was on the border between the work and recreation areas.

The location guaranteed high traffic, and therefore guaranteed that anyone walking the clearly marked corridor to the door that led to the upper level had a high likelihood of being noticed, remembered, and remarked upon later to any investigating parties. It also wasn't the kind of place where you could wait for the middle of the night, when things would be quieter, and hope to get there relatively unnoticed.

Nethrayne was a city that existed on a planet of constant daylight. Though the days here were apparently marked by a twenty-hour cycle, there were so many different people, from so many different species and planets, all of them keeping the day/night cycle they preferred, that in practice the city simply ran constantly.

They stopped at the cafe that marked the end of the recreation sector, placing orders and occupying an outdoor table as if they were just another group of friends hanging out after a long workday. It still boggled Nyx's mind that there were enough people on all of Nethrayne, much less on this single level, for their entire party to sit at the cafe without having to impersonate specific people. She'd thought of the level as a small town where everyone would know everyone, but when she'd brought up the issue Morgen had informed her that the population of Level Four was over twenty-thousand.

While that wasn't enough anonymity to risk sitting around wearing their own faces for anyone to recall, it was enough that they'd split the remainder of Seth's pre-made glamours to simply alter their features, saving his active pool of magic for when they really needed it.

They had only located one individual who had access to the fifth level, a scientist by the name of Etherin Lavall. He maintained a rigidly regular schedule, returning from his work on the upper floor at precisely the same time each evening. He was due to pass by any moment now, and his path back to his quarters would take him past this cafe.

Once they caught sight of him and confirmed he was gone, Seth would glamour Morgen in the scientist's likeness, while giving the rest of them the illusion of invisibility. That part made

Nyx nervous—he'd said he wasn't back up to full magical capacity yet. If she got confused and did anything stupid, he was working within a limited budget, so to speak. But the likelihood of her having problems only went up the longer they stayed, so it didn't make sense to sit on their hands for another day or two to let Seth power up.

The rest of the plan involved Morgen—impersonating Lavall and utilizing the Siren half of his abilities—distracting the guard at the elevator door with a detailed story of having forgotten something, while Nyx worked on the door.

They'd debated the alternate route of not impersonating Lavall, of Seth simply obscuring the fact anyone had gone through the door at all. But since it didn't have an alarm system Reyva could manipulate, if the door did log the fact that it had been opened, regardless of whether anyone saw it happen, they'd decided it was better for the guard to remember Lavall going through.

Which was why they were all sitting here, waiting for Lavall to make his daily appearance. Nyx's attention kept wandering back to Beauregard. The focused, almost manic energy he'd had since arriving on her Station back on Earth was…not gone, but tempered.

She had expected his agitation to worsen the closer they came to their goal, but the Beauregard before her didn't look like a man on the verge of vengeance three decades in the making. He looked lost. Pensive, almost haunted.

She couldn't shake the feeling that his reasons for being here were rooted in something deeper than the loss of his wife. Nyx didn't doubt the existence of that wife, as Morgen did, nor did she doubt that wife had been lost in some way to the Kumir. Even now, Beauregard rolled a silver, oval locket between his fingers, and Nyx suspected that if she looked inside, she would see a picture of that woman.

But she thought it took more than a death to drive a person to this. Even Laiveran's drive to the atrocities he'd committed hadn't simply been because Nyaera had died, but because she'd been trapped in an endless loop of agony that he had felt every moment of. That he might *still* be feeling, if Nyx had interpreted what he'd said in the Station's Heart correctly.

She wasn't equating Beauregard's actions with Laiveran's—they were two completely different responses—but the kind of drive it took to sustain their vendettas for this length of time was the same. One born and kept alive from something deeper and more complicated than simple death.

The subtle glances cast in Beauregard's direction from the others at the table told her she wasn't the only one thinking it. But Seth had told her that no amount of pushing, public or private, from anyone in their group had convinced Beauregard's lips to loosen on the subject. At the end of the day, if they were worried—and they were—they'd all made the decision to be here until they saw this through.

If she was afraid Beauregard didn't care if he came out alive on the other side of this, she had to hope he cared enough about keeping Morgen and Maruca alive not to do anything spectacularly stupid. None of them were going back, and she wouldn't leave them here, robbing them of the one admittedly bad chance at getting home that was her.

And no, the part of her that had been terrified to leave the Station because she was worried she couldn't get back was not on the verge of having an anxiety attack. Not in the slightest. She was totally, completely, one-hundred-percent fine.

If her palms were sweating and her heartbeat was up, that was just because they were about to break into a highly-secure area of a highly-secure city that belonged to a councilor.

"Show time," Morgen said.

Lavall strode down the aisle outside the cafe. He was a head shorter than Morgen, with medium-brown skin and straight, fuzzy eyebrows like twin caterpillars. He walked with a short, determined stride, his attention focused on the ground in front of him, as if he didn't want even the potential of making eye contact with another soul. As if his own soul was troubled, and he didn't know how to deal with it.

He passed the cafe and, one by one, the members of their group peeled off, heading for the restroom. Once they were all in, Seth got to work, turning Morgen into the man who had just walked past them, turning the rest of them into nothing.

After the fact, someone at the cafe might remember that seven people had gone into this restroom and only one had walked out, but by then it wouldn't matter. They'd either all be gone by then, or dead.

As he worked, Nyx could see the strain on Seth's face. He'd mastered the trick of making himself appear invisible when he was sixteen. But when he did that, it was only himself he was responsible for. His footfalls, his body, his breaths.

Now he'd added five other people to the mix. Five other sets of footfalls and breaths, keeping track of every movement in order to mask it, and he wasn't operating at his full magical capacity. Still, he wouldn't have said he could do it if he couldn't.

When he was ready, he nodded to the others. Who hesitated. To them, nothing had changed. They could see and hear each other—though no one was talking because they'd already talked about the need to avoid excess sound—because making them all disappear from each other's sight was a recipe for them stumbling into each other and creating more chaos that needed to be illusion-covered.

Nyx had to be the one to get them going. "Every second you stand here is more work for him."

They moved out. Morgen took the lead, the rest of them following in a single-file line behind him, Seth at the end where he could keep track of it all. Nyx walked just in front of him, marking the steadiness of his heartbeat through the Hiding she hadn't seen any reason to remove, and counting their steps.

Thirty from the cafe to the main hallway. Forty down the hallway, then a right turn down a corridor not wide enough for two people to walk down side by side. If they triggered an alarm, or if the guard waiting at the other end of the corridor did, a security gate would slide closed, blocking the end of the corridor they'd entered from, trapping them with no room to maneuver and plenty of time for security to show up.

Morgen, impersonating Lavall, had to be in the lead to reach the guard first. In an ideal world, Nyx would have been right behind him for easy access to the door. But since Seth had needed to be at the end of their party for the walk over, and Nyx needed to be near Seth in case she had a memory skip he needed to contain, she was at the end, too.

Everyone halted except for Morgen, who approached the guard with a sheepish expression on his face, spinning a story of having left something in his office. The story wasn't, strictly speaking, necessary. The scientists who had access to the top level of Nethrayne did not have the Earth concept of business hours. They came and went as they pleased, so even though Lavall had left a mere ten minutes ago, if he wanted to return now, that wasn't for this guard to question.

What the story gave them was time. Morgen's already melodic voice grew even more so as he slipped the barest fraction of his Siren ability into the words. Such a subtle, barely nonexistent trace that it took root easily, enough to prevent any concern the guard might have had as Morgen fed steady drops of power into it.

When they'd discussed this part of the plan, Nyx had been surprised there weren't systems in place to prevent it. Sirens weren't a rare race, so it followed one might want to protect against that branch of magic. She'd been imagining a ward of some kind that picked up on specific magic use and either prevented it or set off an alarm. After all, if there were wards to prevent entry to a place, why not wards of a different kind?

She'd been thinking too technically, as it turned out, thinking of magic like a computer system where traps could be set. If X happened then Y would follow. Magic wasn't like that. Some people, like Morgen, could feel and categorize magic to a higher extent than others. He could look at a working and tell how it was done and what magic was used to get there.

But he was the exception, not the rule, and while it wasn't *impossible* to create something that might detect a Siren's ability in use here, there were dozens of other magical branches, all equal security risks, which would all need their own individual detector. While there was no doubt this area was of enough importance to whichever councilor ran Nethrayne to warrant dozens of magical detectors, the problem with magic was that it tended to entangle itself. Place those dozens of detecting spells, which needed to remain separate in order to function, and they would find a way to merge sooner rather than later, becoming useless in the process.

The real deterrents on Nethrayne were the ones that made it so difficult to reach this point that no Siren unregistered on Nethrayne should have gotten here in the first place. Not to mention pureblood Sirens were the only race with blue skin, and therefore were easy to spot.

Also, as Morgen had said, most Sirens operated with a blunt force approach. Hit a person with enough magic and they crumpled. It usually worked, but it left a trail. And if a person, such as the guard before them, was resistant enough, they would have time to at least recognize they were being magically attacked and request backup.

To Nyx's knowledge, Morgen had never operated with blunt force. He charmed, first with ordinary words and his smiles and his winning personality, and then with magic. He was, to her mind, the definition of a Siren, luring people under his spell so smoothly they didn't even notice they were drowning.

He'd laughed when she'd told him as much, and joked that he simply had to work twice as hard because he was only half Siren. But watching the guard fall under his spell now, she thought she'd had the right of it. The man had gone a little glazed in the eyes, looking eager to please, rapt with attention as Morgen droned on about his supposed absentmindedness.

Nyx waited until Morgen gave a slight go-ahead motion with his fingers. The others had plastered themselves flat against the wall, but she still had to turn sideways and sidestep to move past them down the corridor without tripping or creating a lot of noise for Seth to cover.

He followed, and it didn't matter how good she knew he was, she still held her breath when they reached the door. The landing outside it was hardly larger than the corridor, the passage widening just enough to create a depression for the guard to stand in. With Morgen standing next to him, it left little more than a foot of space for her, still turned sideways, to squeeze in behind him.

Instinctively, she tried to feel the Station and felt nothing. If Seth and Reyva hadn't been so adamant that their experiences with it were like those in Kaliaris, she would have said this was just a door. Standing next to it didn't feel like being on the border of Kaliaris, didn't feel anything like her Station's sphere of influence.

Because this wasn't *her* Station, and she wasn't bonded to it. But when she pushed harder, stretching her senses as if she was reaching for Kaliaris, she did feel *something*. An inkling of a presence beyond herself that was the sentience of the Stations themselves. She glanced at Seth, who nodded to say, *Go ahead, I've got this.*

She couldn't control this Station. She couldn't command them. She didn't know if they could catch her intent without words, the way Kaliaris sometimes could. The only thing she knew to do was talk to them. To hope that they would hear her and believe what she said. To further hope that their Avatar, who would hear her words alongside them, would do the same.

She placed her hand gently against the door, like she might place it on someone's shoulder, and whispered, "Kaliaris says hello."

The words were an opening gambit, and she waited to see how they would be received. She didn't know if the Stations could talk to each other. She did know, from what Calista had said about their own sundering from the ley line network, that the Stations could at least feel one another.

She waited for some response, some indication that she had been noticed. None came. Maybe they hadn't heard her. Perhaps these tendrils of the Station that stretched through Nethrayne were so far from its Heart that it would take her words time to reach them. Or perhaps the words never would. Perhaps this Station slept, as Griff had told her Kaliaris sometimes did, control left in the hands of their Avatar while they whiled the centuries away.

All she knew to do was to keep talking. Keep trying. "I've spoken to Calista, too. They miss their connection to you. To the others. I'm Kaliaris' Guardian. I know that might not endear me much to you, because I know what you are. What you all are, and I am sorry.

"I'm sorry for everything you have lost and been made to endure. I'm sorry that as a Guardian, I am a part of that. I would free you from it, if I could. I am trying to find out how that might be done, but I need through this door to do that."

She waited. The faintest trace of warmth pulsed beneath her palm. Not an answer, not a question, a mere recognition of her speech. Probably the most the Station could directly answer her without their Avatar's help, which brought Nyx to the second problem.

She didn't need to convince only the Station—if she wanted this door to open, she needed to convince the Avatar as well.

"I know your control is not fully yours, but subject to your Avatar, who is subject in theory to your Guardian. But your Avatar can exercise discretion. Please talk to them. Ask them to hear me. Tell them I am working to free *them* too. But I cannot do that if my friends and I cannot get through this door."

She tried not to let her anxiety show as she waited for a

response—somehow she didn't think shuffling in place would fill this Station with confidence—but it was hard not to be anxious when, beneath her Hiding, she could feel Seth's heart rate slowly increasing. The strain of so much consistent illusion magic spread across multiple individuals was taking its toll. And she didn't know how long Morgen could keep up what he was doing without the guard finally getting the feeling, past Morgen's Siren lull, that something wasn't quite right.

"What is taking so long?" It was Reyva's voice, right behind Nyx, startling her into a jump. Seth's heart thumped a little faster, covering the new voice, the new movement. "If you cannot open the door, say so and we will regroup."

"I'm negotiating."

"That does not—"

"Reyva," Seth gritted out in the softest of whispers. "Please be quiet and stay still."

Maybe the wardbreaker heard the strain in his voice, because she did. Unfortunately for Nyx, Reyva obeying meant her staying right where she was. Right where she could hear everything Nyx might say.

Nyx couldn't help but wonder if that was what the woman had counted on. Reyva had been so frustrated by the door in the Station. Of course she wanted another chance to find out how she might get past what she would view as a failure of her own magic.

The Station felt Reyva's presence and recoiled, anger pulsing beneath Nyx's palm. Whatever Reyva had tried with Kaliaris— the thing that had *hurt* and brought Nyx running to curtail any further attempts—she must have tried here, too. And to a greater, likely more painful, extent if this Station's reaction was any indication.

"She won't hurt you again," Nyx soothed. "You have my word on that."

A sharp intake of breath from Reyva.

A wary flicker of heat from the Station, as if to say, *I'm still listening.*

She needed it to truly talk to her, but for that, she would need the Avatar. She couldn't *get* the Avatar, because she wasn't inside the Station. She was touching an extension of the Station. The Avatar could move *through* the door to talk to her, except they couldn't, because they weren't allowed outside the Station grounds, and this side of the door was *not* Station grounds.

She glanced at Seth. He held up two fingers. She had two minutes before they had to retreat or risk a failure in his illusions.

"If you won't let us through, I understand, just tell me so." She tapped twice on the door. "Two for no. One for yes."

Three pulses of warmth came back against her hand. She took them as a *maybe*. As a *convince me*.

What else could she offer? What else could prove her intent? Her hand went absently to her cheek, to the thorns embedded there. Seth's hand lashed out, caught her wrist and jerked it away from the thorns.

The look on his face said, "No. *Fuck* no, don't even think about it."

She rolled her eyes. She'd discarded the idea as soon as she'd had it. Tying herself to Kaliaris was one thing. Kaliaris was *hers*, and they still resented her for it. She wasn't leaving part of herself on Nethrayne, even if it would get them through this door. Which she wasn't certain it would.

She had one other thing. One other option. "I'm going to show you something you won't like. I'm not threatening you with it. But I am keeping it from the people who did this to you. If you can feel what I am, then you know what promises mean to me. So know that I have promised to destroy this, just as I've promised to free you."

She tugged the Harvester out and added the thinnest of exceptions to her Hiding, one meant for this Station alone. She pressed the small sphere to the door and the door—the wall —shuddered.

Searing heat shot through her palm and she jerked both hands away. She'd made the wrong gambit. Instead of convincing them, she'd pissed them off. She was turning to Seth, to motion for them to fall back, when the door shuddered again and slid open.

The beat of Seth's heart sped again as he rushed to cover the sudden movement of the door. Morgen made a self-deprecating comment about losing track of time and pressed his hand to the door's sensor, which Seth followed with an illusion of the door opening for the guard's benefit.

Nyx moved through. Morgen held the door, turning back to the guard for another Siren-laced exchange, giving Seth and the others time to follow. She didn't breathe normally until they were all on the other side, standing in a wide stairwell, the door firmly shut at their backs.

Nyx wasn't sure what she'd expected to find—the passage lined with Kumir every five feet, ready to take out any unauthorized persons?—but it wasn't the six-foot blue-and-white fox sitting placidly on the bottom steps, blocking the way forward.

29

White tufts adorned the fox's ears. Tails—Nyx counted nine of them—curved around her body, the fluffy tips covering her paws.

No one moved, trying to make Seth's glamouring job as easy as possible, but Nyx knew it didn't matter. The fox might not be able to *see* them, but it would have no trouble knowing exactly where they were through other senses.

Slowly, Nyx approached, putting herself in front of Morgen, who was still the only visible member of their party.

"Thank you," she told the Station's Avatar, "for letting us through."

Three of the nine tails twitched. "Do not thank me, for I have not yet decided what to do with you." She glanced at the exact spot where Seth stood. "You may cease wasting your magic, if you wish."

He did. Nyx didn't look behind her to see what anyone else was making of this. The entirety of her focus was on the Avatar, because now that they were here, she understood that this entire area was part of the Station. The rest of Nethrayne might have skeletal fingers, thin veins stretching through it, but here they blossomed into a full expression of the Station.

Here, the Avatar had control. For the first time, the flexibility of the Stations felt like a threat. Nyx might know how they functioned, but it did her little good here, where she had none of the control.

Neutrally, she asked, "Does your Guardian know you are here?" A question that really asked, *If they do, can I trust your Guardian? Have you brought us here only to trap us?*

"This matter does not concern my Guardian. This is between you and I and Altiran."

"Okay." *Altiran.* She relaxed a fraction, committing the Station's name to memory. "What do you want?"

"To know why you are here."

"I told you—"

"You told us of a promise. One it will take some time to reach Kaliaris to confirm. Still, it is such a one that the risk is worth taking. But that does not tell us why you are *here.* Do you know what the floor above contains?"

"The Kumir."

Another flick of the Avatar's tails, two this time, instead of three. "And do you know what the Kumir *are?*"

The obvious answer came to mind: assassins. But that wasn't what the Avatar was asking. "I'm…sorry. I don't."

The fox's eyes cooled. "Then you have no business here. The secrets that are kept here will not help you in the quest you've stated. And I would not let you bring more suffering to what dwells here than they already endure. Take your friends and leave."

"And if we don't?" Beauregard's booming voice.

The fox bared her teeth. "Then I will wake the inhabitants above and, in so doing, wake the hand behind them. I do not expect you will live very long, after that."

The fox turned, as if it was a foregone conclusion that they would not be so foolish.

"Wait," Beauregard said. "I can answer your question. Why we are here. What the Kumir are."

The fox turned back. "Can you? Very well."

Beauregard approached, removing the locket from around his neck as he did. He opened it and held it out to the Avatar, cupped in his palm where only they could view it. "This is what the Kumir are. What they once were, and what I would make them again. This is what has been taken from them."

A bad feeling spread through Nyx as the Avatar's gaze softened. A horrible suspicion crept into her mind. One that wouldn't have occurred to her before she realized that this floor, where the Kumir were held, was part of the Station. That it therefore existed on a nexus like her own, and would have prevented the Kumir from aging.

She'd asked herself what kind of drive could keep a man on a path for half his life and been certain it was more than simple death. As certain as she'd been that the locket Beauregard now held out to the Avatar contained a picture of his wife.

It made sense—the sadness that had been in Beauregard's eyes after the contingent of Kumir had died on his castle grounds. The obsession with finding the source of the Kumir, as opposed to slaughtering as many as he could find in the name of vengeance.

It made sense…and yet it made none. Because how could *one* woman be all of the Kumir?

"James Beauregard, then," the Avatar said. "Yours is a name I heard whispered often, when she first came here. Not so much, anymore."

Beauregard's hand closed into a fist around the locket, clasping it shut.

The fox tilted her head, studying him. "You cannot make her what she was."

"I can offer her a choice."

The Avatar nodded. "See that you honor the one she makes, James. I do not think it will be the one you desire. Such torment as these halls have borne witness to cannot be undone."

"All I ask is the chance."

"Then you have it. But know that I will offer you no aid past what I have given already. I wish to see this ended. But I can interfere no further without being discovered, and my punishment for that might make hers seem kind."

The fox stepped around Beauregard, coming almost nose-to-nose with Nyx. "You have made an impossible promise, Guardian of Kaliaris. Take care that you keep it."

A hole opened in the wall to Nyx's right, leading into a tunnel, and the fox hopped into it.

"Wait," Nyx called. "Can you at least tell us where we should go?"

"When you reach the top of the stairs, both paths will lead to the same place, where they meet on the other side. But you may find the one to your right slightly less disturbing." The tunnel entrance began to close, the fox's final words barely making it through. "Do not underestimate the witch. She sees through *all* the eyes here, when she wishes."

They ascended the stairs, pausing at the top for Seth to re-glamour Morgen as Lavall, and to hide the rest of them from notice. But when he reached for his magic, Nyx reached for his hand.

"Wait." She tugged him down a few steps, far enough away from the others that she could speak softly and not be heard. "You don't have enough left for Morgen *and* the rest of us."

He dragged a hand over his face. "We don't exactly have other options."

"You have me."

He gave her a flat stare. "No."

"If I Hide us, it conserves your magic. They don't have to know it's me doing it instead of you." They'd talked around the mechanism behind Nyx's memory loss, when they'd explained what was happening to her. Even so, she suspected Beauregard had already figured out what she was.

"No. There's no guarantee you won't fall into a memory island in ten minutes and expose everyone, or that using your magic won't cause you to have an episode right now."

"None of my other Hidings have broken when I had episodes." She tapped the Harvester, then the words written in marker on her arm, then her portal magic jewelry, then his heart. "All still there. Through everything."

"And if using it causes you to slip?"

"It hasn't yet." Not when she'd Hidden his heartbeat, or the words on her arm, or the throwing star she'd embedded in the tree back on Earth.

"But what if it does this time?"

"Seth…" She cupped his face in her hand and he covered it with his own, fingers curving around hers. "I *am* going to slip. No matter what you do, no matter what I do or don't do, it's inevitable. I can feel it." Chunks of memory circling her like sharks sensing fresh blood, waiting for an opening to strike. "Let me do something useful before it happens. And catch me when it does."

He closed his eyes, blowing out a long breath. "Okay." He turned his head, pressed a kiss to her palm, and repeated, softer, "Okay."

They walked back to the others, and as Seth's magic slipped over Morgen, returning him to the likeness of Lavall, Nyx's slid over the others, a whispered cloak of Hiding to keep them safe.

The stairwell door opened onto a floor with the gentle curve of a ring, the same as all the ones below, but noticeable here, as if this level was smaller. As the Avatar had suggested, they took the path to the right.

Morgen/Lavall strode confidently down the hallway, projecting the air of someone who knew precisely where he was going, and who had no intention of being interrupted on his way there.

The floor was quiet—eerily so—the hallways empty, but it had a weight that spoke of habitation. Doors lined both walls, square windows cut into them, and as they passed, Nyx looked through.

Kumir stood in rows, like soldiers at rest. Their eyes were closed, faces blank, as if in a trancelike state. As if they were robots, waiting for someone to flip their power switch and input a command.

Chills slipped down Nyx's spine, and she wouldn't have noticed she'd stopped walking if Beauregard hadn't paused as well. The pain etched on his face…

He saw her notice and broke away, his hands clenched fists at his sides. Nyx trotted to catch up to the others just as someone called out, "Lavall! I didn't expect you back this evening but I can't say I'm disappointed. Come in here and take a look at this."

The voice, which to Nyx's mind sounded far too upbeat and normal to have any place on this floor, belonged to a middle-aged white man poking his head out of one of the rooms. Morgen had little choice but to acquiesce, which meant Seth had no choice but to follow, and Maruca took it upon herself to do the same.

They'd barely gone in when the floating islands of memory shuddered around Nyx.

No, not now. This was the point she'd been afraid of hitting. The point where it didn't take anything to trigger an episode. Where they just happened.

"Evra," she managed, as one of the islands broke loose and fell toward her, "I think you might want to lock me down."

30

There was an arm around Nyx's throat. She reacted on instinct, jabbing her elbow hard into her captor's abdomen. They grunted, but otherwise barely acknowledged taking the hit.

"Nyx, calm down." A woman's voice, steady and strong. "We've been through this several times, now. If you would look at—"

Nyx wasn't listening, too busy running through her options. Her captor was physically stronger and larger than her, and had been anticipating retaliation, if the way she took Nyx's strike was any indication.

Nyx could keep fighting, or she could try another approach. She pretended to faint, letting her entire body drop unexpectedly. For a brief second, the person holding her relaxed. Nyx used the opening to tuck her chin, jerk down on the woman's arm, and pull her head out of the hold as she pedaled backwards.

The second she was free she dragged a Hiding around her and ran. Wind kissed her arms as the woman lunged for the place where Nyx had disappeared from sight. The initial drain on her magic was fierce, but once she was no longer in the place the woman had expected her to be, it took significantly less magic to keep herself Hidden.

She felt threads of her magic trailing behind her, connected to the very people she ran from. No one was supposed to know Nyx—and her Hidden abilities—existed. Yet these people did, and they'd clearly coerced her into using her magic for them. Had all her focus not been on fleeing, she would have cut the threads to them that instant.

But her focus *was* on flight. Then she passed a door with a window cut into it, and her focus was on something else. Because through the window she'd caught a glimpse of identical people—identical women. Terror flooded her veins with adrenaline.

Kumir. That was what they had to be. Her mother had told her the stories, the description of those women. The assassins who had hunted her people to extinction.

How had Nyx ended up here—wherever *here* was—with them?

She slowed as she approached what looked like an entryway, darting eyes noting a door to her left that look like it might lead out. The problem was that it didn't have a doorknob. She skidded to a halt, pushing, then digging her fingers into the seams and pulling, but attempts to slide it had no effect.

The sounds of pursuit pounded closer and she abandoned the door, running on. They couldn't see her through the Hiding, but if they physically ran into her, it would be too solid of a feeling for her to Hide.

She ran past more windows that showed more rooms, like the ones that had held the Kumir on the other side. But what she glimpsed in these was nothing short of horror.

At first, when she looked into the ones closest to the entryway, she thought they held wounded Kumir. The naked bodies lying on the beds within were certainly all the same body. They were just missing things. Feet or legs, arms or hands. Except none of those missing things were bloodied or bandaged.

The more rooms she passed, the more pieces the bodies within the rooms were missing. In this one, both legs. In that one, both legs and an arm. The next, half the torso missing as well.

Her footsteps slowed as revulsion overcame her, her flight response unable to remember that she was supposed to be running when it was starting to look like she was in a house of horrors with nowhere to flee *to*.

She wanted to stop looking but she couldn't. And when she came across the room where the bodies contained only an arm, a shoulder, a neck, and half a face, her feet just stopped. She stared, bile clawing free of her stomach and into her throat, acid burning the tender lining.

Three people rushed past her—the blonde white woman who'd been restraining her, a black-haired-woman with tiger's stripes on her tan skin, and an older Black man—all oblivious to the fact that Nyx had stopped. She barely noticed as they ran on. She stared through the window, her gaze fixated on a single body within the room. The portion of a face that had before been complete only up to the bottom lip grew more flesh, more bone, more tissue. It crawled up the sides, filling out the cheeks a little more, then the upper lip.

More footsteps pounded down the aisle and someone crashed into her, their arms wrapping around her in a hold meant to prevent her from fighting, from running. She tried neither, the lightest brush of a feather earring tickling her cheek.

"Nyxi?" Seth's voice. Seth's arms, stronger than she remembered, his body bigger than it should be. But in everything she was surrounded by, she didn't have it in her to question it. Not when the very fact he'd known unerringly where she was said that he was *Seth*, the ever-present exception in her Hidings. And since there was no point in keeping that Hiding anymore, she let it go. Only to realize there was another one beneath it, Hiding her from everyone except Seth and the five people who had just rushed by her.

She couldn't take her eyes off the horror in front of her. "They're *growing*," she whispered. It was the only word she could think of to describe what she was seeing. Both like and unlike plants sprouting from a seed, trees growing from a cutting.

"No." A new voice, a beautiful one, tinged with the same horror she felt. It didn't sound like it belonged on the face it came out of, and she sensed Seth's illusions at work. "They're regenerating."

The three individuals that had rushed past her earlier returned, and the man with the beautiful voice turned his attention to the older Black man. "A hydra? The Kumir are spun from a full-blooded hydra?"

That face—what was in that man's face was terrible. "Yes."

The first man shook his head, as if he couldn't accept the confirmation. "This is not...even before the full-bloods were wiped out, they were only capable of regenerating their own body. They didn't spawn copies of themselves."

The older man shook his head. "We don't have time for—"

"Yes"—this from the blonde—"we do. I think I speak for everyone here when I say we aren't going further until you explain this."

The man's jaw clenched. His shoulders slumped. "One case. There was *one* case of a bisected hydra in which both halves regenerated. The consciousness of the individual remained in one half. The other was a shell, a replicant tied to the other.

"Certain parties became interested in seeing if this replication could be forced from something less than a perfect bisection. Needless to say, the hydra race wasn't exactly clamoring at the gates to be subjected to unnecessary mutilation in the name of science.

"They received it anyway, and that is how the pureblood hydras died out." He swallowed. "There were twenty of them left when someone developed a compound. A blend of magic and medicine that gave the experimenters what they wanted—

the ability to spur regeneration from something as small as a finger, then halt that regeneration once the body was complete."

He gave a mirthless laugh. "After all, if your goal is to have an army of identical assassins, it doesn't do any good for them to start regenerating on the battlefield and have people understand what they are. Better for the soldiers to die on the field, their origins a myth.

"The only problem was, the replicants only lived so long as the original did too. Nineteen of those twenty remaining hydras died. The Kumir are made from *one* woman—Severena Kumirava."

He looked at the first man. "You get that much of an explanation because you are of my blood and I owe it. But I will waste no more time. My wife has spent thirty years in agony. I will not let her suffer any longer."

He turned and walked away. The others, their faces identical expressions of mute horror, followed. Nyx numbly let Seth pull her along. His lips pressed against her ear and he whispered, "I know nothing makes sense to you right now, but just trust me, please."

"Okay." She didn't have the option not to. She was surrounded by people she didn't know, somewhere she was certain wasn't Earth, and she was desperately trying to convince herself that this was a lucid dream. That nothing of what the man had said about the bodies in those rooms was true. That those bodies didn't even exist because this *wasn't real*.

Pinching herself didn't make her wake up, though. Did that even work? Or was being able to have the thought and follow through on the action proof enough that you weren't asleep, and that was why people did it?

They rounded a curve and her brain quit thinking altogether. Just...quit. To her right, walls gave way to a catwalk that stretched across a sheer drop, ending at a circular glass island maybe fifteen feet in diameter.

It wasn't the narrow width of the railless catwalk, or the fact the ground several hundred feet below appeared to be molten lava, that made her stomach flip. It was the woman hovering five feet off the glass floor of the island. She looked as if she were asleep, her eyes closed, the weightless way her auburn hair floated around her face giving the impression that she drifted underwater.

It was the same face Nyx had seen in the rooms before on multitudes of still forms, their expressions blank. Except this woman's face was not blank, her body not still. Her eyes roved behind their lids, as if forced closed when she wanted them open. She jerked and contorted within the web of magic that held her aloft, fighting.

But her struggle didn't stop the ropes of magic that slipped around fingers and toes, severing them with brutal efficiency. Currents of the same magic that held her aloft carried the pieces away, streaming them across the gulf, where they would end up on beds in rooms, continuing this grotesque process.

The woman bled, as the parts in the rooms had not. She jerked harder but didn't scream, and as Nyx watched, her severed digits regrew, leaving the woman whole again. The cutting ropes curled around the woman once more, looping this time around ankles and wrists.

The man who'd told them this story in the hallway—and stars, was that really his *wife?*—let out a strangled noise and surged forward. The blonde woman and the redhead grabbed onto him, holding him back, whispering things Nyx couldn't hear.

They held him back because, standing at the end of the catwalk between them and the floating woman, stood another woman. Her back was to them, hands out at her sides, fingers twitching, fluttering, moving. As if she conducted a silent symphony—or as if she conducted the magic currently at work before her.

"Do you intend to stand there in disapproval all day, Lavall, or do you intend to help?"

Her words were clearly addressed to the one man whose presence was altered by Seth's magic, rather than Hidden by hers. It was just as clear that the man had no idea how to respond. So he didn't.

The woman made an irritated noise. "Your predecessor didn't make nearly such a fuss about the harvesting schedule. Yet I still found him odious enough to do away with." She turned, revealing an almost alabaster-white face framed in wild dark curls. The face wasn't beautiful by the typical standards, but it *was* beautiful. The kind of face that inspired poetry, but all but guaranteed the poem would be tragic.

"Now come—" She broke off, her gaze narrowing. She stalked down the catwalk, stopping in front of the visible member of their party. "You are not Lavall. The illusion is good —some of the best I've seen—but I know Lavall's mind. And yours is so very different from his."

Her elegant fingers twitched madly, spider legs plucking at a web. Instinct born of past pain sent Nyx's brain reaching for a memory of agonizing fire. She was pulled viciously from the memory island and thrust back into her current self. Those loose islands of memory rattled around her and she shoved them back, focusing on the now. On who precisely those restless hands belonged to: Councilor Koral.

She could still feel those fingernails digging into her skull that day in her Station's Arrival Room, remembered the fire that had laced through her at their touch. Those hands rose to either side of Morgen's face now, not touching him and yet he spasmed, as if gripped with a paralysis he was attempting to fight. Nyx reached for Morgen but Seth's arm, locked around her waist, held her back.

He couldn't hold back Evra, Maruca, or Beauregard. They threw themselves at the councilor, only to be halted immediately, as if caught in an invisible web. Like the web that held Severena.

Koral's gaze shot to the place where the three were stuck in her magic. Nyx gasped as power surged out of her, fighting to keep them Hidden in the face of someone who now *knew* they were there.

"You back with us?" Seth murmured.

"Yeah."

"Then let them go. They're already caught."

Nyx did, severing those three Hidings so she could keep the ones over her, Reyva, and Seth intact.

Koral made a *tsking* sound as Evra, Maruca, and Beauregard materialized out of thin air. It was Beauregard her gaze lingered on, recognition sparking in her eyes. She laughed. "So you finally found her. I suppose it's fitting that you'll get to die in her actual presence. I might even let her open her eyes for it. Now, who else did you bring with you?"

She didn't wait for an answer, casting her hands out, magic rippling across the space in a blink. It latched onto Nyx, invisible fingers digging into her skin, her nerves, apparently not needing to know she was *there* to do its job. It gave the feedback of her presence to Koral, and as soon as the councilor knew there were others ensnared in her web, that draw on Nyx's magic opened from a trickle to a flood.

She let the Hiding go. If Koral had been delighted to find Beauregard here, she was practically ecstatic to see Nyx, her pale pink lips curving into a wide smile. "My, my. If it isn't Earth's Guardian. The one who *certainly* had nothing to do with her"— she pointed at Maruca—"coming back from Arkadia. You're a little far from home, aren't you dear?"

Nyx didn't answer. She couldn't. Her vocal cords were as frozen as the rest of her.

Koral's fingers were moving rapidly again, restless with eagerness. "I think I'd like to finish what I started the last time we spoke. There is something I very much want to know."

No. The only reason Koral hadn't succeeded in prying Nyx's mind open before was because Nyx had had someone else's help. If she was right, that someone had been Jevryn. Only he wasn't here to help her this time.

The loose memory islands pressed at her again, as if her fear gave them an opening. As if they were trying to convince her that *here* wasn't such a great time to be, so she might as well pick another. She forced them back, but the mental hand she held them with trembled. Soon, they were all going to come crashing in, and she wouldn't be able to stop them.

Worry about it later, stay alive now, she ordered herself. Maybe she could—

Behind Koral, Maruca crumpled. The way her body hit the ground... For one terrifying moment, Nyx thought she was dead.

But as Koral spun away from Nyx, as if seeking the reason why her magic's hold had failed on Maruca, the redhead sprang back to life. She shot forward, hands latching onto Koral's ankle.

Rage and pain flashed across the councilor's face as Maruca's magic latched on, siphoning energy. The web that held the rest of them immobile pulsed. Maruca spasmed, but she didn't let go.

She didn't move, either. Not even when the councilor ceased attempting to fully re-ensnare her with magic and progressed to physical attacks. Koral kicked with her free leg, vicious jabs to the face until Maruca managed to haul herself forward enough to cover her face and neck with her arms. Then the blows came to her ribs, her back, her stomach.

Let go, Nyx wanted to scream, *just let go.* Because whatever Maruca was managing to drain from Koral, it clearly wasn't enough. And they were out of time.

Footsteps sounded behind them, and Nyx didn't need to be able to turn and look to know who they belonged to. Because this entire floor belonged to Koral and, as the Avatar had said, "The witch sees through *all* eyes on this floor." Or, as Nyx suspected, she controlled all of them. If Nyx had to guess, she'd say that every Kumir on the floor was pouring down the catwalk.

Two of them moved around Nyx, going for Maruca. Nyx

struggled, as she'd *been* struggling, to no avail. The two Kumir were almost on Maruca.

Then a bright pulse of magic burst from Reyva, and the web holding them shattered. Nyx was suddenly, gloriously free. They *all* were.

Morgen immediately dove for Maruca, hauling her away from Koral while Beauregard dispatched the two Kumir—Nyx had to keep thinking of them that way, or else she'd never be able to do what Beauregard was doing right now—then wheeled and sprinted for Severena.

Evra freed her sword from its scabbard with long-practiced ease and swung at the councilor. Koral blocked. Not with a blade, but with her magic, slowing Evra's movement at the last moment just enough to allow her to dodge the strike.

Whatever Reyva was doing to disrupt Koral's magic, it wasn't stopping it entirely.

"How long can you keep that up?" Nyx asked.

"Not long," Reyva gritted out. "The bitch is strong."

"Bigger problem," Seth said. He'd taken up position behind them on the catwalk, facing back the way they'd come. "Too many people to fight."

Nyx finally looked in that direction, confirming the catwalk —and the path back as far as she could see—was filled with Kumir. They weren't engaging—weren't attacking or advancing—likely because Koral thought they didn't need to. Nyx and the others had no hope of getting past *that* many people, and as far as Koral knew, that catwalk was the only way out of here.

But it *wasn't*, so… "We need to get to Beauregard. *Now.*"

Before Reyva's magic gave out and they all got frozen in place again. Before Koral managed to do more than block Evra's attacks.

They fell back. Seth guided Reyva, who was so focused on her efforts she couldn't put one foot in front of the other without stumbling. Nyx's head felt increasingly like a jar of rocks being shaken, her vision swimming as she fought to stay *here*. She blinked hard and her vision cleared.

The Kumir followed them as they retreated, filling every foot of space that Nyx and the others vacated. She reached Beauregard and Morgen, each of whom cradled a different unconscious woman in their arms. In Morgen's, Maruca looked…Nyx shook her head. She would be fine. She *would*. The woman didn't get to save all their damn lives and turn around and die herself.

"Seth, I need the portal stones."

He hesitated, looking from her to where Koral still fought with Evra. "She's a councilor. She knows who you are. Where to find you."

"Then we're already fucked and I'd rather handle this at home." Home, where she had some chance of controlling the narrative. She was counting on the likelihood of Koral following them as directly as possible, as opposed to running to the rest of the Council first. "*Please*. I don't know how much longer I'm going to be me."

That worked. Seth shoved a fistful of portal stones into her hands. Nyx blew on them like they were dice and this was a million-dollar gamble. She looked at the tethers of her Hidings, bypassing the ones that Hid the Harvester and Seth's heartbeat, finding instead the one tied to a throwing star on a far-distant planet.

She pulled a thin thread of portal magic from the necklace, focusing on that star, and crushed the first stone. The spark of magic it gave off was there for the barest flicker of a second, and she cursed herself as she missed her opening. She crushed the next stone and this time sank a spear of magic through it before it vanished, like threading the eye of a very small needle, enough to keep the connection open as she crushed the next stone.

Then the next. And the next. And the next.

She kept going, crushing stone after stone, but the portal didn't *want* to be held open. It was barely the size of a baseball, and she strained under the weight of keeping it from collapsing.

Panic flared in her chest. She hadn't allowed herself the *what if*. What if this didn't work? What if there wasn't a way home this time? She crushed the next stones in rapid succession, her fear and determination growing the portal wider. The size of a grapefruit. Then a basketball.

Her whole body trembled, sweat rolling down the small of her back. Another stone crushed, another centimeter in diameter gained.

Not enough. The portal wasn't large enough to move through. She fought to hold it anyway, as if her sheer stubbornness could achieve what she had neither the magic nor the experience to do.

The edges trembled and began to collapse.

"*No.*" The word was a strangled cry, an exhausted exhalation of pure fury, and then—

A form stalked into view on the other side, black robes fluttering in Earth's wind. Fingers grasped the edges of the portal, and the power—holy stars the fucking *power*—that poured in as another's magic and will joined her own.

The portal stabilized, expanded, and one very pissed-off Jevryn A-Morridahn stepped through.

31

Nyx stumbled back. She'd seen Jevryn angry before. She thought it might actually be his default state of existence. But the fury that sparked in his silver eyes now was practically tangible.

Nyx didn't waste time looking a gift councilor in the mouth. She turned toward her best friend and shouted, "Evra, fall back!"

Evra, bless her, did precisely that without argument, making her way to them with quick backward steps, sword at the ready before her, gaze never leaving Koral.

"I can't hold her much longer." Reyva looked exhausted.

Jevryn spared her a flicker of a glance. "You may cease your efforts, they are unnecessary."

Reyva looked like she wanted to tell him to go fuck himself, and Nyx understood. It was like Reyva had held a mountain pass alone against an invading army for an entire day, and then her general had arrived, patted her on the head and said, "Thanks, but we don't really need the pass."

Reyva looked at Nyx, and it took Nyx a minute to realize she was asking for confirmation. Nyx nodded. Reyva's magic died.

Nyx barely noticed. She was too relieved to see Jevryn. Even if seeing him meant that he'd shown up at her Station with Elena only to find her gone, and she was going to have to answer some uncomfortable questions about that. About this.

She didn't care. If she had worried she was using him as a crutch before, as someone older and more powerful who was theoretically capable of handling any situation, well...the sudden safety she felt at him standing between her and Koral seemed to point to that being a valid concern.

He faced Koral, and the utter lack of emotion he outwardly showed was both comforting and terrifying. It was the same kind of bored annoyance he'd expressed when speaking with the Minethran queen on Amentia Furor. As if he'd expected to have a light work day before his weekend and instead been saddled with an unexpected task requiring actual effort.

She had a feeling if he was standing against a literal invading horde, naked, alone, and with no weaponry, he would still look exactly like this.

"Jevryn." Koral mimicked his expression to the extent Nyx wondered if mastering it had been a prerequisite for becoming a councilor. "You have the most interesting tendency to insert yourself into all matters even tangentially related to Earth. I'm curious, is your fascination with Earth's Guardian a result of your still being so in love with its Avatar, or have your inclinations moved in a new direction?" Her gaze swept over Nyx. "She's pretty enough, I suppose, though practically a child."

Nyx could not adequately describe the sense of revulsion that overcame her at that supposition. It felt wrong on a fundamental level. The brief flux in her emotions caused the memory islands in her skull to rattle against it again, and she strained to hold them.

Jevryn's response came out clipped. "That is utterly disgusting."

Koral shrugged. "I am forced to guess at your motivations, as you have always been the most difficult of us to understand. Even Kiev is simple—he lives to torment you. And you should have been equally simple, but you are not."

"My deepest apologies for upsetting your beliefs on the simplistic nature of individual beings." His voice was jagged ice.

Koral's eyes narrowed. "I will make you this offer only once. You can have her"—she indicated Nyx—"whatever she is to you. I will forget you were here, when you ought not know Nethrayne's location. I might even forget what she can do. In return, the others stay with me."

"No." The word was out before Nyx could debate the wisdom of saying it. She was afraid Jevryn would do it, would take her and leave her friends here.

Jevryn's eyes shifted to her, then back to Koral. He shrugged. "As she says."

"You would let a child make your decisions for you? Have the centuries made you as senile as Councilor Brecht?"

"Hardly. You are the one whose faculties are in question if you expect me to believe that I could see this"—he indicated the Kumir—"and you would let me walk away without a deeper hold over me. I must admit surprise. I always thought the Kumir were Alastair's. To find you at their helm is…unsettling."

The pressure in the room shifted, as if Koral drew something into herself, and it upset the fragile balance of the environment. "We have always avoided each other well enough. I see no reason we cannot continue to do so." Her gaze shifted to Nyx. "Earlier teasing aside, do you really believe I don't know what she is? That I can't guess why you interfered with my initial probe of her mind after the Arkadia incident? It took seeing her again to put it together, took seeing her work, but I have."

Seeing her work. Nyx's stomach hollowed out. Koral knew she was Hidden. Had the councilor somehow felt that it wasn't illusion magic hiding them all when they'd become caught in her web?

Koral's smile was threat and promise. "If you want her to survive, you do not want to make me your enemy."

Jevryn laughed. A single, rough sound that had more in common with a hunting wolf than a man. "I have no intention of making you my enemy. I have every intention of making you nothing."

Lightning crackled over the surface of his skin, his clothes, flickers of electricity that filled the air with static.

Koral's eyes widened. "You wouldn't dare."

Jevryn's magic pulsed, deepened, seeming to turn in on itself and back out, again and again, growing with each movement until it gained such force that Nyx and the others stepped as far back from him as they could. "You know, Koral," he said casually, "I never particularly cared for you."

Koral took a step back before she caught herself. "The others will not let this stand. They will come for you, they—"

Jevryn's magic detonated. The throngs of Kumir behind Koral disintegrated, one second living bodies, the next nothing but ash.

Koral cried out and dropped to her knees, the shield she'd erected around herself buckling under the onslaught of Jevryn's attack. Her hands were thrown out in front of her, as if she physically held the weight of his magic from crushing her.

Her fingers, never still, moved with savage intensity, jerking and straining, plucking again at those invisible strings. The pressure in the room shifted once more and she surged to her feet, shoving her hands outward.

Jevryn grunted, like he'd taken a punch to the gut, but he didn't step back. They stayed locked in that struggle of wills, the air growing heavier and heavier, until Nyx thought it would turn too thick to breathe.

But it was Koral who truly labored, Koral whose knees buckled again, even as she screamed, "Why won't you just *break*?"

Jevryn finally moved, holding his arms out from his sides, bent at the elbows, palms up. "A-Morridahns do not break."

He slammed his palms together. Koral's shield snapped, the flickering of Jevryn's power crackling as he compressed the broken shield around her.

She screamed as it touched her, as something like and unlike flame licked at her skin. Then Jevryn's hands twisted, as if wrenching open a jar, and Koral exploded into ash.

He turned, ash raining down, utterly unfazed by what he'd done. He leveled an impressive glare on Nyx and his mouth opened, no doubt to issue a tirade that would convey how thoroughly irritated he was to be here, and how much difficulty she had caused him.

Maybe he even did. But if so, Nyx didn't hear it. The loose memory islands that had been hovering around her were no longer content to be kept at bay. They fell like meteors, crashing into her again and again, and she was lost in the maelstrom.

S eth could have guessed that dragging a version of Nyx who didn't know what a portal was *through* a portal would turn out poorly, and he would have been right. She turned into a demonic hellcat upon reentry to Earth, kicking and thrashing with adrenaline-backed fury.

She caught him in his eye with her elbow, his groin with her foot, and made it all of four steps toward freedom before Jevryn portaled into her path. He picked her up by the back of her shirt, holding her aloft like a cat with a kitten. The man was seriously stronger than he looked. He carried her over the border to the Station and deposited her into Griff's waiting talons.

Griff said something Seth was too far away to hear, and for a few moments Nyx was calm. Long enough for Morgen and Evra to carry an unconscious Maruca onto the Station's grounds, and for Beauregard to follow with Severena.

Then it all went to hell. Severena was barely within the Station's domain when she started screaming. He didn't think she was truly awake, or if she was, she wasn't fully aware.

Jevryn looked at her, a frown on his lips, and told Beauregard, "She is sensitive to the feel of Stations. And she was kept in one for thirty years."

That was all it took for Beauregard to haul her back across the border, Reyva on his heels. He stopped on the other side, torn between Severena and Maruca.

"We'll take care of Ruca," Morgen told him. "Do what you need to."

But when Nyx shuddered in Griff's hold a moment later, her face blanking before shifting into panic, the Station shuddered with her. The ground pitched violently enough to send everyone but Griff and Jevryn to their knees.

Evra looked at Seth. "Maruca needs the Warlock."

And bringing the Warlock here wasn't a good idea. Not with Nyx in her current state. "Go," he told them. "I've got Nyx."

Which might have been an overly optimistic statement. Because for the next eighteen hours, the only break he, Jevryn, or Griff got was when Nyx was unconscious.

32

Nyx woke to a steady *thump thump thump* in her ear. Her face was smooshed against Seth's chest. He was asleep, his back resting against one of the few bookcases that remained upright in the library, his arms and legs wrapped firmly around her.

He jerked as she shifted, tightening his hold.

"I wouldn't have taken it personally if you wanted to actually tie me up." Her voice came out raspy and irritated. She was so thirsty her lips were cracking, but Seth wasn't releasing his grip on her enough for her to reach the glass of water that appeared on the floor a foot from them.

"Tried that. You don't remember?"

"It's all a little blurry."

He sighed. "First time we tried, the rope was part of the Station and you just had it untie itself. So Jevryn got rope that didn't belong to the Station, and you just used parts of the Station to saw through it."

"Sorry. Can I please have water now?"

He retrieved the glass and handed it to her, all without releasing his death grip on her.

She drained the water in four gulps. "I think I'm okay for a bit. You can let me go."

He grunted. "I'll consider it."

She wondered how pissed Jevryn was, on a scale of one to *I'm-never-helping-you-ever-again*. The look on his face when he'd stepped through onto Nethrayne would live in her mind forever.

Nethrayne. Maruca. Severena.

She jolted to her feet—or would have, except Seth swiped her legs from beneath her and landed atop her in a grappling hold. The resultant noise had the library door bursting open, Griff and Jevryn rushing in.

Griff's wings were drooping, and Jevryn looked the closest to exhaustion she'd ever seen him. Meaning his posture wasn't textbook perfect, and those were definitely shadows under his eyes.

"It's fine," she told them. "Apparently I just moved too fast for Mr. Paranoid here."

"It's not paranoia if you're always trying to escape," Seth said.

"Forgive me," Griff said, "but would you mind telling me my name?"

"Griff."

"My other name?"

"Arradin."

When Griff exhaled, it felt like the entire Station let out a sigh of relief with him.

Seth's forehead dropped to hers. "Could you please refrain from making any sudden movements for the rest of your life?"

"Maybe. Could you get off me?"

"*Maybe*," he said, mimicking the drawn-out way she'd said it.

She shoved him. He grumbled and let her up.

"What happened to everyone?" she asked. "Are they okay?"

It was Griff who answered, his voice carefully neutral. "The Station was extremely volatile when you returned."

She filled in the blanks. "So no one felt safe enough to be here."

"Some people *couldn't* be here. Severena...I do not know if you could call what she did waking, since all she did was scream, but she is one of those people who is sensitive to what it feels like to be inside a Station. And she was kept in one, so..."

So being in *this* Station had upset her.

Seth picked up the thread. "Beauregard and Reyva took her back to his castle. I have no idea what they're telling his followers. Morgen and Evra took Maruca to the Warlock. She was...not in a good way."

Nyx squeezed her eyes shut, worried. Worried about *Maruca*, who forty-eight hours ago no one could have convinced Nyx she would be concerned about. But one half-assed apology to a younger version of herself, coupled with one heroic act, and Maruca had somehow been lodged firmly in Nyx's register of People She Gave a Shit About.

Griff cleared his throat. "Kalvar heard. About her condition."

Nyx closed her eyes. *I broke a kid's heart because I didn't know any other way to save him.* "Where is he now?"

"Waiting for her to wake up. Evra stopped by a few hours ago to update us. She wanted to stay, but with the Station the way it was, Griff didn't think it was a good idea."

She needed to see them. To know that they were alright. That Maruca was healed. That Morgen and Evra were fine. That Kalvar wasn't getting his teenage heart stomped in again.

And Severena...how did a person *live* through what she had? How did a person come out the other side of that? She remembered what Nethrayne's Avatar had said, that Severena might not make the choice Beauregard wanted her to. She realized now the fox had been saying that Severena might not *want* to live after that.

What would Beauregard do if that was the case? What was the right thing *to* do? To let her make that choice? To stop her?

And how was Reyva taking all of this? She'd lost her entire

life to the Kumir. As had every man and woman living on Beauregard's estate. If they saw Severena and he couldn't convince them of what she was, would they try to harm her?

Nyx pushed to her feet—slowly, for the sake of Seth's frazzled nerves—and said, "I have to go. I have to see them."

"*No*," Griff, Seth, and Jevryn all said together.

Griff paced forward until his beak was an inch from her nose. "You are not leaving the grounds of this Station again in your current condition. I feared you would be lost to us all forever, or else killed on Nethrayne. You have frightened me half to death, you have exhausted my nerves, and you will stay right where you are."

"What he said," Seth chimed in, "but minus the fatherly authoritarian overtones."

Griff spared Seth a brief glare, then turned his attention back to Nyx. "Have I made myself clear?"

"Yes?" she squeaked out. So maybe leaving the Station *was* a terrible idea, now that he mentioned it. The last thing she needed was to have a memory skip in front of Ankira.

"Good." Griff spread his wings in invitation for a hug.

She stepped into them, squeezing him tight. "I'm sorry I scared you."

"To think," he grumbled, wings folding around her, "that I didn't believe everyone when they said children would cause me heart attacks."

Out of the corner of her eye, she saw Jevryn shift, as if to leave the room. As if the scene made him uncomfortable.

Well, too bad if seeing Griff have a life that didn't involve *him* was uncomfortable for him. Nyx would rather get the next part out of the way without having to track him down across the Station.

She released Griff and turned to Jevryn. "Were you not able to get her?" She didn't think she had to say *who*, and she wasn't wrong.

"She is here." Jevryn's voice was tight enough to remind Nyx that he seemed to dislike her mother as much as she did.

"Okay." Nyx rubbed her palms on her jeans. "Is she…not willing to fix me?" Given the way they'd all said dealing with Nyx over the past few hours had gone, she was surprised they hadn't knocked her out and dragged her to Elena.

"Her willingness is not the issue," Jevryn said. "The issue is that we have been unable to reach her."

"If she's here, how can she be unreachable?"

Griff sat back on his haunches, tail curling around his paws. "Because you have locked her in a room in the Station and I have been unable to open it despite extreme effort. Even once you passed out, you kept her thoroughly segregated."

Nyx sank into the Station's senses, filtering through them until she found said room. She didn't know the feel of her mother within Kaliaris the way she knew the feel of Seth or Griff or Evra, but the irritated click of high heels on the floor of that room was good enough evidence for her.

"I…don't remember doing that."

"I believe it was an instinctual reaction," Griff said. "You heard her voice through the Station and then she was gone before she could lay eyes on you."

Nyx groaned. "She's been in there since we got back? She's gonna be so pissed."

Then Seth said five words that could change her entire worldview, if she let them. "That's not your problem anymore."

Not her problem anymore. It didn't *matter* if her mother was pissed. It didn't even matter if she was pissed at Nyx, specifically. Because Elena no longer controlled her life.

Now if only she could actually convince herself of that. "Okay." She tilted her head to one side, then the other, cracking her neck and restraining a moan at the tension relief it provided. Her entire body felt like one giant ache. "Let's get this over with."

"You don't have to do this right away," Seth said.

"Yes, she does," Jevryn said. "I am not risking her lucidity failing again."

"If she needs time—" Griff began.

"It's okay," Nyx said. "Jevryn's right."

She led them to the room that held her mother. It was in the same hallway as Liya's room, but at the opposite end. It didn't have a doorway, or windows, and for a moment Nyx just stood there, willing herself to create either of them.

Seth stood behind her, Griff and Jevryn flanking her sides. The councilor felt nearly as tense as Nyx. She remembered what he'd written her—that if he hadn't brought Elena to Earth all those years ago, he'd have strangled her—and thought perhaps he was as reluctant to enter as she. He clearly hated Elena, which was more emotion than she'd ever seen him show for anyone but Griff.

Her mother had that effect on people.

So she was surprised when Jevryn said, "Would you like me to go in first?"

"Yes, but...I need a minute." A minute in which she turned the wall to glass, and watched a woman who didn't know she was being watched.

"She cannot see us?" Jevryn asked.

Nyx shook her head. "One-way glass." Her mother looked... like her mother. Eight years had done little to change her.

No, that wasn't quite right. It was that the changes weren't the ones a person expected to note after a prolonged time apart. Her mother didn't look older. She looked younger. Not physically—there was the hint of lines at the corners of her eyes that hadn't been there before—but in her bearing, her energy.

As if it had been Nyx and Seth and Viktor that had sapped the life from her, and time away had been her restoration.

Nyx's hands clenched into fists. Wherever Elena found herself in life now, it looked good on her. She wore a sleek champagne dress that was a shade lighter than her high heels. Her white-blonde hair was swept into an elegant updo, her makeup flawless. Even the irritated way she paced the floor was somehow aristocratic.

Nyx had forgotten that about her mother. How everything Elena did looked pretty and perfect and flowing. How much Nyx had once wanted to be like that, too. Before it had become obvious she wasn't made for it.

"Where has she been?"

"Are you certain you wish to know? You need not. She can do what she is here to do and be gone from your life without impacting it further."

"I want to know."

He nodded, as if he hadn't truly expected her to decline the information. "She married into the Kormadin royal family."

Nyx's head snapped back. "What?"

Of all the things she'd imagined her mother doing while Nyx was memory-less and alone in Dead Earth, *getting married* hadn't been anywhere among them.

"Her husband is one of the minor royals, though his ambitions within the family have become markedly increased—and markedly more successful—since his marriage to Elena. Enough so that they have been living within the Kormadin palace for the last five years. I believe that was one of her goals with the marriage, though certainly not the only one. Retrieving her was extraordinarily difficult."

She remembered what Diana had said on their first meeting, when Evra had been so angered that a healer had rendered the woman infertile. She'd said that the healer belonged to the Kormadin royal family—*Diana's* family—and that it would take an army to make them bow to any authority.

She understood why Jevryn had been so careful, now. Why it had taken him time. As a councilor, he could have marched in and demanded that Elena come with him. But word of it would have spread. It would have raised questions about why Elena would be so important to a councilor. It would have made the Council itself curious.

"How did you get her to come?"

"I had someone infiltrate her household staff, kidnap her, and bring her to a location I could portal from unnoticed."

Of course he had. "Who?" Who could he have trusted this with, trusted that word of it wouldn't leak to anyone else?

"Kaden."

She stiffened. Of *course*, he'd sent Kaden.

Is he here? The words almost left her tongue, but she already knew the answer. Kaliaris remembered Kaden's presence, and that presence wasn't within the Station's premises.

Is he alright? But she didn't ask that, either.

She conjured a door in the wall, and let Jevryn precede her in.

"I s this your idea of a joke?" Elena's icy voice cut the air, and only once she'd asked the question—of Jevryn—did Nyx truly notice the room. It was an exact replica of the one Elena had inhabited in their cabin, in that small pocket of Earth Between.

"I assure you," Jevryn responded, "I find nothing at all about your presence humorous."

"If you think I believe you've brought me here for that girl, when I've seen no evidence that—"

"Hello, Mother." Nyx stepped into the room. Seth followed, not stopping until his chest was pressed to her back, his left hand resting protectively on her hip. He was as tense as she was.

Everyone was tense, even Griff, standing at Nyx's left side.

If the universe had any sense of fairness, her mother would at least try to apologize. Would show some semblance of guilt for what she'd done. Maybe try to bullshit her with some explanation of why it had all been necessary and for Nyx's own good.

But Nyx had stopped looking to the universe for fairness some time ago.

Elena looked at Seth, following his hand down to Nyx's hip,

and laughed. "I see the puppy ran away from his master, only to realize he didn't want to leave after all." She gave him an amused smile. "I didn't really think you'd have the balls to go crawling back to her, once you remembered it all."

Then she shook her head at Nyx, as if disappointed in her. "Or that you'd be desperate enough to take him back."

Even with her missing memories, Nyx was willing to bet she'd never wanted to slap anyone as much as she wanted to slap her mother then. But since it was patently obvious that riling Nyx was precisely what Elena was trying to do, she ignored it.

"Did Jevryn tell you why you're here?"

Elena's eyes practically danced with mirth. "Jevryn, hmm? Is that what you call him?"

"Councilor A-Morridahn is a mouthful, so yes, that's what I call him." If anything, that response seemed to amuse her mother further. Nyx repeated, "Did he tell you why you're here?"

Elena waved her hand. "You've made a mess of things, and I'm now expected to be inconvenienced in order to clean it up."

Even knowing that her mother *wanted* to infuriate her, Nyx couldn't stop the rage from surfacing. "*I've* made a mess of things? You stole my entire life, dumped me somewhere no one could remember me, took away the only person who cared about me, and *I've* made a mess of things?"

Elena gave her another one of those disappointed looks Nyx had been all too familiar with by the time she was five. "He clearly didn't care *that* much if he chose to forget you and run off."

Seth's hand tightened on her hip and Nyx shifted further back into him.

"Besides, if you'd simply left things the way they were, this never would have happened. I *did* try to stop you, once the Hiding began to fray. I did everything I could to repair the damage, but no. You had to keep cutting away at things, and a parent can only interfere so far. If you insisted on ripping your way out of this Hiding, it's hardly unreasonable to expect you to live with the consequences."

"Un—un*reasonable?*" Nyx's voice shook with fury. "And what part of what *you* did to *me* was fucking reasonable?"

"Watch your language when you speak to me."

Nyx looked her dead in the eye and enunciated her next two words slowly. "Fuck. You."

The veneer of pleasantness slipped from her mother's face. If they'd been alone, her gut said Elena would have slapped her. As it was, all she did was say, "Let's fix the mess you've made so I can be on my way." She held out her hand for Nyx's.

Nyx stared at it, something hot and twisting clawing at her chest. The two parts of that sentence shouldn't have hurt so much. The implication that this was all Nyx's fault, like everything was her fault, was nothing new. And the fact that Elena wanted to get it over with so she could return to her new life shouldn't come as a surprise.

But *fuck.* Seven years alone. Seven years not even knowing her own mind. Thinking she must have done something truly awful to deserve the karmic retribution that was her existence. And her mother couldn't even scrape together an insincere *sorry* or an explanation of any kind. Couldn't even be bothered to understand why either should be necessary.

Elena grew impatient and grabbed her wrist. Nyx jerked it free. "No."

"This is what you had me brought here for."

"I don't trust you. Not inside my mind again. Not without some kind of explanation."

Elena sighed, buffing her fingernails against the hem of her dress. "I'd forgotten how tiresome you can be. An inherited trait, no doubt." She had that hard glint in her eye, the one that preceded her coldest remarks, the ones crafted and honed and saved for the times in which they might do the most damage.

"Perhaps your father can talk some sense into you. You always did seem to do better with male influences."

Nyx quashed the spark of hope that immediately leapt up. This wasn't the moment where Elena finally told her the answer to a question she'd asked over and over again growing up. This was where Elena dangled the possibility of that answer in front of her and expected Nyx would trip over herself, doing whatever Elena asked, in the hopes of getting it.

Well, Nyx was calling her bluff. "My father," she repeated, spreading her hands wide. "By all means, then, produce him. I can't *wait* to hear what he has to say."

A look of triumph spread across Elena's face. She turned on a ridiculously tall heel and arched one platinum blonde eyebrow at Jevryn. "Well? I did the parenting for eighteen years while you kept your hands clean. Surely you have some words of wisdom to dispense?"

A river of ice froze solid down Nyx's spine.

No.

No way, in all the hells in all the universes, was Jevryn her father. She'd begged him to tell her and he'd said...he'd said... *He is not a good person. He chose to have no part in your life.*

Except Jevryn had now snapped so rigid, his face tight as if... as if it was true.

Pieces of the recent past clicked together in ways they hadn't before. Ways she'd had no *reason* for them to before. The fact that he'd come for her on Amentia Furor, when that planet was forbidden even to him. How he'd taught her to use portal magic there when he'd had no reason to. When he'd had every reason not to. That he'd taken the time out of his busy schedule to *make her a sandwich*. That he'd kept her secrets.

He'd interceded with the Minethrans on her behalf and now...oh, now she knew exactly what he'd told the queen in that language her translator spell hadn't known. The way he'd spread his hands wide in that helpless gesture, she could practically hear him saying, "Children. You know how difficult they can be."

There was more. Koral saying she knew what Nyx was, what she was to *him*, because of the magic Nyx had used. She'd thought Koral had realized she was Hidden, but she'd been talking about the portal magic—and the fact that Nyx had inherited the ability to use it from Jevryn.

Her mind raced back, conjuring up Griff as he told her the mercury boots—Jevryn's boots—suited her.

Griff. She turned to him, hoping for refusal, for something he could say that would make this not be true. But there was no refusal, no shock, on his face. Only hurt and resignation.

She wanted to believe he hadn't known. She cared about him enough, trusted him enough, that she would give him the benefit of that doubt. But his reaction told her he'd at least suspected. And he hadn't told her.

She shoved that hurt aside—she only had room for so many, at present—and remembered Seth saying, "Nyx Ilera Mira Fortuna." The middle two names her grandmothers'.

"Griff, what was Jevryn's mother's name?" She'd never told Griff her middle names, never had any reason to.

If possible, Jevryn went even more rigid than he'd been before. Elena laughed.

Griff glanced at Jevryn, but in the end he closed his eyes and said, "Ilera Hedaad A-Morridahn."

She wanted to scream at all of them. She wanted to cry. She wanted to ask *why*. But that would only make her feel like the child she'd once so much hated being.

She wouldn't give Elena the satisfaction. She met her mother's triumphant gaze—of *course* she was pleased about this, doing the maximum damage she could at just the right time—and held it until that triumph dimmed.

Nyx's words came out precise and even and cold. "I am going to leave. You are going to stay in this room. When I come back here, you will fix what *you* broke. You will fix it without attempting to change or Hide anything else, and then you will get the fuck out of my Station. Am I clear?"

She'd like to think it was the tone of her voice that made her mother swallow and say, "Yes." But it was probably the way the room had darkened to a near pitch black, the corners seeming to dissolve into abstractness.

Nyx didn't turn the lights back up as she strode for the door. Griff and Jevryn beat her to the exit, likely concerned Nyx might attempt to lock them in here with Elena.

"What time should I expect you back?" Elena asked. Like Nyx was making an appointment and her mother simply wanted to be prepared for it.

"Whenever I feel like it. So you'd better hope my memory doesn't go sideways before I *do* feel like it, because otherwise you might be stuck in here a very long time."

33

The door swung shut and Jevryn took a step toward her. "Nyx—"

She held out her hand, warding him off. "Don't." *I begged you,* she wanted to say. *I begged you to tell me who my father was and you looked me in the eye and refused.* "Just...don't."

"There is—"

She slammed a literal wall between them, Griff and Jevryn on one side, her and Seth on the other.

Her hands clenched into fists, and Seth covered them with his own. "What do you need?"

She laughed. "To not have parents? To have come into the world fully formed as an adult?"

"Anything I can actually help with?"

She sighed and let her head fall onto his shoulder. She needed a whole lot of things she wasn't going to get. So she'd have to take what she could. "You can keep me company on the back porch while I stare into nothing and send Jevryn through a Station maze until I feel like talking to him."

"I'm sorry. I never thought..." He shook his head. "I mean, you do look like him, but statistically, with all the people in the universe? Of course you're going to look like a lot of them. Even with my you-probably-have-a-rich-dad conspiracy theory I never would have aimed as high as a councilor."

"Thanks."

He grinned. "Do I get to call you 'princess' now when I'm mad at you?"

She lifted her head and glared at him. "He's not a king, so no."

"Close enough. Think I'm going to anyway."

"Only if you want me to bite your head off." And so it went, her letting him distract her as he pulled her out to the back porch. Temerex saw her and trotted over, an excited nicker leaving her throat.

Nyx would like to think that excited nicker was all to do with happiness to see her, but like most equines, it was food-related. As evidenced by the image of qualtez fish the unicorn-dragon sent her.

"I'm a sucker for making you happy," Nyx murmured, and drew up a tub of the fish. "Has she seen…him?" she asked, carefully avoiding Jevryn's name because Temerex knew the sound of the syllables.

Seth laughed. "Oh, yeah. Seen him, eyed him, given him the cold shoulder."

Huh. "Good for you, girl." Nyx scratched her withers. There was an art to scratching a unicorn-dragon without cutting her fingers or dislodging scales, and she'd finally mastered it.

Temerex sent Nyx an image of the unicorn-dragon lying on her heated stall rocks in a sunbeam which, near as Nyx had deduced, was her conveyance of contentment. And that single image made another revelation tear through her.

"Shit."

"What?" Seth asked.

"The images I get from her. The ones no one else here does? Jevryn gets them too." She now understood exactly why he'd ignored the question when she'd asked him about it. She didn't know how communication could be genetic, but then she didn't know the universe-wide history of every type of magic, either.

Was that how Temerex had found her on Amentia Furor? Had she felt, in Nyx, a spark of whatever it was that connected her to Jevryn and so she'd come running? No wonder, when Jevryn dumped Temerex here, the unicorn-dragon had kept sending Nyx an image of the three of them together, and the overwhelming sentiment Nyx had gotten from the image was *family*.

She'd thought Tem just viewed Nyx and Jevryn as *her* family. It had never occurred to Nyx that Temerex could see what she couldn't.

"Are you really going to make him wander through a maze?" Seth asked.

"Yes." It was petty, but she needed it. Not the maze, exactly, not trapping him in it. It wasn't as if Jevryn would be confused about what was happening to him. Nor would she take any particular enjoyment from him running around in it.

She just…wanted to know if he would try. If he would give her that much, that illusion of control, or if he would settle himself in a chair and tell her to fetch him once she'd ceased being childish.

"Wait with me?" she asked Seth.

"Of course."

She settled onto her back in the warm grass and closed her eyes, Seth filling the space next to her.

Currently, she'd separated Jevryn from Griff and put him in a windowless room not unlike the one her mother occupied. She changed it now, dozens of doors and staircases leading out. Then, in the center of the room, she added the single furniture option of a chair.

He ran his fingers over the chair back and turned a slow circle of the room. After a moment, he moved. The carelessness with which he picked a staircase and began climbing told her he knew very well it didn't matter which door he opened, or staircase he climbed. That his task was not to find a way out, but simply to put in the effort.

It shouldn't have mattered to her, which option he chose. The chair or the staircase.

But it did.

S he was still lying on her back, soaking in the sunshine when Jevryn climbed the final staircase and opened the trapdoor at the top, emerging onto the grass next to her. Seth stood and wordlessly left, a gentle squeeze of her hand his goodbye.

Nyx opened her eyes and looked at Jevryn. He'd been climbing for the better part of an hour, solidly ignoring any same-floor doors she gave him in favor of the upward-climbing staircases.

If he'd thought choosing the more physically difficult routes would get her to let him quit sooner, well, damn it he was right. Not that he looked any worse for wear from his physical exertion.

"Have I paid enough penance to be granted a conversation?" he asked mildly.

"Maybe if you climbed another twenty-six years' worth of stairs." One for every year of her life he'd ignored. She rolled up to sit, knees bent, arms resting atop them.

"An expensive conversation." He settled onto the grass next to her, mirroring her position.

"To some people. What's twenty years to you?"

He was quiet for a moment, then, "As you say. My years are perhaps not worth so much."

She wanted to snap at him, to yell at him, but he hadn't given her anything to work with yet. Temerex, who had been sprawled out on her side next to Nyx, jerked awake, rolling onto her stomach.

She saw Jevryn and her ears perked up. She stretched her

neck and muzzle toward him. But as he started to lift his hand to her she jerked back, as if remembering she wasn't happy with him. She gained her feet and turned away, flicking her tail in a whiplike move that forced him to lean out of the way to avoid the sharp spikes in her tail. She trotted away, sparks flying each time her hooves hit the ground.

Jevryn watched her go, looking almost human. Almost hurt.

"What did you expect? You abandoned her. Again."

He offered no response. No defense.

"The images I get from her—the fact I can communicate with her—that's because of you? Because I'm related to you?" She couldn't quite make herself say the words *your daughter*.

"Yes," he answered, seeming relieved to be on a subject that required only a factual response. "She came from a breeder who specialized in genetic tailoring. Her telepathic abilities are specific to my DNA. I suppose yours is similar enough to allow for some transference of the ability."

"Why?"

"I am not particularly well-versed in genetics. Arradin would be better at—"

"Why am I *yours*?"

His hands clenched together. "This is not an easy discussion for me to have. It is one that, frankly, I had hoped never *to* have."

"I don't really care what's easy for you right now."

"No. No, I suppose you don't." He turned his head, looking off into the distance. The sun slanted on his high cheekbones, caught on the silver of his eyes, and it was impossible not to compare herself to him, now that she knew.

She'd gotten the deep black of his hair, but not the perfect silken shine. The high arch of his cheekbones, though hers were slightly less sharp. The tone of his skin, but not its depth. The color of his eyes, but not the shape.

She had always taken comfort in the thought that she must look a great deal like her father, because she looked so little like her mother. That comfort was gone, now.

"The act that led to your conception," Jevryn finally said. "It was not a consensual one on my part."

"She...forced you?"

"Yes." A short, bitter syllable. "She drugged me. I admit I never saw it coming. I was too confident in myself and too dismissive of her.

"When I found her she was, as you know, the last of the Hidden. She was only nineteen. I made allowances for her on account of her youth and what she had been through. I made too many allowances.

"She was from one of the original five Hidden families. Born to an excessive amount of wealth and privilege and raised to expect only more of both. She was never grateful for having been spared the same fate as her family, only angered over the loss of her lifestyle.

"She did not appreciate being told that if she wanted to survive, she needed to disappear. I provided her with accommodations equal to what she was accustomed to, but it wasn't enough. She didn't simply want luxury, she wanted a return to prominence. To be known, and at the side of someone with power and influence.

"And there I was, the seemingly perfect target. Her attempts at seduction were embarrassingly obvious. I thought her childish but not dangerous. I underestimated her."

He stopped talking, and though Nyx didn't want to hear the particulars, she needed to. She needed to understand where she had come from. To understand *why*. "What happened?"

"As I said, I underestimated her. I underestimated the scope of her ambition. The fact that, given the secrecy she lived under by necessity, I was the *only* man within her reach who met her criteria. And if I was uninterested in her, she would simply find another way to bind me to her.

"I had stopped interacting with her, certain that she was well-guarded and that I had no need to. So she fabricated an attack." He shook his head. "No, that isn't quite right. She did not fabricate anything. She leaked her whereabouts knowing the Kumir would come for her and that, when they did, *I* would come as well.

"She understood her magical ability was too valuable in this game to risk. I moved her to a new location, and she repaid my efforts to keep her wretched heart beating by drugging me. With Bloodshot. It is a heavy sedative that also heightens arousal, lowers cognitive ability, and induces short term memory loss.

"I was aware something wasn't right about that night, but I was unaware of the full details of what had happened until after you were born. She didn't want to take the risk that if I knew, you would *not* be born. As soon as she delivered, she presented you to me, along with a healer to verify your parentage, as if you were the winning throw in a dice game.

"I was furious, when I sent her to Earth. More so when I understood what she had done to Viktor. The Hidden had kept that particular talent under tight secrecy, though only a subset of the population are susceptible to it. He was, and there was no undoing it."

So Jevryn had just…shipped them all off to Earth. Nyx dropped her head into her hands. It was either that, or scream at him. What her mother had done to him was wrong. Sickeningly so. But Nyx hadn't deserved to pay the price for that.

"Are you…well?" Jevryn asked hesitantly.

"Am I *well*?" She lifted her head. "My mother forced herself on you so she could have *me* as a bargaining chip. She brainwashed Viktor. She shattered the inside of my mind and I don't even understand *why*. She lies, she manipulates, and she hates, and she thinks none of that is her fault if she's not getting what she wants.

"You *knew that*. You knew exactly what she was and you left me with her. You let her drag Viktor and Seth with us. What the hell did we do to deserve that?"

He flinched. "Viktor was not so far gone as I understood he later became. I would have made different choices then, had I known his condition would worsen. But at the time he still cared for his son and I thought it cruel to separate them."

"And me?"

"Hidden children must be raised by someone of their ability. Until you come fully into your power, it is too easy for you to lose yourselves in it. All it takes is one frightening experience in which you feel the need to hide, as all children at some point do, except you Hide literally, inside yourselves, getting lost in the webs of your own power.

"Without an older Hidden to draw you out, you would be lost forever. There have been Hidden orphans before, lost from their families and it unknown what they were. Until just such a scenario as the one I mentioned occurs and they waste away, incapable of being woken."

Nyx thought of the hours she'd lost on Lehine, following her mother's Hiding. Of the days she'd lost here, recently. She'd thought it was her desire to know her past that had driven her so far into herself for so long. It had never occurred to her that it was the magic itself.

"Fine," Nyx said. "So I had to have her. You never once thought it might be a good idea to check on me? You saw what she was and thought…what? 'That woman's a terrible human being but she'll make a fine mother'?"

A muscle feathered in Jevryn's jaw. "I did the best I knew to do for you."

"By letting me grow up with nothing? With no one save a boy who was as trapped as I was, and two adults who didn't give a damn?"

"I should hardly have considered you to have grown up with *nothing*. Unless of course Elena imprinted her own definition of luxury upon you."

Nyx gaped at him. "In what world is a three-room cabin, so small that Seth had to sleep *in the barn*, considered luxurious? And it's a good thing Seth learned how to cook at *eight*. Because by that point Viktor was so far gone he forgot us half the time, and she didn't give a damn if we ate or not. But forgive me, I guess I'm just a selfish entitled bitch like her."

A hint of uncertainty crept into Jevryn's eyes. "I provided her with more than enough money to ensure—"

"Money?" Nyx cut him off. "You gave a woman like that *money* and thought that would make her a good parent?"

His jaw set. "I hired the contractors that were to build a new residence myself. I had the plans drawn up. I also saw to the selection of a governess and tutors for you *and* the Hawthorne boy. While the residents of Dead Earth may not accidentally find their way into the pockets of Earth Between, there is nothing to prevent them from entering it if they are shown the way, which Viktor was given explicit instructions to do.

"In addition to this, Elena was provided with a generous bi-annual stipend to provide for *all* of your needs."

Nyx couldn't decide if she wanted to laugh or cry. Had he really been that naive about what Elena would do with anything he gave her? Or had he simply wanted to throw money at the problem that had been *Nyx* so he could forget about her, his conscience clear?

"I don't know how to tell you this, but none of that ever happened. I grew up in the cabin. Seth mostly grew up in the barn. The only tutor I had was Viktor and the books he brought back from Dead Earth."

At least Elena had instructed Viktor to go through the trouble of legally "home-schooling" her, though Nyx privately thought the only reason she had her high school diploma was because learning all of the stuff had kept her busy.

There was a storm brewing in Jevryn's eyes, sparks of that magic that had turned so many people to dust flashing like light-ning in the silver depths. "If this is true, I would see it for myself."

"Great. It's a two-day drive by car unless you can portal through the Betweens."

Apparently he *could* portal through the Betweens. He walked off the Station grounds and disappeared. Then he reappeared fifteen seconds later, dragged her beyond the boundary and said, "Forgive me, but you shouldn't be left alone in your condition."

A blink of an eye later she stood once more on the grounds of her childhood home.

The shock on Jevryn's face was almost humorous. If, you know, this hadn't been her life. When he started walking the grounds, as if he was going to find the bones of this other residence he had generously provided for the building of, like she had previously Hidden or burned it to the ground in anticipation of one day providing him with this sob story, she was just annoyed.

She leaned against the exterior wall of the cabin and watched him, trying not to think of how many more unpleasant memories she now had access to than she'd had the last time she'd been here. No wonder Seth hadn't wanted to come back. It was easier to think of it all as a bad dream, or at least as an unpleasant segment of the past that never had to be repeated, than it was to stand here and remember the utter futility her existence had been.

Jevryn stood in the center of the old sand riding arena, overgrown now with weeds. His robes and long, silken hair blew in the wind, hand on the pommel of the sword at his hip. He looked like a mage warrior out of a fantasy painting, and her heart squeezed painfully to think of how in awe of him her younger self would have been. How easily and undeservedly he could have won her love.

All he would have had to do was show up. Maybe when she was older she would have wanted to know why he'd left her here for so long, but back then? Back then she would have run into his arms without question, would have been so *proud* to have him as her father. Would have worked herself into the ground to be whatever he wanted in a daughter.

To be *worthy* of being his daughter, when she understood now that that wasn't how it was supposed to be. She should never have had to think at three or ten or sixteen that if she could just be better—smarter, braver, stronger—her father would have wanted her.

But knowing that—knowing that it wasn't right—didn't help. Because she was still that little girl inside, only now she knew that none of the excuses she'd consoled herself with were true. She'd told herself her father didn't know she existed, or that her mother had stolen her away from him, and when he found out, when he found *her*, he would take her away and everything would be better.

But he'd always known right where to find her. And she'd never been good enough to be worth taking. She would never *be* good enough to be worth wanting.

He stalked up from the field, silent, and portaled them back outside the Station's grounds. The sky within the border was filled with storm clouds, and the moment they stepped within Kaliaris' reach Griff came bounding out the backdoor. Clods of dirt flew as he tore across the lawn, inserting himself between Nyx and Jevryn.

"Are you alright?" he demanded, wing splaying across her shoulders and curving around her, as if he intended to hide her fully from Jevryn's view. As if he was afraid Jevryn might have *done* something to her.

"I'm fine." She hugged him. Or, more accurately, hugged his foreleg, since he was larger than she'd ever seen him, and that foreleg was the thickness of a human torso.

His head swiveled toward Jevryn. "Where did you take her?"

"Nowhere dangerous, Arradin."

"Taking her *anywhere* right now is dangerous. Had you any respect for—"

"Griff, it's fine," she interrupted. His concern might be soothing the hurt, jagged edges inside her, but she didn't want to be in the middle of an argument between him and Jevryn over what her best interests were right now.

It would be too much like listening to her parents argue

while she was in the room and they forgot she was there. A bit of normal childhood trauma she'd once longed for and now preferred to skip. "He's not worth it."

She patted his foreleg and turned toward the Station building.

"You need to let Elena fix this," Jevryn said.

Nyx stopped, squeezing her eyes closed on the wave of rage that crested and broke inside her. Yes, *she knew* she needed to let Elena fix this. But… "How am I supposed to trust her to do that? I didn't trust her before. After what you've told me, I trust her even less."

"You need not trust her. *I* will be there as she does this. Should she attempt to harm you, I will do far worse than end her life."

"So I'm supposed to trust you instead? If I recall, when I asked you about my father, the only thing you deigned to tell me was that he wasn't a good man and I was better off without him." Her hands clenched into fists. "And you know what? You were right." She moved for the Station's door again.

"Wait." His voice rang out with command.

Nyx just couldn't help herself. "Or what?" she called back, continuing to walk. "You'll ground me?"

"Nyx *Ilera A-Morridahn*." His voice cracked across the space between them like a whip.

She turned to look at him then, and she let all her hurt and fury show. "Do you think you can ignore the uncomfortable parts of my life as easily as you ignore the parts of my name you don't want to acknowledge, *Father*?"

He met her stubborn gaze with his own. "You are angry with me, and you have every right to be. But I hid you here so that no one would know you existed. So you *could* survive.

"No councilor's progeny lives long. Do you know how many children the others have brought into this universe over the centuries?"

She had no answer.

"One-hundred and forty-two. Of those, fifty-seven lived long enough to have children of their own before they were killed. From them, two-hundred and eleven third-and-fourth-generation descendants of the All Council line. Do you know how many of those descendants remains alive today?"

Uneasiness roiled in her gut.

"*One*. And she is standing before me now. Forgive me for my callousness if I thought being severed from me was the best method to ensure your survival."

Frustration burned in her throat. She didn't want to allow him any rightness. Didn't want to feel as if he in any way deserved her forgiveness, because the child in her still wanted to forgive. Still wanted the explanation, the perfect words that would make it okay to love him. To *want* to be loved by him.

That sliver of a memory she'd regained rose. The one where she'd hidden in her mother's car, and asked a stranger if he was her father. It was a memory that was still blurred, a stranger's face she still couldn't recall. And she had a feeling that even if her mother fixed what she'd done, this particular event wouldn't be retrievable.

"I have this memory," she said quietly. "From when I was six. I followed my mother to a diner. She met a stranger and I asked him if he was my father. I can't remember his face. I can't remember anything else that happened." She looked directly into his eyes. "Was that you?"

Several beats of silence before he said, "Yes."

The tightness in her chest grew, prickles of pain behind her eyes. He'd seen her. Met her. Talked to her. She might have no real memory of it, but she could guess well enough what she would have said. How she would have begged him to take her—told him that she'd be good and wouldn't cause any trouble—if she and Seth could just go with him.

And she'd made so little of an impression, he'd been so unmoved, that he hadn't even condescended to take the time, while he was *already on Earth*, to see if she was being properly taken care of.

She walked into the Station without looking back. She'd dealt with one of her parents. She might as well get the other one out of the way.

34

Nyx pulled on the Station, drawing herself, Griff, Jevryn, and Seth to the door of her mother's room. She looked at Jevryn, about to say…what?

If you let her hurt me, I'll never forgive you?

He wouldn't care if she never forgave him. He would likely be most pleased if she continued treating him in the manner she always had—like a powerful person who was just being nice to her for a time because they had an agreement to work together. She had nothing else to threaten him with. Nothing that she could *use*, anyway, because she wouldn't use Griff.

But Griff, as it turned out, had plenty to threaten Jevryn with and the willingness to use it. "I told you before what I would do if you allowed any harm to come to her. That promise still stands."

Jevryn's lips pressed into a thin line, but all he did was nod.

"And Jevryn?" Griff continued. "We are operating under my definition of harm. Not yours."

"Of course." Jevryn's voice was perfectly empty. He had retreated from both of them behind his councilor mask, and she couldn't tell if that was because he wanted to be away from them, or because they were outside Elena's room and he didn't want to see her.

Nyx opened the door. Her mother didn't get a single word in before her throat was enclosed in a choker of Jevryn's power.

"Fix her," he ordered. "One wrong move, and I will take an excess of pleasure in ending your life."

The first hint of true nervousness crept into Elena's eyes. "What guarantee do I have that you'll let me go once I do? If I recall, you once told me that after she"—she jerked her head at Nyx—"was an adult, I should run as far away from you as possible. So I did."

"You have my word."

"What is that worth?"

"A great deal more than yours."

"I want—"

"I do not care what you want." The choker tightened. "You believe I will not kill you because she needs you. Allow me to disabuse you of that misconception. Her healer has stated that, given the proper length of time, she will eventually sort this out for herself. That process will be painful and unpleasant, but she *will* come out the other side of it.

"You are merely a shortcut. Never think that you are *necessary*. Refuse to help her, and I *will* kill you. Accept my word that you will return to your life after this, and hope that I keep it."

The choker loosened and Elena sucked in a breath. Pure vitriol burned in her eyes, but she said nothing. She turned to Nyx and held out her hand.

Nyx still couldn't quell her nerves. "Do you understand what you need to do?" She had sent Jevryn the clearest explanation Tobi could give her, in case she wasn't coherent by the time her mother got here. But this was, as the Congregation had repeatedly reminded her, not something any one of their number had ever had experience with.

"I know my own magic. This would never have happened if you hadn't fought me so hard in the first place."

Right. Because forgetting her own identity was such an obviously desirable outcome that Nyx should have just gone along with it without argument. She held her tongue and put her hand in her mother's.

Power poured over her, an ocean of it submerging her into endless depths. It felt like drowning. She struggled—against her mother's physical grip, and against that ocean. Her own magic rose in response, more of it than she'd ever felt, more than she'd ever known she *had*. It crested in her like a wave, building and building and—

A stinging slap cracked across her face. She blinked, the room and her mother coming back into focus, that tide of power within her just...waiting.

"Hold still," Elena snapped, "and stop fighting me. Or would you *like* to end up brain-damaged?"

Nyx froze, her chest heaving as she fought to take in enough air, to think. Her magic pulsed and roiled within her, wanting release, wanting to push the invasion of Elena's power from her. She couldn't let it go. She couldn't do this, couldn't just *submit*, not after everything.

Seth's warmth pressed against her back, his arms snaking around her waist. "It's okay. I have you."

The loose memory islands in her mind shuddered and shifted, threatening to fall. She closed her eyes, focusing on Seth, and let her power go. It had barely settled before Elena's magic was ravaging through her. The flow of it gushed like a roaring river, smaller creeks and streams splintering off from the main force.

Those offshoots reached for the loose islands of Nyx's memories, latching onto them. Elena's magic moved too swiftly for Nyx to follow, mere seconds all it took for every loose piece in her mind to be caught in a sticky strand of Hidden power.

Elena tugged and the islands shuffled, like someone had

dumped hundreds of dominoes into Nyx's skull and shaken them.

It *hurt*.

She was barely aware of Elena saying, "Hold her still, damn it," barely aware of Seth clamping her tighter.

Another vicious tug of power, another shuffle of dominoes. Then the memory islands were hurtling none-too-gently toward that puzzle board in her mind, crashing like meteors. They were jammed into place, ordered there by a hand that knew where they belonged and didn't care how forcefully they were put back together.

Agony blossomed in her skull. She held out—held on—until she was certain they were *right*. Until she looked down at the gleaming, unscarred whole of her mind and it felt solid. And though the renewal hurt, though her mind wanted to shut down so it could settle the weight of her life back within her, she fought unconsciousness long enough for one final act. She summoned the tides of her magic, and shoved Elena *out*.

S eth caught Nyx's dead weight as she dropped. A short, strangled sound came from Elena as Jevryn's power clamped tight.

"She's fine," Elena gasped out. Lines of blood trickled from the flickering choker.

"She does not *look* fine," Jevryn said, advancing on her. "She did not *scream* as if she was fine."

"It's only backlash," she struggled to get out. "She'll wake once it's run its course." She clawed at the choker then jerked her hands back, her fingertips coming away bloody. When Jevryn didn't let up, she looked at Seth.

"Tell him," she pleaded.

Seth almost laughed. That narcissistic bitch was actually asking *him* for help?

Jevryn's gaze followed Elena's, and while Seth didn't feel like defending her, the look on the councilor's face said that not saying *anything* wasn't an option.

"I was out for a day when I got my memories back. Couldn't tell you if that's what's happening now."

Jevryn flicked his hand. The choker of magic disappeared and Elena sucked in a breath, angry red slices criss-crossing her neck.

It was kind of impressive, the way she managed to draw herself up to some semblance of regality and stare down her nose at Jevryn despite being a full foot shorter. "I have done as you asked. Return me to my home."

"Once I am certain she is well. Not a moment before." Jevryn turned his back on her.

Elena laughed. "So the little brat *did* manage to get a foothold in your heart that day. I should have pushed you harder."

Jevryn pivoted, the movement almost too fast to follow. His fist connected with Elena's cheek. She stumbled back, shock on her face. Jevryn followed, his own face a mask of cold rage. He gripped her jaw, his fingers indenting the skin.

"Be grateful," he said icily, "that I do not break my word once it is given." He leaned in closer. His next words were spoken too softly for Seth to catch, but they made Elena's face lose what little color it had still possessed.

Jevryn let her go with a shove, shaking out his hand as if flinging off something foul, and walked from the room. Seth followed, carrying Nyx. Griff came last, sealing the door shut on Elena.

Jevryn turned, his expression smooth and unreadable once more, his gaze dropping to Nyx. He held his arms out. "I can take her."

Seth hefted her closer. "I've got her." The guy might be Nyx's biological father, but Seth was relatively certain he didn't know the first thing about *being* a father.

Jevryn didn't lower his arms. "I will not harm her."

Seth snorted. "All you've ever done is harm her. You weren't there when we were growing up. You didn't have to hear her cry herself to sleep more nights than not and know there was nothing you could do to make anything better.

"So don't think you get to step in now, when it's fucking convenient, and think that being willing to carry her up a flight of stairs is going to make up for anything. You *weren't there*. And if you aren't going to actually be here *now*, then don't give her the hope that you are."

Jevryn's eyes turned from silver to blue. Nyx's had done that once, when one of the horses had colicked and there hadn't been anything they could do. She'd been beyond sad. She'd been in sorrow. Two days later, Seth had dragged her into Dead Earth for the first time, and that blue had finally returned to silver.

Jevryn's arms fell back to his sides. He blinked, and the blue irises faded back to silver. Stiffly, he said, "Alert me when she wakes."

Seth watched him walk away. "Guy doesn't fight very hard for anything, does he?"

"Once, he did," Griff said quietly. "And it broke him."

"I thought 'A-Morridahns do not break'," he said, mimicking the tone Jevryn had used when he'd said as much to Koral.

Griff sighed. "They only think they do not."

The Station shifted beneath Seth's feet, and then they were standing in Nyx's room. "I still haven't gotten used to you guys doing that."

He placed her on the bed, then unlaced her boots and dropped them on the floor. She shifted, and he found the small movement reassuring.

"Give it a few centuries," Griff said. "You'll acclimate."

A few centuries. The words killed what little energy he had left. He dropped onto the bedside chair. "How do you do it?" He rubbed his hands together, trying to relieve the uncomfortable prickling under his skin that had started at Griff's off-hand comment. "You, Jevryn, the Council—how do you live that long?"

He watched the rise and fall of Nyx's chest while he waited for an answer.

"I am not sure you could call what any of us has been doing *living*," Griff said finally. "We are bound rather too tightly to our pasts. It is inescapable for the Council, given how they became what they are, and was for me as well because I had no future to reach for.

"Nyx has given me that future—a friend, a family. That, not time, is what makes all the difference. So if you want my advice —my experience—for whatever it is worth, it is this: if you lock yourself in the past, it is impossible to move forward. And you cling to yours, especially where she is concerned, in a way I am not certain is good for either of you."

"You think I'm bad for her?" It was what he was afraid of. What he'd always been afraid of.

"No. I am saying that if you cannot let go of what you *were*, you cannot be anything *now*. Your past has shaped you both. But it cannot be allowed to define who you are, or who you will become."

"What if I can't let it go?" His voice didn't even sound like his own, hollow and dull.

Griff's talon landed on Seth's shoulder, squeezing gently. "You can. And I believe you will. But right now you are exhausted. Go get some rest. I can stay in case she wakes."

Seth shook his head. "It's okay. I'm not tired."

"You are going to fall asleep in this chair and wake up with a crick in your neck," Griff grumbled. Another gentle squeeze of his talon. "But very well. Call for me if you need anything."

Seth didn't think he'd sleep. But a few minutes later, the exhaustion tugging at his bones proved him a liar.

35

Nyx decided if she never again woke up wondering how she'd gotten where she was and what had happened in the interim, it would be too soon. At least this time it was all easy enough to piece together. She was in her room. Seth, asleep in the chair next to the bed, was a good indication of how she'd gotten here. And she remembered well enough the explosion of pain that had sent her into the all-too-receptive arms of unconsciousness.

That pain was gone now, as were the loose memory islands and the skeleton of Elena's Hiding. She felt whole for the first time in her adult life, and when she reached for her past, it was just *there*. As if it had always been there. As if the last eight years had been a bad dream.

But it hadn't been a bad dream, because those memories were there too, and she wasn't ready for how much more that time alone hurt when it was lined up right next to the others. She thought she'd been ready. She thought she'd been told enough and remembered enough and pieced together enough things that logic would get her through this.

But logic didn't have shit on a lifetime of feelings suddenly settling back inside her. She slipped out of bed quietly, so she wouldn't wake Seth. Or attempted to. She landed on her boots—he must have taken them off for her—and stumbled, grabbing onto the nightstand to keep from falling over. He didn't wake, and that told her how exhausted he was. Unless she was perfectly quiet, he almost always woke when she did.

Unlike everything she'd recalled about him in the last few months, this wasn't just a feeling, wasn't something she knew but couldn't explain. All the memories were there to back it up.

Memories of him, and her, and *them,* and everything that was supposed to have happened—everything they were supposed to become—and hadn't. She speed-walked for the bathroom, making it inside just as the shattering of a dream hit her seven years late.

It wasn't only Seth. It wasn't only never getting to leave Earth, never getting to do any of the things they'd talked about. It was the loss of her agency. Of never getting to live. Of growing up in a cage of isolation and then, the moment things were supposed to change for the better, they changed for the worse.

It was thinking, through every cruel thing her mother had ever said to her, that somewhere beneath it all she had to care. When Nyx had been younger, she'd seen hints of affection. Brief moments that had become more infrequent as Nyx grew, until eventually they disappeared altogether.

It was realizing that her mother was as much a stranger to her as her father was, and that she always had been, because Nyx had never been allowed to know her. As if, at some point, Elena had written Nyx off as a failed investment that couldn't be recovered. But instead of letting Nyx go, she'd erased her.

A sob tore out of her and she crawled into the shower, turning the spray on full blast because she didn't want to hear herself cry. She hugged her knees to her chest as hot water soaked through her hair, her shirt, her jeans. Droplets rained down her face, falling into her eyes.

A crash sounded from the bedroom and Seth's frantic voice called, "Nyx?"

She tried and failed to pull herself together enough to respond. A second later the bathroom door burst open. Seth's eyes, at first wild, calmed now that he'd found her. But as his gaze swept over her, taking her in, they filled with a pain that mirrored her own.

He climbed into the shower, went to his knees and pulled her to him. "I'm sorry, baby. I'm so sorry."

She hated her mother more than ever for how broken he sounded. Seth was never supposed to sound that way. On the surface, he might be the dour one and her the happy one. But beneath the surface, she was the one prone to gray skies and maudlin moods. He was the one who could laugh when the world was burning, who could make *her* laugh even in her bleakest moments.

She buried her head in the crook of his neck, her body shaking with the tears that wouldn't quit. "She just left me. Like I was nothing. What's wrong with me? What's so fucking wrong with me that she tried to erase me? That she had to take everything, that she had to take *you*."

"There isn't a single thing wrong with you." He crushed her tighter. "Leaving is on me. That's *my* fault."

She lifted her head. "That's bullshit and you know it. She put you in an impossible situation."

Her mother had known Nyx hated the way Seth had had to take care of her. She understood exactly why Elena had given Seth the choice of remembering or not. Of staying or going. Because Elena would have been happy knowing that Seth had either left Nyx, or spent the rest of his life doing the one thing Nyx had never wanted him to.

But Seth didn't seem like he was hearing her.

"It's bullshit," she repeated.

"I promised you," he whispered. "On the beach, in Washington, I promised you I'd never leave."

Washington. No wonder Seth had nearly cut his finger off when Griff had brought her back the beach sand from his trip, and she'd told him how she'd always wanted to go to the beach and never gotten to.

Because she had gone. Seth had taken her, to the closest shore they could reach. A month before she turned eighteen, another trip trying to work out the final kinks in Seth's ability to avoid Viktor's tracking.

The memory washed over her in a soft wave.

Lying on the sand, the sound of the waves lapping softly against the shore, Seth ranging over her. "Marry me."

She laughed and rolled her eyes. "Sure. Nothing will go wrong with that."

"You think I'm kidding, but I'm completely serious. Marry me. Not today, not now, but someday."

Laughing again, because he couldn't actually be serious. "Hmm, I don't know. Why should I?"

"Because I'll always be here. As long as you want me, no matter what happens, I'll never leave. You'll never be alone." His lips finally curved, giving way to the smirk that lived almost perpetually on his face. "Consider it my first wedding vow."

She pushed onto her elbows then, finally understanding that he wasn't kidding, and it scared the hell out of her. Because despite all the plans they'd made, despite how much she wanted to believe in that future where they were never apart, she didn't always believe it.

There was a darkness that liked to whisper in her ear, late at night, telling her that they would discover the universe, and he would discover how much more he could be. Without her.

"Make me a second vow."

That smirk on his face deepened as he dipped his head, trailing teasing kisses down the side of her neck. "Alright. What do you want me to promise? Is it dirty? Tell me it's dirty."

"Promise you won't ever let yourself be trapped with me again. That you won't stay when you don't want to just because of a stupid vow."

He pulled back, his eyes searching hers. "I'll always want to stay with you."

"Then it shouldn't scare you to promise."

He shook his head. "I don't like it."

She jabbed him in the ribs. "Vow two, or vow one never happens."

"Ow." He rubbed at his side. "Fine, I promise. Does that mean you're saying yes?"

"It means I'm saying ask me again in ten years."

"Ten," he repeated. "Why ten?"

"Because 'decade' is one of my favorite words." Because ten years was a good testing ground. Because it was long enough to find out how they worked together in the rest of the world. "And if you'll always be here for me, you'll still be here then. So ask me again in a decade."

She let the memory go, the Seth of the past replaced with the one that was here with her now. "We were just kids," she said softly.

"A month," he said. "I promised you and I couldn't even keep it a month."

"I wasn't there to keep a promise to. All that was left in that apartment was a girl who didn't know who she was and didn't know what you meant to her.

"And in case you forgot, I made you make me a second promise. Tell me you wouldn't have felt trapped if you stayed. Tell me you wouldn't have woken up one morning and hated me."

He didn't say anything.

"That's what I thought." She closed her eyes, because she didn't know how to ask what she *had* to ask while she was looking at him. "Do you feel trapped now? Knowing I'm bound to the Station, that I may never find a way to undo this? Do you want to leave?"

He brushed wet hair from her cheeks, his hands cupping her face. "Look at me."

She didn't want to, felt pressure constricting around her ribs.

"*Look* at me."

She did.

"The answers are no, and never."

The aching tightness in her chest eased.

"No, I don't feel trapped. No, I never want to leave you." His thumb stroked across her cheek. "So I need to know if you still want me to stay."

Her answer was a kiss. Deep, and long, and hungry, and he returned it with everything he'd been holding back the last few months. All his hesitance washed away. She lost herself in the way he tasted, the way he touched her. She barely managed a command to the Station to shut off the shower as he hoisted her up, carrying her into the bedroom.

And she discovered they could still laugh when they made love, peeling each other out of wet clothes that were nearly impossible to get off. She drowned in the warmth of his skin and the way he still fit with her, like a perfect complement, even after all this time.

They remembered what was old, and they learned what was new, and she poured into every touch three words she'd never said, and he never had either, because they'd never had to.

36

Nyx had forgotten how utterly blissed out it was possible to feel when your body finally managed to make your brain shut up.

She was completely relaxed and almost asleep again, so naturally someone had to come knocking at her door.

She groaned and poked Seth in the stomach. "You get it."

"Who is it?" he mumbled, also nearly asleep.

"I don't know, I'm too tired to look." Too tired to have all of the Station's senses zooming around in her brain. And she already knew that, whoever it was, she didn't want to talk to them.

Seth grumbled, but he rolled out of bed. Then grumbled some more as he pulled his mostly-still-wet jeans on. He trudged to the door and Nyx dragged the covers over her head as she heard the doorknob turn.

"Oh, it's you." She was pretty sure he used that pointedly vague dialogue just to make her wonder who it was.

"I need to speak with her," a measured voice said.

Of course it was Jevryn.

"She's tired."

There was a pause, then a pointed, "She is, apparently, not *too* tired."

Ugh. This was nine kinds of weird. She decided she was too old to be embarrassed that her father was at the door when it was obvious she'd just had sex. Besides, it wasn't like he'd ever been her *dad*.

"Is the door open enough that he'll see it if I flip him off?" she asked.

The creak of hinges drifted to her. "It is now."

Nyx poked her arm out of the covers and raised her middle finger.

Drily, Jevryn said, "Your manners are, as ever, impeccable."

"I must get them from you," she shot back. Fuck. She was bantering. She and Jevryn *bantered*. Or was it sniping, since she wasn't entirely certain it was good-natured on either side? Either way, it suggested a level of familiarity she hadn't realized had developed. When had that happened, and was it too late to opt out?

"You have two minutes to dress," he informed her. A pause, then, to Seth, "And you. Put on a shirt."

The door swung closed. She yelled after him. "You know I don't have to let you in if I don't want to, right?"

"You know that your Station is alive, right?" he called back. "Which means that it can die. I am not above killing parts of it to get your attention. I have little time and even less patience."

"What else is new?" she mumbled.

She remembered when Laiveran had made a construct from the Station and Jevryn had killed it. Remembered Kaliaris' pain as it died. Remembered how effortlessly Jevryn had killed the Kumir on Nethrayne. Even taking out Koral hadn't made him break a sweat.

What exactly was she descended from?

She rolled out of bed and donned clothes while Seth pulled his shirt on, grinning at her. "I think it's going well. I've definitely got the fatherly seal of approval."

Nyx snorted, raking her hands through her hair. She'd just tamed it into some semblance of order when the door opened and Jevryn walked in. He glanced at Seth. "You may go."

"He may stay," Nyx countered, mimicking his tone. "I'll just tell him everything later anyway."

"Then you may relay it later."

Seth rolled his eyes. "I'll go make sure Cruella's not up to anything." He brushed a kiss to her cheek and walked out.

Jevryn's eyes followed him. He had a look on his face that indicated he wanted to say something, likely of a critical nature. Nyx arched her eyebrows, daring him to presume he had the right to comment on *any* facet of her life.

He cleared his throat. "Koral's death has been noted, and the Council called to convene."

Her brief respite from worry, the one she'd gained from finally having her memories whole and her relationship sorted, vanished. "Are you… What's going to happen to you?"

She hadn't realized she was concerned. But he had come to Nethrayne for her. He'd found her mother for her, and she realized now what that must have cost him. How he must have hated needing anything of Elena.

She knew it was foolish to think he'd done any of it for *her* and not for what he needed from her. But she wanted him to have helped because she *was* his daughter. She wanted that to mean something to him. She wanted him to want to earn her acceptance, to keep trying to earn it even if she told him she hated him every day for the next ten years.

Her life had been a series of wanting things she knew she would never get. But damn it, he didn't get to go get himself executed by Council mandate when she'd only just learned who he was.

He gave her a wry smile. "I am unlikely to meet my end, if that is your concern. There is, after all, nothing left in the way of proof."

Bodies. He meant there weren't any bodies left. "Doesn't that kind of...point towards you?"

"That particular facet of Salyrian death magic was not discussed outside of our own circles. Reducing an opponent to literal dust was seen as an unnecessary expenditure of power. A complete loss of control. A bit like—" He cut off abruptly. "Never mind. That particular analogy is inappropriate and rather vulgar, now that I think about it."

"Is that why you did it?" At the questioning tilt of his head, she added, "So Kiev wouldn't think it was you? I'm guessing you've never *actually* had a complete loss of control in your life."

He'd always seemed to her like the epitome of control.

"No, Nyx. I did it because she threatened *you*." He gave her no time to process that statement before he moved on. "But while there is nothing to point to me, there is also nothing to point to anyone else. The Council has existed in equilibrium for centuries because it has been in our best interests to do so. And because we were once colleagues of a sort, who then suffered common tragedies and made terrible choices together.

"We are bound together by our pasts and our mistakes, and by the knowledge that if one of us was murdered, it would surely spark the next death, and then the next. Our paranoia is already legend.

"It has long been clear that one of our number was behind the Kumir, because the only reason to exterminate the totality of the Hidden was to unearth the remembrance of the Harvester's location.

"And when we all remembered it was in our own Vault, the very last place we would consider looking for it, we knew little peace in our anticipation that one of us would attempt to take it. When it disappeared, we were on the verge of internal war."

And he had taken the fall then, taken the suspicion of its theft, to allow Kaden to bring the Harvester to Earth. He'd spent years in Psionics, and if she still didn't fully understand what that meant she knew, by the way Kaden had refused to talk about it, that she didn't want to. And she wanted to ask now, but she didn't think Jevryn would appreciate her bringing up something he probably didn't realize Seth had overheard him talking about.

"So what you're telling me is you aren't going to be around for a while?" she guessed.

"Not at a moment's notice, no. I am kindly requesting that you keep out of trouble, because I may not be there the next time you get into it."

"I'm never *trying* to get into trouble."

"Yes, I know. That is what makes it all the more worrisome. Why *were* you on Nethrayne? I have come to understand Beauregard's involvement, but why would you involve yourself in any capacity, even if you never intended to go personally?"

"Because the Kumir killed all the Hidden? Because they kept coming for Seth any time he rode the ley lines, which meant they probably knew he was with my mother at one point and were therefore trying to find her? Because if we figured out who was behind them, we'd know who was looking for the Harvester?"

"Why did you not simply bring this to me?"

She didn't answer.

"Ah. So you did not trust that I was not involved, then."

"Nethrayne was a councilor planet. How was I supposed to know you didn't already know about it? I mean, you found me easily enough."

"No, I did not. Nethrayne is not one of the councilor planets I knew the location of. When Arradin informed me of what happened, I still did not believe that was where you had actually gone. From the moment I arrived on Earth, I did one thing. I waited by the anchor Arradin showed me you had made, in the ludicrous hope you would have enough stubbornness to reach through again. Be grateful I did."

"I am."

"Wonderful." He shook his head. "I still do not understand how you reached Nethrayne in the first place. How did you break through the overriding dominance of a Station even if, as I understand it, the place at which you did so was not fully *of* the Station?"

"I was just looking for Seth."

Understanding dawned on Jevryn's face. "You made him into an anchor? You made a *living person* into an anchor?"

"I didn't mean to."

He pinched the bridge of his nose. "You do understand you could have killed him?"

Ice curled around her spine. "What?"

"Drawing on an anchor exhausts the magic in it. When an anchor is inanimate, it simply means that if its help is not enough to allow you to portal to that place, you exhaust the anchor and lose it. But when that anchor is human, it connects you to *them* as a source of energy.

"Had you not had the ability and portal magic to reach him and continued to try anyway, you would have drained that energy from him. You would have *exhausted the anchor.*"

"Shit." She dragged a hand through her hair. "Maybe you should have mentioned all this before you gave me a ton of portal magic?"

"You were not intended to have found it yet."

"I find everything I'm not supposed to find. It's kind of a curse."

"I will note that for the future. In the meantime… Were I more sensible, I would take the remainder of it with me. However, should your involvement in any of this become known, I would not leave you without that means of escape." He hesitated, then withdrew something from his pocket. It was a small disc the size of a quarter, black rock with thin blue veining. "This is tied to one of my anchors. Can you feel the connection?"

She took it, rubbing her thumb over the smooth stone, feeling the warmth of the magic within. If she concentrated, she could feel it tethered to something. Something she could follow, like she'd followed Seth. She nodded.

"It leads to one of my homes. One of the few I am certain no one knows the location of. Go there, if you find yourself in difficulty. You will arrive in the library. Find Arradin's book and remove it from the shelf. I will be alerted to your presence and come as soon as I am able."

He headed for the door. He was just leaving?

"That's it? Call if I need to get bailed out of jail, otherwise I'll see you whenever?"

He turned back. His eyes were not unkind, but they held something she found mildly condescending. "What would you have of me? There is nothing I can say or do that will unmake the past, and had I it to do over again with you, my choices would vary little.

"Let us not pretend to be other than what we are. I cannot be what you want me to be."

"You have no idea what I want you to be. You've never bothered to ask."

"I can guess well enough. You want a father. You want to be loved. You want me to tell you believable lies that will make me into something other than the monster you have already determined I am. You want excuses that will make you accept the necessity of what I have done, and what I will do, so that you can forgive it.

"I can do none of those things. You would do well to accept that and spare yourself any further hurt." He walked out.

She stalked after him. "Am I such a disappointment?"

No answer, not even a falter in his stride.

She sank into Kaliaris' senses, lengthening the hallway so she could continue to trail him down it. "I'm not asking you to throw me a birthday party every year and come to Christmas dinner. I'm just asking you to know me before you decide I'm worthless."

He. Just. Kept. Walking.

She stopped and let him go, feeling pathetic. Feeling like that six-year-old kid she'd been in that diner, at a meeting she *still* couldn't remember. It hit her that this probably wasn't the first time she'd begged him not to walk away from her.

They leave you, a dark voice whispered in the back of her mind. *In the end, everybody leaves you. Your mother. Viktor. Seth. Kaden. Jevryn.*

There was something wrong with her. Something fundamentally broken, because no one ever stayed unless they *had* to. Familiar darkness settled over her, stretching roots into her bones.

Then Griff was there, his wing settling around her shoulder, tugging her close. A small beam of light pierced through the darkness.

"I'm sorry," Griff said gently.

She couldn't be crying again. She didn't *want* to be crying again. She turned her face into his chest, soft feathers tickling her nose, and he wrapped his other wing around her, enclosing her in a soft cocoon that blanketed her from the world.

"We're not leaving," he told her. "None of *us* are leaving."

And that, damn it, made her cry harder. But it also made the darkness retreat.

37

S he finally stopped crying, the cathartic expenditure giving her the necessary relief to remember she had things to do. The Station's senses, pouring through her, also made her realize that, while her father might be gone, her mother wasn't.

"What is she still doing here?"

Griff stretched his wings before settling them back against his body. "I am afraid Jevryn did not have the time to return her personally."

Translation, Jevryn hadn't wanted to be anywhere near Elena again unless he absolutely had to.

Nyx understood that. As pissed as she was at him for personal reasons, she wouldn't wish Elena's company on him. So she got why *he* hadn't taken her, but, "Can't she just leave on the ley lines?"

"Not without a guide. When I suggested she return home immediately, she informed me it was not considered proper for a woman of her status to travel anywhere alone, so she was never trained to do so."

That was just so prissily *Elena* that Nyx couldn't hold back a snort. "Then I'll hire her a guide. I'll hire her ten."

"Would that it were so simple. Unfortunately, I fear her

husband has been petitioning the Kormadin family to rally the army in search of her."

Of course. Nyx's own father wouldn't spare her more than a few hours of his time, yet somehow Elena, objectively awful human being, had a husband who would raise an army in search of her.

Life really wasn't fair.

"I allowed her to write him, overseeing the contents of the message. He is aware of her magical heritage, and therefore aware that she has had previous interactions with the Council. I had her express that her abilities had been necessary in a matter of extreme importance, and that the less fanfare with which she was retrieved from this place, the better. We have not yet received her husband's response."

Nyx took one of those deep breaths that was supposed to be steadying. She didn't want her mother here a single second longer. But while shipping her off to an Earth Between inn was tempting, she also didn't want her mother interacting with the residents of Earth Between.

They were Nyx's. She'd made friends in the town, was building a reputation for herself there. Who knew what Elena might say? How much damage she might do. At least within the Station, Nyx controlled who she interacted with and where she went.

"She asked to see you," Griff said.

"Asked?" Nyx found that hard to believe.

"Very well, she demanded to see you, after I refused to allow her to roam the Station."

"Thank you for that." Stars knew she didn't want her mother mucking about within these walls either.

"Are you going to see her?"

Nyx hesitated, but settled on, "No." She had things she needed to ask. But she just couldn't deal with her mother right now. Couldn't handle the way Elena managed to tear the scabs off every half-healed cut and rub salt into the newly exposed wounds. "I have something else I need to do."

She darted up to her room to replace her used portal magic bracelets with fresh ones—she still wasn't comfortable going anywhere without them—then headed for where the Station ended and Wayfarer's Way began. She thought about asking Seth to join her, but he was passed out in the library. She wasn't sure when he'd last slept for more than a couple hours at a time, and it felt rude to wake him.

That, and if she came close to a panic attack again, she'd rather he didn't witness it. She approached the edge of the Station's grounds with significantly more caution than she'd exercised when she'd last tried to go into Earth Between.

She was ten feet from the border when her heart rate kicked up, but this time she let herself stop. Her left hand went to her opposite wrist, fingers tracing over the two fresh bracelets she'd clasped on. Magic hummed from within the thalacite, a gentle buzz beneath her fingertips.

The portal witch in her was calmed by the feel, the reminder of control. The Hidden part of her reached out, feeling for that throwing star on the opposite side of the Station's border. She'd renewed the Hiding on it, refreshing her anchor to this world. To *home*.

It was a reminder that she'd left, and she'd returned. She carried enough magic to reach either her anchor or the one Jevryn had given her, and that magic couldn't be taken from her because it was Hidden, and no one but Seth could see it. Not even the Council. Not even Jevryn. Not even her mother.

Her heart rate slowed and she crossed the remaining ten feet to the border, stopping as her panic rose again.

Resilience, Viktor's voice whispered in her head, *is what will let you survive. Hone every skill you have, and learn the ones you do not, and so long as you do not accept that you have been beaten, you haven't been.*

It hurt to remember his words. To wonder what had become

of him. He had never been unkind. Unyielding, yes, but not unkind. But there had always been an emptiness in him, in the care he'd taken of her and Seth. Because all the affection he possessed had been swallowed up by Elena's magic.

He'd taken care of them, when he was home and not chasing Elena. He'd taught them everything he knew because that was what he'd been ordered to do, but he hadn't loved them. He hadn't been capable of that much connection.

But he had been the most stable person in Nyx and Seth's lives, his training the only reason she had survived Arkadia and Lehine and Amentia Furor.

Resilience is what will let you survive.

She could be that again. She always *had* been that. It hadn't exactly been easy to see it lately, to feel it, but the proof was in the fact that she was still here. She hadn't given up on Nethrayne, when it would have been all too easy to say that she'd had enough, and her brain was fucked, and everyone could figure it all out without her.

She hadn't gotten stuck there. And she wasn't going to spend the rest of her life too afraid to voluntarily step outside her own Station.

She tugged the thinnest tendril of portal magic from the bracelet, weaving it over and under her fingers, a comforting thing to fidget with. She focused on it, on twirling it around her fingers like a ribbon, closed her eyes, and crossed the border.

Her awareness of Kaliaris disappeared. The air was only air, the ground only ground. She waited for the choking suffocation, for the panic—but it didn't come.

The sound of pounding footsteps did. "Nyx?"

She opened her eyes. Evra ran up Wayfarer's Way, a concerned, determined look on her face. She was moving so fast Nyx didn't get a single word out before the Amazon tackled her, driving her back across the Station's boundary and pinning her to the ground.

"Griff!" Evra called.

Nyx was laughing so hard she couldn't get words out. Nothing screamed *I care* like a full-force tackle from Evra al'Daemon.

Griff swooped in, landing beside them. "Ah," he said, removing his spectacles and polishing them on his feathers. "I see you have found Nyx."

"Is that all you have to say? I found her *outside* the Station, she—"

"Is fine," Nyx finished. Clear skepticism etched across Evra's features. "No really, I'm fine. I'm a real girl again and everything. See?" Nyx hugged her best friend.

"Affection," the Amazon grumbled. "Clearly you *are* back to yourself." Evra patted her awkwardly on the arm.

Nyx showed mercy and let her go. Evra returned the kindness by letting her sit up.

"Is this improved condition permanent?"

"Yep. Courtesy of Elena Fortuna."

Evra arched one eyebrow. "Do I want to ask?"

"Later. I'm all emotionally-processed out at the moment." And she still wasn't sure whether to say anything about Jevryn. About who Jevryn was to her. He hadn't explicitly told her not to tell anyone, but…it might be better off for everyone involved if she didn't.

Seth wouldn't talk about it. Griff wouldn't either. And it wasn't that she thought Evra or Morgen *would* if they knew, but…she already felt like enough of her secrets were out. More than she'd ever *wanted* out there.

It had never worried her that much before, how many people knew she was Hidden. But now that she had the rest of her memories back? Now that she was also the girl who'd had it drilled into her head day in and day out that if anyone found out what she was, horrible things would happen to her?

Yeah, now every time she thought about the number of people who *did* know, she wanted to break out in hives. She didn't think she could handle more than Seth and Griff knowing about Jevryn right now.

She rolled to her feet. "I was actually on my way to find you. How's Maruca?"

"She is recovering. Slowly. The Warlock says she will make a return to full health in time."

That was...not the answer Nyx had been expecting. "Not that I'm suggesting Tobi is a cure-all who should be used all the time," she said carefully, "but he couldn't help her?"

It seemed improbable, given the things she had seen him do. Given what Kaden had told her Tobi had done to save him on Arkadia.

"Shamans will not heal without consent. They do have leeway with those who are too injured to give it verbally, but it seems that, during their time on Arkadia, Maruca expressly forbade him from ever healing her."

"Why would she do that?"

Evra quirked an eyebrow. "You have your memories back. You don't know?"

"Look, I was educated, but it was via the mind of Viktor Hawthorne. Which meant it mostly consisted of ways to kill people, ways not to get killed *by* other people, and ways to survive in unfortunate situations." Now that she knew how far Viktor would have had to travel to purchase any educational tomes on the magic of the wider universe, she understood why she'd had so few of them. "Shamans are rare, from what I understand, and they aren't dangerous, so I'm not surprised he never felt the need to mention them."

Evra laughed. "Shamans can be exceptionally dangerous. You think someone who can heal a broken ankle in a blink can't break it just as fast?"

She...hadn't thought of that. "Isn't that antithetical to everything they stand for?"

"Yes. Which is why, if a Shaman ever does it, they are severed from the Congregation and hunted until the end of their days.

Which tend not to be very long, as most go mad without that connection."

"So Maruca was what? Afraid of Tobi?" That seemed hard to believe. He was hands-down the sweetest kid Nyx had ever met. And sure, she hadn't met very many children, but she'd seen quite a few in Dead Earth, and most of them had struck her as tiny little sociopaths. Adorable, but terrifying.

"Not that he would harm her physically. You must have noticed, since Tobi has now walked into your mind, that he is more…aware of you. That it seems as if he *knows* you, knows things about you that you perhaps would not expect, or want."

Nyx shrugged. "He seemed a lot more comfortable around me, I guess. But it didn't really feel like he knew my deepest darkest secrets, or anything."

"Hmm. Perhaps it was the mismatched state of your brain at the time."

"Thanks," Nyx said drily.

"Any time. The point is, in ordinary circumstances, Shamans learn more about those they heal than those people tend to find comfortable. The more superstitious among us believe that Shamans must take something from us in order to heal. A form of payment, so to speak. A piece of our souls, our vitality—something of that nature."

"And Maruca is one of those superstitious ones?"

"I couldn't say for certain. But it is clear that she would rather die than allow anyone that deep inside herself, especially since none of us *know* precisely what occurs when Shamans heal."

Given what Maruca had told her on Nethrayne, Nyx wasn't surprised. She doubted the woman even let Kaden or Morgen truly know her. That she loved them and would die for them, Nyx had no doubt. But Nyx didn't think she let them *in*.

"She sleeps most of the time," Evra said. "But if you'd like to see her, I will take you."

Nyx nodded. "I'd like to see Beauregard first. I want to check on Severena."

Evra hesitated. "I have been twice already. He isn't letting anyone inside."

"I need to try."

Evra nodded. "Very well. Let's go, then."

Beauregard's estate was quiet. *Too* quiet. No guards patrolled the grounds. No one came out to meet them as they approached. It was like stumbling onto a spelled castle in a fairy tale, everything ghostly and frozen and quiet.

They reached the door and Nyx knocked. Waited. Knocked again. Waited some more.

"I have told you," Evra said. "He isn't responding."

Nyx reached for the door handle. She shoved, opening the door all of an inch before Evra's hand landed on hers, halting further progress.

"He clearly does not want visitors."

"It's a big castle. Maybe he didn't hear the knock."

"There are spells for that."

"I know," Nyx admitted. Viktor had always been disappointed her magic was too specialized to be bent to something like a spell to carry sound through a building. He considered such spells useful diversion tactics. But most people used them as the magical equivalent of a doorbell. "But he could need help."

"From the wife he spent thirty years rescuing?" Evra said skeptically.

"More like from himself? From thinking he has to handle everything on his own?" She wiggled the door. "He *did* leave it unlocked. It's clearly a cry for help."

"Or a sign that he isn't thinking clearly."

"In which case we should check on him."

Evra sighed. "We go in. We check. We leave if he doesn't want us here."

Nyx was already shoving the door open. She walked ten feet into the foyer and stopped. The interior was as eerily quiet and empty as the grounds had been. The floating orbs that lit the room were dimmed, barely casting a glow on the shiny black floor tiles. It reinforced the abandoned, haunted castle vibes.

"Where *is* everyone?" Nyx asked.

"Gone." The voice—Reyva's—came from up and to the right. She was descending one of the foyer's two staircases, and she looked tired. Bone tired, like one stiff wind might blow her over. Worse, she looked…lost.

"Where?"

Reyva shrugged. "Wherever people go when they're told their life's mission is complete."

"He just…kicked them all out?" More surprisingly, in her opinion, was that they'd let him. She doubted he would have shown them Severena. Too much potential for things to go wrong with that, and he wouldn't have risked her safety.

"He paid them all a year's wages and assured them the Kumir would never be seen again."

Nyx hadn't realized he paid his guards. She'd thought it was more or less a volunteer position. Exactly how much money did Beauregard have?

Reyva continued. "Anyone who refused to leave was forcefully expelled."

"But he let you stay?"

"For now. I think I'm only still here because I already know everything, and he's more worried about what I might say if I leave."

Personally, Nyx thought Reyva was still here because she'd spent the last few years of her life trying to avenge her family's deaths and, since it hadn't ended the way she'd expected, now she didn't know what to do.

"I wanted to check on Severena."

"He won't like it, but...maybe you can make him see reason. Stars know I can't."

See reason? Nyx and Evra shared a look before following Reyva. She led them straight ahead, to the back of the foyer and through a set of wide double doors that let into a massive inner courtyard.

Nyx immediately understood why Beauregard had chosen this room. It was too large to feel trapped in, easily a few thousand square feet, with a ceiling that stretched as high as the top of the castle and was made of glass, allowing the daylight free rein. Plants and trees and grasses flourished in the space, the ground broken by stone walking paths and fountains.

And there, twenty or so feet ahead, were Beauregard and Severena. She was agitated, her hands constantly rubbing up and down her arms, over her wrists. She shifted from foot to foot, running one over the foot of the opposite ankle, then down to her toes, then switching and doing the same on the other.

Nyx understood why. She wished she didn't. The memory of those white rooms, of severed limbs growing into bodies, of Severena floating as magic cut her and then returned to cut again and again, would haunt Nyx's nightmares as long as she lived.

Beauregard spoke to her in low, soothing tones. Nyx couldn't make out the words, but it seemed like they were helping. Some. A little. Then Severena shook her head, saying something Nyx didn't catch.

She darted sideways and Beauregard caught her. A white patch appeared in his hand. He slapped it on Severena's arm and her eyelids fluttered, her body going limp. Silent tears tracked down Beauregard's cheeks as he gently placed her on a nearby stone bench.

"You may as well ask whatever you've come here to," he said tiredly. Nyx hadn't realized he was even aware of their presence. "She won't be out long. Hydras are notoriously difficult to sedate."

"I just wanted to see how she was." She realized how stupid

it sounded the moment the words came out of her mouth.

"She spent thirty years in agony, watching through copies of her own eyes as she destroyed peoples' lives. How do you think she is?" Nyx didn't get a chance to answer before he closed his eyes, his shoulders slumping, and said, "I'm sorry. You didn't deserve that. She wouldn't even be here now if it weren't for you, but I—" He slumped to the ground, his back resting against the bench that held his wife, and ran a hand over his face. "I don't know what to do. I don't know how to help her. She wants to die." The last words were whispered so softly Nyx almost didn't catch them.

Reyva, her voice not unkind, said, "Maybe you should let her." It wasn't malice in the words, wasn't the sentiment of a woman who blamed Severena for what had happened to her family. It was horror, and it was sadness, and it was compassion. The look on Reyva's face said she wouldn't want to live with Severena's burden any more than Severena did.

"I can't." Beauregard's voice was broken. "She didn't survive all of it only to die. She never got to live. But she can't forget. It's all she thinks of." He wiped a hand over his face and looked at Nyx with haunted eyes. "It's selfish of me, to ask anything more of you than you've already given. But I have to. You were made to forget. You can make *her* forget."

Nyx went rigid. "I'm not sure what Morgen told you about that—"

"He didn't tell me anything. Severena talks in her sleep. I'm sorry. About your family. About your people."

Nyx didn't know what to say to that. She'd never known her people. She never would. So she addressed what he'd asked of her. "I wouldn't wish what was done to me on anyone."

"I understand. But your memories are not hers."

No, they weren't. Maybe hers hadn't been as bad as Severena's, but she'd guessed they weren't cheerful even before Seth had confirmed it. She'd still wanted them back.

Nyx opened her mouth to tell him that, regardless of what he wanted, she couldn't do it because she didn't know how. But the weight of regained memories within her told her it would be a lie. She was her mother's daughter, with everything that entailed. It would never have occurred to her to Hide memories before Elena had done it to her, but now that Nyx had felt and seen the mechanism, now that she remembered the full depth of her ability, she *could* replicate it.

Everything in her recoiled at the idea. She'd felt so helpless, so lost, with her memories erased. How could she do that to someone else? How could Beauregard *ask* her to do it when he'd seen how hard it had been for Nyx to not know? How could he want that for his wife?

On the bench, Severena stirred, hands jerking, face twisting in a mask of pain. She looked so young. Younger than she'd looked in her replicants, though Nyx realized that had nothing to do with the physical age of the bodies, and everything to do with the eyes that had been looking out from behind them.

So young, and she'd never gotten to live.

"Please," Beauregard said. "She deserves more than this. She deserves to be happy."

"I can't rewrite her history," Nyx said gently. "I could Hide only the last thirty years, if she agreed that's what she wanted, but I can't fabricate a memory to explain why her husband has aged thirty years and she hasn't."

Beauregard's eyes were dark pools of resignation. "I'm not asking this for me. I didn't do all of this for *me*. I realized, every time her replicants found me, that she wasn't aging. I did not go to Nethrayne thinking that I would bring her home and she would shrug off her pain like it was nothing and make *me* happy again."

His voice broke. "I went because I love her. I'll let her go because I love her. Let her be free of all of this. Let her live. Even if that means being free of me."

Nyx closed her eyes. Opened them. "Let me talk to her. Alone."

38

Severena woke with more calm than Nyx would have in her situation. Her eyes darted around the room, and only when they didn't find Beauregard did they come to rest on Nyx.

Severena clasped opposite hands over opposite wrists, her fingers digging in. "I've seen you before." Her voice was soft, and sweet. "I tried to kill you, and then you killed me. Once with a sword. Then with a monster."

The Harvester pulsed against Nyx's chest, as if *it* remembered too.

"Then I did it myself, when you held me in the ground."

Nyx remembered the replicants, trapped in the earth of her Station, all holding their breaths until they suffocated. She understood how they'd managed it now. Because they'd been controlled by another hand. By Koral's.

How long had Koral known Nyx was Jevryn's daughter? Had she been fully aware, through the Kumir's eyes, each time the Kumir had seen her? Or were they more like automatons, things she'd given instructions to and then sent off to do her bidding?

She supposed it didn't matter now. Koral was gone.

"I'm sorry," Nyx said. Inadequate words that didn't fix

anything. She remembered blood spilling over her hands, the hazel eyes of the woman before her going dull and lifeless.

Severena shrugged, a jerky, spider-like movement that reminded Nyx of the way Koral's fingers had twitched and plucked. What did it do to someone to have another person in their head for so long? To have their will completely subject to another's?

The woman's hands clenched tighter around her wrists, loosened, tightened again. Over and over. Abruptly, she said, "How do you know James?"

"He's my friend's uncle."

Shadows danced over Severena's face. "Morgen," she said softly. "Janelle wasn't even thinking of having children yet when —" She broke off. "And now the boy looks older than I do.

"It isn't right. None of this is *right*." She squeezed her eyes shut. "You have to convince him to let me go."

"Severena—"

"I can't live like this. In the beginning, I used to dream James would find me. In the middle, I prayed he wouldn't. And by the end, I just wanted it to be over.

"I've seen too much. I've done too much. And he can say that none of it was me, and I know he's right, but it doesn't matter because even though it wasn't me, it *was*.

"I still saw it all, *felt* it all. I still have to live with it. Every day for the rest of my life, I have to live with it."

"What if you didn't?" Nyx asked.

Severena eyed her warily. "What do you mean?"

"Beauregard wants me to offer you something." So she explained. What she could do, if Severena wanted. How it had been done to her. "You should know—this isn't something I would ever choose."

"But you would do it for me?" Severena asked. Her voice had lost some of its heaviness, as if the idea of having her life washed away was a lifted burden.

"I don't know," Nyx said honestly. "Not knowing who you

are? It's a terrible feeling. But my circumstances were different. I didn't choose it. For various reasons, I couldn't make any new connections. I didn't have anyone. I didn't have a life.

"I don't know Beauregard well, but I know he wouldn't let that be your life. You could decide beforehand, what you wanted him to tell you. Who you wanted to be."

Severena drew her knees to her chest. "Isn't it...isn't it like dying? If everything I've lived, everything I've known, is gone, do I not cease to exist?"

Nyx had never thought of it that way. "Maybe. Maybe not. The memories aren't gone, they aren't destroyed. They're still a part of you, they just aren't accessible. You'll still know how to do things. What you like and don't like. I think that, in the most fundamental way, you'll still be *you*."

"So maybe it's not like death. Maybe it's like rebirth."

"It sounds pretty, when you say it like that." Severena stared at her toes. "But you still wouldn't choose it? Even if you'd seen what I have?"

"I wish I could give you a simple yes or no. But I don't know. I think I wouldn't. But I haven't lived your life. And I'm not you. It's not my place to tell you what you should do or how you should feel."

"I think—I think I need to speak to my husband." Severena said it like she hadn't talked to Beauregard since she came back. Maybe she hadn't. Not *really* talked, anyway.

"Of course." Nyx stood.

Severena caught her wrist. "Will you come back in a few days? After I've decided."

Nyx nodded, trying not to look as relieved as she felt that she didn't have to make her own decision right now—because if Severena decided this was what she wanted, Nyx still didn't know if she could bring herself to do it. "Send for me once you make up your mind."

She left Beauregard and Severena to talk, rejoining Evra and

Reyva. When Reyva tried to slink off, Nyx called after her. "You can't stay here."

"Beauregard doesn't mind."

"You know what I mean." There was nothing for Reyva here. Not even company, because Severena and Beauregard were locked in a world that only included them, and that wasn't likely to change any time soon.

Reyva shrugged. She didn't say she didn't have anywhere else to go, but she might as well have.

"Come back to the Station. You can stay until you figure out what you want to do."

"Why would you do that for me?"

"It is just what she does," Evra said. "There is no use arguing with her."

So Reyva didn't. She ran upstairs to pack, and Nyx arched an eyebrow at Evra. "It's what I do?"

Evra nodded. "It is—what do you Earthlings call it?—your thing. You collect lost individuals and shelter them until they no longer need it."

"You make it sound like I'm running a halfway house for aliens having mid-life crises."

"It is not an entirely inaccurate description."

Reyva returned, carrying a small pack and nothing else. They left the castle, but instead of heading straight back to the Station, they ventured farther into Earth Between to check on Maruca. As they walked, Reyva's gaze kept lingering on random people. The more it did so, the more her frown deepened.

They were almost to the Warlock's shop when Nyx finally figured out *which* people Reyva was noticing—those who bore the slave tattoos of the Shadow Market.

"The revolt in the Market a few months ago," Reyva said. "That was you?"

Nyx shook her head. "That was all Kalvar. I just gave them a place to go for a while."

Evra gave Nyx a pointed look that she ignored.

"And…is it true Bryn outlawed the slavers?"

Evra said, "I do not know if 'outlawed' is the correct word. I don't believe the Market can be said to have actual laws. But they have been made unwelcome, to the extent they can no longer operate there."

That was news to Nyx. She hadn't realized Evra was still in contact with the Keeper of Shadows. Or that Bryn was, finally, doing the types of things Evra had said she'd wanted to become Keeper in order to do.

The news caused a visible shift in Reyva's expression, as if a brain that had been entirely focused on a single cause for years was finally scraping the rust off gears and lumbering in another direction.

They reached the Warlock's shop but Evra tugged them past it, across the street to the Wanderer's Inn. Of course it made sense that Evra, Morgen, Maruca and Kalvar hadn't all been staying in the Warlock's home above her shop. Certainly not now that she and Diana had Tobi and Lauralyn with them.

Evra led them inside the inn, up the stairs to a room at the end of the second floor hallway. Morgen was exiting it as they walked up. He looked tired, dark circles beneath his eyes, but he found a smile when he saw them.

"Give me good news, little Guardian. Tell me this excursion means you're all sorted out."

"Back to normal," Nyx said, more cheerfully than she felt, because Morgen looked like he needed a little cheerful. "How's Maruca?"

"Sleeping. I was heading out for food, since Kalvar won't leave her side. The Warlock swears she'll be fine given enough time, but try convincing him of that."

"The Station's open again, if you want to head there." She hadn't missed that he and Evra were still dressed in the clothes they'd worn on Nethrayne, and Reyva was wearing the uniform of Beauregard's former guards, minus the mask.

When Morgen hesitated, she added, "I know Griff would like

to see you." She wagered Griff would also like to convince him to sleep for a couple of hours.

"I notice you don't seem to be including yourself," Morgen said.

"I want to check in on Kalvar, and I have something I need to take care of. I'll be back soon."

Morgen hemmed and hawed, but eventually he left with Evra and Reyva, while Nyx peeked her head into Maruca's room. The redhead wasn't the only one asleep. Kalvar was passed out in the chair next to her. Since Nyx had no reason to wake them save her own curiosity, she didn't. She contented herself with the fact that they were both still breathing, and softly closed the door.

Downstairs, she exited the inn and crossed the street. She stood outside the Warlock's shop, staring at the pretty cursive lettering on the glass front door. Coming here usually made her happy. It reminded her of first becoming the Guardian, when she'd been wide-eyed and excited, and thinking the Warlock's shop really should have cobwebs.

She didn't feel happy or wide-eyed or excited today. She pushed the door open and walked in. The bell on the door chimed, summoning the Warlock from the shop's backroom, Tobi on her heels.

The Warlock's customary smile faltered when she saw Nyx.

Tobi's magic tapped gently at Nyx's mind, asking permission, and Nyx gave it with a nod. He gave her a smile that was all Tobi, zero Congregation.

"You're better!"

"Sure am, Doc. Someone gave me some good advice about making people fix things they've broken."

The kid barreled into her, knowing from previous experience that Nyx was always open to hugs. She squeezed him back and ruffled his hair. "Do you think I could talk to your mom for a minute?"

"Yeah, she's right here." He made no move to leave, obviously missing the unspoken request for a private conversation.

A smile tugged at the Warlock's lips. "Tobi, could you go ask Diana and Lauralyn what they'd like for dinner?" He nodded enthusiastically and zoomed out the back door.

Ankira watched him go, finally turning back to Nyx. "I am glad you are better," she said softly.

"Yeah. Me too." Nyx's voice was sharp. More so than she'd intended, but the sting of the Warlock's previous threat—to her, to her Station—was still fresh in her memory.

"I just wanted to let you know there's no need to have me replaced." She'd wanted to come here—to make sure Ankira knew there was no need to follow through on her earlier threat— but that was *all* she needed to do. She turned for the door.

"Nyx, wait." Ankira came around the sales counter. "What I said to you before. I didn't mean for it to come across like it did."

"Like what? Like you were threatening to take away everything I have, everything I love?"

A flicker of regret crossed the Warlock's face, but she said, "I have things I love too."

"I know. I brought two of them to you. And no," she said when Ankira's face paled, "that isn't a threat to take them away. *I* would never do that to you."

"Nyx—"

"I understand that I seem younger than I am. I understand that because I'm nice, and I want people to like me because I want to like them, that people seem to think that means I'm stupid, too. I am neither.

"So while I won't threaten you, let me explain something you may not have thought out. Because of Tobi, you know what I am. For you to convince the Council to remove me, you would need to explain *why* they would need to remove me, which involves explaining what I am and what was done to me.

"Depending on which councilor received that message, one of two things would happen. One, I would die." Or get locked into councilor servitude, but she could leave that out for the sake of brevity. "Two, you would die. Diana likely would too. I don't think the councilor who would take that action would kill children, but I honestly don't know." Where Jevryn's moral compass found north was anyone's guess, and he'd already told her it wasn't in alignment with her own.

"But even if Tobi and Lauralyn weren't killed, they would be left with no parents. Again. Not to mention some fresh trauma to layer over the mountain of it they already have. I don't want any of those outcomes to happen."

The Warlock's face was drawn, and she looked like she didn't know whether to believe Nyx. Or maybe it was just that she didn't want to believe her. She dipped her head. "I'm sorry."

Nyx was sorry too. Sorry that she didn't know whether the apology was meant, or simply uttered because Nyx had finally shown that she might not be harmless after all. Sorry, because she'd wanted to believe Ankira was becoming a friend.

Maybe she had been. Maybe, if that apology was genuine, they still could be. Six months ago, Nyx would have accepted it in a heartbeat, so desperate for connection. Now life—and opportunity—had taught her to wait and see.

She pushed the door open, let it swing shut again without leaving. Because she *wasn't* a vindictive sort, and she'd realized there was something else she needed to let Earth's Warlock know.

"Diana might want to make herself scarce for a bit. I have a member of the Kormadin royal family in my Station, and while I'd like nothing better than to get rid of her, I'm not sure when that will happen."

The Warlock's already bloodless face paled further. "Are they…"

"They aren't here for Diana. They have no idea she's here, and I'm certainly not going to tell them. Nor am I going to let them leave the Station. I just thought Diana should know not to drop by." The former royal liked to spar with Evra.

"Thank you," was all Ankira said.

Nyx nodded and left. She hoped she and Ankira would find their way back to, if not friendly, at least neutral, ground. But whether that happened or not mostly depended on Ankira, now.

G riff met Nyx at the Station's border, an envelope clutched in his talons. "From your mother's husband. It arrived by special courier an hour ago."

Nyx broke the royal seal—yes, that was actually a thing, though this one was magical rather than stamped wax—and read. It wasn't the irate response she would have expected from an important man who had fought to ready an army to retrieve a woman, only to find out said woman was in no actual danger.

My love,

—Nyx gagged—

I am relieved to know you are safe, and that this was all a misunderstanding. I am equally relieved the Council left you on a planet with which you are familiar, and trust they have given you proper accommodations.
I have a few matters to finish here regarding the Savine matter. Given your interest in its conclusion, I trust you will feel it more important that I tend to it before coming for you.
Expect me in four days, by Earth's calendar.

Yours,
Emerik

Nyx reread it twice to make sure she understood. Elena's *husband* was coming for her. Personally. The dreaded stepfather.

Did he...know about Nyx? But how could he? Her past had

been erased from the public knowledge base—not that there had really been anyone to erase it *from*. Even if he had bothered to look up the name of Earth's Guardian and discovered that Nyx's surname was that of one of the prominent Hidden families—his wife's family—that wasn't unusual.

Nyx had looked up the Fortunas of the universe and discovered there were a *lot* of Fortunas in the universe. So many that there were over three-thousand Nyx Fortunas. The same went for the other four original Hidden surnames. Once Hidden magic had gained prominence, there had been a glut of families changing their names, hoping to be mistaken for being one of *those* Fortunas or Graves or An'Vitores, Ketais or Nichtovens.

So…no. Nyx highly doubted her stepfather knew who she was, unless Elena had told him that she had a daughter. And Nyx was guessing that was something her mother didn't want him to know. It was, in fact, something she was guessing her mother might very well do anything to prevent him from knowing.

Griff was looking at her expectantly.

"Her husband will be coming for her in four days. We're stuck with her until then."

"I see." Nyx suspected the displeasure in Griff's voice was not all on her behalf. And it was easy enough to guess why he would have a personal dislike of Elena.

"Can I talk to you?" she asked. There was something she needed to know. And there was something *he* needed to know.

"You can always talk to me."

"You know what I mean. Can we talk about things you might not want to talk about?"

"I must reiterate that you can always talk to me. I am not only here for the easy discussions."

And there, in the simplicity of the statement, in his boundless patience with her, in the way he'd always put himself between her and everything else—even Jevryn—was the father she'd always wanted. And it made what she had to ask even harder.

"Did you know? That I was his daughter?"

"No." He closed his eyes. "But I did have suspicions."

That hurt. More than she wanted it to. "Why didn't you say anything?"

He stretched his wings, resettled them. "I considered broaching the subject. Many times. I knew how much you wanted the answer to your parentage. But I had no evidence to suggest that I was correct. All I had were my own suppositions. And I am hardly impartial where Jevryn is concerned.

"Of course I noted the similarities in your appearance. But you are not the first person to come through the Station who bore the requisite number of similar features for me to see them and think of him.

"I admit I was curious when he interceded for you with Koral, when he offered you his aid. But I thought, as you did, that he offered that for me. That was the first time in centuries I had remembered enough of myself to even recognize him. Had you been a stranger to him, he might yet have offered it to keep my attention.

"Later… You would often do things that reminded me of him. But again, it is hardly unreasonable that, even thinking it only the slightest possibility you were his, I would look for the best parts of him in you. I had nothing to suggest I was right."

That made sense, up to a point. "But then I could portal."

"Yes. I was fairly certain, once you left Lehine under your own power, that you were *a* councilor's progeny."

She bit her lip. "Where was the confusion at that point? Do I look like another councilor?"

"Yes. As much like another as you look like Jevryn."

Oh. Kiev. How, in all this mess, had Jevryn's twin slipped her mind?

"I should have told you my suspicions when you returned from Amentia Furor. I should have asked Jevryn myself. I couldn't bring myself to do either. If I told you, you would ask him. It would hurt you, if it was true. It would hurt you more if you were Kiev's."

Yes, it would have. After what Kiev had done to Lana and Fari, after what he'd voted to have done to *her*...she did not know that she could have handled being his.

"And while your being the daughter of a councilor was the most logical explanation for your abilities, there was always the possibility that you did not belong to any of them. There *are* other families of portal witches, and just because they are not inherently as strong doesn't mean they could not produce a one-off strong enough to manage what you managed on Lehine.

"What if I told you my fears—that you were Jevryn's or Kiev's—and I was wrong? What if I put you through all that hope and pain and worry for nothing? And by then... Even before you shared with me how you felt about our relationship, I had already begun to think of you as mine." He closed his eyes, briefly. "I always wanted children. Whenever I brought it up, Jevryn would put me off with *maybe next year* or *when things calm down.*

"So then you were here, and you were mine, and I didn't *want* you to be his. I am not naive. Whatever Jevryn does or does not feel for me, I hardly expected him to be alone these many centuries. Nor would I have wanted it of him.

"But it...hurts. That he gave someone else, someone like *her*, what he was never willing to give me. I didn't want to learn you were his, Nyx. It was selfish of me, and it wasn't the only reason, but it was the strongest.

"I understand if you cannot forgive this of me. But I promise you that if I had known for certain, if I had had proof, I would not have kept the knowledge from you."

It was what she'd needed to hear. She put a hand on his shoulder. "It's already forgiven." He hadn't withheld what he thought he knew in order to hurt her, or because he thought that her wanting to know was foolish. It was more than she could say for either of the people who had contributed to her actual DNA.

If he'd been certain and not told her, she would have to consider it more thoroughly. But she could well imagine the doubt that lived in Griff's mind regarding anything to do with Jevryn. The doubt and pain that Jevryn having a daughter was causing him now.

She squeezed his shoulder. "You should know—he didn't choose to have me."

Griff's voice was gentle. "He is not the kind of man to be forgetful and make mistakes of that nature."

"No, but—just ask him about it, okay? It's not something that's my place to tell, but if you asked him, I think he would explain it. And *I* want you to know." She was allowed to have her own turn being selfish. To not want Griff to feel the hurt of betrayal every time he looked at her. He would never show it, would never allow it to affect how he treated her, but it would be there between them, and she didn't want it to be.

"If you wish me to," he said finally, "I will ask."

39

Nyx spent the four days leading up to Emerik Kormadin's arrival pretending that her mother didn't exist and wasn't in the Station. Easy enough to do when she could provide Elena with all the basic necessities required by human decency without another person actually having to interact with her. If anyone deserved to be stuck with nothing but their own thoughts for company for a few days, it was that woman.

Nyx's hopes of relaxing in the intervening time were dashed by the dramatic rise in Departures that were scheduled when all of Beauregard's former guards realized he was serious about disbanding his army. She booked herself a little more solidly than she needed to, in order to get them all out before Emerik Kormadin arrived.

The official travel request for him had come through, not only with his name on it, but with a Serenity Kormadin as well. Was Serenity his sister? His mother? How ingrained in the Kormadin family was Elena if two members of the royal family were willing to travel all this way for her?

She kept meaning to look up the genealogy on the Kormadins and kept letting herself get distracted instead. By Seth, by Morgen and Evra's frequent trips between the Station and Earth Between as they checked on Maruca, by anything at all that let her forget she was avoiding her own mother.

Reyva had departed yesterday. Nyx hadn't expected her to stick around too long—she'd had the look of a woman who didn't fit where she was and desperately wanted to find the place she did—and hadn't been surprised when Seth told her Reyva had asked for one of his portal stones to the Shadow Market. Nyx had a feeling if she ever visited the Market again she would discover that Bryn had a new right hand, and that right hand's name was NuReyva Duraven.

She was envisioning the level of mayhem those two could cause together when a pair of boots stepped onto the Station's grounds. They were familiar to her, by now. A long stride. Confident steps.

She wasn't the only one they were familiar to, and so wasn't surprised when Griff intercepted Jevryn within a few dozen feet of the Station's border. She didn't know what had brought Jevryn traipsing back across the galaxy to Earth—if he knew Elena was leaving within the hour and wanted to make sure she did so, or if the timing was coincidental—but she was glad Griff wouldn't have to wait any longer to get the answers she'd told him to find.

Resigned to her own need for answers, she forced her feet on the path to her mother's room. Seth had wanted to accompany her, but Seth and Elena mixed like fire and gasoline. She'd never get any answers out of her mother if he was there, and she had two she wanted. Needed. Just two questions, and then she told herself she could finally let all this go. Let her *mother* go.

She suspected Elena Fortuna was a wound that would never fully heal. But it was a wound that Nyx at least wanted to cease reopening. So, to continue with this gross analogy, she needed to purge it one last time.

Bracing herself, she opened the door to Elena's room. Her mother had a look on her face that said she'd spent the last four days crafting the perfect speech about how she was not to be treated this way.

Nyx curtailed it before it could begin by throwing a small glass bottle at her mother's face. Elena's elegant, fine-boned hand shot out and caught it.

"For your face. And your neck. Compliments of Seth." There was a purple and yellow bruise on Elena's cheek from where Seth said Jevryn had punched her, and thin scabbed-over lines on her neck.

"I don't have to explain to you why you're going to put the glamour on, right?" The last thing they needed was Elena's influential, smitten husband getting affronted that she'd suffered physical injury.

Elena's nose wrinkled. But she wouldn't want any more fuss in this regard than Nyx did. "No." She dutifully dabbed some of the bottle's contents onto the afflicted areas, checking the room's mirror for the final results, and pocketed the remainder of the glamour. "Am I finally to be allowed to leave this room?"

Nyx nodded and led her into the cafe. Elena seated herself primly on the edge of one of the barstools, as if the seat was covered in filth she did not want her clothing to touch. As if everything about Nyx's Station was beneath her.

Nyx took a deep breath and reminded herself it didn't matter what her mother thought. Reminded herself that she wasn't here for an apology. She already knew she would never get one of those. At this point, she only wanted answers. So she could tidy it all up in her mind and move on.

She didn't address Elena right away. It had never been in her nature to fill a silence, as it seemed to be in most people's, and her mother had always found the tendency unsettling. The way Nyx could stare into nothing and say nothing, perfectly content, was a trait her mother had considered unnatural.

Nyx used it to her advantage now, milling about the kitchen, making a drink she didn't want just to occupy her time, until her mother couldn't take it anymore and said, "Aren't you going to offer me anything? I've been trapped in that room for days."

Days in which she had been provided with adequate food and water, and more comfort than she deserved.

"Remind me of a single time you ever made me so much as a peanut butter and jelly sandwich, and maybe I'll pour you a glass of water."

Elena threw her hands up. "This is why you were so difficult to raise. Everything was about fairness with you. Did this equal that? Was a thing right or wrong? It was so childish."

"I *was* a child. You couldn't let me be one for five seconds?"

"I would have done you no favors had I let you believe the world operated that way. People don't get what they deserve, they get what they can take."

It wasn't the first time her mother had told her that. It was just the first time she *remembered* that her mother had said it before. Often.

Nyx leaned against the counter farthest away from Elena, folding her arms over her chest, baiting her trap. "I remember the speech. Only do what's in your best interests because that's what everyone else will do."

Elena straightened, dusting invisible dust off the bodice of her dress. "Precisely."

"Then why did you keep me? Jevryn told me, you know. How I came into the world."

Annoyance flashed across Elena's face. "Did he? I assume he played the victim, then."

Played the victim? "You raped him."

"Is that what he told you?" Elena scoffed. "As if he didn't want it. They all do."

"Really? He wanted it so much you had to drug him?"

Elena waved her hand. "I needed to ensure I got you out of the deal, and he's so damn magically attuned I could never have deactivated his contraception spell if he was in full control of his faculties. But if he tried to convince you the rest was unwarranted, he's manipulating you, dear."

She leaned in, as if finally deigning to impart some motherly wisdom on her daughter. "Men aren't like us. Sex isn't emotional for them, it's just something they do to pass the time. If they avoid it, it's only because they fear the repercussions of sleeping with the wrong woman.

"That's all it was with Jevryn. And like any man, once the consequences set in, he pretended he never wanted it."

Nyx was barely aware of drawing on the Station. The seat beneath Elena collapsed, sending her sprawling to the ground. Nyx left the floor inflexible long enough for the impact to hurt, then let it turn pliant, swallowing Elena up to her chest.

Nyx towered over her. "I'm going to do you a favor. I'm going to tell you to *never* repeat the sentiments you've just expressed ever again. Certainly not on my Station's grounds. Because while I know you well enough to know that you never feel remorse for anything, there is another here who *doesn't* know you that well. But they do know Jevryn, and on his behalf they might feel like seeing if it's possible to beat some virtue into you."

Elena sneered at her. "You always did think you were better than everyone else. Just like *him*. I could feel it when you were growing in my womb—that you'd turn out to be a walking, talking, holier-than-thou replica of him. I should have done myself a favor and gotten rid of you."

"Yeah?" Nyx released her from the floor. "Why didn't you? I didn't get you what you wanted from Jevryn, so why not cut me loose?"

Her mother's face was a mask of blankness that hid cold rage as she picked herself up. She eyed the unbroken barstools warily and chose to remain standing.

"Why did you bother with me?" Nyx repeated.

The rage and blankness disappeared from Elena's face, her expression shifting like a chameleon's colors as she tried on a new look. One that didn't suit: contrition. "Hidden children must be raised by Hidden parents. You wouldn't have survived if I'd dropped you on a stranger's doorstep. Especially *you*, with your propensity for sticking your nose where it oughtn't be. I understood I bore a responsibility for bringing you into this world."

Nyx gave her a hard look. "Yeah. Try again."

"I'm telling you the—"

"Try. Again."

Elena sighed, the earnestness leaving her face. "Have you ever considered how much nicer your life could be if you would simply *let* people tell you pleasant lies?"

"No."

"Oh, fine." Elena's mouth twisted like she'd just bitten in to something sour. "You want to know? I grew up with hundreds of other Hidden in existence. We feel each other's magic. We *need* it. We take comfort in it. Do you have any idea how hard it was for me when they were suddenly gone? All of them killed within a span of years? How hard it was for me to be alone?"

Nyx gaped at her. Did *Nyx* understand how hard it was to be alone? Was her mother fucking kidding her right now?

"I couldn't stand it, and there was only one way I wasn't going to be alone forever. But there was no point in having a useless child, so I chose Jevryn as the father. He seemed like the ideal choice, but then he had to go and be so obstinate and make it pointless.

"You were supposed to elevate me and you did the opposite. Worse, you landed me on *Earth* for eighteen years. And while you took the edge off, you still weren't enough to fully drown out the magical isolation. A second child would have, but I wasn't going to make the same mistake I'd made before.

"I wasn't going to have *another* useless child." Elena's eyes turned calculating. "Although, once you were old enough, sometimes I thought about Hiding that boy's contraception spell, just so there would be at least one more. To give me time to plan."

She wrinkled her nose. "But you would have been insufferable as a parent yourself."

Nyx opened the nearest cabinet, pulled out a bottle of tequila and a shot glass, and downed an ounce-worth of the clear liquor. Her mother had seriously considered Hiding Seth's contraception spell so Nyx would get knocked up, just so Elena "wouldn't feel so alone." She poured another shot and knocked it back.

This was fucked up. This was *beyond* fucked up. Elena had only condescended to raise her own daughter because she was a magical junkie who needed a feedback loop. And because she was getting a lot of money for it. Money Jevryn had sent that Nyx had never seen a cent of.

"What happened to the house that was supposed to be built?" she asked. "The people Jevryn hired?"

Elena waved her hand dismissively. "A waste. What's the point of building a mansion in a wasteland? Of educating a child who isn't going anywhere? You must know he would never have acknowledged you publicly." A malicious gleam entered her eyes. "I'm guessing he still hasn't."

Nyx didn't give her mother the satisfaction of responding to that. "So you just...what? Went to the contractors and asked for a refund?"

Elena sighed. "In essence, yes. The non-magical are so susceptible to manipulation, even in Dead Earth where our magic is weakened."

On impulse, Nyx asked, "And the portal stones Jevryn bought in the Shadow Market?" They'd been in the Keeper's registry under Viktor's name, one for every planet in the verse.

Elena laughed. "That's what a sense of 'duty' and 'honor' does to a man. He didn't really care about you, but you were his daughter, so he felt honor-bound to protect you. That purchase was supposed to convince anyone looking that there wasn't a councilor involved, because what need would *he* have of portal stones?

"And of course he wasn't going to leave you on Earth

without an escape plan. If anyone found us and we had to run, he wanted Viktor to be able to get us away. And if we never needed to use the stones, Viktor was ordered to gift them to you, once you were old enough.

"I wasn't ever supposed to know about them, but the idiot man didn't count on me having the brains to ask Viktor if there was anything Jevryn hadn't told me. And of course Viktor couldn't lie to me."

Nyx really wanted another round of tequila. Then she reminded herself that she was a lightweight, and abstained. "So, what? You used the portal stones to find the Kormadins, and the money to buy your way in?" It was the only explanation that made sense for why her mother hadn't used much of the money on Earth. Whatever her mother said about a nicer home being a waste, Elena hated poverty, ugliness, and simplicity.

They'd lived a subsistence lifestyle, and maybe Elena hadn't had to do any of the manual labor to make that possible—maybe she had splurged on pointless things to make her own life more bearable—but the only reason she wouldn't have allowed herself to live in the full luxury Jevryn's money would have bought her was if she felt a better future could be won by abstaining. By hating her life on Earth as much as she possibly could.

Elena scoffed. "You can't *buy* your way into the Kormadin family. They have no need of money and even their least descendants can spot a fraud from miles away. But I couldn't come to them empty-handed, either. I needed to comport myself with the grace and dignity to which I was raised, and that requires a certain amount of affluence.

"I needed to present Emerik with my true self. A wealthy woman of high birth with the requisite training to be highly useful to a man like him. The Kormadins do not understand mercy. If I had come to him as a pauper, I should never have won him."

"I'm so glad you did," Nyx said sarcastically. "He sounds like a real prince."

"Do not be insulting. Princes are as plentiful as pebbles in the Kormadin family. Emerik has not ranked so lowly in years."

Fine. Whatever. Nyx didn't know what the power structure of the Kormadin family was, and she didn't need the story of how her mother had clearly gone fishing for Emerik and caught him. She didn't care. In fact, the less she knew about her mother's new life, the more her recently-restored sanity was likely to stay intact.

Elena drew herself up. "And when it comes to my husband, you will not say a word to him about any of this. He doesn't know about you, and I want it to stay that way, are we clear? His family has very traditional values."

And just like that, Nyx knew the answer to the question she hadn't yet asked. "That's why you did this to me? Why you Hid me? You wanted me kept around because I was the only other Hidden for your feedback loop, but you couldn't risk the Kormadins finding out about me? Couldn't risk that I might look for you and...what? Open my mouth about being your daughter?"

"You're incapable of keeping it shut," Elena snapped. She notably didn't even try to deny it. "You always had to give your opinion on everything, never could let anything go."

"So that was worth taking away my entire life?"

"I spent *years* cultivating Emerik. Do you have any idea how hard I had to work? Sneaking away from that wretched place to meet him? And Viktor *always* dragging me back."

The last statement cut through Nyx's anger, because it didn't make any sense. "Why did you let him?"

"Excuse me?"

"Viktor. Why did you let him bring you home? You were the one in control, weren't you? You said jump and he asked how high? So why did he go looking for you every time you left? Why did you let him?"

"It's unimportant."

"I think it is. Explain it to me."

The set of Elena's mouth said she wasn't going to.

"Talk," Nyx ordered, "or I pen a letter to my stepfather letting him know how *delighted* I'd be to become part of your family, now that previous circumstances are no longer preventing me from doing so."

The words practically poured out of Elena after that. "Viktor had become a problem. He was the head of my guard when Jevryn still had me under lock and key. I took him because I needed his help to ensure no one talked about my pregnancy until after you were born.

"Then, when Jevryn reacted by sending me to Earth, he thought it was fitting to leave me with Viktor and his brat of a child as punishment. The problem with keeping someone ensorcelled for that length of time is that you can't simply stop.

"I was warned about that growing up. The ability is meant for small adjustments, a nudge here or there to make someone sympathetic towards you. Withdraw the power and the affected party is none-the-wiser.

"But use it daily on someone for months? I couldn't withdraw it without driving Viktor insane, likely resulting in my own death at his hands. But the longer I used it, the more obsessed he became. I had to keep him distracted, so I gave him you and Seth. Told him how important you both were to me and how worried I was for your safety. That I wanted you to be able to defend yourselves when you were older."

She laughed. "It kept him busy. Kept you all busy. And you and Seth running away like clockwork certainly helped. By that point, whenever I left, he was so ensorcelled he was incapable of *not* tracking me down.

"So I used that with Emerik. He'd lost his wife a few years prior and he wasn't over it. But if there's one thing a man likes to feel like, it's a hero. He'd been impotent to save his wife from an illness even the best healers couldn't cure. But me? A pretty woman who'd lost her entire family only to be stalked constantly by a madman? Oh, he could save me from that, if I could only trust him enough to let him do it.

"I had to be convinced, of course. That I wasn't putting him in danger, that I needed his help. And when the timing was right, I allowed myself to be convinced." A smirk formed on her lips. "He slew the monster and I, so grateful to be saved, couldn't possibly refuse when he offered to make me his wife."

Nyx's stomach turned. *He slew the monster.* "He killed Viktor? Because you convinced him Viktor was some kind of psychotic stalker?"

"Don't look so appalled. Viktor *was* a psychotic stalker."

"One magically created by *you*."

"Oh please, ensorcelling him wouldn't have worked half so well if the tendency wasn't already there. I saw the way he looked at me when he was only part of my guard. He wanted me. I used that. His death was a mercy. Even if I'd released him, he'd never have been functionally sane again. At least this way he did something useful with his death."

"Do you even hear yourself when you talk?" The deep thrumming that pulsed through Nyx's ears could have been the sound of her own fury, but it wasn't. Her hour was up, and the waking thrum of the Station's portal heralded the arrival of Emerik Kormadin.

"Doesn't that sound mean you have work to do?" Elena snapped, her inflection making the word "work" sound like an insult.

"Yes." Nyx smiled. "Yes it does."

She hadn't yet told Elena that her husband was coming to take her home, so when Nyx left for the Arrival Room, her mother didn't follow.

Nyx didn't know exactly what she was going to do when she met Emerik Kormadin, but she was eager to find out.

40

The form that rose up from the portal was oddly shaped. Human, yes, but as if it had a growth on the side, or—

The ley dust sloughed off, and for a moment Nyx stared, stunned. The man wasn't what shocked her. Emerik Kormadin was perfectly ordinary. A couple inches shy of six feet, warm brown skin and wiry black hair cropped short. A man in his mid fifties who wore it well and could have past for his late forties.

No, it was the little girl, held on his hip, who caught Nyx's attention. Serenity Kormadin was not Emerik's sister or mother. She was his daughter. Nyx could see it in the shape of her jaw and the angle of her cheekbones, how they matched his, but the rest of her features…

Well, in the same way Nyx had inherited most of her physical appearance from Jevryn, Serenity had clearly inherited most of hers from her mother. Lighter skin and bright blue eyes, blonde hair so white it was almost blinding.

She wore a pink dress, hair held back in a bow of matching color, little hands holding on to her father's shoulder. She gazed around her with avid interest but no hesitance, as if this excursion was new, but she had never been taught to fear new things and so she only had room for delight.

Serenity's gaze went to the doorway. Her eyes lit up and she squealed. "Mommy!"

Emerik set her down with a laugh and watched her run to the doorway. The doorway Elena had appeared in. Elena, who smiled with what looked like genuine delight and bent down to receive the rushing child into her arms, swinging her up.

"Mommy, I missed you *so* much."

"I missed you too, sweetheart." The warmth in Elena's voice, the light in her eyes... Nyx wanted to believe it was feigned. That Elena Fortuna had gotten the promising match she'd wanted in Emerik and was now playing her role to the hilt, even if that role included doting mother.

But her happiness wasn't fake. She didn't get that telling tightness at the corners of her eyes, didn't stiffen as Emerik walked over to wrap them both in a hug. Elena had another daughter—Nyx had a *sister*—and Elena loved that child as she had never loved Nyx.

Nyx must have made a sound of some kind, because fear flitted across Elena's face. As if she'd momentarily forgotten all about her other daughter.

Part of Nyx wanted to open her mouth and say, "Introduce us, mother." But any satisfaction gained from it would be temporary. She wouldn't win anything from the exchange. Emerik might not even believe her—it was easy enough to see he wouldn't want to—and even if she did convince him, to what end?

She had the answers she'd needed, and that was all she wanted from her mother. She didn't want to be tied to her for the rest of her life. The only thing she might want would be to know her sister. But with Elena's voice whispering in her daughter's ear, Serenity Kormadin would not appreciate Nyx's existence either.

"My apologies," Emerik said, breaking away from his family with a rueful grin, taking his papers to where Nyx still stood by the podium. "I seem to have forgotten the formalities in my enthusiasm."

Elena urged her daughter to follow, watching with cautious, narrowed eyes as Nyx took his papers and verified them. As mother and child moved away from the doorway, Nyx felt a now-familiar presence waiting just beyond it.

"No worries," Nyx said. "I'm sure you're eager to take your wife home. Should I process your Departure now?"

Serenity looked up at her father with big, pleading eyes. "Daddy, can't we stay? Just for a little while? Nanna said they have Gliblin birds here. I wanted to see them."

Emerik smiled, obviously unable to resist her. "Well, I am sure we can manage—"

"Absolutely not." Jevryn A-Morridahn's unyielding voice came from the doorway.

Nyx hated the relief—the validation—she felt as he came to stand behind her. He was not a good substitute for the happy little family in front of her, that she had never had and never would, and yet she was so stupidly grateful he was here. Because even if he was no more a decent parent than her mother had been, at least he was, at the moment, backing *her*. And there was some satisfaction in having the scariest bastard in the room on her side.

"Councilor A-Morridahn." Emerik bowed hastily, and Nyx finally managed a smile when Elena was forced to do the same, as deference was exactly what the proper wife of a wealthy man from a family of traditional values would be expected to show.

Emerik straightened. "Forgive me, I had no idea you would be here personally."

"I wanted to ensure your wife's safe departure. And to make certain there were no misunderstandings between us. Her assistance in this matter was, after all, invaluable. I would hate for the Kormadins to harbor any…ill feelings about the matter."

"No, of course not. Our family is always happy to assist the Council, as you know. We pride ourselves on that relationship."

"I am pleased to hear it. So I am sure I need not explain that your immediate return—and discretion—is called for."

"Yes. We will return at once." Emerik turned to Nyx. "It seems we will need that immediate Departure after all."

Elena's gaze darted between Nyx and Jevryn, calculation in her eyes. She opened her mouth, but Jevryn cut her off. "You have a lovely daughter, Mrs. Kormadin. You must care for her very much."

Elena's hand went protectively to Serenity's shoulder, drawing her close at the implied threat. "Yes. I do."

Jevryn smiled. "It is good to care for one's child, is it not? To do what is in their best interests, even if it is not what *you* want to do. That is, after all, how we keep them safe.

"Take care not to forget it, as the years pass. Time slips by so swiftly. Before we know it, our children are grown and independent, too old for us to protect them at every turn."

Emerik laughed uneasily. "Too true. The years seem to pass faster the older I get." His words were lightly spoken, but his genialness was forced. He hadn't missed Jevryn's threat, even if he didn't understand its cause. "We'll be on our way. I assure you, you needn't worry about our discretion."

Nyx watched in silence as they stepped onto the portal floor, ley dust swirling to cover them as they sank down. Elena and Jevryn were locked in a staring contest until the very end.

Nyx waited until they were gone. Then she met Jevryn's gaze, speaking clearly so he couldn't mistake her. "The next time you want to threaten her, don't pretend like you care about me in order to do it."

For a moment, she thought he might say something. In the end, he only nodded.

"Why are you here?"

He hesitated. Then he reached into his robes and pulled out a stack of papers. "I promised you these."

Identification papers. For Kalvar, Tobi, and Lauralyn.

"Thank you," she managed to grit out. "You didn't have to bring them yourself."

"I had a few minutes. It was no trouble."

She wondered if she would ever think of portaling across worlds as "no trouble." Like it was the same as getting into a car and driving across town.

Maybe she would. She'd already done it enough that the universe felt much smaller than it once had.

He cleared his throat. "I also brought Kaden to retrieve his sister. We will be leaving shortly."

"Right." It was…strange, to think about Kaden here. To know he'd been the one to get her mother. To know that, without him, her mind wouldn't be in its current neat working order. "Is he… coming here, then?"

"No. I will be collecting him on the outskirts of the city."

She wondered if the relief she felt showed on her face, and what Jevryn would make of it if it did. If her father even bothered to notice her facial expressions. If he even thought of her as his daughter, or if he'd separated the biology of her existence from his reality of it.

Probably the latter. Enough that it wouldn't occur to him that it might be awkward for her that her ex-boyfriend was constantly at his beck and call. Then she decided that it didn't have to be awkward, because she didn't have to see Kaden. There was no law decreeing that she had to acknowledge he was here. It would probably be easier, for both of them, if she didn't.

Part of her wanted to say goodbye to Maruca, but it wasn't necessary. She'd seen her once, while she was awake, and it had been weird. Not bad, just weird. They'd wiped the slate clean between them, but they probably weren't ever going to be BFFs. Which was fine, and meant Maruca wasn't going to care if Nyx didn't personally stop by to see her off-planet.

Jevryn cleared his throat. "There is another matter I have to tend to. I wish to apologize." At her blank look, he continued. "I needn't have been so curt with you, before. This situation is not fair to either of us, and I—"

"You don't have to apologize." She could feel the warmth in her cheeks, the embarrassment of remembering how she'd chased him down her hallway, pathetically hungering for a scrap of his attention.

She ruthlessly crushed the hopeful voice that said, *Maybe he does care.* He didn't. All he'd wanted that day was to get away from her. His current apology was likely a direct result of him coming to her fresh from a conversation with Griff, who probably would have told Jevryn he had a responsibility to her, whether he liked it or not.

But she didn't want to be Jevryn's responsibility. She'd rather be someone he worked with, someone he might come to respect if she proved herself useful enough. And fuck if that wasn't just another version of wanting his approval. Even if now she wanted it so she could say, *See? I turned out just fine without you.*

He was waiting for her to continue, so she did. "You've made it abundantly clear that you have no interest in being my father, in any capacity. That's fine. I don't need one." *Liar. Liar, liar, liar.* "As far as I'm concerned, we can return to the way things were. You're invested in what I'm doing because of Griff. I need your help because, frankly, you got me involved in this mess when you sent Kaden here with the Harvester. I'll accept it until this is finished, and then we can go our separate ways."

A brief flicker of blue crossed Jevryn's eyes, then disappeared. She remembered, then, that his eyes had been blue on Amentia Furor. Remembered Seth once telling her that her own eyes had turned blue, but she'd been too sad to care enough to check.

Jevryn cleared his throat. "Very well. It seemed tactless to ask before, but have you made any progress with Laiveran?"

She blinked at the sudden coolness in his voice. The remote councilor tone. What had she expected? That he'd argue with her? Actually put up a fight? He hadn't put up a fight for her at any point in the last twenty-six years, so she didn't know why she'd hoped he would now.

Still, she hadn't expected him to switch right back to the business part of business as usual. She'd more been envisioning him leaving and her having a few months to stop thinking, *Fuck, I can't believe that's my dad*, before she had to talk to him again.

She pulled it together and said, "I have a name. Laiveran still isn't very coherent, but I think it might be the name of the person who helped him build the rings of the Harvester. I'm sure they've been dead a long time, but if we can track down one of their descendants, maybe they'll know something about it."

"What is the name?"

"Gharew."

"Surname?"

"Gharew was all I got out of him. I don't know if it's the first or last name."

Jevryn's brow furrowed. "It sounds familiar, though I cannot place it."

"That's pretty much what Griff said."

His frown deepened. "I have some thoughts. May I check something in the Station's Archives before I leave?"

"Knock yourself out."

The corner of his mouth twitched as he turned away. "I never did understand that phrase."

She'd barely been alone a whole two seconds before Griff came in. "I'm sorry I wasn't with you. While you sent her off."

"Pretty sure I forbade you from being present or listening." She'd known the circumstances of her conception might come up, and hadn't wanted to put Griff through it. "Did you talk to Jevryn? About what I told you to?"

"Yes. I am grateful that you pushed me to ask." The tone of his voice said he also didn't want to discuss it any further.

"Well," she said, trying for lightness, "then you know. I have the world's worst mother. Please tell me you had normal parents? Kind, loving parents who only screwed you up a little bit? I need to believe someone did."

As she'd hoped, the tenseness in his body eased. "I did, actually. Minimal amounts of damage inflicted. We only ever truly disagreed on one thing." He cocked his head at that angle she'd come to equate with a half-smile. "Care to guess what it was?"

"Jevryn?"

"Indeed. They wanted me to marry a nice boy from home. They even had him picked out. His name was Gilthas. He was very respectably employed at the local Historians Guild, and his parents and mine were good friends.

"We dated for a while, in a dutiful attempt to make them happy. We were ill-suited, but neither one of us was quite willing to break it off. Just when I feared he was going to propose out of obligation, and I was going to accept for the same reason, Jevryn happened. I spent weeks off-planet finally realizing what I'd been missing while, unbeknownst to me, Gilthas was having a remarkably similar experience with the town baker.

"It worked out for the best, in the end, but needless to say my parents were less than thrilled when I returned home after my disappearance with a dark-haired stranger from another world."

"Did they come around?"

"In time. And they were never rude to him, despite how difficult Jevryn can be. They were good people. I regret that I never reached out to them after I became the Avatar here. But I didn't know what to say. I didn't know if I could bear their sorrow on top of my own. I felt it would be easier on them if they thought I had died, so that is what I asked Jevryn to tell them."

Nyx frowned. "Did they move away from your homeworld?"

"No. They never understood my wanderlust, and certainly had none of it themselves. They would have died there. I should like to visit, if I can ever sort through my feelings enough to do so. We do not have cemeteries, as this country does—we return the ashes of our people to the sky—but we do have halls of remembrance. I should like to pay my respects in the one that bears their names."

Nyx's stomach hurt. He talked about going home as if he thought he could. She remembered he'd said something similar before, when she'd first bargained with Kaliaris for his right to leave the Station. He'd said then that he'd never thought to see his homeworld again, but now he had the opportunity.

The only problem with that was that Jevryn had told her Laiveran had Harvested Griff's homeworld.

"Griff…" She trailed off. How was she supposed to tell him this?

"Have I said something unsettling?"

She swallowed. "I think there's something you need to know. It's about—"

"*Nyx.*" Her name was a short, commanding syllable, coming from where Jevryn stood in the cafe entrance. Had he always sounded that parentally authoritative, or was it a new development? "I need a word with you. Now."

She looked between Griff and him. "Fine. But it isn't going to change anything." She followed him into the library—she was going to rename the library "the conveniently available room for private conversations" if things kept going at this rate—and crossed her arms as the doors closed behind them. "You lied to him. He thinks his homeworld still exists."

"Yes, I lied to him. Because he'd just had his freedom and even his body stripped from him. Was I supposed to tell him, at his weakest moment, when he'd already endured far more loss than he should have, that his family, his planet, his entire race, were gone?"

"I don't know. But you could have told him at *some* point." *Keep it professional. Don't make it personal.*

Fuck it. "You can't just lie to people and expect to never have to deal with the consequences."

A muscle feathered along Jevryn's jaw. "If you succeed in

freeing him from this place, *then* I will tell him and deal with the consequences. Until then, what point is there in hurting him?"

"For one, because he deserves to know, and for another, because he's thinking of visiting now."

Jevryn's eyes darkened. "You say that as if he can leave this place."

Nyx held up her hand, showing the number three traced in black over her skin. "I don't just bargain for myself. I bargained for him, too. Tell him. Before he tries to go there and realizes it's gone. How did you even hide it for this long?"

He looked away. "The Station's Archives hold no records of the time before the ley lines. Therefore there is no record of his world's demise to be accessed. From there it was a simple matter of altering this Station's map of the connected planets. It was easy enough to add one that is not there. Earth Between sees such little traffic that there are several planets no on ever arrives from or departs to via this port, so the fact he's never met any of his people is no cause for suspicion."

The library door swung open. Griff stood on the threshold, the black streaking his feathers making it clear he'd overheard.

Shit. Why hadn't she been paying attention to the Station? What was it about arguing with Jevryn that consumed the whole of her attention and short-circuited her connection to Kaliaris?

Griff needed to know about his homeworld, but she hadn't wanted him to find out like this, overhearing her and Jevryn yelling about it. She'd wanted him to hear it *from* Jevryn, because he deserved that.

"Arradin..." Jevryn took a halting step forward.

Nyx was capable of recognizing when a situation required her absence. She left, touching her palm to Griff's wing on the way out in silent support. She thought she understood a little how he must be feeling now, learning his planet, his people, had been destroyed.

Maybe Earth was technically her homeworld, being the place she'd grown up, and it was still here. But Jevryn's—her father's

—world was gone. It was an entire half of her history erased, a half she would never have a chance to know, and it had only just occurred to her to mourn it.

Nyx walked into her room and found Seth lounging on her bed.

He flashed her his customary grin. "Is the wicked witch gone? Did I walk around the block enough times to avoid the big argument?"

Nyx didn't have a return grin in her. How he managed to smile through everything was beyond her. "She's gone. Her husband came to pick her up with my half-sister in tow."

He sat up. "I'm sorry, with your what?"

"Half-sister. About this tall." Nyx held out her hand to indicate how high. "Blonde, adorable, thinks Elena's the best mother in the world. Probably has a host of dedicated servants that call her princess."

Seth's lips twisted. "How did any man meet Elena and think, 'Damn, I'd like that woman to be the mother of my child'?"

Nyx snorted. "To explain that, I'd have to explain the very elaborate ruse she used to lure Emerik Kormadin, and to explain *that* I'd have to explain—" *Shit.*

She dropped onto her bed. How had she forgotten long enough to *joke* in front of him?

"Hey, you okay?" He knelt in front of her, his hands resting on her knees.

"No." No, she wasn't okay. She had a moment, a brief one she didn't want to acknowledge, of understanding *why* Jevryn hadn't told Griff about his parents. When he'd been listing those reasons to her mere minutes ago, they'd felt like excuses. Like things he'd told himself because he hadn't wanted to do the hard work.

But now, looking at Seth, she understood. He'd already been

through so much. She didn't want to add to that. Especially not now, when they should finally have a moment to breathe. To just be.

She could tell him tomorrow. Or next week. And then next week might turn into next month, or next year.

She wasn't her father. She'd be damned if she started making his mistakes.

Her hands closed over Seth's. "There's something I have to tell you. It's about Viktor."

EPILOGUE

One Month Later

Nyx dove forward, hands clenched together in front of her, and dropped to her knees in powder-soft sand. The screams of the people around her faded into the background, her entire focus narrowed to a single goal as she slid forward, arms reaching—and popped the volleyball straight up into the air.

Seth jumped, catching the ball with a swift overhand spike that sent it hurtling down on the other side of the net. Morgen lunged for it and—thank the motherfucking stars—missed.

Nyx collapsed on her back in relief as the screams of encouragement from the onlooking crowd turned to cheers. Seth's face swam into view above her, his trademark grin in place.

"That is not the pose of a champion."

"I'm not a champion. I'm dead. Remind me to never, ever play Morgen and Evra in beach volleyball ever again." Not when getting the necessary two-point lead on them was almost impossible. They were a vicious power couple.

Nyx's limbs ached, her breathing was ragged, and her t-shirt was now soaked through with sweat and stuck to her chest. She should have just lied about the rules. It wasn't like they would have known.

"Come on." Seth held out his hand to help her up. "The victory rounds must be made."

She groaned, ignoring his hand and closing her eyes against the brilliance of the sun. "Do them without me."

She highly doubted the good people of Earth Between cared if she preferred to lie here in the nice sand and fall asleep. Beach volleyball wasn't the only entertainment at the Station's first ever Neighborhood Barbecue Day, and there were plenty of other things to distract.

Hands closed around her waist and she found herself rudely dragged up from her comfy bed of sand. She shrieked as Seth threw her over his shoulder. "Seth Connor Hawthorne, put me down right now!"

"Sorry, Nyxi darling"—she could *feel* his damn grin—"but the people want what the people want."

"I'm relatively sure the people don't want to see my ass. Put me *down*."

The son of a bitch actually slapped her on the rear before complying with her request, and then wisely darted out of punching range.

"For the record," Evra told Morgen as she walked up, "if you ever do anything like that to me, I will destroy you."

Morgen got a speculative look on his face that said he might enjoy being destroyed. Evra looked—as she usually did post any physical exertion that made Nyx want to cry—fresh as a damn daisy.

"Are you physically incapable of sweating?" Nyx demanded.

"Do not be ridiculous. If I were incapable of sweating I would overheat quickly and be useless in combat."

Morgen clapped Nyx on the shoulder. "Wicking spells, little Guardian. Her entire wardrobe is coated in wicking spells."

Huh. "Is that why you insist on doing your own laundry?" Nyx asked Evra. It had always struck her as odd, considering the

Amazon was the least domestic person Nyx knew. "Are the spells in the wash? Is there a specially-formulated detergent for badasses, guaranteed to make you look like you don't belong with the rest of us mere mortals?"

"Yes," Evra deadpanned. "Be nice, and perhaps I will buy you some for your birthday."

They made their way through the throngs of people to the Station's back porch. Nyx was still surprised so many people had come. Yes, she'd been making regular trips into Earth Between since she'd become the Guardian, hoping to build connections and a friendly relationship between the Station and Earth Between's residents, but she hadn't realized she'd been successful.

It was clear, given that she was pretty certain every single person in Earth Between had stopped by at one point or another, that she had been. That, or everyone had been curious about what Neighborhood Barbecue Day entailed. Nyx had made it a kind of over-the-top exploration of what she considered the quintessential suburban activities of the US.

There was the barbecue aspect, where they'd grilled every kind of food that could be grilled, and paired it with every potluck-appropriate side Nyx could think of, most of which she'd never tried. As it turned out, she hated coleslaw. She'd completed the food portion of the event with coolers of beer placed strategically around the Station's grounds.

For the activities portion, she'd gone on to add pretty much every family or neighborhood game she could think of that she'd never gotten to experience. Badminton. Volleyball. Basketball. Swimming pool. Bicycles.

For the younger kids, she'd set up bubble stations, massive drawing pads, and a tub full of water guns she suspected their parents would never forgive her for introducing them to. Especially not Ankira and Diana, who were both half-wet because Tobi thought water guns were *great*.

The Warlock noticed Nyx and nodded at her. Nyx nodded

back. That pretty much summed up the state of their relationship these days. They were perfectly polite whenever cause called for them to interact, but the budding friendship that had been there had cooled.

Nyx had the feeling that every time Ankira looked at her, she was remembering Nyx telling her that Tobi, Lauralyn, and Diana could all have died if she'd gone to the Council. Nyx hadn't intended it as a threat, but regardless of whether Ankira had taken it as one, the Warlock seemed to have come to the conclusion that Nyx was a person it was safer to know from afar.

As Nyx reached the patio, Temerex nickered, demanding attention. The unicorn-dragon stood behind an electric fence festooned with multiple signs that read, *Please do NOT feed or pet the horse.* She was, of necessity, glamoured to look like an ordinary horse, but Nyx didn't want anyone reaching out to pet her and feeling scales instead of fur. Or any small children getting their fingers chomped off when they inevitably wanted to feed her.

The unicorn-dragon had at first been miffed about the fact that she was confined to a paddock. But soon enough she'd found the events of the afternoon so enthralling that she'd ceased sending Nyx images of imprisonment, and simply settled in to watch the spectacle. Nyx spent a couple minutes scratching her neck, then dropped into a lawn chair on the back porch and fished a beer out of the cooler next to it. She'd barely twisted the top off when Seth plucked it from her fingers and took a long pull.

"Hey, that's mine!"

He grinned at her. "I thought you were getting it for me. Is it really a neighborhood barbecue if women aren't fetching beer for men?"

She crossed her arms. "I was choosing to leave out the patriarchal expectations that are rampant on this planet."

He grinned at her, retrieved a fresh beer from the cooler,

popped the top and handed it to her. "For the sake of equality. Am I forgiven?"

"Maybe."

He leaned down. "What about now?" His lips brushed hers and—okay, fine, he was forgiven.

A loud groan came from her left, where Kalvar sat at the patio table, his nose buried in a textbook. "Could you guys not? I'm trying to study over here."

Seth magnanimously took pity on Kalvar and stopped kissing Nyx. "You aren't supposed to be studying, kid, you're supposed to be having fun."

It had taken all of Nyx's pleading and wheedling to even get him outside. He hadn't stopped studying since the minute Nyx had given him his new identification papers.

Kalvar looked up, a healthy dose of skepticism on his face. He pointed at the spectacle taking place before him. "Fun? This is all weird. What about putting dogs on sticks is normal?"

Nyx pinched the bridge of her nose, then jerked her hand away because it was such a Jevryn thing to do that it irritated her. "For the last time, there are no actual dogs involved in corndogs. Typically they're sausages fried in corn batter, but these are vegan. They're faux-sausage. No animals were harmed in the making of these corndogs."

Kalvar shook his head. "That only makes it weirder. And I don't have time for fun. I'm trying to absorb a lifetime of knowledge in six months."

Kalvar had set his sights on taking the next available Proficiency Exam for Universal Merit. Higher education in the wider universe took many forms. Every planet had their own academic standards, as did the countries or kingdoms on those planets, the same way it varied from country to country on Earth.

However, there was an overarching universe-wide education system run by something called the Governance Board, and the degrees they conferred were accepted in every territory on every planet. As such, their curriculum was exhaustive, intensive, and they were exorbitantly expensive. They would also accept anyone who could pass the proficiency exam, regardless of their prior academic credentials.

Ever since Nyx had told Kalvar that any schooling he wanted was paid for—she'd held Jevryn to his promise of financial aid— Kalvar had had his heart set on joining the next Governance Academy entering class. She'd lost count of the number of books he'd ordered, and these days he surfaced almost as rarely as Liya did.

Though the girl had done just that today. She sat next to him, her blue hair tumbling over her shoulders in loose waves. There was something different about her that Nyx couldn't quite put her finger on. Maybe it was only that when she'd first come to the Station she'd hidden her face behind her hair, and her body behind baggy clothes, whereas now Nyx had no trouble seeing the vivid eyes that matched her hair, and the baggy clothes had been replaced with a lightweight dress.

That didn't quite feel like the totality of the difference, but Nyx didn't want to stare at her trying to figure out what it was. The girl was still shy about anyone looking too directly at her, and virtually everything about her was a mystery. She had a tendency to run away when asked even the most seemingly harmless of questions.

"You're going to do fine," Liya told Kalvar. Wherever she came from, her education had apparently been stellar, and she'd spent the last month tutoring Kalvar. As had Morgen. And despite the hardship of Kalvar's early years of life, he'd had access to free education resources on his planet, so he didn't have as much to make up for as he might have.

"Absolutely fine," Morgen agreed, reaching over to close Kalvar's book. "And if you don't take a break, your brain will start leaking out of your ears and you'll never get to take the test."

Kalvar gave him a look full of teenage scorn. It bounced right off Morgen, who pointed across the Station grounds to a group lounging beneath the shade of a giant oak. "Look," he said, as if pointing out the sighting of a rare wild animal, "youths of a similar age to you. Your peers, if you will, obviously just as annoyed their parents have dragged them here as you are that Nyx has. Go forth and make friends. Engage in juvenile delinquency."

"What could we possibly have in common?" Kalvar grumbled. But despite his tone, he didn't look entirely opposed to the idea. He also looked like he had no idea how to go about it.

Liya obviously sensed his split feelings. While she seemed to have a pathological aversion to interacting with anyone inside the Station aside from Kalvar, Nyx had the suspicion that might stem from the fact that she was obviously highly aware of others' moods. She opened her mouth and said the most un-Liya-like thing Nyx had ever heard come out of it. "It could be fun."

Kalvar gave her a dumb look. "You're going to go?"

She shrugged and stood. "Why not? Are you coming?"

"Uh...sure." He stood, shoved his hands into his pockets, and followed her across the grounds.

Morgen sighed dramatically. "They grow up so fast."

Nyx's gaze caught on a couple approaching from the eastern side of the festivities and she straightened, doubting what she saw. "Is that...?" She turned to Morgen. "Did you know they were coming?"

He shook his head mutely in response.

Beauregard and Severena had stopped at the edge of the goings-on. Severena's auburn hair had been dyed a pure silver, but even from this distance it was obvious it was her from the way Beauregard looked like he would murder anyone who came too close to her. He scanned the crowd, saw Nyx and the others, and leaned down to whisper in Severena's ear. She nodded and they made their way to the porch, Beauregard keeping a guiding hand on Severena's back.

Nyx hadn't seen either of them since the day Beauregard had

asked her to Hide Severena's memories. She'd received a letter from Severena a few days after. It had thanked her and basically said, "I'm taking some time to think about things."

Nyx had hoped that was a good sign, hoped that maybe the possibility of having all the badness wiped away had given Severena room to breathe. To try to come to terms with what she'd been through. Nyx didn't pretend she could have any idea *how* to come to terms with something like that but she felt, like Beauregard did, that Severena deserved a chance at life. A chance at something better.

And she hoped, selfishly, that that chance didn't involve her Hidden magic.

They approached and Nyx noted other differences in Severena's appearance. Her eyebrows, dyed the same silver as her hair, had been thinned and arched. Previously hazel eyes were now brilliant amethyst. The dusting of freckles on her face were gone, and skin that had once been pale was now tanned to a dark gold, as if Severena had spent every minute of the last month beneath the sun's gaze.

No one would ever look at her now and connect her to the Kumir. Privately, Nyx thought she could have changed nothing about her appearance and never been connected to the Kumir. Her replicants had always been sent in force, and it was by the appearance of multiple identical women that they had been recognized for what they were. But Nyx also thought maybe Severena needed to distance herself from that image—to look in the mirror and see a different woman than the one Koral had used.

Nyx smiled at her. "You got my invitation." She hadn't thought there was any point in sending it, but she was glad now that she had.

Severena smiled. "This is my first neighborhood barbecue."

"Mine too. I'm glad you came."

"I was hoping I could speak with you. In private."

Nyx's stomach sank—she wasn't surprised that Severena

hadn't actually come here to mingle with strangers, but she'd hoped. She nodded and led Severena through the French doors into the library. They were barely past the threshold when the woman stopped, looking back outside.

"Is it alright if we stay here?" she asked.

"Of course. I'm sorry about the Station." Severena frowned, so Nyx added, "I don't know how to make it feel any different."

Her frown lifted. "Oh, it isn't that. Now that I'm a little more in my right mind, the feel of the Station doesn't bother me. Especially now that I know what Nethrayne's Avatar did for me. It's James." She nodded her head at the glass door, where on the other side Beauregard was talking with Morgen while looking back at his wife every five to ten seconds. "I'm not very comfortable with having him out of my sight yet."

"It seems mutual."

The corner of Severena's lip curled up. "Yes, I suppose it is." The beginnings of the smile faltered and died. She ran her hands over her wrists. "I wanted to thank you. For what you offered me, even when it must have been painful to you to offer it. Knowing I could be rid of it all without dying, without putting James through that—it helped.

"I'm still not okay. Not really. But I finally think I might be some day. And that's because of you. I wanted to give you something in return."

Nyx shook her head. "You don't owe me anything."

Severena canted her head. "I owe you everything. Without you, James would never have reached me. I would never have left Nethrayne, and even had I, I would never have escaped Koral's search for me."

Nyx scuffed her foot on the floor. "I'm not exactly responsible for that last one."

Severena was quiet for a moment. "Did you know that Councilor A-Morridahn offered me reparations?"

Nyx's head jerked up. "He did what?"

A ghost of a smile lit Severena's lips. "I thought that might surprise you. I do not know what your connection to him is, but I do know he came to Nethrayne for you—not for me. He has offered material compensation for what I have been through for *you*, not me. So while it may have been his hand that destroyed Koral, I am free because of you.

"So I do owe you, Nyx Fortuna. And it would be unkind of you not to let me repay it."

Nyx blew out a breath. "Okay."

"My replicants were sent to destroy the Hidden. While I don't fully understand why, I am aware there was an object of power involved. I do not know—and do not *want* to know—if you are in possession of that object. But I suspect you are.

"So you should know it was Koral who sent my replicants to Earth, chasing Morgen when he came here. Koral who ensured the order to retrieve him was sent to you—a new Guardian, inexperienced and guaranteed to fail—instead of to Earth Between's city guard, so that my replicants would have time to find him and learn what he knew of the item she sought.

"But Koral did not act alone. She was close with two other Councilors—Alastair Moon, and Zurin Helidax. How much she told them of you, I do not know. And I would say it was information you wouldn't need, with Councilor A-Morridahn backing you, had he not asked me for it himself."

"Did you give it to him?"

Severena shook her head. "As I have said, I do not know what his connection to you is. I thought it should be your choice, whether you wished to pass the information on to him or not."

"Thank you," Nyx said, and meant it.

Severena didn't immediately leave. She looked out the door, watching as Beauregard reluctantly allowed Morgen to drag him over to the badminton court. She looked a mixture of happiness and sorrow. She still fidgeted as she had in Beauregard's castle, hands running over herself, as if in reassurance that all her limbs were still there.

Softly, she said, "He thinks I am the only one who lost thirty years, you know? But he lost them, too. We were both held captive, in different ways." Even softer, she said, "He wants me to leave him."

Nyx hesitated, but Severena was the one who'd brought up the subject. "Can I ask why?"

"Foolish reasons. He thinks he will be a reminder of what I went through, when he is a balm to it. He thinks he will hold me back, when he's the only thing holding me here. He thinks it's wrong that he looks old enough to be my father, that he'll die long before I do. But we are the same age. It's only my body that's younger. And I don't want a life without him.

"I love him. I always have. I know we can't be what we were. I know I'll lose him long before I would have if none of this had happened. But I don't care. He never gave up on me. I don't think he ever would have.

"Am I wrong for wanting to stay? Am I crazy for thinking it could work?"

Nyx found her own gaze traveling to Seth. "I don't think so. Maybe you're right, and you can't be what you were. But that would have happened no matter what. Even if the two of you had been together for the last thirty years, you still wouldn't be now what you were then. People change, even together. That isn't a bad thing.

"So you can't be what you were. But you can be something different. Something that, maybe, is even better than what you would have otherwise become."

"Thank you." Severena's voice was choked, and the fingers she dragged beneath her eyes came away wet. Nyx didn't know what to say, but she was spared from coming up with a response when Severena continued. "I think I'd like to find my husband and learn what a barbecue is." She ran her hands over her wrists and arms again. "I don't—I don't know how long I can stay. People are still difficult for me. I hope you won't be offended."

As far as Nyx was concerned, it was a miracle Severena was

this put together and managing a public appearance at all. "Stay as long or as little as you like."

Nyx watched her rejoin Beauregard, thread her fingers between his and tug him off the badminton court. She noted with some satisfaction that Severena was pulling him toward the vegan corndog Station. Nyx didn't care what Kalvar thought, those damn things were delicious.

Rather than immediately returning outside, Nyx stood for a moment, watching everyone through the window pane, her heart experiencing an odd juxtaposition of happiness and loss.

Happiness, because she had forged for herself what she'd always wanted—a family made of Griff, Seth, Evra, Morgen, and Kalvar—and she'd given herself, and them, something else she'd always wanted to experience: a day in which the only thing that mattered was spending it with them. A day to make memories they could look back on and smile.

But she felt the loss, too, because even though she had the family she'd chosen, and they were worth so much more than the one that hadn't wanted her, there would always be some part of her that ached for the childhood she should have had. She didn't think it would ever stop hurting—for her or for Seth—but she was slowly beginning to realize that that was okay.

That she could have the hurt and the happiness side by side. That it was okay to feel bitter about what she'd missed out on while still appreciating what she had.

Her mother had never looked at her with the affection of the woman who was currently showing her daughter how to blow bubbles across the Station's lawn. Jevryn had never hoisted a three-year-old version of herself onto his shoulders like the man who spun in circles through those bubbles, making the child scream in delight. She'd never gotten to run around with other children her age playing made-up games.

But she had Griff, who had given her a home, who had put himself between her and danger, and who made her feel like he was proud of her. She had Evra and Morgen, who had crossed worlds for her.

She had Seth, who somehow didn't blame her for the fact that she was the only reason he'd grown up as he had. That she was the reason his father had been turned into a spell-sick zombie. That she was, ultimately, the reason his father had died. She had Seth, who loved her, and who was walking toward her now with that gleam in his eyes that said he was going to haul her back outside and into the fun.

She might have a lot of unpleasant memories. But they had all brought her to this point, right here, right now. And she wouldn't trade what she had right now for anything.

WONDERING WHAT HAPPENED IN THE DINER SCENE NYX CAN'T REMEMBER?

Do you want to know what was going through Jevryn's head when he met Nyx for the first time? That bonus scene, along with all my others, is available exclusively to my newsletter subscribers. You can get it by signing up for my newsletter at:

https://michellemanus.com/newsletter/

If you enjoyed the book, it would be beyond super awesome of you to leave a rating and/or review at your retailer of choice. Reviews really are one of the best ways you can help support authors.

Thanks so much for reading!

ABOUT THE AUTHOR

Michelle lives in a desolate land with a dark wizard, a unicorn, and a feline overlord. Despite certain stereotypes you may be familiar with, the dark wizard is not holding her captive, nor does the unicorn require virgin riders. The feline overlord, however, may well be evil.

You can find Michelle on her website: Michellemanus.com or join her newsletter for updates on new releases, and to receive exclusive bonus content.

ALSO BY MICHELLE MANUS

The Aspect Society Trilogy

Siren's Song

Valkyrie's Call

Truthfinder's Promise

The Nyx Fortuna Series

Guardian of Chaos

Guardian of Shadows

Guardian of Madness

Guardian of Torment

Guardian of Defiance

www.ingramcontent.com/pod-product-compliance
Lightning Source LLC
Chambersburg PA
CBHW060729190726
48285CB00001B/134